48 HOURS

A City of London Thriller

J JACKSON BENTLEY

Publishers Note

J Jackson Bentley originally wrote originally wrote 48 Hours in 2010 and it became an instant best seller, with well over a million copies downloaded in the following year.

The first Edition was originally published in 2011 and when it was announced that it would be re-issued in 2020 in a box set to celebrate Twenty Years of the publishing house, JJB insisted on re-writing the book to make it more relevant to the current day and to take account of historic intervening events.

The story and characters that made this book such a huge success in 2011, remain largely the same.

The first of the acclaimed City of London Thriller series, it has won fans across the globe from Northumberland to North Korea.

Now, published in this special signature edition by The Fidus Press , we invite you back into the world of Josh Hammond and Dee Conrad to discover where that heroic partnership started.

The new simple, but dramatic, book covers were specially designed for us by Scandinoir Design, an elegant and stylish addition to any bookshelf.

Sue W, Publisher.
The Fidus Press

©J Jackson Bentley 2021

All rights reserved.
Without limiting the rights under copyright reserved above,
no reproduction, copy or transmission of this publication may be made without written
permission of both the copyright owner and the publisher
of this book.

~

This Fourth Edition published by www.FidusPress.com in the United Kingdom 2021
First published on Kindle by Fidus Books in the United Kingdom 2011
Fidus Books is an imprint of:

The Fidus Press
Chorley. England. UK

~

This is a work of fiction. Names, characters, places and incidents are either the product
of the author's imagination or are used fictitiously, and any resemblance to actual
persons, living or dead, or to actual events is entirely coincidental.

~

Kindle edition is set in Calibri 10 & Candara 12

~

A CIP catalogue record for this book is available from the British Library

First Edition Acknowledgements & Authors Note

For authenticity, I have kept locations and places exactly where they appear in real life. Obviously in any work of fiction it is necessary to have fictional locations but where this has been done the fictional locations are situated on real streets or in real areas of London. Most buildings given a historic background exist and can be seen by walking around London. One is fictional and it is for you to find out which one.

I have taken very few liberties with the transport arrangements mentioned in the book, and most journeys can be travelled as described. Believe me, I have travelled many of these routes hundreds of times.

I am grateful to the experts in gems, firearms, physical combat, loss adjusting, insurance and banking who freely and enthusiastically give their time to allow us authors to maintain authenticity.

I reserve my most grateful thanks for Sue W, my editor, who has proofread and improved all of my books since my first book was published by Macmillan in 1994.

Finally, I acknowledge the assistance given by Fidus Books on taking the City of London Thrillers into electronic format for the Kindle.

J Jackson Bentley, London.

Prologue
Threadneedle Street, City of London, Wednesday, 11am

The rain was persistent but not heavy. It drizzled down like sugar onto strawberries. At first the tiny droplets sat on the wool worsted of my suit as if on a newly waxed car. Then, within seconds, capillary action sucked the water into the fabric until it became saturated. I hadn't moved far along the slick pavement before the rain had soaked through the lining of my jacket and into my thin summer shirt.

It was still warm, and the rain that hit the warm concrete paving vaporised, sending a thin mist swirling around the feet of the people rushing for cover. The skies were darkening by the second, but not as rapidly as the mood of the commuters struggling to unpack pocket sized umbrellas that took longer to erect than Ranulph Fiennes' Arctic tent.

A Starbucks coffee shop was quickly looming on my left. The dull green lighting scheme seemed to brighten as the contrast with the naturally lit street increased. I stepped into the doorway and shook the excess water droplets from my jacket in much the same way as a wet dog shakes its sodden pelt. The windows in the shop were already steaming up, and a long line of men in ruined silk ties and women with flattened hair queued to order a serving of comfort in a cup.

I waited patiently as the machines coughed and spluttered out order after order, sounding like some geriatric patient in a hospital waiting room. The rich, dark coffee odour was thick in the air. There was no need to ingest the caffeine. You could just breathe it in.

My spirits lifted as I held the hot cup in my hands and blew gently across the surface of my Caramel Macchiato, as if my breath produced some super cooling breeze that would make the scalding brew instantly consumable. With no tables available I propped myself up against a shelf and set down my drink next to a blueberry muffin.

I sighed and let the tension flow from my body. I was about to lift my cup and see how many layers of skin the superheated concoction would dislodge from the inside of my mouth when I heard three successive beeps. A text message had arrived on my cell phone.

I took my new iPhone from my pocket immediately, as we all know it is important that you don't offend your mobile phone by ignoring it, even for a few seconds, and so I flicked a couple of buttons to reveal the text message:

"Mr Hammond,

If you do not pay me £250,000.00 in the next 48 hours, I will kill you after noon on Friday! Check your emails for instructions."

Chapter 1

Starbucks, Threadneedle Street, London. Wednesday, 11:10am

I was still wondering which of my certifiable friends had sent the text message when the phone beeped again, this time sounding a long single throaty tone. I had an email. I crushed the last of the muffin into my already full mouth and struggled to chew as the cake dehydrated my mouth to the extent that swallowing became almost impossible. I thought I might choke, and then when I read the email, I did.

"Hi Josh,

OK, here is the deal. You pay me £250,000.00 (details of bank account to follow) within 48 hours and you get to live. If for any reason I don't get that money you die by noon Friday. I appreciate this is a shock and perhaps you are wondering if I am serious. Please see attached photos.

Regards,

Bob

PS: Usually blackmailers tell you not to call the police etc. etc. This is both boring and unproductive as people always do. Feel free to call the police or anyone else you care to, the fact is it will take you 48 hours to persuade them that this isn't a wind up and by then you will either have paid me or be awaiting your fate."

I sipped my coffee nervously, the base of my glass cup tinkling against the ceramic saucer as I waited for the attachments to open. The phone told me that there were two pictures to display; josh1.jpg and josh2.jpg. It took a while, but they slowly began to appear. Line by line, left to right, the pictures were revealed. The process reminded me of the old BBC teleprinter, revealing the soccer scores as they happened on the TV screen on a Saturday afternoon.

The first picture was a head-and-shoulder close up of me walking along the street. It had been taken less than an hour earlier, and I appeared to be looking straight at the camera. I thought it was rather a good picture of me. Anyone who knew me would instantly recognise my fair hair with its tousled style, the blue eyes in my clean-shaven face, and the lean, muscular build I had acquired as a result of playing in a local squash league. The definition was so good I was sure I could actually see wispy hairs growing out of my ears. Bob, my new friend, had also rather worryingly photo-shopped red crosshairs onto my forehead.

The second photo was equally sharp and showed me sitting in a client's office earlier that morning. I seemed to be leaning back in the chair, one hand scratching the back of my head. I recognised my shirt, the one I was still wearing. The buttoned cuff had ridden up a little as I stretched, showing my watch. This one had a target superimposed onto my back.

The fact that the background of both photographs was out of focus suggested to me that the depth of field of the camera lens was narrow, which suggested a long telephoto lens had been used to take the snaps. Clearly, I had no recollection of being photographed, but these days even small compact cameras had zoom lenses capable of magnifying sixteen times without having to resort to digital zooming. The photographer could have been some distance away when he took the pictures. If a camera could shoot me so easily without my being aware of it, I wondered what else could, and I didn't like the answer to that question.

While I was examining the photos, a seat became free by the window, and I sat down. I won't be sitting by any windows after Friday noon, I thought. I looked at my iPhone again and tried to work out what information I could glean from these brief messages.

Firstly, I thought, it could still be a joke, but that seemed less likely now. Secondly, someone had clearly been following me and clearly, they could have attacked me at any time during the morning. Like most of us going about our daily lives, I was vulnerable whilst I was unaware of any threat. Thirdly, the relatively paltry sum of money that had been requested in exchange for my life was almost impossible for me to raise, but not quite, although how I could gather those funds in just forty-eight hours was a concern. Finally, Bob was not worried about me calling the police; either that, or he was bluffing. Unfortunately, I had to assume that he was right. I could easily waste much of the next forty-eight hours in police stations begging to be taken seriously if I'm not careful, I thought.

So, what to do? Pay up or wait and see?

I am, by nature and training, a decisive man and so I quickly concluded that if I began the process of raising the money straight away, then at least I was keeping all options open. I didn't have to actually hand it over if I didn't want to, after all.

Unthinking, I wiped the condensation from the inside of the glass window with the side of my balled right hand and saw that the rain had stopped. Bright rays of August sunshine were cutting through the clouds, seemingly spotlighting individual Londoners going about their business. Now that the sun was beating down again, the smiles quickly returned to the faces of the pedestrians and they looked as if they didn't have a care in the world.

I did. I had forty-eight hours to live unless I could raise a quarter of a million pounds.

Chapter 2

Dyson Brecht Loss Adjusters, Ropemaker Street,

London. Wednesday, 12noon.

I heard a clock chiming the noon hour as I sat outside Toby Baker's glass walled office. The church clock tower bell had been discordant and tuneless for as long as I could remember, but no-one ever seemed to do anything about it. The old doorman we'd had when I started this job years ago told me that it had never been the same since it had been damaged during the Blitz, so it was the Germans' fault. Ironic, since my company was founded by a German and an American.

My eyes were fixed on Toby's office, where the morning meeting was breaking up and individuals were gathering their papers and belongings. There was a round of ritual handshaking and fake smiling, with everyone putting aside the bitter arguments of the morning for the sake of maintaining the prospect of an amicable settlement. Toby ushered out his guests and looked at me with a puzzled expression. To be fair, I rarely sought him out in person. We had even conducted my annual review over the phone whilst we were both just a mile apart in Dubai.

As the last of his guests walked towards the bank of elevators I stepped into Toby's office and closed the door behind me. Toby sat at his desk, leaned back in his mega expensive *stressless* office chair, and visibly relaxed. He placed his hands, fingers interlocked, on his ample stomach.

Before I had a chance to speak, Toby screwed up his face as if he was in pain and said, "You're here to hand in your notice, aren't you?"

"No," I replied instantly. "It's more important than that."

The expression on Toby's face slackened and a possible smile crossed his lips on its way to becoming a smirk. "Nothing's more important than that, Josh."

I slid a sheet of letter sized paper across his desk. There were four items printed on it: the text message, the email text and the two photographs. Toby lifted his Armani glasses off his nose and rested them on his head as he squinted to read the text without the help of his prescription lenses. After a moment he laid the paper flat on the desk. His expression seemed halfway between a smile and a frown.

"Surely this is a joke?" he said, clearly unconvinced. I did not reply in words, but simply shook my head.

"No. Maybe not, then," he said as he took a second look at my printout.

Toby was by far the brightest man I knew, only a year older than me at thirty-four years of age. Most people assumed he was actually older, as his dark hair was already showing signs of greyness at the temples. His expensive glasses framed deep brown eyes which always seemed to twinkle with a hint of mischief, but he could be deadly serious when necessary. He wasn't particularly well qualified, but he was so well informed on every subject that he gave the impression of brilliance, tempered by laziness. Not one for unnecessary exercise, or any at all if it could be avoided, Toby was often described as 'larger than life', a polite way of saying that he was borderline chubby. He liked to research everything to death. If he met a quantum physicist in a bar he would study quantum physics for days on the internet, in libraries and in magazines until he could converse intelligently with his bar buddy, should they ever meet again.

It is this love of detailed research which has made him such a brilliant loss adjuster. Along with a photographic memory, his research enables him to know as much about an insured loss as the insured. By the time a paint manufacturer attends a settlement meeting for an insured loss relating to a fire at his factory, Toby will have found out what products were mixed to make the paint, their flammable qualities, the appropriate regulations for safe storage, the factory regulations relating to fire protection and safety, and the current market price for the paint produced.

Toby believes that knowledge is power, and he has been proved right so many times that most of the major insurers rely on him to ensure that they never overcompensate their customers. Despite his hefty fees, the money he saves his clients every year swamps the sums he commands in payment for his services.

After another few seconds glancing at the printed sheet, he sat forward in his chair, rubbing his chin thoughtfully. He looked me in the eye, his expression signalling to me that he had already arrived at a conclusion.

"Do you want my advice?" I nodded. "OK, this is what we do."

I took notes on a yellow legal pad faintly lined in blue, each page serrated along its length so that it could be torn out and filed. By the time he had finished speaking I had a long list of 'to do' items. He spoke slowly, in his quiet and reassuring voice, and I jotted down what he said almost verbatim.

1) Your flat may be small but in Greenwich it still has to be worth £250k, and as you own it outright, you can raise a £200k loan on that, try Roddy at Chartered Equitable, he'll get your application processed fast and at a preferential business to business interest rate.

2) You have at least £50k in accrued bonuses, paid holiday leave and expenses due by the end of the year, I'll get those advanced.

3) The mortgage will take weeks and so you will sign a promissory note in my favour, using the flat as collateral and I'll loan you the £200k from my partners account for 60 days.

4) I'll call the my contacts in the City of London Police, the Metropolitan Police will be too slow to act, and I should be able to get you in to see someone today. Tell them everything, including your plans to raise the cash.

5) I want you watched 24/7 to see if we can spot your blackmailer. I suggest you call Vastrick Security, tell them to bill the firm, we can sort out the costs later. I want someone on your tail by the time you leave the office tonight.

6) I'll cancel my afternoon and do some research, this must have happened before and if it has the insurance companies will know about it.

When he had finished speaking he asked me to read back the list, which I did, with Toby elaborating further on each point I recalled. By now Toby was sitting upright, his glasses back on his nose. He was staring intently into my face.

"Josh, it's taken me ten years to train you, to get you to where you are now, so don't you dare waste all of that effort by getting yourself killed, all right?"

I assured him that averting imminent death was already a priority for me, and on that note we parted. We both had things to do, if I was to live long enough to see West Ham losing yet again on Saturday.

Chapter 3

Hong Kong Suite, City Wall Hotel, London: Wednesday, 2pm

The hand that clutched the gold Cross fountain pen was not that of a young man; it was heavily veined and had a mat of dark hair across the back of the hand spreading down each finger as far as the knuckle. The fingers were long, slim and well-manicured. Nor was this a manual worker's hand. At each wrist was a crisp white double cuff, held together with simple gold cufflinks in the shape of a square. The Egyptian cotton shirt from Thomas Pink in London was tailored to the wearer's needs, and so the cuffs were perfect in length and the left cuff was cut more generously to accommodate the heavy bracelet and case of the watch that banded its wearer's tanned wrist. The time on the Breitling Old Navitimer Mecanique displayed two o'clock as the writer signed off the letter with a flourish. The signature read Bob, but Bob was not the name of the writer. It was a simple, common and unremarkable nom de plume.

'Bob' checked his Samsung phone, but found nothing worthy of his interest, and set it back down on the antique desk that was part of the exquisite furniture which adorned his five hundred pounds per night suite. Opening the drawer, Bob revealed six basic, no-contract mobile phones, each with a white label adhered to its rear. He picked the phone with the label that read "Josh", reinserted the battery and switched it on. It was time for another message.

"Josh,

Hi, it's Bob again. Just a reminder that time is at a premium. I hope that you realise the seriousness of your position. If not, you will get a reminder later today. Best not to wear your favourite suit for the next 24 hours.

Bob."

The man pressed the send button on the unregistered Nokia pay-as-you-go phone, bought with his grocery shopping at Sainsbury's yesterday. When the message had been sent, he switched the phone off again, removed the battery and laid it in the desk drawer between another Nokia carrying the name Richard and an Alcatel phone labelled Sir Max.

Bob stood up and walked over to the bed, where he bent down and retrieved a briefcase from underneath. The case was black leather and as anonymous as the phones. It was monogrammed with the letters PD. Not that these were his initials - they weren't, they were simply the first two adhesive letters he had randomly alighted upon from the sheet of adhesive gold leaf letters supplied with the case. He clicked open the case and laid it on the red Oriental silk bedspread over the likeness of a Chinese dragon picked out in golden thread. Inside was an odd looking gun - perhaps rifle might have been a more accurate description. The gun had a shoulder stock, eighteen inch barrel and a bulky magazine. Bob checked the magazine with its odd projectiles and replaced it in the briefcase. He was unconcerned about leaving his fingerprints or DNA on the gun or the case as, in common with ninety-nine per cent of the population, he knew that the authorities did not have his biometric details on record.

Bob walked across the deep pile carpeting and slipped into his Burberry mackintosh. It was London, it was August, and rain seemed inevitable. Carrying the briefcase, he exited the suite and headed towards the West End to do a little shopping before his five o'clock appointment.

Chapter 4

City of London Police HQ, Wood St, London: Wednesday, 2pm

I sat in the lobby on an old carved wooden bench in the historic building that housed the City Of London Police, and which probably had not changed much in the last hundred years. Unlike London's busy Metropolitan Police stations, this station was quiet, and the occasional uniformed policeman who passed by me was exceptionally smartly dressed. The plain clothes police here would have looked at home in a bank anywhere in the City.

A man approached the bench. He was smiling. I took in the smart suit, the pale blue shirt with the cutaway collar and the dark blue woven silk tie. My contact looked like a Conservative politician. He was perhaps in his mid-thirties, rather tall, with short cropped hair and steel coloured eyes He came to a halt in front of me and so I stood. The man extended his hand.

"Mr Hammond." It was said as a statement. "I am Inspector Boniface; perhaps we could talk in my office." I accepted the invitation to follow the Inspector to his room, and we walked side by side along a sterile corridor with walls half tiled in sickly green glazed tiles which would not have looked out of place in a Victorian public lavatory. The woodwork was dark stained and equally gloomy.

The policeman followed my gaze, and seemed to read my mind. "Awful, isn't it? But we can't change it. This is a listed building and the interior fixtures are of historic interest, apparently." His tone of voice suggested that he didn't share that viewpoint. I rather liked him already.

We reached an office with a half glazed door and walls. The glass was ridged with bevelled vertical strips that were frosted to permit light transfer to the corridor without invading the privacy of the office's occupants.

The policeman ushered me inside, where the modern office furnishings and technology appeared starkly incongruous. This was a room that Sherlock Holmes might have used for consultations. The outside windows were glazed with the same small opaque panes of glass used elsewhere in the building, and they were raised at least four feet from the ground, so that no-one could see out or in easily. The radiator was of the old hospital column variety, and set in the back wall was a black painted Victorian fire surround and grate.

I sat down in a modern chrome and leather swivel chair, and he took his place in a matching chair on the opposite side of the modern beech desk. At the invitation of Inspector Boniface I retold my story so far, even though it was obvious that the Inspector was familiar with events to date. When I had finished speaking I waited hopefully for his response. A look of resignation crossed the Inspector's face, and I guessed what was coming.

"Mr Hammond, I have to be honest with you here. I'm not sure that there's very much we can do to help you yet."

"You mean until after I've been killed?" I replied. The tension in my voice was tangible.

"Not exactly, although I realise that this must be rather upsetting."

"Upsetting!" I felt anger rising inside me. "Upsetting is losing your house keys. Being killed for no reason whatsoever is a little more than upsetting."

"I really do understand," the Inspector sympathised. "The problem is this; you have received an anonymous threat by text, which may or may not be a sick joke. I know you don't see it that way, but we have no evidence to suggest it could be anything more serious at this moment in time. From this Police Station alone, the City of London Police have had to handle over a thousand death threats of all kinds in the City since the banks were bailed out by the government. Some were very specific, others were very graphic, but they all came to nothing, despite time and effort spent trying to find the culprits. As a result, it is our official position that such threats are almost always made by people who are simply letting off steam." He paused for breath, and to gauge my reaction. "However, I accept that your threat may be a little more credible because it asks for money and because you have clearly been specifically identified and targeted. With that in mind, I propose the following.

First, I'd like you make a detailed statement – while you're at home this evening will be fine - outlining the threat and naming anyone you can think of who may harbour unfriendly feelings towards you. Concentrate on your business dealings to begin with. For example, your pursuer could be an insured person whose claim you reduced or rejected. Second, we sit you down with a high tech specialist who will try to track the person threatening you by tracing his electronic communications, and third, we will help you with the transfer of the money, being sure to electronically tag it and trail it. That, at least, should help to keep you safe, if the threat turns out to be credible."

The Inspector was interrupted by three short beeps from my phone. "Perhaps you'd better take a look at that, given the circumstances," he suggested.

I took out the phone and glanced at the message. I felt my heart rate increase as I recognised the source. I looked up at the Inspector before saying, "It's from him." I read the message out loud. It didn't make any sense to me, but I felt more afraid than I wanted to be.

"What the hell does that mean? Don't wear your favourite suit!" I bellowed in the direction of the policeman.

"Josh – er, may I call you Josh?" I nodded. "Whilst you work in the City, you live in Greenwich, and there is very little chance of me persuading the Metropolitan Police to arrange twenty four hour protection for you on the basis of these threats today. We simply don't have the manpower, for a start. So, let's stick to the plan for now. Go home and make your statement, being as thorough as you can. Come here first thing tomorrow morning and we'll see what we can do. The tech guy you'll see tomorrow is an outsourced sub-contractor and not a police officer, but he is excellent at his job and he will be able to help. Until then, I believe you've been told that you will be accompanied by a private close protection operative, is that correct?"

I answered in the affirmative.

"Good. Look, Josh, I'm sure that this is nothing to worry about. It's probably just an unbalanced individual who has neither the capacity nor the will to hurt you. Try not to worry unnecessarily, and tomorrow maybe we'll be able to track him down and lock him up, if we have to."

I couldn't help thinking that Bob knew exactly what he was doing when he allowed only forty eight hours for the whole process. His forecast about my experience with the police was right on the money. How much else was he right about?

I shook hands with the Inspector, who placed his hand on my shoulder, smiled and told me again not to worry.

I was signing out of the building by writing my name again in the visitors' book when an attractive young woman in a tailored grey business suit approached the desk. The jacket was short and fitted at the waist, and sat above a skirt which was short enough to be interesting, yet long enough to be modest. She had shapely legs and wore low heeled shoes, which made her just a little shorter than me. I guessed her height at around five feet eight, give or take an inch. Under the jacket she wore a plain white blouse, buttoned just low enough to reveal a hint of cleavage. There was a fine gold chain around her neck, with some kind of stone set in the pendant. When my gaze eventually moved upwards to her face, I saw an auburn shoulder length bob framing high cheekbones. She appeared to wear very little make up, and it was my opinion that she didn't need it, anyway. She had a friendly smile and incredible hazel eyes, and she was looking directly at me.

"Josh Hammond?" she enquired in a crisp Home Counties accent.

"I am indeed," I smiled as I shook her outstretched hand.

"I'm Dee Conrad of Vastrick Security," the young woman responded, "and I am your bodyguard."

Chapter 5

Greenwich, London: Wednesday, 4:30pm.

Bob had never been to Greenwich before and he made a mental note to come back in the future when he had some leisure time, to visit the sights. The place seemed to be awash with maritime heritage and references, as well as being the base for the meridian, upon which all world time was measured.

Bob walked up Langdale Road and away from the Underground station. He was heading south. He walked long the Greenwich High Road, occasionally stopping to browse in shop windows. He passed the Greenwich Playhouse and the Pitstop Clinic, bluntly described as a clinic for men who have sex with men. Bob crossed the busy road and headed up Egerton Drive past the Molton Brown Emporium, and as he did so he reflected on the numerous times he had stayed in hotels around the world and used bathrooms furnished with Molton Brown toiletries.

Shortly after the turn off for Ashburnham Grove Bob turned into a small mews development, built in the late eighteenth century when the sea was still king in London. The mews was typical of its type. The buildings were in terraces accessible directly from the pavement, and all were three storeys high with an additional basement or garden flat below. Between each pair of houses was a small alleyway, with a wrought iron gate which led into the rear gardens.

Bob opened the gate between an occupied house and a house being refurbished. He walked between the buildings and checked that the rear access was just as he had remembered. It was. When Bob had first scoped out the ideal position for his venture this location had proved to be ideal. The occupied house was not usually populated until after 6pm most days, when a woman and several children returned home in a Lexus SUV. Around one hour later the husband and father arrived on foot.

Bob took up position in the alleyway and opened his attaché case. Where he stood he would only be visible to a person in direct line with the alleyway, and as the street was deserted he felt quite secure where he was. While he waited for his target, he assembled the odd looking rifle and loaded it with ammunition. Once satisfied that he was ready, Bob leaned against the wall and enjoyed the late afternoon sun.

***

I am always at my desk by seven in the morning, and often much earlier. It is the only way to beat the rush hour these days. In the years I have been commuting from Greenwich, the rush hour has moved further forward and now I need to leave the house at around six fifteen if I want a journey time of forty five minutes or less. Still, it has the theoretical advantage of allowing me to leave the office at four in the afternoon, missing the worst of the commuter traffic on the way home. It also means that I miss the London Tube weirdos. It seems that six in the morning is too early for the crazies, who are presumably resting up and preparing for a day of tormenting fellow passengers, most of whom just want to get to work without speaking to anyone or making eye contact.

Normally my busy work life means that, on work nights, I drop in at home, get changed, and arrive at the gym, swimming pool or the squash centre by five thirty. As I grow older I have discovered that I have to be in bed by eleven if I want to have any chance of making the early Tube, and so my midweek socialising is strictly limited.

As the Tube train rattled into the Greenwich station, Dee, my new close Protection Officer (bodyguard), set out the plan for our return to my house.

"Josh, just take your normal route back, walking at a steady pace, and I'll hurry ahead, taking a short cut through Ashburnham Place. I should get to Ashburnham Mews before you. I'll leave the front door on the latch, and then I'll go up to the first floor and check out your flat before you get there. We can't be too careful."

I couldn't help smiling as I agreed to the cloak and dagger scheme that seemed to me to be both overly complex and melodramatic. Nonetheless, Ms Conrad did have a point. If she went on ahead, anyone watching the house would think she was another tenant and would be unaware that I was being guarded.

***

Bob heard the 'clack clack' of a woman's heels coming along the street at a brisk pace; he opened the gate and pantomimed the checking of the lower hinge. His face was obscured by his bent back as Dee passed by. As soon as she had passed him, Bob stepped back into the alley and closed the gate again. He watched her as she walked along the street. Her skirt was tight enough to show that she was all woman, and the way she walked showed some class. Bob was still watching when Dee opened the door to one of the three story properties that were split into four or more flats. He was interested to note that she lived in the same building as Josh. Living in Greenwich obviously had its advantages.

If Bob had lingered on Dee's rear any longer he would have missed seeing Josh round the corner into the mews. Bob had to work fast. He took the gun and pressed himself against the wall of the alleyway with the gate closed. The gun was concealed by his side. There was too much background noise to hear Josh's loafers lightly treading the mews pavement, and so Bob had to rely on his eyes. A moment later Josh passed by the alleyway, staring straight ahead, seemingly lost in thought.

Bob stepped out onto the pavement with one large step, levelled the gun and fired three shots in quick succession into Josh's back. There was virtually no sound, just the pop, pop, pop of three projectiles leaving the barrel.

Bob saw his target go down, and watched as three bright red patches bloomed on Josh's back as he lay on the pavement. Bob stepped quickly back into the alley and shut the gate, locking it with a padlock he had brought with him. The owners would be annoyed when they discovered that their gate had been padlocked and they had no key, but Bob couldn't care less about that. He did it simply because it ensured his safe getaway. In the end the padlock proved to be unnecessary, as it seemed no-one had witnessed his part in the unfolding drama.

Bob packed the gun into the attaché case as he strode through the back garden and walked fifty metres along a cobbled backstreet onto Devonshire Drive. Once he was sure no-one was following, he slackened his pace and moved casually towards the bus stop, about a hundred metres away on Greenwich Street. A bus was already taking passengers on board and so Bob hopped on, swiped his Oyster card and sat down. He didn't know where the bus was going, but he would eventually get to an Underground station he recognised, and soon after that he would be heading back to the City.

***

I rounded the corner into the Mews just in time to see Ms Conrad close the door to the house. It was certainly a pleasant sight. Far from being worried about my blackmailer, I was mildly excited. I was looking forward to an 'evening in' with the lady who was protecting me and whom I fancied like mad. As I walked along the path I planned my moves for the night ahead. Perhaps the ransom demand wasn't all bad, after all, if this was a consequence.

I had just walked past the Pattinsons' house, which was being refurbished after a fire, a fire for which I was the loss adjuster - very convenient for site visits - when I felt what seemed like a punch in the back. It was followed by two more hits before I found myself gasping for air and dropping to my knees. Feeling dizzy from a lack of oxygen, I fell face forward and in another few seconds blackness overtook me. Oddly enough, just before I passed out, the last thing I remember thinking was, "How does Bob expect to get his quarter of a million pounds now?"

***

Dee checked the apartment for intruders or any unexpected messages or parcels. The apartment was clear. It took no time to check because there was virtually no furniture in the place. What little furniture Josh had was minimalist but stylish. The apartment was bright with light neutral colours dominating. The decor was neither masculine nor feminine. It looked like a show home, rather than the archetypal bachelor pad she had been expecting.

Having satisfied herself that the flat was clear she walked to the first floor window to look for Josh, and that was when she saw him. He was lying face down on the pavement, his dark suit punctuated with three closely grouped hits to the back that were bubbling bright red. Dee's heart skipped a beat. She flung off her shoes and ran barefoot down to the ground floor and out of the door.

***

I wasn't at all sure how much time had passed, but when I next became aware of my surroundings I was sitting on the pavement with my back against the wall. An assortment of concerned and curious neighbours had gathered around. Dee was kneeling at my side, encouraging me to breathe deeply. I looked at her hands. They were covered in red. "Is that my blood?" I asked, not really wanting to know the answer. She looked concerned, guilty even, as she answered my question.

"No, Josh, it's paint."

I wasn't sure I understood, or whether I had heard her correctly. The neighbours looked puzzled, too, and I was somewhat irritated to note that some of them even seemed a little disappointed that this wasn't the drama they had thought at first. Dee explained.

"Someone apparently thought it would be amusing to shoot you with a paint gun. You're not hurt, Josh, just winded."

The neighbours were already speculating amongst themselves, something about it probably being kids from the council flats up the road, but I was totally bemused. I voiced my thoughts.

"I've been paintballing a dozen times and nothing hurt like that. I thought I was dying." Dee helped me to my feet.

"Josh, the paintball guns used for those games are toys. This gun was probably the army version. High velocity paintball guns are used in the Middle East, mainly by the Israelis, for controlling violent crowds. I suspect that's what was used here."

"Don't wear your best suit." I quoted Bob's email out loud.

"My thoughts exactly," Dee replied. "Come on, let's get you home."

Chapter 6

Ashburnham Mews, Greenwich, London: Wednesday, 9pm.

Dee stood up and stretched, walking across the room to draw the heavy damask curtains against the darkening summer sky. The two of us had shared a pasta meal and Dee had asked a colleague to bring around an overnight bag for her. She informed me that as a result of the paintballing incident she had no intention of leaving my side before noon on Friday. I found myself thinking for a brief moment that maybe it had been worth it, after all.

The last three hours had been amongst the most enjoyable of my tenure in Greenwich. The two of us had eaten in companionable silence. Afterwards, Dee had rubbed salve into my bruised back and then we had written a long and laborious statement for the police, covering the day's events. Dee guessed that, after this evening's attack, a continuous police presence would be pretty much guaranteed.

The question of where the gunman had sprung from seemed to have been solved when the Doland family returned home at six to find that their gate was locked with a padlock for which they didn't have a key. Fortunately the police were still in the area, having been called by a concerned neighbour who had assumed the worst when she saw me lying on the ground, and they removed the padlock with bolt cutters before placing it in an evidence bag. The police would have stayed longer, and would have been more insistent about a statement, had it not been for the telephoned intervention of Inspector Boniface of the City of London Police, explaining that he had the situation under control.

My guess was that, before the end of the week, the Police would raid the council flats nearby and, whilst they would not find the paint gun, they would find plenty of drugs and illegal weapons to make their trip worthwhile. The elderly residents of The Ashburnhams would then feel safe again.

"Dee." The gorgeous young woman turned to face me, trying to anticipate my question. "Why do you think this Bob character risked exposure or even arrest by shooting me with a paintball gun? I mean, it's not as if the time limit is up yet. I still have forty hours left."

Ms Conrad pulled up an upholstered footrest that matched the sofa and sat down, facing me. We were less than a yard apart and my heart was beginning to race. She spoke quietly but with an assured tone that inspired confidence.

"We can't know for sure, Josh, but I suspect that our blackmailer enjoys the game rather more than he actually needs the money." She paused. "Despite all of the controls we have over electronic banking these days, the fact is that if you pay up we will probably never see the money again. So, as long as Bob is clever and doesn't leave an obvious electronic trail for the police to follow, he might never be identified. To take a risk like he did tonight suggests to me that he enjoys the thrill that comes from terrifying his victims."

"Well, he certainly scared me," I conceded. That was something of an understatement. I could still remember vividly how I had felt when those paint pellets had hit me. I had believed I was dying, and it had shaken me very badly, although I was trying my best not to show it. I could not shake off the worrying realisation that, had the sniper chosen a different weapon, I would now almost certainly be dead. First had been the camera; then came the paintball gun. What might it be next time? I tried to put it to the back of my mind, but it wasn't easy.

The next two hours were spent in intimate proximity, in my mind anyway, as we, the guard and the guarded, watched TV. At eleven, Dee stood up and stretched her limbs.

"We need to sleep. We might have a long day tomorrow." With that she took a pillow and blanket and laid, fully dressed, on the recliner. "Put the light off on your way to bed." She smiled at the look of disappointment that undoubtedly crossed my face. I would never make a good poker player, I thought, especially if one of my opponents was a stunningly attractive woman.

I sat on my bed and shook physically. Perhaps it was delayed shock. Perhaps it was the thought that at best I was about to lose all of my life savings, and at worst I could lose my life. I felt panic rising in my chest. My heart was beating uncontrollably and I began to hyperventilate. Slowly I regained control as I breathed through my nose and sipped chilled water from a bottle by the bed.

"Why me?" I thought, but no matter how hard I tried I could think of no reason why anyone would choose me for such a scam. I eventually fell asleep with the question rolling around in my befuddled brain.

Chapter 7

City of London Police HQ, Wood St, London: Thursday, 9am.

I was sitting in Inspector Boniface's office watching a young man setting up his laptop and some associated cables and gizmos. Dee Conrad sat beside me. I stole a quick glance at my iPhone. There were no new messages but the newly installed countdown application clicked onto twenty seven hours as I watched.

After a restless night, punctuated by nightmares, I had awoken early before Dee had a chance to rouse me from my fitful sleep. We were in my office by seven fifteen. Dee watched as I cleared my messages and post before we set off for the police station to meet the technician, who was now settling down into the chair on the opposite side of Boniface's desk.

"Right, Mr. Hammond," the young man said. "My name's Simon, and I'm a forensic computer analyst. I've been shown the messages you have received to date, the texts and the email. I am also aware of the paintballing incident last night, which must have been terrifying for you."

"Not as terrifying as the real thing," I countered.

"No, I guess not."

I watched Simon as he set up his equipment. He was in his mid-twenties, I guessed, perhaps six feet tall and dressed in jeans and a polo shirt. He wore metal rimmed glasses and a friendly smile, and the word "geek" could have been invented to describe him. The forensic analyst turned to his laptop which had now booted up. A thin, square black box, connected to the laptop by a USB cable, showed a glowing green diode which had been flashing but was now steady. Simon tapped the keyboard and turned the laptop around so that the screen would face us.

"If I have an enemy in this game it isn't the criminals, it's Hollywood and the TV producers. They give the impression that a computer genius can access anything anywhere and find addresses for the police to raid. Unfortunately, that isn't generally true. Let me start with the email." Simon touched a key and the email came into view, exactly as I had remembered it. "Now, keep your eye on the header." We looked intently at the lines which denoted my email address as being the recipient of Bob's email. Simon clicked a few more keys and the header lengthened to cover half the page.

"This is the email address that sent your email….. 'paymaster@48hrs.co.za', which is a South African domain. As you can see, there is a large amount of routing information in the header. This lists the IP address where mail was sent from and the addresses of all intermediaries until it arrived with you at your IP address at Dyson Brecht. The unfortunate thing is that the email was sent from the IP address of Quadrille Hotel Services, who supply public area internet access and room internet access to hotel customers in the City of London. With further investigation it's possible that we could get Quadrille to narrow the address to the actual hotel, but as anyone in that hotel could access the internet from the lobby, restaurants, gyms and so on, it's unlikely we can do much about identifying the blackmailer with that information alone."

Dee asked for clarification. "So, Simon, what you are saying is that, even if it's possible that we could get Quadrille to identify the hotel the message was sent from, that doesn't necessarily mean our man ever stayed there. He could simply have used their internet access to mislead us."

"Yes, that's exactly what I'm saying," Simon agreed. "Put yourself in his shoes. He would try very hard not to leave a trail to follow. Also, it's rather unlikely that Quadrille would get back to me with that information today, or even tomorrow. The chances are the internet access is subcontracted out to another company somewhere in the UK, and the IT guys who could track this data back might be freelancers, working for the subcontractor from home. I guess what I'm saying is that it's a long shot, and it would not necessarily guarantee us any worthwhile data in any case."

I shook my head. "On the BBC last night, the Silent Witness team did what you just described in 20 seconds and traced the message to an individual office in a block of offices."

"Artistic license," Simon replied. "It simply doesn't work like that in real life. Let's turn to the texts and the phone records and see if we can find anything useful there." With a few more keystrokes the screen changed again. "We know the number that sent the texts, they all came from the same phone, but guess what...."

"It was an unregistered pay-as-you-go phone," Dee guessed out loud.

"Spot on," Simon acknowledged with more than a little admiration in his voice. "It gets worse, though." The analyst paused as he flicked more buttons. "From the phone number we can tell that the phone is a new Nokia 3310 and that it was acquired recently. The records show that it was first activated yesterday and it may only have been on the shelf of the shop where it was bought for a matter of hours, rather than days or weeks. I draw that conclusion because that particular telephone number was only allocated earlier this month. We are waiting for confirmation, but my guess is that it was bought at a supermarket in the London area. Some place where they sell phones by the dozen and the sales assistants will have no idea who bought it. Unless Bob is a bit dim, he'll have paid cash for it. No credit card which could be traced. But you never know. Sometimes people are careless."

My mind had been racing while Simon had been speaking.

"Simon, you're probably right to think that the email and texts were sent from the City. That makes sense when you consider that I was photographed in the City yesterday and shot with paintballs in Greenwich last night. I was wondering, can't we trace where the phone is now? I understand we can track mobile phones by triangulation or cell location or something."

Simon looked directly at the two of us facing him. He looked into my eyes as he spoke. "Josh, we've pinged that number, by computer, every thirty seconds since five o'clock yesterday, and we haven't had a hit. That suggests to me that Bob knows exactly what he's doing. If he's seen any Hollywood movies he will know that we can track a phone, even when it's switched off, or on standby to be more accurate. However, if you remove the battery......" he let the thought hang in the air.

I looked at Dee, my mood plummeting. "This is hopeless," I said.

Dee tried to find some positives from the meeting. "If you ping the phone when it's switched on, can you trace it?"

"Yes, given enough time," Simon answered, "but Bob has, so far at least, kept his messages short and not so sweet. Nothing he's sent so far would have given us enough time to track him." Simon hesitated before offering more negative news. "To be honest, people think that we can get an address from a phone's location, and sometimes that's possible in a rural area, but in a place the size of London the best we can do is narrow it down to a diameter of two or three hundred yards. A radius like that will include thousands of people on the street, in shops, offices and hotels, and hundreds of those will be using phones at any given moment."

"So, what are you saying?" I asked, my frustration bringing hoarseness to my usually controlled voice.

"I'm afraid, Josh, that as an analyst I can't give you any more information than you could guess for yourself. My guess is that the blackmailer lives or lodges in the City, and is probably within a mile of us right at this minute, but we simply can't trace him electronically."

"Wait a minute," Dee interrupted. "What about his email address, 'paymaster@48hrs.com', or whatever it is? It sounds like he might have set up his own domain. Can't we track him that way?" Simon leaned over and his hands quickly rattled the keys on the laptop until a new screen appeared.

"The web domain was set up from an IP address in South Africa, Johannesburg actually, in 2018, during the England Rugby Tour. The IP address leads back to the Intercontinental Hotel which, according to the information on lastminuterooms.co.za, has seven hundred and eleven rooms, all of which would have been full at the time." Simon clicked again on the keyboard and a page entitled 'whois' appeared on the screen. "The site was registered and is maintained by "CoolestDomains" in Thailand. They don't speak much English but they told us that the owner paid for four years' worth of domain hosting and for ten email addresses up front by credit card. They gave us his address and card number."

"We've got him then?" I asked hopefully as I sat forward in my chair.

"I'm afraid not," Simon sighed, obviously reluctant to pile yet more agony on me, recognising that my life span could potentially be measured in hours.

"The address they gave us belongs to Thomas Cook Travel Agency in Uxbridge, where an agent sold a prepaid Mastercard to Michael Lambaurgh, an England Rugby fan who booked a trip to South Africa with them."

"Surely, they must have a record of where he lives?" Dee interjected.

"Yes, I'm afraid we're ahead of you again there. The Metropolitan Police who look after the crowds at Twickenham on match days know Michael Lambaurgh very well. It seems that Michael ran out of money after two weeks in South Africa, and was caught causing trouble by British Police who'd been drafted in to help police the World Cup. To avoid his arrest and prosecution in South Africa, he agreed to be deported. Unfortunately for us, the night before he flew back a man with a heavy Boer dialect, probably fake, offered to buy his card from him when it was refused for payment at a bar. The man offered him three hundred rand, about thirty pounds, for the card. Michael took it happily as there was less than a pound of credit left on it." Simon picked up a printed email that had arrived earlier that morning.

"According to the credit card company, the card was topped up with five thousand rand cash at a Thomas Cook Foreign Exchange point in Johannesburg the next day. An hour ago Michael Lambaurgh described the man who bought the card as white European, about six feet tall with receding dark hair. He couldn't remember much else about that night, as he was falling over drunk, to use his own words."

"So," Dee said, looking at me and then Simon. "We're nowhere." Simon frowned again but held his palms up submissively. "I'm afraid that about sums it up. Unless Bob starts to make some serious mistakes, we won't find him before Friday at noon."

Chapter 8

Dyson Brecht Offices, Ropemaker Street, London:

Thursday, 12 noon.

I was unhappy about my personal mobile phone being cloned by Simon, but eventually accepted that it was necessary. Simon informed me that he would be able to monitor all incoming and outgoing calls and messages in real time, which would hopefully assist in locating Bob. Despite all of this, neither Simon nor Dee were confident that Bob would be found before the deadline expired. I decided I would just have to be careful how I used the phone until Simon terminated the shadowing of my calls and texts.

The countdown on my iPhone had reached twenty-four hours. It had been only twenty-four hours since I had spilled the beans to Toby, my boss, but it already seemed like an eternity. I was now sitting in a conference room with Dee. We sat in silence, each alone with our thoughts.

The door to the conference room opened and Toby walked in with another man. I immediately recognised the second man as Roddy McDougall, the Dyson Brecht contact at Chartered Equitable Building Society. Roddy sat and acknowledged me with a nod. Toby broke the silence.

"Miss Conrad. It's very nice to see you again. This is Roddy McDougall. He is helping us raise the money for the ransom demand, in a manner of speaking."

Roddy, a chubby redhead who looked out of place in a suit, spoke directly to me in a Scots accent. "I don't know what to say, Josh. This is a crazy situation. I suppose all I can realistically do is make your life a wee bit simpler by raising the loan agreement as quickly as possible. To that end I have these papers prepared. Take your time to read them, if you want, but they're all as we discussed yesterday." Roddy pushed a sheaf of papers across the table towards me. Toby spoke.

"Josh, I've asked Terry in Legal to agree the terms of your loan agreement on your behalf so that we can spend time on finding a solution that doesn't ruin you financially." He paused whilst he looked at a sheet of paper lying flat on the table in front of him.

"Your flat will be valued at around three hundred and twenty thousand pounds, which is actually quite generous given the current housing slump post Covid 19. You will borrow two hundred thousand, repayable over twenty five years at a rate tracked to one percent over base. It's the best we could do." Toby looked at Roddy for confirmation, and Roddy nodded and smiled. I appreciated that this was an excellent deal in the circumstances.

"Subject to the valuer's condition survey confirming the initial valuation, the cash can be paid to you on Tuesday next week. Until then you are mine, buddy boy. I own you." Toby smiled, and the others in the room joined him as the mood lightened. "With my two hundred grand partner's loan account money and your fifty-grand advance against bonus and benefits, you will have the necessary quarter of a million quid in your account later today. Just be sure to leave your passport on the way out." Dee looked surprised, but he grinned.

"Just kidding! Now, how do we deal with Bob, whoever he is?" Toby looked around the room for ideas. Dee had already explained that the Police offered little hope of finding Bob, even after the money had been paid. When the room remained silent, Toby continued.

"OK. I guess it's down to me. I've had a few thoughts. Let me brainstorm them for a few minutes." Toby stood up and walked to a large flip chart on an easel. He picked up a blue marker pen and began to write. I have watched this brilliant man develop new strategies on the hoof with just a pen, a whiteboard and his agile mind hundreds of times.

I hoped that Toby's ingenuity would help us find the elusive solution to my problem.

Toby wrote at the top of the first sheet; BOB KNOWS YOUR FINANCIAL POSITION. He then drew angled lines lower down the page. At the end of the first line he wrote; HOW? He looked at the rest of us in the room expectantly. Roddy started the brainstorming session by suggesting "The Bank". Toby wrote it down and numbered it. Dee called out with "Friends and neighbours". Toby duly wrote that down and added one of his own, which he numbered three. He wrote "Employers". The exercise went on until the list comprised eight possible ways that Bob could have found out about my financial position.

"OK." Toby said, as he picked up a red marker pen. "Let's see if we can eliminate some of these possibilities." I stood and walked to the board, looking at each line intently before commenting on each in turn.

"Number one; 'The Bank'. I think we can scrub that one, as I use an internet based account and so they have no idea that I own my flat. Also a large part of my earnings are paid into investment funds and pension funds, and so no-one at the bank could have any real idea of my monthly income, let alone my net worth." Toby drew a line through 'The Bank'.

"Next, I think we can rule out friends. They have no idea what I earn. To be honest, most of my friends probably imagine I earn around a third of my actual income. Only a few close friends have been to my flat, and I think they just assumed it was rented. I never felt it necessary to disabuse them of that view." Toby crossed the second line out, too.

"Three and four can stay for the moment." Toby's pen hovered over item five, 'Inland Revenue'. "I think we can rule them out, too," I said, "as they know about my income but they have no idea that I own other assets like the flat. They only know what's on my tax return, and that information is unremarkable." Line five was scrawled out.

"Line six; 'Relatives'." I thought hard before dismissing this one. "Only my parents and my brother have any clue as to my financial position, but even they probably underestimate my income. Dad is forever offering to lend me a couple of grand if I ever get into trouble living in London. Pete, he's more switched on. He probably realises that I earn over a hundred thousand a year, but he probably thinks I have a huge mortgage, just like he has. No. I think we have to eliminate family." Another crossing out in red marker followed that conclusion.

"Ex - girlfriends." I smiled wanly before dismissing line seven. "I'm afraid none of my girlfriends stuck around long enough to understand my financial position, so that's a non-starter." It was eliminated in red.

"Last one." I considered 'Lenders and credit agencies'.

"Well, I don't have any loans, and my credit rating is good but, again, there is no way they could know I own a flat worth over three hundred grand. That line has to go as well."

The people in the room perused the list which now consisted of '3) Employer' and, '4) Accountant'. Before I made my opinion known, the other three had alighted on their own preference, which in all cases was the accountant.

"Toby," I said, "the only person at Dyson Brecht who knows about my finances is you, and I trust you with my life. I guess we need to look more closely at Atkins, Garretson, and Palmer, better known in the City as AGP." I paused. "More specifically, I need to speak to Andrew Cuthbertson, who does my accounts." Toby crossed out number three, 'Employer', and flipped the page before writing at the top 'WHY JOSH?'

**

Sandwiches, juice and fruit having been consumed, the four of us assembled in the conference room and set our minds to answering the question "Why pick on Josh?"

Using the same flip chart as before, we listed and discarded all but one reason. Out went Envy, Hatred, Prejudice, Revenge and Ideology. It looked like a list of most of the seven deadly sins, but none of them seemed likely as a motive.

Toby summarised the discussion, which had taken almost an hour and which had been very deep at times.

"Dee, gentlemen, we are left with one category standing; Greed. I have to say that, before we began this exercise, that was my view anyway. Josh, the fact is, the texts and emails you have received have been dispassionate, even jokey. There has been no attempt to make you suffer, no rambling theses about the evils of capitalism or suggestion that you need to repent of your evil ways. No. I think that you were chosen simply because you were available and you had the funds." The others nodded in agreement.

"I have to agree," Roddy said. "You should see the anonymous hate mail we receive in the post. It's as disgusting as it is inaccurate. We are accused of stealing taxpayers' money to pay huge bonuses, but we have never been given a penny of government money and our CEO is paid a fixed salary, with no bonus at all. All of our bonuses go to the staff who run the society, and they earn modest salaries. Our profits are fed back into the mutual for the benefit of our customers. If Bob was on a mission to destroy you, or if his intentions were anything other than simple extortion, you would know about it by now."

Toby spoke as he tore off the used flip chart pages and folded them. "Josh, Dee, the money is ready and there are still twenty two hours to go. I suggest that you speak to Andrew Cuthbertson as soon as possible and see if he can shed any light on how Bob managed to obtain your financial records."

The meeting adjourned and, after a good deal of handshaking and best wishes, Dee and I were left alone in the room with a tray of curling sandwiches and ripening fruit. I spoke quietly.

"OK, let's grab a cab and go see AGP."

"Will they see us at such short notice?"

"Dee, I potentially have less than twenty four hours to live. They'll see us."

Chapter 9

Atkins Garretson Palmer, College Hill, London: Thursday, 3pm.

Meeting with Andrew Cuthbertson was not as simple as I had hoped it would be. Despite my explaining the death threat and the deadly timetable to the receptionist, Andrew's PA and Andrew himself, AGP were having difficulty excusing the accountant from an allegedly important meeting. It took a call from Toby to ensure that Andrew met us at all, and when he did he did not look at all happy.

We were sitting in another anonymous conference room almost identical to the one we had just left. Even the view across London was similar. Andrew strode into the room and threw his pad down onto the desk before sitting opposite Dee and myself. He wore an expensive suit and a cream linen shirt, finished off with a red silk tie. His cufflinks matched his tiepin. His brown hair was immaculately styled, as if he'd just auditioned for a shampoo commercial. He was good looking in a rugged sort of way, and usually his brown eyes twinkled with friendliness, but not today. The accountant did not exchange any pleasantries, nor did he ask who Dee was or what she was doing there. Instead, he glared at me and spoke harshly.

"OK, Josh, you have managed to drag me away from a very important meeting for fifteen minutes, so I'd start talking, if I were you." Andrew looked at his watch and pressed a button on the side of the watchcase. I guessed it was a timer, but it was also meant to signal to us that he would not be staying a minute longer than he had to. Dee was looking puzzled, as I had described Andrew Cuthbertson as a friend, an easy going squash partner and sometime five a side teammate. The man sitting opposite was wound up like a spring and frowning as if trying to win a prize for gurning. Faced with this hostility I kept cool and spoke quietly but assertively.

"Andrew, as you have heard I'm being blackmailed by someone who has an intimate knowledge of my finances..."

"So I hear," Andrew interjected sharply. I continued, ignoring the interruption.

"Well, there are very few people who know my financial circumstances. In fact, apart from me, AGP are the only people who know all the details of my earnings, savings and property holdings."

Andrew's face reddened noticeably, and in one swift movement he stood up, pushing his chair back against the wall with a bang, before placing both palms on the conference table a leaning over towards me. The next words were spat out with the kind of venom I had never seen before in Andrew Cuthbertson.

"Let me see if I can guess where this is going. You are about to suggest that someone at AGP is either blackmailing you or passing information onto your blackmailer. I suggest that before you slander yourself you give some careful thought to your next choice of words." The accountant glared at both of us sitting opposite him and, without reducing the level of vitriol in his voice, he continued. "You drag me out of an important meeting and subject me to these baseless accusations. That's rich, Josh, really rich."

I could not remember the last time that I'd lost my temper to such an extent that I had lost all control, but I could feel anger welling up inside me. It began with a tightening of muscles around the stomach. I could feel adrenaline rising and my heart was beginning to race. Dee Conrad placed her hand on my arm as a signal that I should remain silent, and then she spoke calmly but firmly.

"As I recall this conversation, Josh has accused no-one of anything. He pointed out that your firm are the only people that know his finances, as well as he does himself, except for the blackmailer. Now, the blackmailer must have obtained this information from somewhere, and you have obviously considered the possibility that it may have leaked from here, hence your outburst. We're leaving now, as you are clearly not interested in discussing this calmly, and you can answer these awkward questions directly to the police instead. Your directors can answer those same questions to the regulatory bodies. No doubt when all of this is finally made public, your major clients will wonder how trustworthy AGP really are." Dee stood up and spoke to me.

"Come on, we're going. Your friend here is hiding something, and we'd better let Inspector Boniface find out what it is." Dee turned to the accountant. "And you had better consider what will happen if Josh is murdered, and whether you're prepared to spend life behind bars as a co-conspirator."

Andrew Cuthbertson paled visibly, and I thought I could see him trembling. I was shaken too, but I stood up and followed Dee to the door. Andrew spoke up, calling to us to wait. Suddenly he seemed a lot more cordial; in fact, there was a pleading in his voice that was quite unexpected.

"Look, can't we sit down and talk about this? Perhaps I spoke rather hastily. I'm sorry. It's been a bad morning, that's all. Perhaps I can see what we can do about freeing up some funds to get you out of this hole."

"Mr. Cuthbertson," Dee interjected sharply, before I could reply. "Go back to your important meeting. I think we're done here. I suggest you think carefully about what Josh has told you, and if you want to tell us how his personal information could have fallen into the hands of his blackmailer, call him at home. You have the number."

Dee ushered me out of the room, and the frame rattled as the door slammed behind us.

***

Dee was sipping her orange juice when I returned to the table with my Grand Latte. The coffee shop was nearly empty. I set my cup down and looked at my new friend with a new found respect.

"It'll be weeks before Andrew finds his balls again, and when he does they'll probably be crushed beyond any reasonable expectation of future use," I remarked.

Dee Conrad smiled, and I suddenly realised that she had been as stressed by the afternoon's events as I had. She cared. "Josh," she whispered conspiratorially. "Andrew Cuthbertson is as guilty as sin. It was written all over his face. His behaviour was a classic display of guilt. He was very defensive - way over the top, wouldn't you agree? I would offer good odds that not only does he know more than he's telling you, he's almost certainly the man behind the leaking of your personal details."

I pondered the prospect of one of my closest friends selling me out. The thought was both unwelcome and unattractive. There are some things you don't want to know, not because you want to be protected from a harsh reality but because, once you lose faith in your closest allies, what does the future hold for you? Who can you trust?

"Before this night is over you'll receive a desperate phone call from Andrew Cuthbertson, I guarantee it. I would say that someone is forcing him to cross a line that he's uncomfortable with. I could read conflict all over his face."

Dee paused and looked directly into my eyes. "If, as I believe, you're a good judge of character, and you've chosen your friends wisely, then Mr. Cuthbertson will struggle with himself for a while and then make the right decision."

Chapter 10

Blacksmiths Hall, Lambeth Hill, City of London. Thursday, 5pm.

Bob strode down Queen Victoria Street towards Lambeth Hill. He was fuming. He lifted the Alcatel pay as you go phone from his pocket and looked at the message one more time. The words on the screen did nothing to enhance his mood;

"Dear Bob, or whoever you are, please sod off and don't bother me again. You are not getting a penny from me. Should you try to hurt me in any way I'll be the one dishing out a sound beating, with a coward like you on the wrong end of it. Now curl up and die."

The white phone had a label stuck on the reverse, which read: 'Sir Max'. Bob removed the battery and dropped it in an ornamental black cast iron waste bin carrying the shield of the City of London. As he walked along the main thoroughfare he removed the sim card and dropped it into a roadside drain. Finally, as he approached the next waste bin, he placed the handset on the ground and stood on it, crunching it under the heel of his shiny Church's Roach lace up evening shoes, before collecting up the pieces and dropping them into the bin. He felt a little better.

A minute later Bob had reached Lambeth Hill, so he turned left and walked down towards the River Thames. After walking a further one hundred and fifty metres he reached the Blacksmith's Hall, a medieval hall that had been rebuilt many times in its history. The most recent version faced him now. The hall had been built in the early 19th century for the Worshipful Company of Blacksmiths, in a mock gothic style, which gave it the look of a church. Specially commissioned stained glass showed scenes of ancient smithies at work on some of London's famous landmarks.

Bob stepped inside the cavernous hall and handed his invitation, bag and coat to an attendant. He received a ticket in return, which he placed in the right hand pocket of his dinner jacket. Before removing his hand he checked one last time that he had the vial of clear liquid safely secured there.

No-one ever entered the great halls of London without being awed by the enormity of the space, the incredible craftsmanship of the masonry and the complex network of roof timbers, many of which had been reclaimed from old warships. The great hall looked just like the dining hall at Hogwarts, as depicted in the Harry Potter films.

A young man in a white linen jacket approached him and offered him a glass of cheap champagne. Bob took the bubbly, along with a flyer emblazoned with the words "The Maximillian Rochester Fund for Sick Children".

Bob began to circulate, but it was proving rather difficult as the floor was crammed with people. The charity event had been blessed with a huge turnout. As he headed towards the top table, where he would shortly be sitting, an older, grey haired man called out to him in a plummy voice.

"It's the scholarship boy!"

"It's the thick rich kid!" Bob responded, in a pronounced and exaggerated Lancashire accent.

Forty years had passed since Bob had boarded at Harrow on the Hill Catholic College for Boys. He had won his place there as an eleven year old on a scholarship awarded by his father's trade union. The scholarship's aim was to improve social mobility, but it actually resulted in social misery. The paying boarders such as Max never let the other boys forget that they were unworthy of such an elite establishment. Even now, Max believed that greeting Bob in this way was just a measure of friendly camaraderie. He had no idea of the resentment that Bob harboured for his old prefect, either then or now. Still, it had always suited Bob to play along. That role playing, however, was about to come to an abrupt end, after Max's earlier text message.

If Sir Max had suspected that his blackmailer was in the room, and he had lined up every one of the five hundred people present this evening, hoping to find the culprit, he would have failed miserably, doubtless alighting on the real Bob almost at the last pick. Sir Max felt safe and comfortable among his friends, and would certainly not have suspected any of them capable of doing such a thing.

The older man took the scholarship boy by the shoulder and led him to a quiet alcove. "Listen, old chap, I really must thank you for having a word in the PM's ear. We received a significant contribution under the government's 'Big Society' plan. That is really going to help put the hospices on a firm footing."

"Not at all, Max. As a trustee it was my duty," Bob replied. "Now, what are you drinking? I'm off to the bar."

"I'll have my usual, thank you, but do ask for the twelve year old malt, there's a good chap, otherwise they'll serve up any old tosh. Oh, and make it a double, if you would." Sir Max winked. Bob smiled and fought his way to the bar.

***

Bob flushed the empty vial down the toilet, then left the cubicle and washed his hands. A few minutes later he was back in his seat, just two places away from Max. The aging malt whisky sat untouched in a glass in front of his old College prefect. Bob tried not to stare at it.

Sir Peter Maitland-Buckley opened the proceedings, which would auction off donated goods, experiences and outings to rich lawyers and bankers and bring in a large amount of much needed cash for the charity.

"Before we begin, I'm delighted to welcome our patron, Sir Max Rochester, who has agreed to say a few words," he announced.

Sir Max picked up his whisky and sank it in one gulp before he stood. The whisky mixed with the potassium chloride and slid smoothly down his throat, warming his insides, as the applause died down.

"Ladies and gentlemen, on behalf of the Maximillian Rochester Fund for Sick Children I would like to extend a warm welcome to all of you who are attending this event. May I thank you all for turning out in such numbers. I trust you have all brought suitably large amounts of money with you." There was a ripple of laughter, and Sir Max smiled with satisfaction. He cleared his throat, then brushed a hand across his forehead as he continued. "Now, ladies and gentlemen, let us remember why we are here. Most of us present will count ourselves blessed to have enjoyed comfortable and healthy childhoods, for the main part, and so now is the time to show our largesse and bring some joy into the lives of those children who are sick and dying." Sir Max paused and shook his head as if trying to clear it. "Ladies and gentlemen, please join me in welcoming our charming guest auctioneer this evening, the English born Hollywood actress Kate Jarret."

The actress stood to much applause, and raised the wooden auctioneer's mallet for the cameras. Such was the concentration on this beautiful young woman and her daring strapless dress that no-one noticed Sir Max. He sat down rather heavily, feeling decidedly unwell. He dabbed at the perspiration on his forehead with his handkerchief. A pained expression crossed his wrinkled face as he rubbed the top of his left arm and grimaced, but the pain seemed to pass and he sipped at a glass of water.

It was a nerve wracking two minutes before Sir Max finally succumbed to the clear liquid that Bob had introduced into his whisky. Eventually he tried to stand up, clutched at his chest and collapsed. There were gasps and cries of dismay, and chairs scraped against the floor as other guests jumped to their feet nearby. Bob was the first to his side, apparently making the old man comfortable as he breathed his last. Amid the noisy chaos Sir Peter made an announcement over the PA system, asking if there was a doctor in the room. There were half a dozen, and they began to hurry forward, but they were already too late. Bob ushered everyone back whilst cradling the old man's head. Max tried to utter a few words, but they were little more than a whisper. Bob leaned in to listen. Then he leaned over Max and whispered in his ear.

"You should have paid me the five million, Max. You can't spend it now."

Max's eyes widened in horror as he listened to the words, then he breathed his last breath, his expired body relaxing into Bob's arms.

Chapter 11

Atkins Garretson Palmer, College Hill, London: Thursday, 6pm.

Andrew Cuthbertson was sitting at his desk pondering his options. He had noticed his colleagues staring at him all afternoon. It seemed that a couple of people had addressed him and he hadn't answered. He hadn't even heard them; he was absorbed in his own thoughts. They were concerned that the usually ebullient Andy appeared so withdrawn. He knew that in the next half hour the place would begin to clear and he could have the floor to himself. He needed to do something, but he didn't know what to do.

After the meeting with Josh that afternoon, Andrew had decided to call the blackmailer off. Perhaps he could threaten him with exposure if necessary, but he had to try to keep him away from Josh, at least. Andrew had never believed the man would kill anyone, anyway. He was wealthy in his own right, he had connections at cabinet level, and he was well respected around the world. When Andrew had asked him why he was doing this, there had been no explanation in reply. He was told simply to supply the information required or his wife and daughter, and his employers, would hear about the girl in Bangkok. In fact, they would see the photographs of the very young girl looking scared and bemused, not to mention bruised, after Andy had finished with her. Andrew had been stunned at the threat. How could anyone have found out? Why couldn't they have held the Partners' conference somewhere else, somewhere where young girls weren't offered to you for sale as if they were a fake Rolex?

Andrew had been so caught up in his own misery that he had not noticed the stir in the office. The senior equity partner on the floor was being hemmed in by staff, and eventually he gave in and picked up the phone.

Andrew walked over to see what was happening. The senior partner said into the phone, "It's true then? …… All right. Thank you. I'll let my people know." He replaced the receiver, clearly shaken. Eventually he looked at the expectant faces and addressed the office.

"Please listen, everyone. It seems that the rumours are true. The 'Twittering' is accurate, for once. Sir Max Rochester collapsed and died at Blacksmiths Hall an hour ago." There was an audible gasp. Sir Max was this group's largest client.

Andrew wandered back to his desk in a haze. "It has to be a coincidence, it can't be true," he said to himself. Then he looked at his watch. Sir Max's forty eight hours had expired four minutes ago.

Chapter 12

Ashburnham Mews, Greenwich, London. Thursday, 8pm.

Dee turned the laptop around so that I could see the screen. My bank account looked healthier than ever before. I had over two hundred and fifty two thousand pounds sitting in my current account.

"OK, Josh, it's all there. Now we just wait for instructions. I guess he'll text something in the morning, just to make sure that you're going ahead with it."

Dee was right. With sixteen hours to go we were ready, but I doubted whether Bob would call. He seemed to want to create as much anxiety as possible. He would probably wait until just before noon to contact me and then make me jump through hoops to transfer the money.

I was still considering how I would react to giving away a quarter of a million pounds when my cell phone rang. 'Unknown Number' showed up on the screen. We had placed my cell phone on a small unit provided by the police which looked rather like an iPhone charger with built-in speakers. I pressed the button to answer, and the red light flashed as the unit began a digital recording. I leaned over the unit and spoke into the microphone.

"Hello?" There was silence for several long seconds and I thought that Bob was teasing me, unless he guessed somehow that the call was being recorded.

"Josh, I'm sorry." Andrew Cuthbertson's voice was cracked and faltering. "My life is over, Josh. I've lost everything. Tomorrow everything will come out and I'll be ruined." He was rambling, but I said nothing.

"I did give your details away, you were right, but I was being blackmailed too. You have to believe me. He had me over a barrel, Josh." There was a pause as he sobbed; the man was on the verge of a breakdown. "I need to see you, to tell you the whole story. Tomorrow morning, early, before everything hits the fan."

"OK, Andrew, just stay calm," I said. "Who is this Bob, anyway? Do you have any idea?"

"That's just one of his names, and none of them are his real name. I can't tell you over the phone. I need to see you in person, to explain."

"All right, Andrew. Get a good night's rest and we'll see if we can sort this out tomorrow. Where do you want to meet?"

"Let's meet at the pedestrian footbridge at Butler's Wharf, next to the Chop House Restaurant. It should be deserted there at seven tomorrow morning."

"I can do that, Andrew," I assured him. "I'll take one of the riverboats, but it might be a few minutes after seven when I get there."

"I understand, but try not to be too late. I'll be waiting. Thanks, Josh." He hung up, leaving me wondering just what my friend had got himself mixed up in.

Chapter 13

Butlers Wharf, Tower Bridge, London. Friday, 6:45am.

Alarmed by Andrew Cuthbertson's phone call last night, and by his sudden show of conscience, Bob kept watch over the former warehouses which now housed modern apartments set around an ornamental Japanese Garden. The sun was up and the ducks on the pond were making a racket. Bob was amazed that people would pay upwards of three hundred and fifty thousand pounds for a two bedroomed apartment in an old warehouse in what used to be a rough area of London.

The complex was security gated, entry by a key fob, and so Bob stood out of sight of the pedestrian entrance gate in one of the narrow passages that still led to the waterside. He was very disappointed with Andrew. No matter how much he threatened, Andrew refused to meet him to discuss the situation. Bob had felt sure that another look at the photos of the pathetic pre-pubescent Thai girl would bring the young accountant back into line. He was wrong. Andrew had made it clear that it was too late for that, and so Bob had been waiting outside the Cuthbertsons' apartment for an hour.

***

Andrew hadn't slept a wink. He had decided to tell his wife everything when he arrived home, so that the blackmail threats would be useless, but as soon as he saw his perfect wife, Charlotte, and their daughter Zoe, he knew he couldn't do it. They would find out soon enough, and then he would try to explain, if they gave him the chance.

After a quick shower in the family bathroom, so as not to disturb Charlotte, he dressed and let himself out of the ground floor flat quietly. Not that any noise he made would be heard over the ducks. One of the attractions of the flat, in addition to the security, was the fact that the buildings were grouped around a quadrangle which sported oriental gardens and small ornamental bridges over manmade ponds. His apartment had a wooden deck beyond the patio doors, where they could sit and eat in the warm weather. In the winter the ducks would come and peck on the patio doors, brazenly looking for food. Their comic antics always entertained Zoe. Andrew imagined the scene and smiled through his sadness.

The accountant exited the security gate and walked across the lane to the wooden ramp that led onto the wharf. In ten minutes the story would be told and Josh would be safe.

Andrew walked through the brick tunnel and emerged into the bright early morning sunshine as Tower Bridge came into view. Ahead of him stood a modern, stylised stainless steel pedestrian bridge with steel grating walkway. It was no longer than five metres because the only thing it spanned was an old disused unloading bay. The small pool underneath the bridge was flooded by the Thames at high tide, but now it was just a muddy quagmire with the occasional wave lapping in.

A few yards away a wooden jetty ran out into the Thames to accommodate the river taxis and tourist boats. It was still deserted. The first boat of the morning had not yet arrived. A light mist hovered low over the surface of the water, already dissipating in the morning air. The scene was bathed in the golden light of the late summer sunrise, and the few trees in the area were already beginning to show the first hint of autumn in the yellowing leaves, but the air was fresh and cool and the rays of the sun cast long shadows across his path.

Andrew was entirely alone apart from a grey squirrel which was hunting around for food, and a jogger who was moving at a pace that could easily have been exceeded by most people walking briskly. Why do they do it, he asked himself. Run or walk, but that slow jog is pathetic.

The jogger was dressed in a grey fleece training suit, his hood up against the cool river breeze. He stopped a few yards away from Andrew and did some hamstring and calf stretches, using the railings for support. Andrew leaned against the handrail to make room for the jogger on the narrow bridge. The jogger reached the small bridge and the accountant felt it move with the extra weight of the new occupant. The jogger was moving towards him, fists shadow boxing the air.

"Loony," thought Andrew, and looked away to avoid eye contact. The jogger stopped directly behind him. Andy could feel his presence and turned around to tell him to clear off. When he saw the face beneath the hood, he froze.

***

Bob saw the shock on Andrew's face and took his opportunity. A leather sap, or cosh, filled with lead pellets swung up and caught the young accountant directly under the chin. Bob saw the young man's eyes roll back into his head and his body go limp. He knew he didn't have long. Having scoured the wharf for signs of life a minute earlier as he'd feigned stretching, he knew they were alone. Taking the weight of Andrew's body, he leaned him against the railing and tipped him over.

The young accountant toppled face down into the muddy quagmire as Bob looked on. After a few seconds Andrew shuddered and began to come round. Thrashing wildly, he could do no more than pull himself deeper into the mud; his manic efforts to save himself did not last long, and after a few moments one had to look hard to see a body at all.

Bob looked up as a maritime horn sounded. The first Thames Clipper of the day was approaching. He turned his back and walked away in the direction he had come from, as though nothing at all had happened.

Chapter 14

Butlers Wharf, Tower Bridge, London. 7:05am.

We picked up the Thames Clipper at Greenwich at five minutes to seven, and the high speed catamaran skimmed along the Thames at the speed limit for less than ten minutes before we reached our destination. On those occasions when I took the glass sided Clippers, with their spectacular views of the bridges and the city, I always promised myself that I would use them more often and abandon the overcrowded Tube. On a morning like this, with a clear blue sky and just a light breeze, it seemed especially appealing.

We alighted at Tower Bridge and I looked around in the early morning sunshine, searching for Andrew.

Dee hadn't been to this area of London for a decade and was surprised at how upmarket it had all become. Two of London's most popular restaurants were within a stone's throw of where we stood. We walked along the South Bank in the direction of Butler's Wharf and the stylish post-modern pedestrian bridge. There was no sign of Andrew, but it was only just after seven, so we agreed to give him until seven fifteen before calling him.

We stood on the bridge for a while, taking in the fresh air and just talking. I explained how the Shad Thames area had turned from a derelict warehouse district into a thriving community occupied by aspirational professionals. As I looked around, I noticed that many of the businesses and buildings which we could see housed companies which were in our company insurance portfolio.

Dee was becoming concerned, and suggested that we call Andrew. By now it was almost seven fifteen. I called Andrew's number up on my list of most recently called numbers and pressed the green telephone symbol.

Almost immediately I heard a sound like an old fashioned telephone bell. Assuming that Andy must be somewhere close by, I looked around for him but couldn't see him. Dee looked around, too, clearly as puzzled as I was. The ringing stopped and my call went to voice mail. It was definitely his phone which we had heard ringing.

I rang the number again and we listened carefully. The tone seemed to be coming from underneath the bridge. Dee looked through the steel grating that formed the walkway and saw the phone lighting up with each ring. She caught her breath and pointed at it. I rang off and, kneeling down, I looked more closely. The phone was lying on debris at the bridge parapet, just inches away from the muddy water which was splashing around down there. Dee held my jacket as I climbed over the guard rails and stood on the exposed muddy bank. I had to hold onto the bridge to avoid slipping into the quicksand-like mud in the basin. I picked up the mobile phone from amongst the stones. It was dirty but it appeared largely undamaged. I was checking that it was still working when another Thames Clipper passed about fifteen metres away and the wash pushed river water into the basin, washing over my feet and soaking my socks and shoes. I swore loudly. Then I thought I saw something in the muddy morass.

As the river water washed over the mud I was sure I saw a face appear just below the surface, but then the water withdrew like a receding wave and the face was gone. I was convinced that I must have imagined it, until I noticed the toe of a brown shoe breaking the surface of the mud just a few metres away. I didn't want to believe what I knew must be true.

I climbed back onto the bridge and told Dee what I had seen. She looked into my eyes.

"Is it Andrew?" she asked.

"I hope not, but it does seem to be rather too much of a coincidence," I replied, feeling a depth of sadness that surprised me.

Dee dialled the number for Inspector Boniface and twenty minutes later we heard the River Police boat approaching, sirens blaring.

***

An hour later the body had been recovered from the mud before the tide could come in and sweep it away. I unofficially confirmed it was Andrew, and Dee nodded her agreement as I spoke. The official identification would be done by Charlotte later, after the body had been cleaned and a cause of death had been established.

Dee and I were sitting in a police transporter with Inspector Boniface.

"Josh, this is outside my jurisdiction, it's a job for the Met boys, so be wary. Remember, you have a motive and also opportunity, so you are bound to be questioned."

"I have Dee as an alibi," I responded, feeling mildly annoyed that anyone would consider me a suspect in Andrew's death.

"I understand that, Josh, but…" he looked at Dee. "….Ms Conrad was heard threatening Andrew less than twenty four hours ago. I'm just warning you both to be prepared for some hard questioning. Now, I'm going to take you both back to the City Police HQ. I've told the investigating officer that you are crucial witnesses to a blackmail plot and potentially two murders."

"Two murders?" Dee looked puzzled.

"Yes. When the Scene of Crimes Officers looked at Sir Max Rochester's phone last night they discovered a number of texts." I guessed what was coming, but I let the Inspector continue unabated. "The upshot of it is that he, too, had been given forty eight hours to deliver a rather larger sum than yours, and he refused to play ball. He died within a few minutes of the deadline expiring."

"My God, this man is serious about killing his victims!" Dee Conrad seemed surprised, but I wasn't. I fully expected to die if I didn't pay. Otherwise why would I shell out a quarter of a million pounds?

"Obviously this is a working theory at the moment because the death looks like natural causes, possibly a heart attack, but hopefully a toxicology report will provide some answers." Boniface paused for the inevitable question. I asked it.

"Is it possible for someone to induce a heart attack, then?"

"The short answer is yes. It doesn't strictly cause a coronary infarction but you can interfere with heart function with a sufficient dose of potassium chloride. They use it as one of the components for chemical executions, more politely referred to as lethal injections in the USA. Anyone who knew that Sir Max had heart problems could reasonably assume that a large dose of potassium chloride would be enough to kill him."

"Does it have to be injected?" Dee asked.

"No, but it's colourless, and in a strong drink such as whisky it would be almost undetectable. Another reason for suspicion is that by the time the paramedics arrived on the scene, Sir Max's whisky glass had disappeared from the table."

"So it was murder," I concluded.

"We may never get to prove that, Josh. It's touch and go at the moment."

"But what about toxicology? Won't that find the chemicals in the body?" I couldn't believe that the team in CSI Miami wouldn't have known with certainty it was murder. Boniface had an answer for that, too.

"The trouble is, Josh, that when someone has a heart attack the levels of potassium are often raised in the body immediately afterwards. It's a natural chemical reaction, caused by an enzyme being released into the bloodstream. So, higher levels of potassium may not be conclusive evidence of murder."

"And what about Andrew Cuthbertson? Are the police treating his death as suspicious?" Dee asked.

"Suspicious, yes, but for the moment it looks like either an accident of some sort or a suicide, and if it wasn't - well, you two will be considered prime candidates for interview."

Strangely enough I really could imagine Andrew ending it all after hearing his frantic call last night, but who would commit suicide by jumping ten feet into mud? No-one.

We were suddenly interrupted by Andrew's phone ringing. Boniface lifted the phone from the clear plastic evidence bag using a latex gloved hand. By the time he got it free of its container it had stopped ringing. The screen announced a missed call from Work. While he had the phone in his hand Boniface scrolled down the recent calls list. The last call was to a person listed as LH. The call had been made late last night, after he had called me.

"LH. That could be the blackmailer." I realised that I sounded a little desperate. Boniface lifted the phone to his ear after dialling the last number called. The phone rang out without an answer and went to an anonymous woman who asked us to leave a message after the tone.

"I'll get a trace on that number straight away. Maybe LH, or Bob, has made his first mistake." Boniface stepped out of the van, holding his own phone to his ear and speaking urgently.

***

Bob felt the phone vibrate in his pocket as he stepped onto Beech Street and headed back to his hotel. He knew who was calling. That cheap Nokia was reserved exclusively for speaking to Cuthbertson, and he was dead. The police had probably found his phone. Bob switched the phone off, and for the second time in twenty four hours he dismantled and discarded a cell phone.

Chapter 15

City of London Police HQ, Wood St, London. Friday, 9:30am.

The old fashioned office carried the vague aroma of lavender furniture polish. Obviously the cleaners had been in. I let my gaze wander around the office walls. There was a good deal about the Force on view, but very little about the man. A single certificate hung on the wall behind the desk. It appeared that Inspector Boniface had completed a course with NYPD on counter terrorism in urban environments. I wondered idly whether it was a serious course or whether it had been something of a jolly.

The door opened and Boniface walked in. "Well, we have some news, but it's not particularly good, I'm afraid," he stated. "The phone I was calling for LH has been switched off, probably permanently. However, as your threat comes from Bob and Sir Max was threatened by Bob, too, I think we can assume that LH might be the blackmailer's real initials. Also, it appears that our late friend Mr Cuthbertson was being blackmailed as well. This is the text of an email sent to Andrew by LH." Boniface laid a sheet of paper on the desk. It read:

Andrew,

The information on our first female client is late. Hope you aren't getting cold feet. Don't know what the wife would say about the little Thai girl. Was she much older than your daughter? Send the info, don't be a martyr.

LH

I knew that Andrew had been in Bangkok at a partners' conference some months before and told Boniface about it. He already knew. I guess we were both thinking the same thing; the photo must have been pretty bad to have worried Andy enough to become drawn into a murderous blackmail plot.

"Josh, Dee. We are not making sufficient progress in identifying Bob to say with any certainty that you would be safe if you didn't pay the money." Boniface left the decision on whether to pay up or not to me, in the full knowledge that official police policy was always to refuse to pay blackmail demands.

Dee spoke to me directly. "Bob hasn't sent you the bank details yet. Maybe he's running scared after the Andrew Cuthbertson debacle." She didn't sound very convincing, even to herself.

We sat in silence for a moment and then discussed the arrangements for the bank transfer, should it be necessary. The money would be transferred from my account, temporarily, to an account held by the Serious Financial Crimes team. They would then send the money electronically to the bank account Bob nominated. The transfer file accompanying the money would have an invisible electronic tag which carried a code, alerting the bank and overseas law enforcement agencies that this was a tracked payment and that the tag must be left in place for subsequent transfers or transactions. Apparently the major banks have an arrangement with the law enforcement authorities that precludes them from notifying their customer that the money is being tracked.

Now it was simply a question of waiting.

**

Bob had showered and shaved. He felt refreshed after the morning's tribulations. He was back on track. His clothes from his morning jaunt were with the hotel laundry and, when returned, would be donated to the Salvation Army. There was no point in taking any unnecessary risks.

Bob looked at his Breitling watch and read the time as ten thirty. Time for a couple of calls, he decided. He took the phone labelled with the name Josh, inserted the battery and switched it on. He dialled the last number called. The phone rang out for a moment and a man picked it up.

"Abasi Nour speaking. How may I help you?"

"Hello Abasi, this is Josh Hammond. Are we still OK for twelve noon?" Bob's voice was higher than normal and carried the dialect most associated with the East End of London. Bob was rightly proud of his convincing range of dialects.

"Mr Josh, yes, I am ready. The goods are here." The Egyptian paused for a moment. "I will confirm that this is a private transaction, between two men of honour?"

Bob replied and confirmed that he would pay the money directly into Mr Nour's personal bank account and not into the business account. The merchant gave Bob his bank account details and wished him well until they met at noon.

**

It was almost half past eleven when Josh's phone buzzed with a text message. The phone was back on the docking station that the police were using to trace the caller. Josh, Dee and Inspector Boniface peered at the small screen.

"Hi Josh,

Just an half an hour to go until payment is due or…… well we won't go into that. Here are the details of my bank account. If I don't hear that my account has been credited by noon the deal is off. By the way, make sure that your money is labelled as coming from you. There is a lot of activity in my account and I wouldn't want to miss your payment.

Bob."

Boniface was reading the bank account number from the screen and repeating the numbers and the sort code to someone on the other end of the telephone line.

"Right, Josh, your money will be there in five minutes. As soon as we receive the electronic receipt we'll trace the account holder and start tracking the money. My guess is that it will bounce around the world for a few hours and settle In Grand Cayman or Switzerland overnight."

Boniface seemed confident that the money could not escape the police net. I was not so sure. It seemed to me that Bob had been a step ahead of us all along, and whilst I didn't know how it could be done, I suspected that Bob had found a way of transferring the money - my money - without leaving a trail. I had an uncomfortable feeling that I would not be getting it back.

Chapter 16

Nour Jewellery Design, Hatton Garden, London. Friday, 11:50am.

The shop was small but beautifully furnished. It had the appearance of a consulting room as there were no gems on display, but each of the two magnificent carved walnut desks carried a brochure showing exquisite jewellery. Abasi Nour was a neat Egyptian man with a pencil moustache and a linen suit which was unsuited to the weather. He rose from his chair as Bob entered the shop, having been buzzed in through the security door.

"Mr Josh, how nice to see you again," the shop owner said cheerily as he greeted the tall moustached man with the unconvincing toupee. His own hair was dyed jet black and carefully styled to cover his whole head.

The two men sat down and Bob handed over his business card. It read "Josh Hammond, Senior Loss Analyst."

"Mr Nour, as you know this first transaction...."

Mr Nour held up his hand to stop Bob speaking. "Halima, could you leave us please?" The spectacularly attractive olive skinned girl at the other desk rose, smiled and exited through the door at the back of the shop.

"Sorry, Mr Josh, but we cannot be too careful. Now, you were saying."

"Mr Nour, this is the first bonus payment of the year. There is another due later in the year, which will be a little larger, I hope. And I would like to do the same again if this transaction is beneficial."

"Yes, indeed, London City bonuses are both legendary and generous to humble merchants like myself."

"Shall we get on?" Bob prompted. "The money has been transferred."

"Yes, sir, I will just confirm." The Egyptian pressed a button on his phone and waited. After a moment he spoke a few sentences in Arabic before switching to English. "Asif, I am so distressed to disturb you on this special day but can you confirm that the funds are cleared to my account as agreed?" He listened to the reply for a moment and then bade his bank manager farewell in Arabic.

"My bank manager is sitting at home with his laptop and has confirmed payment, so we may now proceed."

Abasi Noor opened a secret drawer in his desk by sliding back an intricately carved panel. He reached in a brought out a velvet pouch.

"As you requested, I have purchased only the very best round diamonds from Antwerp. These are all classified as colourless category D, or what we call best blue white. They are also internally flawless, they are extraordinarily rare. They have been cut for maximum brilliance, not for maximum carat size. But as you will see they are all large diamonds. You may not know that a diamond that is twice the size of another is usually almost three times more expensive. Please, take a look."

Even under the harsh fluorescent lighting the diamonds looked magnificent. Bob had acquired them to sell on, but he was reconsidering now that he had been besotted by their beauty.

"I have the invoice from Antwerp. Losi Van Serck cut these diamonds personally as a favour to me and the certificate attached to the invoice shows the quality, cut and carat."

Bob looked at the invoice made out to Mr Nour. The Egyptian had paid two hundred and twenty five thousand pounds for the jewels, making an easy mark-up. Usually he would have to integrate the diamonds into a unique designer gold necklace to achieve a mark-up like that. But Bob was happy. These diamonds could easily be transported anywhere in the world and were ready to be traded.

A few minutes later Bob was walking along Greville Street in the direction of the Farringdon Tube Station, sending the last text on the "Josh Phone" before discarding it. After a short tube journey to Kings Cross, where he removed the glasses, moustache, hairpiece and garish City boy's tie in the gentlemen's toilets, Bob hailed a taxi and headed back to his hotel for a celebratory lunch.

Chapter 17

City of London Police HQ, Wood St, London. Friday, Noon.

Dee was chatting and joking to try to distract me, but it wasn't working. It had been over half an hour since the money was transmitted, and all we had seen or heard was Boniface taking an urgent call. He had yelled "How did that happen?" and stormed out of the office without another word.

I had a horrible feeling that my money was gone forever. My phone was still in the dock and it buzzed again. I read the message aloud.

"Thanks Josh,

That was easy. Perhaps I didn't ask for enough. Next time I'll be more realistic. You'll be hearing from me again.

Bob"

I put my head in my hands. Dee put her hand on my back.

"He's winding you up, Josh, now that he's got what he wanted. In any case, I wouldn't be surprised if he's apprehended over the weekend. This is a murder investigation now."

What Dee said made sense, but I wasn't convinced. I was still pondering her remark when Boniface appeared, his face like thunder. He spoke calmly despite his agitated appearance.

"Josh, first of all let me assure you that your money is safe. We are tracking it, but we have a problem. The account we sent your money to is held at the Sharia Islamic Bank of Arabia close to Regents Park. Unfortunately we can't raise them on the telephone to find out the customer's details because it's Friday and the Bank is closed for the Muslim weekend. It's also Ramadan, and so getting hold of people at home is going to be tricky, as the London Central Mosque has a variety of activities going on today."

I wondered whether Bob had done this deliberately, or whether he was just a lucky son of a bitch.

The day meandered on at a snail's pace. The police were as frustrated as I was. Bob was still their best suspect for a double murder, after all. Tracking my money seemed the best way to track the man. The IT guys had pinged his mobile phone several times without success. I had a sneaking feeling that we would find it in the hands of a homeless man sometime next week.

The good thing was that the money had not moved and so, theoretically, I still had my quarter of a million pounds. It was almost two o'clock when Inspector Boniface's phone rang again. Before the caller was put through, Boniface put the call on conference and began recording it. He held his finger to his lips as an instruction to us to keep quiet.

"Inspector Boniface speaking. How can I help you?"

"Hello, my name is Asif Al Maheel. I am the manager of the Regents Park Branch of the Sharia Islamic Bank of Arabia. You have been leaving messages for me."

"Thanks for calling back, Mr Al Maheel. First of all, let me apologise for interrupting your weekend. I wouldn't have done so if this was not an urgent matter. If it is at all possible, I need you to go to the bank and check whose account had two hundred and fifty thousand pounds paid into it at noon today."

"Oh, I don't need to go to the bank for that information; I was expecting a payment of that amount by noon today from a Mr Josh Hammond. It arrived on time and I called my customer to inform him so. But I am afraid I cannot disclose his details without a very good reason, or maybe a warrant. I would have to speak to our legal department on Sunday."

"Mr Al Maheel, we don't have time to wait until Sunday, I'm afraid. We are hot on the trail of a double murderer, and your customer may be in danger."

There was silence on the other end of the line for a moment. "Inspector, please, I hope you are being honest with me. In good faith I will give you his name, but on the condition you do not involve the bank."

"I can assure you, we just want to speak to your customer. We are happy that the bank is not involved."

The speakerphone chirped again.

"My customer, and my friend, is the owner of Nour Jewellery Design of Hatton Garden."

"Will he be at his premises today? I believe it is the Sabbath?"

"Oh, yes. Abasi is not the good Muslim that he might be. Please call me if you have any problems. I am at your service, Inspector. Goodbye."

***

As we waited on the pavement for a car to pick us up, Dee took me to one side. Her hazel eyes were bright with intent. Her face was perfect. Dee was probably in her early thirties. Her hair always shone. She had a pert nose and a generous mouth beneath it. Her make-up was generally understated, but her great cheekbones made cosmetics largely redundant. I had never really met a woman like her before. No more than five feet eight inches tall, she looked elegant and well proportioned, but I had been assured that in a fight she could take out men twice her size.

"Josh, theoretically my assignment is over but I want you to know that I'm going nowhere until I think you're safe. Are you comfortable with that?" I nodded dumbly. I could have kissed her, but then again I had felt like kissing her since we'd met.

An unmarked car pulled up and Boniface slid in beside the driver, leaving Dee and I to take the back seat. As soon as the doors were closed we moved off at speed towards the Barbican. The driver could easily have been a cabbie; he knew all the shortcuts. We drove down Long Lane before cutting up onto Charterhouse, avoiding the one way system. A minute later we were skirting around St Etheldreda's Church and onto Hatton Garden. About half way up on the right hand side we found 'Nour Jewellery Design'.

We left the car and walked towards the shop. Unlike every other shop in Hatton Garden, which is famous throughout the world for its wall to wall jewellery stores, Nour had no jewellery on display, just large decals showing the most lavish pieces I have ever seen. The writing on the windows made it clear that Nour would procure the best diamonds and finest gold for you and then fashion them into unique works of art that you could wear.

Boniface pressed a button on the wall and held his warrant card against the glass. The door buzzed and he pushed it open. We followed him in. A stunning olive skinned girl sat at the desk facing us.

"Can I help you?" she asked. The accent was more East End than Middle East. Boniface asked for Mr Nour and the girl slipped her long perfectly manicured fingers under the edge of the desk, almost invisibly. A moment later Mr Nour opened the door at the back of the shop. He beamed in anticipation of doing business with wealthy customers.

"Welcome, gentlemen. How may I help you?" He stopped beaming when he saw the warrant card. In fact, I thought I saw fear in his eyes as he looked quickly from the Inspector to me. That was not unusual. Some of my Middle Eastern clients only ever saw their police when they were about to be taken into custody so that they could be given the opportunity to confess.

"You are Mr Abasi Nour, with a bank Account at the Sharia Islamic Bank of Arabia, Regents Park?" The nervous Egyptian nodded. "You have just had two hundred and fifty thousand pounds transferred into your account from a Mr Josh Hammond?" The man nodded again. "Then meet Mr Josh Hammond in person." Mr Nour blanched, and collapsed into his chair.

**

Five minutes passed whilst Halima made her ashen boss some hot sweet tea. Mr Nour was normally a swarthy man with typical Middle Eastern colour, but now his complexion was pallid and yellow. He looked ill.

Inspector Boniface had explained earlier that there was no chance that Mr Nour was Bob. He simply didn't fit the profile. He was sure that Bob had used Mr Nour to break the chain between me and my money. With any luck we would get our first description of Bob.

Under gentle questioning from the Inspector the whole story unfolded. Just over forty eight hours ago, Wednesday afternoon, Mr Noor had received a call from a man claiming to be Josh Hammond. He said he had been recommended by Sir Max Rochester, who was a respected customer.

This Josh had been paid a bonus of a quarter of a million pounds (I wish) and wanted to hide it from his ex-wife's lawyers. He wanted to convert it into something small and transportable that he could hide easily. Diamonds had seemed the perfect option. The trouble was that he needed to do it quickly, because next week the auditors would be looking to split the marital proceeds.

Mr Nour had agreed to purchase the finest diamonds available from Antwerp, apparently the world centre for the supply of fine, cut diamonds. He had even managed to procure diamonds cut personally by Losi Van Serck, the leading artist in the field of diamond cutting. The diamonds had arrived this morning, and Josh Hammond had apparently collected them.

'Mr Hammond' had visited the shop twice and on each occasion he had stayed for only a few minutes. Mr Nour handed over a business card. It was my business card, or at least on first pass it looked like my business card. On closer inspection it had different phone numbers. The landline number was correct, but it had a red pen stroke through the middle. The fax number and the mobile number were not my numbers.

"He told me not to call him at work because calls could be recorded," Mr Nour explained.

"Presumably you asked for some form of identification?" Mr Nour's eyes brightened as if he had suddenly been redeemed. He opened a drawer and withdrew two sheets of A4 paper. On the first was a scan of a driving licence; on the second was a scan of a passport. In both cases the name was Josh Hammond but the details were all wrong. The photo was of a middle aged man who looked nothing at all like me, with a mane of unkempt hair and a big moustache. Neither photo was flattering.

"He emailed those to me when he made the order. It must have been a different Josh Hammond. This has all been a confusing error."

"Mr Nour, do you have CCTV coverage of your meeting with Mr Hammond?"

The Egyptian disappeared into the back of the shop and returned a moment later with a shiny CD Rom.

"This is today's CCTV coverage," he explained, handing over the CD. Boniface laid it to one side and spoke quietly.

"Mr Nour, the money you received for your diamonds will be frozen in your account until we have resolved whether or not it is yours to keep." Boniface saw the look on my face and shook his head almost imperceptibly, inviting me to remain silent. "If this man contacts you again you must call me immediately. Now I need three things - a police technician to examine your computer, a description of the man who claimed to be Josh Hammond, and a full description of the diamonds you handed over."

"I have a photo of each of the diamonds and their certificates. Halima can email them to you. As for the man, he appeared very much like you see in these pictures. I would say he was almost six feet tall, a little overweight, he wore a badly fitting toupee and he was wearing a Breitling Navitimer Mecanique wristwatch. I have been selling Breitling watches for thirty years and the Mecanique, a French version, is very rare now, and very valuable."

It was typical of a jeweller to be able to describe a watch with precision and yet only be able to give a vague description of the wearer.

"Thank you, Mr Nour. My understanding is that Breitling watches are individually numbered. Is that correct?"

"Yes, each one is registered to protect the brand against replicas and fakes. But obviously I did not see the number."

I thought that was too much to hope for, but nonetheless Bob had slipped up. He was fallible after all, and I took heart from that.

"Thank you, Mr Nour," Boniface said, shaking his hand. "A technician will be here within the hour. I can assure you that we will try our level best to find your gems and also the man who misled you."

Chapter 18

City of London Police Station, Wood St, London. Friday, 5pm.

I was exhausted. It had been a long day.

The police had eventually managed to freeze the money in the Sharia Islamic Bank of Arabia but there was some doubt as to whether I would ever get it back. Mr Nour had sold the diamonds in good faith to a man who had two hundred and fifty thousand pounds delivered to Nour's account. The Egyptian had even made sure that 'Josh Hammond's' money was in his account before he let the diamonds go. Finally Nour had copies of a scanned passport and driving licence that probably would have fooled me. Either he lost a quarter of a million pounds' worth of diamonds, or I lost the cash, and if I was being honest I had traded the money for my life, which was now hopefully safe from Bob, who was potentially a double murderer.

Boniface and I were covering the emails Bob had sent to Nour and the fax number on the business card. Neither led anywhere. The email had been sent from josh.hammond@48hours.co.za which we had known was a dead end since yesterday morning. The fax number was a *Scanfax* number, a free service that allows email users to have faxes converted to email and forwarded on. The number led straight back to the email address.

I was still in Boniface's office reading through my statement concerning the morning's grim find when Dee came in with a Detective Sergeant from the financial crimes team. Boniface gestured to them to sit down, but they both seemed excited. They handed a sheet of paper to me and to Boniface and asked us to read it to ourselves. It read;

Breitling Research: Dee Conrad & DS Peter Fellowes.

The Navtimer watch was introduced in 1952 and went out of production around 2003. The Old Navtimer edition was produced in the period 1993 to 2002. The Mecanique was a special French limited edition of just 1000 pieces. Breitling HQ is in Grenchen, Switzerland.

DS Fellowes has been in touch with Breitling HQ in Grenchen, Switzerland and they confirmed that the majority of owners do register with them to guard against theft and forgeries. They said, "When you are paying thousands of pounds for a watch you want to know it is genuine."

Each Old Navtimer Mecanique is marked with the model reference number, A11022 and a unique Breitling registration number. Of the 1000 Mecanique watches 143 are unaccounted for or have never been registered. Most are registered in France, where they were predominantly marketed but 78 are registered to people currently living in the UK, 66 of the UK based owners are French nationals and 4 are known Breitling Dealers. That leaves 8 in British private ownership. Unfortunately Breitling cannot give us names or addresses without an international warrant, which is unlikely to be granted as we are on a fishing expedition here.

However, there is a ray of hope. Breitling watches are serviced and maintained at Tonbridge Wells and Dee Conrad has been in contact with the manager there. He has maintenance records of 12 watches bearing the reference A11022. He was not keen to share that information but after a bit of sweet talking he agreed to email Dee a list of the names and the towns to which the serviced watches were returned. He said we will need a warrant if we want any more than that. Here is the spreadsheet he sent.

NAME	TOWN
D. Allinson	Edinburgh
S. Bentley	Oxford
F. Cozee	London

A. Hickstead   Leeds

L. Houlier   London

D. Julliard   St Helier

H. Laurent   Manchester

T. Morrissey   Wigan

K. Pascal   Glasgow

N. Van Doren   Rotterdam

G. Weissman   London

A. Wasir   Birmingham

I decided to be the first to make an observation.

"If my reasoning is correct, we have potentially eight watches registered to individuals who are not French and are not dealers. The spreadsheet you've procured has eight people who appear to be non-French. Even if I'm wrong on a couple of the names, it means that our man is almost certainly on that list."

"That would be right if it was not for the fact that one hundred and forty-three of the watches were not registered. Those unregistered watches could all be in London," DS Fellowes countered.

"Or none of them could be in the UK at all. It is at least a lead," I said optimistically.

Dee chirped up. "Am I the only one seeing this? The fifth name down, L Houlier of London, whose initials are LH."

The room fell silent.

Chapter 19

Pendolino Train, First Class Carriage, Kings Cross. 5pm.

Bob sat in the seat and relaxed. The East Coast line was experimenting with the Pendolino that had proved such a success on the West Coast route. When not locked down by a pandemic as he was last year, Bob was a regular rail traveller across Europe and found the Pendolino less comfortable than the Eurostar or the old GNER 225s.

He closed his eyes and pondered as the odours of dinner cooking in the dining car permeated the carriage. This line was one of the last to preserve the dignity of passengers by offering a Silver Service dinner in a dedicated dining car.

Bob idly wondered whether the slimy Abasi Nour was in jail yet. He doubted that the Egyptian would ever get his hands on the two hundred and fifty grand that had been used to secure the diamonds. Sir Max had once let slip that Nour had provided him with some investment gems, no questions asked, along with a legitimate diamond studded tiara for his daughter's 'coming out'. Bob remembered being amazed that Debutante Balls for the privileged classes still took place in the twenty first century.

The diamonds were now secure in a safety deposit box in London, and all signs of Bob, his alter ego, had been eliminated.

Bob was content that neither the CCTV nor the photos in the passport or on the driving license could be used to trace him. He had barely recognised himself with the glasses, wig and moustache. He imagined that the best description the police would get from Abasi Nour was that his 'Josh Hammond' was a tall middle aged man from East London.

Of course, Bob couldn't have done all of this on his own. Faik Al Khufi, his faithful young friend, an Iraqi asylum seeker, had proved to be a talented photo editor. His photoshopping skills had produced a masterful passport photo page and a convincing photo card driving license.

Bob would use his influence to keep Faik in the UK, at least until he had outlived his usefulness. He began to drift off as the train left the station. He was looking forward to a weekend with the family, and soon Richard Wolsey Keene would receive his forty eight hour ultimatum. Bob had little doubt the spineless banker would pay the one million pounds he was demanding, especially when he discovered that Sir Max had paid such a heavy price for being stubborn.

Chapter 20

Brompton Place, Knightsbridge, London. Friday, 6:15pm.

As we turned off Brompton Road into Brompton Square I marvelled at the beautiful buildings facing me. They were town houses, but town houses that were so large it was hard to imagine that they could exist in London, where property was so expensive.

DS Fellowes and Dee had driven into the City to speak to Andrew's boss before he departed for the weekend. Inspector Boniface, his driver and I were looking for the house where Mr L Houlier lived.

The car pulled up outside a magnificent porticoed house with four floors. The house was immaculate. The grey granite stone walls had been cleaned and renovated sometime in the recent past. The stone steps were worn. They were rounded at the edges and the entrance to the house itself had a depression in the stone where generations of tradesmen, deliverymen and visitors had stood, waiting to be attended to. Inspector Boniface left the police constable in the car and walked up to the door. I tagged along. The Inspector was just about to press a white pearlescent button surrounded by a ring of intricately cast brass-work when the door opened.

A young man of Latin appearance stood inside looking at us. He smiled.

"I saw you coming up the steps on the CCTV," he said, answering our unasked question, pointing at a carved Lion's head which looked as though it might have been an original fixture but which, on closer inspection, contained a tiny lens in the lion's open jaws.

"Mr L Houlier?" Inspector Boniface asked.

"I'm one of them," the young man replied. "My father is also L. Houlier. He is Leon and I am Luc. Which one of us do you want to see?"

"Actually we would like to speak to whoever owns an Old Navitimer Mecanique watch."

"Ah, my Grandpa's old Pilot Watch, the Breitling, yes?"

"Indeed. May we come in and have a chat about the watch?" Boniface showed the young man his warrant card and introduced me as a colleague.

"So, you too are French, Monsieur Boniface?"

"Not for three generations, Luc." The Inspector fell silent as we stepped into the cathedral-like space that served as the entrance hall. It was a glorious pastiche of gold and Italian marble. Every metal surface was gilded to an identical patina and had the look of ancient, much buffed gold. But it was a clever deception because the air conditioning grilles looked exactly the same. The marble flooring did look original, as it was the same kind of old brown marble flecked with grey that one associates with London Museums. In places it had cracked and had been expertly repaired. The wooden staircase, the tall skirting boards and carved picture rails were a rich dark hardwood and in the middle of the edifice was an astounding chandelier, which was suspended from two floors up by a long gold coloured rod and chain.

Luc could see our astonishment, and filled the silence with an explanation.

"Yes, it is very grand. I sometimes forget how impressive it appears to visitors. When you live here all of the time you become complacent and take the grandeur for granted."

Luc explained that the house had been created from two houses that backed onto one another. It had a front door on both streets. The houses had been bought and refurbished by Dmitri Lubenov, the Russian oil and gas billionaire better known to the English for his patronage of a Premiership soccer team, unfortunately not my team, West Ham.

"We live here because my father is the London representative of Muscovia Natural Resources. Also because when Dmitri took up residence he found that his Rolls Royce would not fit in the garage, despite the architect specifically designing it for the car. That architect was found floating in the Thames a month later." Luc winked and smiled at his own joke. "Our place in Paris is a simple apartment and so this is a big step up for us."

Luc led us into a reception room that was ornate but modern. There was a flat screen 4K TV that must have measured all of seventy two inches, and it was surrounded by speakers and a computer console. Luc invited us to sit down. We took a seat on Chesterfield sofa, the leather of which was so highly polished that it was difficult to sit on without sliding off onto the floor.

Inspector Boniface spoke. "You said the watch was your Grandfather's. Is he still around?"

"Non, he passed away ten years ago, when I was still quite small, but he left his watch and memorabilia to me. My father was not overjoyed, as I suspect my Grandpa knew very well. They had a strained relationship."

"When you say memorabilia........" Inspector Boniface began.

Luc stood and beckoned us to a display case in the corner of the room. One shelf was filled with medals, framed pictures of a young pilot and in the middle an Old Navitimer Mecanique watch; the much discussed Breitling.

"My Grandpa was a pilot in France. He was a test pilot for the Super Entendard before a career flying for Air France. He was an adventurous man and he saw my father as being too boring. He had hopes of me continuing the Houlier's buccaneering adventures." Luc smiled with affection but his eyes betrayed his sadness and loss.

"Do you or your father ever wear the watch, Luc?" I asked.

"Father never, me rarely; I would be frightened to wear it regularly, knowing it is probably valued at five thousand pounds. It is better on display here, as a tribute to Grandpa Houlier."

"Could we just check the back of the watch, please?" the Inspector asked.

Luc walked over to a box concealed in a wooden panel in the wall. A small panel opened out of the wall on hinges. It had been invisible before Luc pressed the panel to open it. The young man flicked a switch and took out a key fob.

Standing in front of the display case, he pressed the key fob and a minuscule diode changed from red to green. Luc then unlocked the door with the key. He reached in and took the watch with a care and reverence that spoke more of its sentimental value than its cash value.

Boniface took the watch from him carefully and looked at the rear of the case. It was marked A11022. It was the real Mc Coy but, sadly, probably not our real McCoy. Nonetheless, Boniface took no chances and as he passed the watch back to Luc he asked, "Has the watch been here all day?"

Luc relocked the cabinet and replaced the key fob, resetting the alarm.

"Of course. I have been here alone all day and in any event the watch has not been out of the case for months. Is there something wrong with the watch, Inspector?"

"Nothing at all, Luc, it isn't the one we were looking for. If I were you I'd take good care of it. Your Grandfather was obviously a special man and the watch is a fitting tribute to his affection for you."

Boniface extended his hand and Luc shook it. I shook hands with the young man too as we made to depart. Just before we left Boniface said, "Where are your parents, if that is not a rude question?"

"If you watch the news tonight at ten o clock, you will see them. They are with the French contingent celebrating with the remaining Battle of Britain pilots in Kent. They will be back tomorrow if you need to speak to them."

"No, that's OK, Luc. You have been very helpful."

It was true he had been helpful, but we hadn't, and he must have been left wondering what our visit was all about as we left the house.

"Well, that was a washout," Boniface said, when the front door had closed and we were walking down the path. "Let's hope the other two are having more success."

As keen as I had been for one of the Houliers to be Bob, once we had seen the photo of Luc and his father, at a Baccalaureate awards ceremony, we knew Leon Houlier was not our man. He was a rotund man, at best five feet six inches, a good six inches shorter than his son. Dead end. The search continued.

Chapter 21

Atkins Garretson Palmer, College Hill, London. Friday, 6pm.

DS Fellowes had decided that walking would be the quickest way to get to the late Andrew Cuthbertson's offices. A phone call an hour ago had confirmed the news that Andrew was dead, and his colleagues were in shock. All had agreed to stay until they had been questioned by the Detective Sergeant.

Dee matched the young detective's long stride and they arrived at AGP on the dot of six. Five minutes later they were sitting in the Partner's office discussing AGP's staff and clients. An hour earlier they had made certain requests and the Partner, though initially reluctant, had arranged for a full print out of the Personal Tax Group's staff and clients to be made available to them.

A young blonde girl entered the office and placed the lists on the conference table between the DS and Dee, who were facing Anthony Craven, partner responsible for this group.

"You don't have anyone on these lists called L Houlier, do you?" Dee asked. DS Fellowes had introduced her as a consultant on financial crimes.

"No, no staff called Houlier at all, no personal tax clients called Houlier. We did have a French corporate client called Bernard Houlier, but he has returned to France now that we have sold his business." Dee made a note.

Tony Craven, Dee and DS Fellowes scanned the lists for any LH. After ten minutes or so they had found only two people with those initials. They were Lucy Huang of the Singapore Office and Lars Halvorssen from Helsinki office. A quick check with the relevant offices showed that Lucy Huang had been at the office all day but had left six hours ago, as Singapore was eight hours ahead of London, and Lars was still at his desk.

No clients had the initials LH, so just to be thorough they also checked the initials HL and came up only with Harriet Levershulme.

Dee Conrad was convinced that someone connected with AGP was involved, probably someone at the Partners' conference, otherwise how would they have known about Andrew and the Thai girl?

"Tony, do you have a list of people who attended the partners' conference in Bangkok recently?" she asked, hoping that this would help.

The accountant reached into his desk and pulled out a table menu. On the reverse of the menu were seating assignments. This was the definitive list of Partners who attended. It seemed that attendance was compulsory at such events, if you valued your future.

They scoured the list for clues but all to no avail. DS Fellowes collected together all of the data, including the menu, and looked across at Dee. Her face wore a defeated expression. They were about to leave when the Detective decided to try one more approach.

He pulled out the spreadsheet with the list of Breitling Old Navitimer owners without saying what the list showed.

"Do you recognise any of the names on this list, by any chance?" he asked.

Tony Craven studied the list with concentration. He really wanted to help find the person who had driven Andy to suicide.

"Only one, I'm afraid. At least, I'm assuming it's him." He pointed to A Hickstead of Leeds. "If it's who I think it is, the A stands for Arthur. He should be on the client list but he is also on the Management Board.

He's a much admired character in here, despite his having been a left wing trade unionist in his early days."

Dee's interest was piqued. She asked, "Wouldn't he have been at the conference too?"

"Yes, of course, all of the management board were there."

"It's just that he doesn't appear on the seating list," she noted.

"No, he wouldn't be on the list, as he was on the top table. When he comes into the office he insists on being called Art, and he acts like one of the lads, but when he's on company business it is Your Lordship all the way."

Dee Looked Puzzled. "His Lordship?"

"Yes of course. Arthur Hickstead. You must have heard of him, surely? Lord Hickstead of Brighouse."

DS Fellowes raised his hand for a high five and Dee slapped it as they both spoke simultaneously. "LH. Yes!"

Tony Craven looked at them, trying to work out what he had said that was causing so much jubilation.

***

The car was silent as we drove back into town. I think we were both disappointed at what had seemed to be a firm lead. We were heading towards College Hill to meet up with the others when Inspector Boniface's phone rang. It was DS Fellowes calling. The Inspector pressed the loudspeaker button and answered.

"OK Fellowes, you're on loudspeaker. We're just coming into College Hill. I'm afraid we hit a dead end."

There was an electric excitement on the other end of the phone that transmitted across the ether just as surely as did the voices.

"We think we might have found LH," Fellowes said, almost in harmony with Dee. They were keen to tell us all, but Boniface asked them to save it for the car as we were pulling up the AGP's offices.

A few moments later Dee and DS Fellowes virtually sprang out of the doors and headed to the cars, laughing and chatting as if they were having fun. I felt a pang of jealousy.

They opened the car door and slid into the seat next to me. As soon as they were seated they began explaining how they had uncovered an LH after all, and when they explained that the L signified Lord and was not in fact a name, both Boniface and I took a sharp intake of breath.

It seemed incredible that a Lord would stoop to blackmail. Moreover, why choose me? Lord Hickstead. It was unfathomable. Yet something seemed to tug at the furthest recesses of my memory. I knew that name from somewhere, I was sure. Then something clicked, the realisation hitting me like a train.

"Oh, no, no, no!" I said out loud, and everyone in the car looked at me.

"What is it?" asked Dee. "Are you all right?"

I was fine, but I had just put the pieces together and it hit me like a revelation from the heavens. I now knew why a peer of the realm would target me, a mere loss adjuster.

Chapter 22

Dyson Brecht Offices, Park Street, Leeds: Friday 15th June,

6pm. Nine Years Earlier.

Some people go Barbados for the summer. Some go to Spain. I get to go to Leeds. Now, there is nothing wrong with Leeds. It's a great city; plenty to do, plenty of women, but somehow I would have preferred Barbados. Unfortunately, as Toby explained to me, the Barbados office didn't have a manager in hospital with a burst appendix, whereas the Leeds office did. That was how I found myself standing in, holidays on hold, looking forward to a few weeks in Yorkshire. My main regret was that, as the football season had already ended, I would not get the chance to watch Leeds United at Elland Road.

Norman was the last to leave the office on that particular day, as he usually was. A typical dour Yorkshireman, he was steady and reliable. If I were in Toby's shoes I would have left him in charge rather than sending in a relatively inexperienced 23-year-old Londoner. I packed my briefcase and headed towards the door. The Balti House on the ground floor was opening up in readiness for its evening customers, and the cooking smells wafted in through the open windows. Up on the sixth floor it smelled delicious.

I closed the last window as the phone rang. It was the landline. I reluctantly picked it up, dread hanging heavy in the pit of my stomach like an undigested meal. "Dyson Brecht, good evening."

"Josh, Josh, Josh, you're a lifesaver!" The voice was heavy with local dialect. I recognised it as belonging to Eddie from Dale County Insurance, the Leeds office's biggest customer.

"I haven't agreed to anything yet, Eddie," I replied.

"I know, but you'll help us out on this, won't you, lad? It's my anniversary this weekend, and I promised the wife I'd take her somewhere nice. You know how it is. Anyway, that fire I'm supposed to be looking at, well, I can't really do it, but you can, can't you, lad?"

I sighed. Another excuse. Two weeks ago it had been his daughter's birthday which had prevented him from attending to his work duties. I wondered what he might come up with next. I hoped his grandmother was in good health, or she might well be the reason why he couldn't cover the weekend yet again, in two weeks' time. Grannies do tend to have a habit of passing away at inconvenient moments, especially when a good excuse is required.

"OK, Eddie. Give me the details, and please tell me it's not out in the wilds." I looked at the address I had written down. It didn't get much wilder. But hey, it was a balmy evening, almost midsummer. It wouldn't be fully dark until nearly midnight, if it got dark at all. It seemed like a great opportunity to go for a nice drive in the green, rolling hills of Yorkshire.

***

The road up to where the house was situated wasn't even on my SatNav map, and I would have struggled to find it at all without the pall of smoke and flashing blue lights to guide me. A makeshift sign read Cobben Lane, and I was looking for Crest House. I drove up the badly rutted road that mainly served farm vehicles, worrying every inch of the way about my deposit on the hired Volvo. At the very least the suspension would be wrecked, and at the worst I would tumble down the hillside, the edge of which seemed to be no more than six inches from my wheels.

I drove past a stone built longhouse, typical of the rural buildings in this area. The longhouse had proved to be the ideal farmhouse in days gone by. The animals would be stabled in stone barns either side of the house, the warmth from their bodies providing extra heat as well as a wind barrier to the human habitation in the middle.

Ahead of me stood the smouldering remnants of a house. The occupants had clearly enjoyed a magnificent view across the valley from their windows. I parked up and strode over to the firemen who were cooling down the embers. I didn't recognise anyone, so I hand signalled 'who is in charge' knowing that my spoken words would be lost amidst the noise of the pumps and the gushing water, and would not penetrate the protective headgear of the firemen. They nodded towards the second fire tender. As I passed the fire engine I spotted the red van parked on the tarmac. Inside was Rodney Killip, the area fire investigator. He signalled for me to join him in the van. I climbed in. He was filling in a pro forma fire report that was bulldog-clipped to a piece of plywood.

"Can't they give you a proper clipboard, then?" I asked frivolously.

"Spending cuts," he grumbled. "They'll be asking us to bring our own water next, you mark my words. By the way, why did you come down that old rutted track? Why didn't you use the tarmac road? Much better for your fancy car, I'd have thought." Rod pointed to a beautiful tarmac road leading off into the distance. He smiled when he saw the frown on my face.

We sat and chatted for around five minutes. It seemed that the lady of the house had been clearing rubbish and had decided to pile it all up and start a bonfire; not a great idea when the landscape is tinder dry, after a particularly dry winter and spring. In Rod's view she hadn't built the fire properly, and when the wind swung around it blew flaming debris and flying sparks onto the roof of the single storey extension. The flat roof was still littered with dried leaves and twigs from the previous autumn, and these quickly caught fire. The lady panicked and, instead of securing the house, she ran next door for help. By the time help arrived, in the shape of the fire crew, the flat roof was well ablaze and flames had leapt in through an open window and ignited the curtains. There was little left to save. At least no lives had been lost. The owners had moved out earlier in the week, and the lady of the house had been tidying up the grounds for the new owner.

"You'll be needing to speak to Brenda; she's the owner and the policyholder. She's next door with Mrs Withers," Rodney told me without lifting his eyes from his report.

***

Brenda was a slight woman unsuited to her name, in my opinion. I don't know why, it just seemed to me she would have suited a more delicate name like Emma or Florence. She had obviously been pretty in her younger days but she had aged quickly. She was forty seven years old but could have been ten years older. Perhaps her appearance owed more to her distress over the house burning down. Her eyes were puffy and red with crying. Her face was smudged with soot.

Obviously in this business you learn to show sensitivity as you are often dealing with people who have suffered a loss of property, and sometimes a loved one. I eased into the questioning by asking Brenda if she had lost anything irreplaceable in the fire, although I already knew that the house was empty. She brightened immediately as she began to realise that, disastrous though the fire had been, she had lost only a house that they were vacating in any event. Her belongings had been moved out, and were all safe.

After more, gentle questioning I was able to determine that the house had been sold and contracts should have been exchanged last Friday. She told me that she should have been in Brussels by now. Unfortunately the exchange had been delayed and was now due to take place on Monday. Somehow I couldn't see that happening.

"Brenda, this is the situation," I began. "Once contracts are exchanged, the new owner is responsible for insuring the property, and so if you had exchanged last Friday it would have been their problem and probably a legal argument would have ensued. To be honest, this way is simpler. Can you tell me what you insured the buildings for? The rebuilding costs, I mean?"

"Yes, the insurance is set at half a million pounds, for buildings only," the weepy lady replied.

"OK, Brenda. That should be more than enough. I think that the RICS Rebuilding index will probably suggest around a hundred and seventy five thousand, but we need to add around twenty five per cent to that because the house is so far out in the countryside. Even so, we're only talking two hundred and twenty five thousand or so, depending on the standard of finishing you had inside."

"Oh, it was beautiful inside, always was, and Brenda had all the bathrooms and the kitchen done last year, didn't you, Brenda?" Mrs Withers interjected helpfully. Brenda looked close to tears again as she nodded her agreement.

I discovered that Brenda was due to fly out to Brussels to join her husband, who had bought a flat in the Belgian capital so that he could fulfil his new role as the EU Commissioner for Labour Relations. I was impressed.

My phone rang, which was amazing way up here in the hills.

"Josh, are you alone?" It was Eddie from Dale County Insurance, Brenda's insurer.

"Hold on," I said as I excused myself from the presence of the two middle aged women. "OK, I'm outside, and I'm on my own."

"Josh, I'm sorry to do this to you, mate." I knew what was coming and I dreaded it. "The duty staff at head office have dug out the policy and they thought that they had better call me at home."

"Come on, Eddie," I sighed. "Don't tell me there's a problem with the policy. The poor woman is in pieces already."

"Look, mate, I'm going to see what I can do, but she doesn't have a policy with us anymore. She wrote to us last month, cancelling the policy as of last Friday, and we have already refunded the balance of her premium."

I sighed, and swore under my breath. When would people learn? They decide to terminate their insurance, the sale date slips and they aren't insured against loss. I see it time and time again. People save fifty pounds on the premium, but then something goes wrong and suddenly they are faced with a bill of tens of thousands.

Eddie and I spoke for a few moments more and then, feeling sick to my stomach, I went back inside to see Brenda.

***

It was a month since I had seen Brenda driven away in the ambulance. I had tried to be positive and I explained to her that the insurers would see what they could do, but to no avail. Brenda started hyperventilating and then she passed out.

In the intervening period the insurers had been under extreme pressure from the new EU Labour Relations Commissioner, and they may have given in had it not been for a stubborn refusal by the underwriters to accept the loss.

I personally took calls from the local MP, a Minister at the DTI and the Insurance Ombudsman. Nothing could change the facts. Brenda had cancelled the policy a week before the fire.

Eddie rang, his voice panicky. The tone of his message was that Brenda was back in the UK, staying with her sister whilst her husband calmed down. He blamed her, the grasping insurers and the unconscionable loss adjusters, according to Eddie, who had just put the phone down after a tirade from Brussels.

"You're next on his list, buddy. Prepare yourself."

I reviewed the papers on the case. The house was due to be sold for four hundred thousand pounds, and as the owners had neither the time nor the funds to rebuild, the plot was now being offered for sale, with the plans, for just one hundred and fifty thousand.

Between the three of us - Eddie, Brenda and me - we were bearing the brunt of the blame for the loss of a cool two hundred and fifty thousand pounds.

The phone rang and I picked it up. "Josh Hammond speaking."

"Please hold for the European Commissioner," a slightly accented female voice requested. A moment's silence followed, and then barely controlled anger.

"Is that Mr Hammond of Dyson Brecht?"

"Yes it is, Mr Hickstead."

Chapter 23

Peppers Restaurant, Woolwich. London. Friday 9:30pm.

Once I had explained how I had first encountered Arthur Hickstead, the others acknowledged that it was probably enough to provide him with a motive for a blackmail attempt, especially as the amount of money he had lost was exactly the same amount that the blackmailer had demanded from me. However, the others did not see his arrest as imminent. I suggested that, had the blackmailer been an unemployed bus driver, he would have been on his way to the police station by now with his hands manacled behind his back. No-one disagreed, but they patiently explained that they had a long way to go before Bob could be taken before a court.

We had no actual evidence that he was the one blackmailing me. It was merely supposition. There was no physical evidence at all linking him to Andrew's death or that of Sir Max.

What we did have, in my view, was some convincing circumstantial evidence. I reviewed the evidence with Dee over the table at Peppers Restaurant, one of the most underrated and overlooked eateries in London. We had already ordered and we were sipping a nice 2008 South African Merlot, a fruity red wine from the Western Provinces.

I ran through what we had on Arthur Hickstead.

"His Lordship is on the board at AGP; he knew Andrew well, he knew Sir Max very well. There were text messages on their phones showing that they were being blackmailed. One of those messages was from someone Andrew referred to as LH, which has to be Lord Hickstead.

Lord Hickstead was in Thailand at the same time as Andrew, and could certainly have known about the Thai girl. Thailand was also the home of the domain name 48hours.co.za.

Lord Hickstead was six feet away from Sir Max when he died, probably from poisoning, and he wears the same type of rare watch that we know the blackmailer wears.

Two people can identify him, Abasi Nour and that soccer thug guy who met him in South Africa.

If we were to raid his home, all we'd need to do is find the diamonds or one of the cell phones, or even a credit card receipt for those phones, and we'd have him cold."

Dee smiled and reached across the table. Taking my hand, she held it in both of hers and I suddenly realised what beautiful hands she had. They were pale and smooth. They were perfectly manicured, nails short and polished with a clear varnish.

"Josh, I love your enthusiasm, and I love listening to your heartfelt views, but we have to be realistic. Lord Hickstead was a leading trade unionist and an associate of the former Prime Minister. He was an EU Commissioner and he has been ennobled in the outgoing PM's resignation list. My guess is that he will still be welcome in Number 10 even under the new regime." She paused as the first course arrived at the table.

"If we're going to take him down - and we will - it will take cast iron proof."

Dee lifted her fork and buried the prongs into her Caesar Salad. My goodness, I thought, she really is gorgeous. I froze for a moment when she looked up at me. I wondered if I had inadvertently said the words out loud, but she simply asked me why I wasn't eating my French Onion Soup. "Too hot," I said, covering for my embarrassment.

The meal was terrific. We both had hot roast red snapper with coconut, chilli and lime salsa, cooked in the Caribbean style. I had grown accustomed to being single, with just the occasional girlfriend, but I now appreciated how good it would be to have a permanent partner; someone I could share every day with. Someone, maybe, just like her.

We were still laughing and talking after the last customer left, and we were alone with Vincent, the owner. I called him over and paid the bill.

"You're good for him," he said to Dee. "Josh is a good customer but we're getting tired of him taking a whole table to himself when we could have two covers."

We laughed and stepped out into the hot and sticky night air, heading for my flat.

***

I spent the pleasant walk home pondering on our relationship, if indeed there was one. Would tonight be the night to make a move? I needn't have troubled myself because others made the decision for me.

As we approached the flat Dee interlocked my arm. She spoke quietly.

"Josh, just chat to me casually as we walk. I want to take a good look at the car on the left hand side of the road."

A dark coloured saloon was parked in a resident only parking space and had two occupants, both of whom I could see quite clearly. As we came closer Dee spoke again. Her voice was quiet but urgent.

"Get ready to run on my say so. Get into the house and call the police. I'll handle these two."

As we drew level with the car, the driver's side door opened. Dee stood in front of me and faced down the driver. He looked puzzled for a moment and then flashed a warrant card. He spoke directly to me.

"Metropolitan Police. We would like you to join us at the police station. We have questions about a suspicious death you may be able to assist with."

"Am I under arrest?" I asked.

"No, but that would be the next step if you refuse to accompany us to Southwark Police Station."

Dee and I conferred, with our backs to the officers, and decided to go along with them, after making a phone call.

"Can't this wait until tomorrow?" Dee asked. "It's been a long day."

"Obviously not," the plain clothes policeman responded. "But that isn't my decision."

Toby picked up the phone as soon as it rang; there was music and jollity in the background.

"Josh, I've heard you made good progress today."

"Not that good, Toby. I'm being taken to Southwark Police Station to be interviewed in relation to Andrew's death."

"Right," Toby said, taking immediate control of the situation. "Don't say anything, either in the car or at the station. I'll get a lawyer to meet you there as soon as possible."

Chapter 24

Southwark Police Station, Borough Rd. London.

Saturday 12:20am.

The Metropolitan Police accommodations were not as quaint as the London City Police Station in Wood Street. The room we were waiting in had bare plastered walls with some kind of shiny paint that may have been blue at some time but which now looked faded and grey.

The furniture, however, was new and the chairs were comfortable and brightly upholstered in a wine coloured fabric. The desk and chairs were probably chipboard but they were faced with the blonde wood so beloved of offices everywhere.

The lighting was provided by a number of spotlights on two tracks on the high ceiling. The odour was provided by an over-zealous cleaner who had obviously disinfected the room before our arrival.

Dee gripped my hand under the table and smiled at me. She had made me agree that I wouldn't say a word until my lawyer arrived. I accepted her advice, which was timely because I soon spotted the CCTV camera in the corner and I had no doubt that the room was wired for sound.

We had been cautioned in the car and we were warned that anything we said could be written down and used later, and that if we chose not to answer questions our silence could be considered by a court in deciding our guilt or innocence.

I asserted my right to representation and explained that I had already let someone know where we were. So, now we were waiting for our lawyer to arrive.

We had been in the room about twenty minutes when the door opened and Inspector Boniface stepped inside.

"Josh, Dee, I'm sorry about this. I had my chief petition the Met's Superintendent in Charge but they wouldn't give way. They wouldn't even hold off until Monday. So, my advice is to tell the truth and get out of here as soon as you can, and come and see me Monday."

He crossed to the door, squeezing my shoulder as he went, and made a beckoning gesture. Just before the beckoned person arrived at the door Boniface smiled at me and said, "Look who I found lurking in the corridor."

A man of around forty in a Savile Row suit and a silk tie that cost more than any of my suits entered our little room. The last time I had seen him he had been wearing white sports kit and he was thrashing me at squash.

"Colin, I never expected to see you." Boniface closed the door as Colin and I hugged; a manly hug, admittedly, but a hug nonetheless. I turned to Dee.

"Dee, meet Colin Penworthy, senior partner at Kellaways." Dee shook hands with my close friend and squash partner, a man who had famously represented an errant member of the Royal Family against her creditors.

"Colin, I thought you were civil cases only, or I would have called you myself."

"Josh, Toby sends his regards. I was at his house partying when I got the call. Luckily I'd gone their straight from work, hence the togs. Anyway, if you both agree I will represent the two of you." We gave our assent.

Colin turned to the CCTV camera and said, "Can I see the officer in charge, please?" Within a minute an untidy man in his late forties appeared and introduced himself as Detective Chief Inspector Terry Coombes. He had short hair which was a mixture of dark and grey, and carried a little extra weight than might have been advisable for his height, which was similar to mine. He wore a suit which looked as though he might have slept in it, although his white shirt was crisp and his tie probably silk. A man not to mess with, I concluded.

Colin rose and shook his hand. "I need a few minutes with my two clients and, as the conversations are privileged, I expect the camera and audio to be switched off, is that clear?"

"Yes, I'll see to it," the policeman answered, in a rather surly manner. He departed, closing the door with an ominous click.

***

For the next ten minutes we explained exactly what had happened in relation to Andrew and his part in the blackmail plot. Now Dee was in another room and I was sitting with Colin, opposite Detective Chief Inspector Coombes and a Detective Sergeant Scott. A digital machine nearby was recording our conversation. The DCI introduced us all, stated the time and asked if I was happy that I had been properly cautioned. I accepted that I had been, twice.

I was asked to explain the events surrounding Andrew's demise, beginning at my visit to his office on Thursday afternoon. As I ran through the story, DS Scott scribbled wildly on a writing pad.

"Mr Hammond, let me be clear here. We don't want any misunderstandings." He said the last part looking at my lawyer. "The initial examination of Mr Cuthbertson shows that his lower mandible is broken. It is likely that the blow that inflicted this damage also rendered the victim unconscious as there are signs of a serious concussion in the brain pan. The forensic scientists suggest that, having been rendered unconscious, probably by someone he knew – no defensive marks present – he was pushed over the railing, falling face down in the mud.

The marks and abrasions on his back are consistent with the joining piece on the bridge hand rail. Do you have any comment on that, Mr Hammond?"

I was about to answer when Colin gripped my knee under the table.

"Mr Hammond obviously does not want to speculate on the manner of Mr Cuthbertson's death, as he was not present, but I am sure that for the purposes of this interview he will accept the scientific evidence of how events unfolded."

I nodded at the appropriate time.

"Thank you," the DCI said without meaning it. "We are of the opinion that to break a man's jaw would take a significant blow from a fit man of at least medium height. In fact, Mr Hammond, a man not unlike you. Could I see your hands, please?"

At Colin's nod I showed my hands palm up. Coombes turned them over to examine my knuckles. The policeman looked closely and set my hands down, thanking me.

"Let the recording show that my client Mr Hammond's hands displayed no signs of injury, damage or abrasion when examined some seventeen hours after the death of Mr Cuthbertson." Colin smiled and the policemen scowled.

"Mr Hammond, it is also possible that someone trained in unarmed combat might also be capable of causing such an injury, even a woman. You had Ms Delia Conrad with you when you met Mr Cuthbertson this morning, didn't you?"

"First of all, Mr Cuthbertson was dead by the time we arrived at the bridge, and secondly Ms Conrad and I were together the whole time and I can assure you that neither of us caused anyone any harm. She will confirm that."

The DCI spoke whilst looking down at a file in a brown manila folder.

"This is not the first time Ms Conrad has appeared in this station for questioning about an assault on a man." He looked up to gauge my reaction, and I suppose I registered surprise. Colin interjected.

"Josh, you will recall that the Detective explained that she had been 'questioned', not arrested or charged. It would be unusual for a close protection officer to go through her entire career without having to restrain someone. What was the exact outcome in the instance you are referring to, Chief Inspector?"

"I don't know," he answered sullenly. "It wasn't my case." He closed the file. "I think that will be enough for now, unless you have any comments."

"You do realise that I have been working closely with the Police in trying to apprehend a blackmailer and possible murderer?" I pointed out.

"Yes, I do realise that. In fact, it's the acrimony between yourself and Mr Cuthbertson, relating to his alleged betrayal of you, which gives you a motive for his manslaughter or murder. My own feeling is that someone got angry enough with Mr Cuthbertson to punch him so hard they knocked him out, and in their anger they tipped him into the river to teach him a lesson. Perhaps they had no intention of killing him. It may even have been self-defence. A confession at this stage would almost certainly be looked upon favourably when deciding on charges."

Colin spoke for me. "Thank you Chief Inspector. If we happen to find the killer before you do we will be sure to mention those options to him or her." Coombes muttered something under his breath.

With that my interview ended and I left the room, to be replaced with Dee, or more correctly, Delia. I wasn't sure how I felt about her full name.

***

I waited in the corridor for the interview to conclude. I desperately wanted to be in there protecting her, making sure she was comfortable, and then I remembered that she would consider two burly men as no competition and three burly men to be a challenge.

It was almost two in the morning when we shook hands with Colin and he noted that his fee invoice would be in the post. I hoped he was joking, as I knew he charged around four hundred pounds an hour and I was already two hundred and fifty grand poorer than this time yesterday.

We took a cab back to my flat, and with late night supplements it came to nearly thirty five pounds. I was dead on my feet and forgot to wait for my change, so the cabbie escaped with a five pound tip.

Inside Dee said she was desperately tired and asked if she could sleep in the bed tonight.

"Of course," I agreed gallantly. "You've been a star today. I'll take the sofa tonight."

"No need," she said, flinging off her shoes. "It's a double bed."

Chapter 25

Stratford DLR Station, London. Saturday 1pm.

We had taken the DLR from Greenwich up to Stratford and then walked across to the London Stadium. I had a Royal East season ticket, with a padded seat in the mid-tier, close to the halfway line, it came with a three-course meal before the match. It had not been difficult getting an additional seat for Dee, and it would not be until West Ham started seeing some real success. The craziness that was the 2019/2020 season and the lockdown, had really hit attendances in the new season. It might have been economic issues, or it may just have been that people simply grew out of the habit of watching live football every second week of the season.

In truth I missed the old ground, I had enjoyed walking along Green Street past the kebab shops and seeing the ground come into view. I always got a great feeling as I looked along the road and saw the old stadium with its claret railings and blue roof trim. The twin castellated towers at the entrance, enhanced by West Ham shields. OK, they were a bit Disneyworld, but that ground had something special, it was once a field of dreams, and the supporters surrounding as we walked towards the new stadium, hoped that one day the London Stadium would see the same success in the future.

On the journey we had been comfortable sitting together in silence. That had given me time to contemplate the events of last night. I would have liked to remember the night as being filled with slow but passionate love making, each of us investigating the other's body, taking time to feel textures, absorb fragrances and grip one another tightly in ecstasy. Sadly, the reality was that we made love clumsily, quickly, with an urgency that was unnecessary, laughed at our amateur performance and promptly fell asleep.

Dee had awoken first at around ten; she just lay in bed waiting for me to stir. When I did it took us a while to make it out of the bedroom. We moved quickly once I remembered it was West Ham United versus Wolverhampton Wanderers today and that I needed to buy another ticket.

We arrived at the ground and Dee looked suitably impressed. She confessed that she had not attended a football match before. I was a taken aback. First I find her name is really Delia, and now I find she isn't a football fan. Could this relationship work? Yes, after last night I knew it most certainly could.

We walked in through the glass fronted main entrance and made our way to the restaurant, where a superb three course lunch was served from one o'clock on match days. The lunch was served carvery style, and so we helped ourselves from large silver domed tureens. The food was generally plain and simple but beautifully cooked.

We took our seats and I introduced Dee to the regulars at our table. Actually I didn't, she introduced herself when I suddenly realised that I couldn't really describe her as my close protection officer and the term girlfriend seemed too presumptuous. Dee filled the silence by saying that she was a colleague. Why hadn't I thought of that?

As we ate and drank our Foster's lager, Dee chatted nonstop with Ron and Danny, lifelong supporters who lived for their families and West Ham, not necessarily always in that order. Danny and Ron were plant fitters at the Ford plant in Dagenham and they invested a goodly proportion of their wages on these twenty one matches a season, in the best seats. We had nineteen home league games and the ticket also included the first three matches of the Carling Cup and the FA Cup.

I often cursed commentators and pundits who pointed at decent hard-working guys like these and dismissed them as corporate guests who were not really interested in the match but only interested in the hospitality. All because they chose to pay for the best seats from a relatively small income. These guys were real supporters.

This was our second match of the season, after an undistinguished placing in last season's unfinished programme. We had lost the first away match at Villa Park in the battle of the claret and blues, and we were all hoping that the first home match would be one we could celebrate properly.

***

We took our padded seats in the West Stand. Dee chose to sit between Ron and me, taking advantage of Ron's running commentary and smiling at his occasional cries of despair.

Wanderers had a reputation for the long ball game, but it seemed to me that they never played that game when I watched them. They played the ball through the midfield with some slick passing. In fact, Liverpool play more of a long ball game when they visit. I think that there is some prejudice that augurs against the less popular clubs in the league, even when they are playing well.

The London Stadium, as we were now expected to refer to it, was bustling with over fifty-five thousand fans attending. West Ham started well enough and looked in control when we were awarded a penalty; a penalty that our best player missed. The disappointment seemed to resonate with the players as much as with the crowd, and the Wolves, started to dominate the play.

We reverted to the bar at half time for a Coke and a comfort break. The match was still tense. But at nil-nil we were still controlling the play. It would only be a matter of time until our efforts were rewarded, we decided after a round table discussion.

We took our seats for the second half and were just settling down when Bolton went on the attack. The ball broke and headed towards the Bolton striker. Our reliable centre half seemed to have the situation covered, but then he was pushed and knocked the ball past our goalkeeper for an own goal. I jumped up, outraged. It was a clear foul and I yelled my opinion at the referee fifty yards below me. I looked around to confirm that Dee too was suitably disaffected, and I saw her smiling. VAR did nothing and the goal stood.

"It isn't funny," I protested, perhaps more harshly than I intended.

"No," she agreed, "but you are." I had to smile.

When the second Wolves goal went in twenty minutes later the crowd could see the writing on the wall. There was a brief respite when we were awarded, and scored, a second penalty, but five minutes later Wolves scored again.

We didn't stay long after the match, as it was too depressing, and so after the crowds had subsided we made our way back to the Tube station. We were just about to exit onto the main thoroughfare, immediately outside the ground, when we saw a potential flare up. A young lad of around sixteen or seventeen had unfastened his windjammer jacket to reveal a Gold soccer shirt bearing the Wolves logo. He looked terrified as three older West Ham fans confronted him. Two of them looked uncertain but one was apoplectic with rage.

Before I could stop her, Dee was at the young man's side.

"Are you OK?" she asked the young fan, with concern in her voice.

"Nuffin' to do with you, darlin'," the enraged Hammers supporter said, sizing up the attractive brunette facing him. Dee was slightly built at around five feet eight in her trainers, but there was something in her eyes that flashed a warning. The Neolithic fan didn't see what the rest of us saw and took his chance. His right arm stretched out to grab the young Bolton fan by the collar. The next move was so quick I almost missed it. Dee shot out her right hand and grabbed the man by the wrist. Her thumb on the back of his hand, she twisted his hand counter clockwise. He yelped with pain as the pressure on his wrist and elbow increased. Dee pulled his hand down, keeping intense pressure on the wrist and elbow, and unless he wanted a wrist or elbow injury he had no choice but to follow. In a few seconds she had him on his knees. He was silent now; he didn't know what was coming next.

"Now, why don't you go home and drown your sorrows? Don't make a bad day worse." Dee then released her grip and helped the man to his feet. She massaged his wrist and said, "I haven't done any damage, the soreness will wear off before you get home." She smiled at the defeated supporter and I wondered whether he would unwisely seek retribution. He didn't.

"I was just having a friendly discussion about the match. I wouldn't do nothing," he said, rubbing his elbow.

"I know," Dee said sweetly. "That's why I didn't break your arm."

The three Hammers supporters walked away chanting at the tops of their voices, restoring their bravado. A car pulled up and the young Wolves fan took his place in the passenger seat. He waved at Dee as the car drove away.

Did I display those same doe eyes when I looked at her, I wondered, and concluded that it was quite possible.

Chapter 26

Ashburnham Mews, Greenwich, London. Sunday 10pm.

This had been the most enjoyable weekend I could remember for a long time, although it would have been perfect if West Ham had won. We had both agreed not to mention the blackmail or my sudden indebtedness over the weekend. If I am being honest, I was quite relieved about being alive and free from Bob and his twisted machinations.

We had spent our time together in eating, sleeping, taking long walks and watching talent competitions on TV. As we sat relaxing on the sofa listening to Norah Jones, the door buzzer sounded. I wasn't expecting guests.

I picked up the phone, determined not to buzz anyone in who would disrupt my evening.

"Hello, Mr Hammond, my name is Jayne Craythorne." The name didn't mean anything to me. "I am the daughter of Sir Maxwell Rochester." I buzzed her up and explained how to find my flat.

I told Dee who the visitor was, and she transformed from a relaxed girlfriend into a bodyguard in a matter of seconds. Dee let Jayne Craythorne into the flat and invited her to sit on my easy chair. I sat on the sofa and Dee took the footrest. After accepting our condolences on the recent death of her father, she explained the reason for her visit.

"Josh, Dee, I'm sorry to interrupt you this late at night but I wouldn't be able to sleep anyway. The police wouldn't tell me anything, but Dad's network of contacts was extensive and this evening I was told that the Metropolitan Police are working with the London City Police on a possible link between Dad's death and the blackmailer who had been pestering him. They have told me that Dad might have been murdered, but that no-one knows for sure at the moment, and they may never know with certainty." She paused for breath. "My contact said that you had been interviewed by the police and had claimed that you too were being blackmailed. Another contact was able to get your address for me. I was hoping you could bring a little clarity to what is otherwise a terribly confusing situation."

Dee decided to take centre stage.

"Jayne, it appears that a man, possibly known to you, by the name of Lord Arthur Hickstead, has been blackmailing people in the city."

Jayne Craythorne's jaw dropped open and tears filler her eyes. Dee offered her a tissue. Our visitor was sobbing.

"I'm not sure that I can believe that. The man you refer to as Lord Hickstead has been known to me since I was born. He and Dad were at school together. Do you have any evidence of his involvement?"

"I'm afraid so," Dee said. "The facts are these. Your Dad was blackmailed by a man emailing from the domain 48hrs.co.za, and so was Josh. Your Dad was texted by an anonymous mobile phone, probably bought at a supermarket in central London, and so was Josh. Andrew Cuthbertson died on Friday. He was your Dad's accountant and he is also Josh's accountant. Lord Hickstead's initials were found on Andrew Cuthbertson's mobile phone, attached to a text blackmailing him to reveal financial details of a client. A jeweller identified the blackmailer as wearing a rare watch. Lord Hickstead owns such a watch, one of just eight in circulation in the UK, and none of the others belong to a man fitting the jeweller's description of the blackmailer. There are more remote links between Hickstead and the domain name, but he was in the right countries at the right time when the domain was established."

Jayne's tears had dried. She was probably my age, very stylishy dressed and superbly made up. Her modern short hairstyle was probably designed by a hairdresser whose name appears on bottles of expensive shampoo. All in all she bore all the hallmarks of a wealthy woman.

"So why haven't the police arrested him yet?" she asked.

"We wondered the same thing, but Inspector Boniface thinks we need more evidence before we can show our hand, or we take the chance that he shuts up shop and we never get to him." I hoped that this explanation gave her more comfort than it gave me. It became clear that it didn't.

"Josh." She seemed tentative. "I would like the two of you to continue your investigation until Arthur Hickstead is arrested. If you agree, I will ensure that you get your money back, one way or another." I was surprised.

"Jayne, I have to tell you that we intend to pursue him anyway, because he's a danger to us all as long as he remains free. In his last email to me he said he would be back for more. Quite frankly, I also want my money back."

"My offer is still open, Josh. Dee, do you have a view?" Jayne looked at Dee, who seemed uncertain.

"I have to say I think you're both a bit mad, but if you are both determined to snare this callous bastard, I'm prepared to run interference for you."

We spoke for a few more minutes and then Jayne left, but not before kissing us both on the cheek and promising to keep in touch. When she left I mentioned to Dee that as well as being Sir Max's only heir she seemed to be wealthy in her own right.

"You know she's married to Jonas Craythorne, don't you?" Dee said.

"No, I didn't know. Who is he?" I asked.

"Have you ever had a burger served in an expanded polystyrene box?"

"Of course. They were everywhere at one time."

"Well, his family owned the license for the design and the manufacture of those boxes throughout Europe. Not only is he one of Vastrick Security's clients, he's a multi-millionaire!"

Chapter 27

Vastrick Security Offices, No 1 Poultry, London. Monday 8am.

Dee and I had taken the Tube as far as Bank Station and we came out into the bright sunlight at the junction of Cornhill, Threadneedle Street and Poultry, an odd name for a city street, I always thought, but I expect there is an explanation for that.

What I do know was that there had been a road and buildings on this site since 60AD, the first buildings being burned down in the Boudican revolt. The one hundred mile long Roman Road to Bath began close to where we were standing. This rebuilt part of the city was burned down twice more, in the Roman Hadrianic period and in the Great Fire of London in 1666. Luckily the buildings had not burned down since I had become the loss adjuster.

We approached the postmodern building at No. 1 Poultry, designed by James Stirling, the great neoclassical architect. The imposing corner site had an arched entrance with a tower and a clock. The structure was a mass of curves, constructed from reinforced concrete and blockwork faced with red and white stone horizontal bands and glass curtain walling.

Taking the lift to the second floor, we followed the signs for Vastrick Security. The office was surprisingly busy for eight o'clock on a Monday morning, but Dee explained that many of the operatives here were shift workers. Some would have been there all night.

I was signed in by Dee and given an electronic key card that monitored my movements in the building and gave me access to selected areas. We walked into an office befitting the founder of a successful security company. On the wall was original artwork by Katy Moran, whose work I had seen before. The canvas was a swirl of bold reds, blues and black. It was quite dramatic.

Robbert T Vastrick came into the office. He was an imposing man, over six feet tall with the beginnings of a paunch, but very young looking for his sixty two years. He held out his hand and offered me a card. I asked why there were two b's in Robbert. Vastrick explained that whilst he was American, his parents did not want him to lose sight of his Dutch heritage. He was named after the original Robbert Vastrick who settled in New Netherland, on the east coast of the USA, in the mid 1600's.

"If I understand Dee's email correctly, the two of you want to try to get either the diamonds or the money back from this crooked Lord. And you would like to use my facilities to do it. Is that a fair summation?" He didn't sound terribly enthusiastic, and so I was about to explain that I was happy to pay for the service, until Dee touched my arm and shook her head.

"Tom is winding you up, Josh, don't rise to it." Obviously Mr Vastrick used his middle name. "That is a good summation, but there's a lot of money floating around out there and I dare say we'll get a share of it."

Tom Vastrick looked at a printout on his desk. "One of the night guys did a search on Lord Hickstead, and already I don't like him. Four reasons. One, he went to a poncey school; two, he was a trade union activist; three, he was a Eurocrat; and four, he was made a Lord for no good reason except patronage." He paused and then added, "Oh, and five, he is a blackmailer, lowest of all the criminal classes, apart from the sickos, of course."

By nine o'clock we had a plan of action and we had been allocated "Operations Room 3", a secure, darkened room so filled with electronic gadgetry it looked like Jack Bauer's CTU in the TV series 24.

As we settled into our new room, I called Toby and told him I needed a few personal days off from work. He agreed to my request without question. I think he was still relieved that I wasn't leaving.

A young man wearing a Vastrick polo shirt handed me an electronic screen with buttons on it. "You might want to borrow this," he said.

"I might if I knew what it was," I replied, and Dee laughed.

"It is a Kindle E Reader, it displays electronic books. I've loaded up a book you may be interested in." Dee leaned over and switched it on. It was a large screen with navigation buttons for page turning. The screen showed black print on a white background, just like a real book.

The book title page came up as we all looked. It read "Red Art – An Unofficial Biography of Arthur Hickstead by Robin Treadwell". Treadwell was a right-wing journalist for a well-known tabloid. The book was published by Cornwell Books, a reactionary publishing house with a deeply conservative bias. Dee showed me how to use the Kindle Paperwhite and I started to read whilst she set up the case on the Vastrick System. I could have laughed when I saw the code name she had chosen for the computer files, and for the case as a whole - "Peer Down".

"Josh, don't mention our investigation to anyone, because if DCI Coombes gets wind of our involvement we can expect another midnight interview."

"Dee, I agree, but we have to continue to help Inspector Boniface where we can. He's been a real friend."

"Of course we will, but he knows better than anyone that to bring down a peer of the realm he will need irrefutable evidence, or he will be jumped on by everyone from the Home Secretary down."

In three hours we were due to meet with Boniface, and so I decided to skim read the biography of the blackmailing Lord Hickstead.

Chapter 28

Breakfast Car, London Bound East Coast Train. Monday 8am.

Lord Hickstead was feeling quite pleased with himself. Jim and Bob had gone, along with all links to the individuals they were blackmailing. So far his revenge plan had netted him one million pounds in cash and diamonds. Of course his big pay day, five million from Sir Max, hadn't worked out, but at least the old bully who'd made his life hell at school was now dead, which was fair compensation.

The peer finished his Great British Breakfast - too late to worry about the calories or the cholesterol now - and looked at his Samsung phone. He had meetings lined up all week, and on Wednesday he would fly to Rotterdam from London City Airport at five in the evening, returning early the next morning. He already had a buyer for the gems. He was surprised at how affected he had been by the glittering diamonds; he had even contemplated keeping them. There was a hypnotic attraction to their cleanly cut beauty. He knew that he had no option but to sell them, though. They were evidence.

As the train drew into Stevenage he smiled to himself. By the time the Dutch buyer had paid the agreed sum for the diamonds - in US dollars - into his Cayman Islands bank account, exchange rates would mean he had banked almost exactly a quarter of a million pounds.

Reaching into his pocket he retrieved a cheap white mobile phone that had been allocated to the terrorising of Richard Wolsey-Keen, banker to the rich and famous. Former chairman of the collapsed Bank of Wessex, he had persuaded Arthur Hickstead to join him on the board and invest five hundred thousand pounds, which he guaranteed would double. The bank had thrived for a couple of years, but the government had to bail it out at the start of the credit crunch, and the shares were now worthless. Arthur was livid when the man who led the bank into near bankruptcy escaped with a hefty pension and a new job with an Investment Bank in the City.

"Dear Richard,

12 hours to go. By way of reminder I don't accept any excuses for delay. By the way, best not wear your favourite suit today.

Sam

Lord Hickstead sent the text message to the banker and looked forward to an outing to Clapham Common, which he felt sure would secure Richard Wolsey- Keen's one million pound ransom demand.

Chapter 29

City of London Police HQ, Wood St, London: Monday, noon.

The sign on the door said 'Detective Chief Superintendent Boddy'. We were on the first floor of the police headquarters for the first time. I noticed that the decor and furnishings were more lavish up here.

The young constable ushered us into the room where Inspector Boniface and an older heavier man in full uniform were sitting around a small but well-polished conference table. They both stood, in deference to Dee, I supposed, and offered their hands. We shook hands with the new man who, I had correctly guessed, was DCS Boddy.

We sat down and the DCS spoke up straight away.

"Mr Hammond, Ms Conrad. On behalf of both the City Police and the Metropolitan Police, I would like to apologise for your treatment on Friday night. It was unnecessary, and the use of old school detective tactics is to be regretted. DCI Coombes will continue his investigations into the deaths of Andrew Cuthbertson and Sir Max, and we will cooperate wherever our paths cross. Inspector Boniface has assured the Metropolitan Police Assistant Commissioner that you will both help with our enquiries, but for the time being if they need to speak to you again it will be here, and in conjunction with the Inspector."

"Thank you." Dee and I responded almost simultaneously. There was a pause.

"Now, how are we going to manage this little rat's nest of aristocratic villainy? What on earth is a Peer doing blackmailing folk? It's beyond belief, and if he's directly involved with either death, well...." Boddy let the thought hang. "Mr Hammond, you said on the phone that you had found out some historical facts about Lord Hickstead that might assist the investigation."

"Yes," I replied, conscious that the information was in the public domain. "It boils down to this, really. Arthur Hickstead was born in 1954 at Brighouse, close to Halifax, which is just off the M62 in Yorkshire. His parents were active in the Labour Party and when he was eleven years old his father's Trade Union offered him a scholarship to study at a public school. They had an arrangement with Harrow on the Hill Catholic College, where scholarship boys could board at special low fees. Both sides were keen on social mobility. However, Arthur hated it, according to his biographer. He felt as though he was little more than a slave for the richer boys, and he suffered bullying and persecution because of his accent and the fact that he was a "stig", the nickname they used for a scholarship student.

He followed some of his peers to Cambridge University and Professor Tony Bartlett was his tutor. Bartlett was arrested many times on demonstrations in the 1960s, and in the 1980s it was thought he had been working for the Soviets.

Oddly, the young Arthur chose to go into the Army for officer training at Sandhurst. The book suggests that in 1976 jobs in the City were hard to find, but retired Army officers were always sought after. He was soon disillusioned by the Army, as he saw it as an extension of the public school. He served in Northern Ireland, and was horrified at the way the officers always managed to escape punishment when a riot turned into a bloodbath, yet the ordinary squaddies would find themselves in the brig.

In 1982 he left the army, but didn't go for a job in the City. He was head hunted for the job of Deputy to the President of the Oil, Gas and Offshore Workers Union. The unions were replacing moderate leaders with hardliners as quickly as they could, to take on Margaret Thatcher.

By 1997 he was President of UNIFY, a conglomeration of his old union and two larger unions who represented skilled tradesmen. His new position meant that he wielded enormous power in the Labour

Party, but he hated New Labour with a passion, according to the book - something he denies.

Anyway, as part of the union amalgamation deal, he could only serve as President for four years, then the President of one of the other merged unions took over the reins.

In 2001 the PM found Arthur Hickstead a role in Brussels, well away from British politics, where he had been ruining the image of New Labour that the spin doctors were building. He was there for eight years before having to return to the UK. The bank where he was a director went down, and although the government saved it, all of the shareholders lost their money. It's thought that he lost in excess of half a million pounds, which was probably most of his pension fund.

In May 2010 he was made a Lord in the PM's resignation list, and despite his former left-wing leanings, Mrs May's government asked for his help on re-structuring the benefits programme to target poverty more universally." I don't think that the new PM is all that keen on Lord Hickstead, as he was quite unhelpful when the country was in turmoil with the Coronavirus.

I passed copies of my research to the two policemen. I say my research, but a nerdy lad at Vastrick had done a lot of the work for me by scanning the book with a 'special algorithm' he had invented. I didn't ask what that meant, I just pretended I knew.

"DS Fellowes has picked up a lot of this from the internet, too," Inspector Boniface noted. "I have to admit, it answers a lot of questions."

Detective Chief Superintendent Boddy took charge of the meeting again.

"I think this confirms what we were all thinking. This man is fireproof unless we can find rock solid evidence that condemns him. I suggest we use the rest of this meeting to discuss tactics, what we know and what we need to know."

Dee and I settled into our seats for a long session.

Chapter 29

Clapham Common Park, London. Noon.

Arthur Hickstead saw Richard Wolsey Keen approach the deserted all-weather football pitches and look around nervously. 'Sam' had texted the banker and told him to come here if he wanted the photos Sam had of him treating pretty young boys to dinner in the less fashionable restaurants.

Richard was standing with his overcoat over his arm, waiting.

Arthur had selected this spot because it was a well-known haunt for men to meet up for 'friendship'. Obscured by trees, Arthur snapped some photos for good measure. He had his camera in his hand when a young Arabic boy came into the frame.

Richard turned to face the boy, who was smiling at him.

"Looking for a friend, mister?" the boy asked in a heavily accented voice.

"No, I'm meeting someone," Richard responded.

"I'm prettier, more cooperative and less money," the boy teased, straightening the banker's tie. Richard was tempted for a moment. There was no-one around and the boy was attractive. Then he remembered what was at stake and he politely dismissed the boy.

To his surprise the boy produced an envelope which had "8 hours" scrawled on the front. The boy waited as he opened the envelope. He leafed through the contents, alarmed to see images of himself sitting in various restaurants, fawning over rent boys. He was stunned. There was no doubt what anyone would think if they saw these pictures, but he knew that it wasn't like that. He just liked the company of young boys. He liked to treat them and listen to their lilting foreign accents. He liked touching them. But nothing more.

He was considering what the tabloids and social media haters would do with these pictures when any remaining thoughts became a blur as he felt three blows to his back in quick succession, and he found himself gasping for breath.

***

When he came round he was looking into the face of a spotty youth with a ragged attempt at a beard and a pony tail.

"What happened to me?" Richard asked, still dazed.

"You've been punk'd, mate."

"What? I don't understand."

"Someone shot you three times with a paintball gun. Suit's a write off, I reckon."

The young Arab boy had gone, as had the envelope, but Richard knew what he had to do.

***

It was three o'clock - five hours to go to his deadline - when the Banker arrived back at the London Mercantile Investment Bank Headquarters at Canary Wharf. He was sweating and red faced due to having to wear his overcoat on a warm day. How else could he cover the red stains on his suit jacket?

Melanie, a blousy middle aged woman with a Hertfordshire accent, approached him.

"Ah, Richard, you're back. Shall I take your coat?"

"No!" he snapped. "Just leave me alone. I have things to do in my office. No calls or visitors. Understand?"

Melanie was taken aback, but these rich bankers were a strange lot even on a good day and so she returned to her desk, wondering why her boss was wearing his overcoat indoors.

Richard did not have a million pounds. Nowhere near it. He had a big pension pot which he couldn't touch for another five years, and he had sifted away some money over the years, concealing it from the prying eyes of the taxman and his spendthrift wife. Nonetheless, if he didn't pay up he would die, and that was a strong motivation. Even if he wasn't killed, once those photographs came out he might as well be dead. Sam was in control, and Richard was smart enough to know it.

Given enough time Richard could have filched a little money from here and there, built the million up slowly, written off some as client investment losses and covered his tracks, but there was no time for finesse. He would have to wire the money now and find a way to make it up later.

Nervously he tapped the keyboard and a new window opened on his screen. He tapped another key and the Bank's bespoke software package opened.

"Cordex SecSoft welcomes you, Hello Richard."

Richard ran down the client accounts until he reached Sylvia Patterson. The lady had two point eight million pounds of cash in her account waiting for the new trading period to begin, but more importantly, she was in a care home and her investments were audited just once a year.

Richard transferred one million pounds into the temporary trading account which bore his name.

"Nature of transaction?" the machine asked.

Option for purchase of development land in Seychelles, Richard typed.

"When are the securities expected?" Richard decided to give himself some time.

14 day settlement account, he typed.

"Select bank from drop down list?"

Yes. Then Richard selected the bank Sam had nominated. He typed in the account number he had been given.

"Transfer to daily accounts or hold position?" This was the last step.

Hold position, he typed.

That should be enough to keep the internal security boys from finding the transaction until he had covered his tracks. He pressed the final confirmation button, and one million pounds left his trading account and whizzed across the ether to Switzerland. With one million in from Mrs Patterson's account and one million going out, Richard's suspense trading account would show up as zero again, for the time being.

Satisfied that he had covered his tracks as well as he could, Richard now had fourteen days to find Mrs Patterson some land options or return her money. That was more than enough time.

Chapter 30

The Queen's Room, House of Lords, London: Monday, 3:25pm.

The advantage of being in the Palace of Westminster at this time of year was the relative peace and quiet. The MPs and the Lords were on their long summer recess, and the staff took the opportunity to have a break themselves.

As a result the magnificent Queen's Room, where library staff and Peers normally interface, was empty apart from Lord Hickstead who was using the internet to do some research. The few librarians who were on duty were in the main library, restoring some of the ancient tomes to their rightful places on the shelves, ready for their Lordships and Ladyships to disrupt the orderly regime again on their return.

The Peer looked around the historic room. It was like a library in itself, with shelves ten feet high, the top shelves accessible only by wooden ladders. The walls were panelled with the same wood that had been used for the shelving. The highly polished surface shone with hues of red and yellow that suggested rosewood to his inexpert eye.

Around the tops of the shelves and at the juncture with the ceilings intricate carvings gave some relief to the panelling. High above the shelves and embedded into the wall panelling were the coats of arms of many of the famous Lords who had graced this place over hundreds of years.

His Lordship's eyes moved to the floor, where a brightly coloured carpet adorned the room. Predominantly reds and browns in an Axminster type pattern, it reminded him of the carpet in his grandmother's front room. A room reserved for visitors, not for the use of grandchildren.

Even the air in the place felt old. He would miss it when he retired, and retirement was not far away. He was tired of it all. Arthur Hickstead had stopped being an active socialist and committed politician years ago; he liked the high life too much. Looking back, he was now faintly embarrassed by his antics in the Trade Union Movement. Ironically, now he was wanted by the Conservatives reshuffled from the last cabinet to report on the benefits culture, a poisoned chalice if ever there was one.

Richard had already confirmed by text that the money had been transferred as he had requested, and he now awaited one more call and the blackmailing scam would all be over. Well, almost.

The white mobile phone allocated to Richard's case vibrated. Looking around, Lord Hickstead ensured that he was alone when he answered.

"Richard Wolsey Keen." The accent he used was clearly West Country.

"Mr Wolsey Keen, just a call to let you know that the money is in our account and your purchase is ready to collect. Though, of course, we would be more than happy to deliver it to your offices."

"No, I would prefer to collect it myself," he answered. "We don't want an item of such value in the hands of some philistine security man in the office, do we?" He was warming to the character he was playing, and the accent became more noticeable.

"Indeed not, sir. In that case, just call in at your convenience. We had already arranged to stay open until nine to accommodate you."

"I'll be there within the hour."

Chapter 31

St. James' Gallery, Ryder Street, London: Monday, 4:20pm.

Despite its name, the St James' Gallery was on Ryder Street just off St James' Street, a stone's throw from Buckingham Palace. Surrounded by the historic buildings that populated the Green Park/St James' Park area, the Gallery occupied the ground floor of a modern office building. There were two marked private parking spaces outside and the taxi pulled up and parked in the first space.

Lord Hickstead gave the cabbie a twenty pound note and asked him to wait, using his pronounced West Country accent. The Peer was back in role playing mode. He was wearing a charcoal suit with a wide pinstripe. He was wearing red braces on his trousers and a matching red handkerchief flopped effeminately from his top pocket. The look he had adopted screamed effete city banker.

Kelvin De Montagu, the gallery owner, smiled effusively as his customer entered the shop. The man was a typical city spiv. The customer's toupee was poorly fitted, and contained much less grey than the rest of his hair and moustache. His glasses had thick black frames with tinted lenses.

"Mr Wolsey Keen," gushed the owner. "So nice to see you again. As I said on the telephone, the fee was paid into my account a short while ago. Of course, I never expected anything less from the acclaimed London Mercantile Investment Bank."

Lord Hickstead handed over one of Richard's business cards.

"Sorry I didn't have one of these handy at our last meeting. Did you receive my ID papers?"

"Yes, Mr Wolsey Keen, they were popped through my letter box the very next day. Thank you." The documents were identical to those he had given to Mr Nour, except for the name change, of course. Faik had worked his magic again, and the colour copies of the forged passport and driving licence once again went unquestioned.

Kelvin disappeared for a few moments and returned carrying a titanium case with the dimensions of an oversized briefcase. He laid it on the counter, opened it and turned it around to face his customer. Inside, protected by inorganic wrapping and embedded in foam, was a painting approximately sixty centimetres tall by forty centimetres wide. It was entitled 'Chartwell Sunrise with Horse', and the signature was that of Winston Churchill.

"I think this will be a fine addition to the Bank's collection, sir. It would grace any city boardroom," Kelvin suggested. "All of the provenance papers, and the documents from the painting's last sale at auction, are in an envelope under the foam padding. Works by Churchill have doubled in price in the last ten years, sir, and I think this will be a great investment as well as a beautiful piece of art. It is rumoured that he was painting this very piece whilst unsuccessfully campaigning against Clement Atlee and the Labour Party in 1945."

Kelvin closed the case and passed it to his customer, who signed a form to say he had received it. After promising to visit Kelvin again in a month or two with a view to securing a further investment piece, Lord Hickstead left with a one million pound painting in his possession.

***

The taxi dropped the Peer off at The Royal Horseguards Hotel, a magnificent Victorian edifice which had once been the home to the National Liberal Club. He could have gone straight to his flat, but taxi drivers always seemed to have incredible memories when questioned by the police. He might just as well leave a false trail, in case anyone decided to follow it later.

After a quick drink in the Churchill Bar, the irony of which made him smile, and still in character, he slipped into the exquisitely appointed men's toilets and removed his braces, toupee, glasses and moustache. Depositing them in the refuse bin, he smoothed his thinning hair and picked up his case.

He left the hotel and walked the short distance to his flat in Whitehall. He would be glad to rid himself of this tawdry City style suit, purchased from a Tesco supermarket back in Yorkshire.

***

Sitting comfortably in his borrowed flat, swishing brandy around in a large balloon shaped glass and admiring his new painting, Lord Hickstead picked up the white mobile phone and dialled a preset number. It was answered immediately.

"Hello, Picture Desk."

The Peer followed his prepared monologue and delivered it perfectly in a Cockney accent that would have put London actors to shame.

"I have pictures of that rogue, Richard Wolsey Keen, picking up a rent boy on Clapham Common and with some of his other young friends."

"OK. And if we decided to use them, how much would you want?" the sub editor asked.

"Nuffing at all. Just to see that slime bag banker suffer, that would be enough. We all bail the bank out and he walks away wiv a massive pension. It just aint right. I'll email 'em to you now."

The sub editor was surprised, but if the photos were genuine he wasn't going to worry about why a punter didn't want any money for them.

Chapter 32

London Mercantile Investment Bank, Canary Wharf, London: Monday, 6:25pm.

A warning message had flashed up on Nicky Taylor's screen over two hours ago and, in the absence of his boss, he investigated the warning. Convinced that there was a problem he couldn't resolve, he was nervous; agitated. He had never uncovered a problem of this magnitude before, and he did not have the courage to interrupt the Director of Security whilst he was meeting with the Chairman. Nicky was just about to leave another message when the door opened and his boss walked in.

"For Pete's sake, Nicky, I've only been gone a couple of hours and I've got three missed messages from you."

After five minutes listening to what Nicky had to say, the Director of Security was also beginning to feel unsettled. He consulted an internal telephone directory and dialled.

"Richard Wolsey Keen speaking."

"Ah, hello Richard, this is Michael from Security. We have a bit of a problem. Can I come down and see you?"

"Look, Michael, I was just about to leave. Can we do this tomorrow?"

"No, I'm afraid it can't wait," said Michael Grazeley, Director of Security, leaving no room for discussion.

***

Shortly after six thirty Richard Wolsey Keen sat facing his tormentors from security. He was still wearing his overcoat and he was still sweating. Michael Grazeley spoke. There was respect in his tone of voice, and Richard relaxed, but only a little.

"The thing is, sir, you exceeded the daily floor limit of a million pounds today. That's a good thing, really, because if it had been a million or less the system wouldn't have flagged up this potential problem."

Richard listened and frowned as if puzzled. "Whist your purchase is for a million pounds, you paid to express clearance of the payment and a fee of four thousand pounds was charged by the clearing system. It was the fee that pushed the purchase over the floor limit."

"Well, really! Surely you haven't made me wait here just because I expended a few thousand pounds that the client will pay anyway?" Richard tried to sound angry.

"No. That isn't the real problem. Nicky here tried to clear the warning by raising an exception notice, which you could have signed in your own time, and all would have been well. But the system wouldn't accept the exception notice because your purchase was for land in the Seychelles, but the bank account you paid the money into was in Switzerland and belongs to an art gallery."

Richard had no idea who owned the account that 'Sam' had nominated for his million pound payoff. He had automatically assumed that it would be Sam's own account. The banker needed time to think. He tried a bluff.

"Michael, you know what things are like here. They change by the minute. About five minutes after I typed the request and sent it, I had a call to say that the land was off the market and so I diverted the investment into fine art for the client. I managed to pick up a marginal sale, and so Mrs Patterson pays one million and four thousand pounds, plus our fees, and she gets artwork worth approximately one point one million. We all win."

"Richard, we are not questioning your judgement. I am sure you will make the bank and the client money. No, the problem is the artwork itself. It appears that you arranged to pick it up in person."

Richard was now in deep water but he had to propagate the lie. "Yes, I wanted to deliver it personally."

"Well, that's the problem. Nicky checked your swipe card. You haven't left the office since mid-afternoon."

"That's right." Richard wondered which direction this was going, and whether he was clever enough to stay ahead of the security chief.

"When Nicky rang the gallery to confirm they had received our transfer, the owner told him you had already picked up the painting. The description the owner of the gallery gave of his Richard Wolsey Keen does not fit you. It appears that our artwork has been stolen. We need to call the police."

Richard said nothing. The colour drained from his face. The security director squeezed his shoulder gently.

"Don't you worry, Richard, we will get to the bottom of this. We'll get your artwork back."

The security team left, and Richard dropped his head into his hands. It was all over. Tomorrow the whole story would come out. He was ruined.

The phone rang. He answered it.

"Hello, Richard. This is Callum Rogerson of UK Newspaper Group. We were wondering whether you had any comment on tomorrow's front page."

Richard knew all too well that UKNG owned two scurrilous tabloids as well as their broadsheet papers and radio interests.

"How would I know? I haven't seen it, and even if I had I wouldn't give you the time of day." He slammed the phone down. How much longer would the debacle at Northern & National Bank make front page news? When he checked he saw that new mail had arrived in his inbox from Callum Rogerson. He wanted to ignore it, but he knew he couldn't.

Richard clicked on a PDF file attachment called 'Front Page' and a piece of software called Adobe Reader opened on his desktop. Slowly a facsimile of the newspaper front page built before his eyes. The headline was bad enough:

"The Fabulous Banker Boys!"

Below the headline was a telephoto shot of the young Arabic boy touching Richard's tie. The photo was taken from such an angle that the boy's face was obscured, but such was the young man's short build that he looked even younger from behind. The soft, puppy dog expression on Richard's face made the photo even more damning.

The text of the article had been carefully worded.

"....assignment on Clapham Common at a place known to be a regular haunt of older men looking for younger partners." "Dinner at the intimate Carannas Restaurant where the clientele is almost exclusively male..."

The reference to further photographs inside chilled the banker to the core.

Richard realised that more damage would be caused by what was not said than what had actually been written. Readers already enraged at his big payoff wouldn't hold back; they would fill in the blanks with their own sordid story. Couldn't people see that he was treating these poor boys, not exploiting them?

The banker did not know how he could hope to face his wife or children again, especially his teenage son, when they had no idea that he had a predilection for attractive young men. His friends and colleagues would not understand, either. They would be shocked, possibly disgusted, and he foresaw only social exclusion and humiliation.

Richard took off his overcoat and jacket. His shirt was stained red at the back but he didn't care about that any more. He opened his desk drawer extracted a half full bottle of whisky and a smaller bottle.

Within a short time, the banker was lying down on the sofa in his darkened office. The whisky bottle in his hand was almost empty, and tears streamed down his face.

Chapter 33

Vastrick Security Offices, No 1 Poultry, London. Tuesday 8am.

We had spent much of yesterday afternoon with the City Police, and so I was surprised to get a call from DS Fellowes on the stroke of eight the following morning. The young policeman wanted to meet with us urgently, and would be bringing along an ex colleague. He was reluctant to say what this was all about on the phone, and so we invited him around.

Dee and I were gradually becoming more intimate as the days passed. I was hoping that this was a continuing trend, although I did occasionally have doubts when I remembered that sick people sometimes fell in love with their nurses. I wondered if the Florence Nightingale syndrome extended to bodyguards.

We sat in the operations room, each at our own console, working through the evidence until our visitors arrived. We gathered in the conference room and the Detective Sergeant introduced us to a former police inspector who now worked in private security.

"Josh Hammond, Dee Conrad, this is Michael Grazeley of the London Mercantile Investment Bank." We shook hands and sat down. "I'm going to let Michael explain, and then we can decide what we need to do."

We sat back as Michael Grazeley explained that at nine o'clock last night he had been called back to the office because Mr Richard Wolsey Keen was discovered lying dead in his office, with an empty whisky bottle and an empty bottle of pills. A note apologising to his wife and rambling on relatively incoherently lay on the printer in his office. It was an apparent suicide.

The police, in cooperation with Michael and his assistant, sought answers as to why the banker might have taken his own life. Their first thoughts centred on the loss of a painting which he had bought for a client, but that was before they looked at his phone and computer.

Martin Grazeley opened his briefcase and removed a printed copy of the front page of one of the country's most scurrilous tabloids. The story was sordid and suggestive, probably ruinous for the banker's career, and yet the photos were relatively innocent on the surface, more suggestive than explicit. Nonetheless, the message was clear; rich banker exploits young men for sexual favours.

Dee spoke out first. "I saw the front page of that paper on a news stand on the way in this morning, and it had a different headline."

"Yes. When we found the front page we rang the paper and asked them where they got the photos. They were emailed anonymously from..." Michael looked down at the file to find the domain name.

"Someone@48hrs.co.za?" Dee suggested. She was brilliant at this.

"Absolutely right. The name used was Sam," Martin said, looking impressed.

"It would seem that, in view of the circumstances, even this awful excuse for a newspaper decided it would be in bad taste to run that front page," DS Fellowes added.

I was now full of questions and so I cut in quickly. "Was there any indication of a specific threat to his life, or was it just the pictures?" Michael looked at DS Fellowes for permission before he answered. The DS nodded his assent.

"He had been threatened by Sam around forty eight hours earlier. The pictures were first mentioned in a text yesterday. Someone - we believe it was Sam -shot Mr Wolsey Keen three times with a paintball gun. His shirt and jacket were stained and his back was bruised."

"We know the blackmailer as Bob," I added. "How much did he ask for?"

"He asked for a million pounds to be express transferred to a Swiss bank account in the name of a London art gallery. He then picked up the painting yesterday, claiming to be Richard. We appear to have lost both the money and the painting. There'll be hell on in the office today."

"Let me guess," said Dee. "The man was around six feet tall, slimly built, bad toupee, moustache, glasses and an East End accent."

Michael showed less surprise this time. "Almost right, except that he had a strong West Country accent."

"It seems His Lordship changes his accents with his names." Those of us who knew what she was talking about nodded in agreement.

Fellowes spoke. "That makes three suspicious deaths now, and a small fortune in ransoms paid. The Chief is really on our backs over this. In fact, the inspector is probably being bawled out at this very moment."

Dee looked thoughtful, and then she smiled as she passed comment. "Either the man is reckless, or he has no idea that we know who he is. That has to be in our favour."

Chapter 34

City of London Police HQ, Wood Street, London: Tuesday, 11am.

We were back upstairs in the more lavishly appointed part of the police HQ. On this occasion we sat at a large walnut conference table which held a tray of different kinds of mineral water and two plates of biscuits. I had never really thought about the police sitting around a conference table having the same kinds of boring minuted meetings that were held in the rest of the City. There was also a video projector on the ceiling and one of those black conference table telephones with microphones on four sides.

I was sitting with Dee and DS Fellowes. Sitting opposite us was DCI Coombes of the Metropolitan Police, along with his sidekick from Friday night, Detective Sergeant Scott. The bigwigs were outside in the corridor, talking.

After a few moments the door opened, and Inspector Boniface entered followed by two uniformed policemen with plenty of silver decoration on their blue serge tunics. One of them had his highly decorated hat under his arm.

The two uniformed men took their seats at the head of the table and Boniface sat next to me. I recognised the first uniformed man, and recalled that he was the London City Detective Chief Superintendent, DCS Boddy. He stood and introduced himself and then his uniformed counterpart from the Met, Assistant Commissioner Bryn Evans, former Assistant Chief Constable for South Wales. Boddy sat down, and Assistant Commissioner Evans took the chair and spoke clearly and concisely in that pleasant sing song manner associated with soft spoken Welshmen.

"Gathered around the table here today we have representatives of the two London Police Forces, and one of the victims of this blackmailer and possible murderer. To date the Metropolitan Police have restricted their investigations to the death of Andrew Cuthbertson, with the City Police looking into the blackmail allegations. These two cases are strands in the same rope, as far as I can see." The AC picked up a sheet of paper. "We also have two other deaths to consider. The death of Sir Max Rochester, which the toxicology reports suggest may be a suspicious death, and the apparent suicide of Richard Wolsey Keen."

The Welshman paused to look around the table. "Whilst the toxicology report indicated high levels of potassium in Sir Max's blood, Sir Max suffered from heart problems and had recorded high potassium levels previously in routine blood tests. Nonetheless, we are not ruling out foul play, especially in the circumstances. Mr Keen's demise, on the other hand, is probably what it appears to be, which is suicide. Excessive amounts of alcohol were found in his bloodstream and stomach, along with a huge number of painkillers. The pills he took were prescribed to him by his doctor, and they contained codeine, which can apparently convert into morphine in the human body. As few as six could kill, and he had taken almost four times that amount. I'll now hand you over to Inspector Boniface, who has some new information."

Inspector Boniface passed around a profile of a man we all recognised, although his photo did him no justice.

"This is the profile of rock star and humanitarian Don Fisher. He came to prominence in the late 1970s with his band 'London's Burning'. After one major mainstream hit they played mainly to their own fans. At that point they may have faded into obscurity if Don had not married a high profile bleached blonde rock journalist who was making a name for herself by swearing on mainstream television in a popular punk rock programme. Three oddly named children later, he teamed up with a few others and launched one of the most successful charities in recent history. Anyone under forty will probably not remember his singing career, but they will certainly know him for his charity work and high profile daughters."

We were all of an age where Don Fisher was known to us; his violent language on live TV, urging people to donate, had become a favourite clip on TV news items whenever his name popped up in connection with a charity event, or when one of his daughters managed to attract the attention of the media for some sort of unwise comment or misdeed. Boniface explained why we were looking at the CV of the former rock star.

"In accordance with money laundering regulations, the banks always let us know if they see any suspicious activity. Just over a week ago they contacted the Financial Crimes Unit and reported that Mr Fisher had asked for one million pounds in cash. He wanted it within forty eight hours. The bank tried to persuade him to use bankers' drafts or electronic transfer, but he refused, and turned up with two heavies to pick up the money in cash. The Financial Crimes Unit followed up with Mr Fisher the next day, but his solicitor told them to mind their own business and the enquiry was put on the back burner, until DS Fellowes saw the file when he searched the Serious Crime Database for related cases this morning."

DCS Boddy interjected with some further interesting snippets.

"An hour ago Mr Fisher agreed to discuss the matter with us, in the presence of his solicitor, later today. What we do know, courtesy of the paparazzi, is that his eldest daughter was the victim of an apparent prankster last week, who shot her with a paintball gun as she exited her favourite nightclub by the rear exit to avoid the Press. Photos of the tearstained daughter, covered in red paint, appeared in the celebrity columns on Saturday."

It seemed that everyone else in the room was doing the maths, as I was. His Lordship had apparently netted a million in cash, a million in art and my quarter of a million in diamonds.

The meeting continued for another hour as assignments were made, and we were asked to remain available but not to hinder the investigation. The codename for the operation was to be Operation Peer Pressure. How many more neat sound bites could be extracted from this heinous man's campaign of hate, I wondered?

Chapter 35

Vastrick Security Offices, No 1 Poultry, London. Tuesday 2pm.

Dee and I were enjoying a late sandwich lunch in her office. The sun was shining and the air conditioning was trying to keep up. At last we were enjoying a glorious spell of late summer weather in the Capital. We were actually having fun, despite the seriousness of the case. We felt comfortable together; we were a good fit, or at least I thought so. I intended to speak to Dee at some point about our 'relationship' but I hadn't found the right time yet. Perhaps I never would. Like all of my relationships, I would have preferred it if the girl just got the message without my having to say it out loud.

Perhaps I had been tainted by my experience with Julie Tate. What a great time we'd had together. We were compatible in every way. Then, when I decided to verbalise what we both felt and where it might go, she smiled kindly and touched my arm. She didn't need to say anything, I knew already, but she said it anyway.

"Josh, of course I love you, but like a brother!"

The door to the office opened, snapping me out of my reverie. A young woman walked in. She looked to me to be about fifteen, but she was in her early twenties. I must be getting old, I thought. Her name was Alana and she was pretty and slightly built. She was one of Vastrick's best investigators, and her nickname was Nancy Drew.

Alana sat down at the desk with us. I cleared away the empty Prêt a Manger sandwich cartons and made some space for Alana's file. Alana's excitable manner of speaking convinced me she really must be fifteen after all.

"I have something here that should be of interest." Alana sat down and opened the file. "I searched for a link between Lord Hickstead and Don Fisher on the internet but found nothing. I word searched all biographies and autobiographies, but they don't mention each other. In the end, I had to laboriously trawl through the NaNA."

"What is Nana?" I asked, showing a degree of ignorance that the other two could not comprehend. Alana patronised me with a patient explanation.

"NaNA is the National News Archive. It attempts to scan all of the newspapers published and digitise their content. It goes back to the 1800s now and is relatively complete back as far as the 1960s."

"I'm afraid I've never heard of it," I admitted, not understanding how such a valuable resource had escaped my notice.

"That's probably because it's a subscription service on a secure server, and the subscription is between six hundred and two thousand pounds a year." I must have looked shocked because Alana tried to explain. "It's good value for money if you are a foundation member, like Vastrick. We get complete access to both the digitised archive and the hard copies. We can print as much as we like and as we pay so much we are allowed to use the universal search engine, which will look for a word or phrase or person anywhere in the archive. The regular users can only search for a particular edition, and they have limited printing rights."

"OK, I accept I might be ignorant. What did you find?" The front page of a long defunct newspaper was pushed in my direction. It had a blue banner with white lettering that proudly proclaimed "TODAY, Britain's only colour newspaper". There was a wide angle photo which showed three well known rock stars, including a young looking Fisher, with five more soberly dressed men behind them. In the background we could see the crowd of over a hundred thousand excited rock fans.

"Look closely, Josh, on the back line, on the extreme left. That is a young looking Arthur Hickstead sharing the stage with the stars of Rock Relief 98, twenty two years ago."

Alana explained that the concert had been held in July and that the shadow cabinet had all been on holiday and so they were represented by a member of their party's ruling National Executive Council, Arthur Hickstead. As the Trades Unions were donating one million pounds, Arthur was being interviewed just before Elton John came on stage. The TV audience at that point was a UK record and, as it was a simulcast with the USA, Hickstead had a chance to address more people than the Prime Minister could hope to reach and he obviously relished the task. When the camera came to him he was beaming, and he began a short prepared piece about helping Africa's workers in being represented. But within seconds of him beginning his speech, Don Fisher stormed into the tent studio, grabbed the camera lens and looked straight into it. He might have been high on something, but he said, and I quote: 'This is all bollocks, there are kids starving out there, get your hands in your flaming pockets and give 'til it hurts. The suits will give their money because it looks good on the balance sheet but we want your cash and we want you to care.' Arthur never appeared on camera again because, after the foul mouthed outburst, Fisher used another F word, not flaming as I just said. The producers cut Arthur's speech and had the cameras cut away to Elton John.

In the Guardian the next day, Arthur Hickstead was described as being livid when he was quoted as saying 'We have given a million pounds to this charity and we expect more respect. That foul mouthed yob won't get another penny from us.' Behind him a crowd of young adults booed him and, according to the reporter, he stormed off and boycotted the after concert event."

That could have been a good motive for blackmail, I supposed, being humiliated in front of the UK's biggest ever TV audience. We thanked Alana for her help and were about to go back to the operations room when my iPhone rang. The screen informed me it was Inspector Boniface.

"Hello, Inspector."

"Josh, can you come to the station as soon as possible? Don Fisher wants to speak to you."

Chapter 36

City of London Police HQ, Wood St, London. Tuesday 4pm.

I have to admit that at school and college I was a radical. I was very anti-establishment, but there was something that irked me even more than the establishment, and that was sell-outs. I loved punk rock music and its sentiment, but I naively believed that the bands were shunning riches, the high life and celebrity that they claimed to hate so much. So, when they all made their money and joined the very establishment they had purported to be rebelling against, I was disgusted and disappointed. To me, principles are for life, and I know some very rich people who are still radical and anti-establishment. To see millionaire pop stars living the high life they raged against when they were struggling sickened me.

In my opinion Don Fisher was both a sell-out and a hypocrite. He looked like a rebel, his grey and receding hair usually worn in a ponytail, suit jacket over torn jeans, unshaven, but he wasn't a rebel at all. I recalled seeing him in an interview on TV two years ago, when he told working class parents not to take their families to McDonald's or out to dinner but to give the money to his charity instead. The interviewer, who had been a well-known left wing agitator in his youth, asked Don why his eldest daughter was out on the town wearing six hundred pound shoes and carrying a designer bag of equal value if he was so concerned about families wasting money. Don replied that his kids were grown up, and they made their own choices. The interviewer pointed out that two of his kids were in full time education and one had an internship earning her fifteen thousand a year. He must be subsidising their jet set lifestyle, he suggested. Don hadn't liked the questions about his family or his partying with the very establishment figures he made his reputation disparaging, and stormed out of the interview.

It was mainly for this reason that I was unlikely to be star struck by meeting a singer who had made most of his fortune by being a famous foul mouthed charity promoter, and not by his singing.

***

Dee was still not leaving my side, and so when I went into the conference room she came with me, of course. I think she also wanted the chance to see Don Fisher close up.

We were ushered into the room, and Don Fisher was polite towards us, shaking hands and flirting with Dee. Then in an instant he changed, and with a wave of his hand he dismissed his solicitor and the uniformed policeman who had been taking his statement.

"Get out; I want to talk to these two alone." In their position I would have slapped him, but they left the room somewhat meekly, smiling deferentially. When we were alone he leaned forward and spoke quietly.

As I looked at him I realised that he looked much older than his fifty six years. His complexion was beyond pale; his hair was grey, wiry and lacked condition. I noticed that his eyes were rheumy and yellow in the corners. His face was heavily wrinkled, especially the eyes and forehead. He had the lines most associated with those who have squinted through a lifetime of smoking to keep the smoke out of their eyes. His thick Birmingham accent seemed more pronounced as he kept his voice down.

"This bastard threatened my daughter and I'm going to see him dead. Are you going to help me?"

"No," I answered, equally quietly.

He frowned, paused and hissed. "If I was you I would cooperate." There was a distinct threat behind the words that made me angrier than I had ever been.

I answered in a barely controlled voice. "How do you even know it was Lord Hickstead who blackmailed you?"

"Who else would it have been?" he snarled.

"Oh, I don't know," I postulated, unable to keep the sarcasm out of my voice. "Maybe it could be one of those lowlifes who shag your daughter on a one night stand, take sordid photos of her and post them on the internet for everyone to see."

The aging rocker leapt to his feet, his face purple with rage. I stood up and faced him, ready for a fight. Dee pushed me down in my seat.

"That's enough, Josh. He might be rude but he's a victim, too, and that last comment was below the belt." She turned to Don Fisher next. "And you can sit down too, before I put you down."

He sat down abruptly, and I apologised, quietly. I felt calmer now.

"I'm sorry. Your daughter is still only twenty, and we all make mistakes when we're young. She's a pretty girl and no one deserves to have their life threatened."

He was calmer, too, when he spoke. "Bloody kids! My parents told me 'what goes around comes around' when I was rebelling and making their lives hell. I hated them then, now I realise I love them more than life itself and always did. Wisdom comes a bit too late for some of us. My two youngest won't get the same freedom."

Dee brought us back to the point.

"Look, Don, I don't know if you remember Arthur Hickstead?" He shook his head; he had no idea who Arthur was. "Well, in 1998 at the Rock Relief concert he was giving a live TV interview, and was about to take credit for a million pound donation when you burst in and made your famous, 'get your hands in your pockets' rant. He felt humiliated, according to the newspapers the next day."

"I remember the rant, as you call it, but possibly because I've seen it so many times on TV since. I don't remember interrupting anyone, but

I wasn't entirely lucid at the time. I did that after I'd taken a little something to keep me awake. It had been a long and stressful couple of days."

Dee spoke as the calm intermediary.

"So, you and Josh are going to get payback, but not by attacking anyone. This man is powerful and well connected; he enjoys his position and the power it brings. The best punishment would be his fall from grace, imprisonment, loss of freedom and the removal of his title. If you want to help, tell us what happened to you and we'll explain what we know."

We then sat and listened as the angry father in Fisher came to the fore, and he described how he had been in bed reading a book when a text came through on his business iPhone. He almost ignored it because that was the number used by the media and his business contacts, and he didn't want to be bothered at that time of night. Nevertheless, he did look at it, and the picture that followed, and he had been shocked beyond words. There on his screen, looking glamorous in a long, low cut dress, Lavender Mali Fisher smiled for the camera. Crosshairs had been added to her forehead.

Jim the blackmailer had allowed Don Fisher forty eight hours to raise one million pounds, but realistically it would have to be paid before the bank closed and so he had around forty hours in reality. Then, for Twenty four hours out of those forty, the banks would not even be open. Nonetheless, he raised the cash – his personal fortune has been estimated at over a hundred million pounds, after all - and arranged to have it picked up. Until the payment had been confirmed, Angel, Lavender and Tawny were told to stay either in their flats or at home. Seemingly, Lavender got bored with being stuck indoors with nothing to do, and went out to a nightclub which had sent her an invitation to attend the reopening of their refurbished electro pop dance room. She was advised by a guy in a tuxedo to leave by the back door, as the press were waiting for her at the front. She complied, and got paint balled. It was just one shot, but a painful one, on her bare back.

Don Fisher had one of his men drop off the bag with the guest at table nineteen at Cosmo's Seafood Restaurant, on the Strand, as instructed. The man at the table was little more than a boy. He appeared to be Arabic, and this was confirmed when he thanked the man for bringing his bag with the words:

"Tell Don that Jim is grateful for his cooperation."

Don's man waited in a shop doorway across the street and watched the restaurant, but the boy with the bag never emerged. Don never heard from Jim again, and had been surprised when he found out that the police knew he had been blackmailed.

We told the rocker what we knew, and he concluded that it was a slam dunk that it was Hickstead. I agreed with him, but noted that the police needed an iron clad case.

To my surprise, Fisher told us that the police were going to pick up Hickstead for questioning and perhaps get a warrant to search his accommodation. The problem was that no-one knew where he was staying. His credit card had not been used since he had used it to buy rail tickets to and from Leeds on Friday.

Chapter 37

City of London Police HQ, Wood St, London. Wednesday 8am.

DS Fellowes tapped on Inspector Boniface's door before entering. As soon as he was in the room he was sharing his good news.

"Inspector, we were checking Hickstead's credit card purchases to see if we could find out where he was staying and we came across this item. I've highlighted it in yellow." Boniface took the printout and read that the card had been charged two hundred and eighty six pounds by VLM Ticketing.

"Who are VLM?" Boniface asked.

"They fly daily from London City Airport to Rotterdam, and it seems that Lord Hickstead has a flight booked at five this evening, with a return flight early tomorrow morning."

"He must be selling the diamonds," Boniface said, thinking out loud.

"That's what we think, sir."

"OK, Fellowes, this is what we do."

The inspector laid out a plan to track and find the diamonds, a plan which he was optimistic would produce results.

***

Dee was concerned at how tired both of us were feeling and so she reset my alarm without me knowing. As a result, I slept until almost eight, whereas I was often up before six.

We ate a relaxed breakfast and neither of us were city ready, still in our lounging clothes. Dee suggested that we head in mid-morning, and I agreed. As we sat and chatted, she asked about my family. I told her about my parents up in the Midlands, and my brother, all of whom felt responsible for me because I was the youngest and had no wife to take care of me. Dee thought that was amusing, given the perils I had faced this past week. She then asked if she could see pictures of them, and so, for ease, I went to www.flickr.com on my laptop and opened my account. My albums were all listed. I opened the one which I had ingeniously named Family Album.

"Do your worst," I said as I turned the laptop to face her. She spent a lot of time grinning and laughing out loud at the photos of me from childhood to the present day. Many of the older photos had been scanned by my parents, but most had been taken with a digital camera.

Having scrolled through the photos, she alighted on a picture of me dressed as Charlie Chaplin at a fancy dress party.

"When was this taken?" she asked. To be honest I could barely remember the event. I think I might have been helped home by my friends that night.

Underneath the photo was a button headed 'more info', and I pressed it. A new panel opened up and we could see that the photo had been taken on February 14th 2004. We could also see that it had been taken with a Canon Eos, for a 60th of a second at f16, and that the flash had fired.

Dee looked closely at the data before asking a question. "Do all digital cameras do this? I mean, do they all record this type of data?"

"Yes," I answered. "Well, at least all of mine have. The information is stored on the memory card automatically."

"In that case we've almost certainly been missing some crucial evidence linking Hickstead to the deaths and the blackmail attempts," she stated.

I realised that she was right. The Peer had taken pictures of Lavender Fisher, myself, and Richard Wolsey Keen, and we had access to all of the emailed photos. If His Lordship had not removed the data before sending the pictures, we could hopefully extricate some valuable evidence from them.

I spun the laptop around and closed the open windows before clicking on My Photos and opening the two photos of me that had been sent by the blackmailer to my mobile phone. I right clicked on the thumbnail of the photo that showed me with crosshairs on my head, and clicked 'properties'.

There it was in front of me;

DSC100145

Saved by: Photopaint 10:08

Taken: 11/08/2010, 9:12

Nikon Coolpix P100

Autoflash on. Not used.

1/125th sec

F5.6

This was picture number 145 taken on the Nikon Coolpix on the day my first threat had been received. It had been manipulated using Corel Photopaint, image editing software.

Whilst I found out what I could about the camera on the internet, Dee called DS Fellowes. She was becoming closer to him than I would have liked.

"DS Fellowes is emailing the other photos to your email account now," she said as she hung up.

It appeared that the Nikon Coolpix P900 was a new model which had only recently been released by the manufacturer, and that as it was a 'bridge camera', a camera that comes somewhere between a compact and a full sized Digital SLR camera, and as such it had a limited market. Nonetheless, I guessed that they had probably sold thousands of them.

My phone pinged several times in quick succession, indicating that I had email.

For the next ten minutes Dee and I looked at all of the photos, printed them with their details and assembled the print outs. We were both excited about our findings.

Each photo was numbered in chronological order. The first photo was of Lavender, numbered DSC100131, and the last was of Richard in the park and was numbered DSC100153. They had all been taken with a Nikon Coolpix P900 and most had been edited by Photopaint.

Dee summarised the value of the evidence we had uncovered, but I had already worked out for myself what it meant.

"If Hickstead owns a Coolpix P900, a quick look at it would tell us whether the camera numbering sequence matched the photos we have from the blackmailer. If he has a laptop loaded with Corel Photopaint, that would be even more convincing. And, with any luck, a forensic examination of the hard drive would confirm that those pictures have been on his computer."

She paused and breathed in deeply. "Josh, we might have him."

Chapter 38

City of London Police HQ, Wood St, London. Wednesday, Noon.

Inspector Boniface was grinning from ear to ear as he read from a note which had just been passed to him. He then pressed the intercom.

"You can send DS Fellowes in now."

We had been so elated by our find that we immediately contacted the police and emailed them all of our data. They promised to act on it straight away, and asked us to call in for an update.

"You two are regular Miss Marples. I guess that someone would have come up with this information, given time, but you were there first. What's more, I think our follow up research will cheer you up no end."

DS Fellowes came in and shook our hands. Everyone in the room was smiling. It was contagious. The Detective Sergeant gave us a rundown of what he had discovered.

"Somehow, we need to link Lord Hickstead to these photos, and if we can't do that, we need to be able to link him to the camera that took the photos. So, when you sent me the information on the Nikon Coolpix P900 my first thought was, who stocks them and have they sold many? The bad news is that they are stocked all over the UK in their thousands. Nevertheless, I called Nikon UK, who are based at Kingston on Thames, who confirmed that it could take months to check the retailers' records. But then I got a call back ten minutes later."

He paused for effect, and grinned even more widely than before. "Bad luck for Hickstead but good luck for us. Nikon are running a launch promotion that gives purchasers of the camera £50 Cashback and a second year's full warranty free of charge if they register online or by phone. They estimate that around ninety five per cent of owners are taking advantage of this offer, but that is still over eleven hundred people so far. They couldn't supply us with the details of everyone who registered. However, they said if I gave them a name, they would be able to tell me whether that person had registered a Nikon Coolpix P900 with them. It turned out that Arthur Hickstead registered for the two-year warranty on a Coolpix P900 in July this year. We know from his registration that he bought it at the camera shop in Heathrow Airport Terminal Four. I contacted the shop directly, and from their records they were able to confirm that he bought it using a credit card and, for duty free purposes, his boarding card. The boarding card was for a Johannesburg flight just before the Rugby Tour."

He beamed at all of us, and punched the air as if he had won the World Cup all by himself. Boniface brought us all back down to earth.

"Before we all get carried away, there are eleven hundred people with this type of camera. It isn't quite a slam dunk yet, but we are getting close. Let me tell you about our plans for later today."

Inspector Boniface then explained his strategy for Hickstead's visit to the Netherlands.

If all went according to plan, His Lordship could be in custody by tonight.

Chapter 38

London City Airport, London. Wednesday, 4:30pm.

Lord Hickstead stood beside his carryon luggage and checked his travel documents. There wasn't a seat to be had in the overcrowded lounge; even standing room was at a premium. He had travelled this route hundreds of times in the last decade and the lounge was busier each time. The success of the airport owners to attract new flights was commendable, but they needed to make some changes to the facilities to accommodate the growing number of passengers.

There was a garbled public announcement directing him to the gate ready for his flight to Rotterdam. As he walked through the narrow passageway he noticed two plain clothes customs officers taking people to one side. He looked straight ahead, making every effort to avoid being selected.

The woman two places ahead of him was stopped and taken to a cubicle. Then he felt a hand on his shoulder, too.

"I'm sorry about this, sir, but we have heightened security today and I have to select someone from each flight. You are the lucky one," the officer said, in a clumsy attempt at humour. "We won't keep you long, sir."

The Peer stood with his arms outstretched and was patted down, the contents of his pockets in a blue tray next to his open carryon bag.

"Thank you, sir. Could you boot up your laptop now, please? While that is booting up, could you please stand in the scanner booth? I am obliged to tell you that you will not be subjected to any harmful rays, but if you decide not to be scanned we reserve the right to do a full body search."

"The scan will be fine, officer. We have to keep the skies safe, after all," Lord Hickstead said, without meaning a word. The scan took less than a minute.

The customs officer tapped a couple of keys on the laptop to ensure that it was a fully working computer, and then he allowed its owner to repack his case and board the plane.

***

A minute later the customs officer was standing in a small windowless office with Inspector Boniface.

"Inspector, I have to tell you that Lord Hickstead is not carrying any diamonds. I did a thorough pat down and I searched his bag. Both he and his bag were then separately scanned; there was no sign of diamonds or anything else unusual, for that matter." There was finality in his tone. "Oh, but there was one thing. As requested I had him boot up his laptop, and he does have an Icon for Photopaint on his windows opening page."

***

The decision not to carry the diamonds with him had been a sound one. It only needed one random security check, such as the one he'd been subjected to, to blow the whole scheme. He would meet with an old colleague from his EU days and enjoy a leisurely dinner before embarking on the late night meeting that formed the real purpose for his trip.

As was bound to be the case, the buyer, Mr Van Aart, turned out to be a shady character, and so not carrying the diamonds was probably a good thing. In any case, Mr Van Aart had his own methods of moving diamonds around the world and Arthur Hickstead didn't want to know what they were.

Chapter 39

Cafe Zwart, Schiekade 640, Rotterdam. Wednesday. 11:45pm

Hickstead knew that the potential buyer already had the certificates, the photos and that he had spoken to the diamond cutter. Van Aart had confirmed that he was satisfied that he could move the diamonds at a profit, as long as Arthur was prepared to be reasonable.

Arthur had chosen to stay at, and eat at, the Best Western Crown Hotel, which was conveniently close to the rail link for the airport. He was now sitting in a coffee shop less than a hundred yards from his hotel, waiting for the Dutch buyer.

The door opened and a bell suspended on a wire jangled as it was displaced by the head of the door. The man who entered was well over six feet tall, and completely bald. More accurately, his head was shaven. He did not seem at all threatening, however, and he smiled under a typically bushy Dutch moustache. Arthur hadn't bothered with a disguise, but he wore a hat and glasses which obscured much of his head and face.

"Mr Bob Smith?" Van Aart asked as he stood at the only table occupied by a customer. Arthur nodded, and they shook hands. Van Aart shouted something in Dutch to the owner and then turned to his seller.

"Bob, I am very impressed with the gems. I am even more impressed that they are legitimate and not stolen. This makes resale more....." - he struggled for the word in English - ".....profitable."

The cafe owner brought a coffee over, along with a pastry containing half a peach covered in white icing. "Fruit; you have to get it where you can, eh, to stay healthy and to live long." Arthur suspected that the sugar in the icing alone made the Dutchman's efforts at hitting his 'five a day' redundant.

The negotiations took almost fifteen minutes, and as soon as they had shaken hands on an agreed price they heard a melodious clock strike twelve. Arthur was a little disappointed at receiving only a quarter of a million Euros rather than a quarter of a million pounds, but it was still around two hundred and ten thousand pounds. Van Aart would pay the money directly into an account in Brussels, held under the name Euro Union Financial Enterprises. That particular account was already heavily loaded with money and expenses accumulated over the last ten years, and kept well away from the inquisitive noses of the UK Exchequer.

Tomorrow morning the Peer would go to his safety deposit box, remove the diamonds and hand them to the courier in the shadow of Nelson's Column in Trafalgar Square, and the transaction would be complete.

***

Ever the gentleman, Lord Hickstead held open the hotel door for the attractive Dutch lady who had come in behind him. She smiled and thanked him before heading to the bar. He wondered whether he should follow her. After all, it had been a successful trip so far, but he had to be up early for his flight and so he took the elevator and headed off to bed.

As soon as the elevator doors closed the woman, who had been following him since he had left the airport, watched the display above the doors, recording that it stopped at the sixth floor. She took her mobile phone out of her pocket and walked to a quiet spot in the lobby.

"Commissaris, this is Imka. The target has left the hotel only once for a meeting in a coffee shop, and now he has retired to bed, I think."

"Good work, Imka. I will tell the English Inspector. They are one hour behind us, he will still be available."

"Commissaris, the man he met with was Walt Van Aart."

"Are you sure, Imka? I have surveillance photographs of him in Paris this morning, sent to me from Europol."

"I am certain it was him, Commissaris. I was on the surveillance team in Delft when he met with the Russians."

"Thank you, Imka. I will send the English police his file, summarised of course. We cannot jeopardise our own prosecution for the sake of a few diamonds."

Chapter 40

London City Airport, London. Thursday, 8:30am.

DS Fellowes stood on the platform at the City Airport Docklands Light Railway Station. He was waiting for the next train to Bank Station in the City. His mobile phone rang. The voice was one he knew well.

"Sarge, our man has arrived and is heading to the DLR station as predicted, so I am now handing him over to you. He should be standing on the platform any second."

Fellowes saw Hickstead arrive on the platform, and smiled in approbation when he noted the next Bank train was scheduled in one minute's time.

"Okay, thanks Andy, I'll take it from here." Fellowes ended the call just as the driverless train approached.

No matter how many times he travelled this route, Arthur Hickstead felt uncomfortable about riding a train with no driver. It was disconcerting to stand at the front of the train and watch as the rails passed beneath it at fifty miles per hour. In the middle of the carriage sat DS Fellowes, apparently immersed in the pages of a fantasy novel. The chances of losing His Lordship were nil, but they didn't want to risk missing a clandestine meeting where diamonds could change hands.

Brad Fellowes wondered whether the Peer knew who he was getting into bed with when he was dealing with Walt Van Aart. A quarter of a million pounds in diamonds was small beer to a crook like Van Aart; the Dutch Police seemed surprised that he would bother to meet Lord Hickstead personally. Unless, of course, Van Aart was aware of the real identity of the seller, and felt that he could use His Lordship's European political clout to his own advantage at some time in the future.

The file said that Van Aart led an organisation known as the Geest Mafia, which in English means the Ghost Mafia. The trafficking of people, diamonds and drugs in the southern half of the Netherlands, including all of Amsterdam south of the river, was their speciality. Another gang called the Matroos, or the Seamen in English, ruled the northern half of the Netherlands. Van Aart was dangerous.

The train terminated at Bank station and Brad Fellowes tailed the Peer until he stood on the platform waiting for the next westbound Circle Line train. So far they had guessed his route correctly, and Brad nodded to DS Scott of the Met., DCI Coombes' sidekick, who would take up the trail from here.

DS Fellowes left the tube station and headed towards the Vastrick Offices at Number 1 Poultry, less than a hundred metres away.

Chapter 41

Vastrick Security, No. 1 Poultry, London. Thursday, 9:30am.

Dee Conrad's Operation Peer Down and the Police Operation Peer Pressure were going well. Our own file was thick with incriminating evidence, albeit mostly circumstantial. Inspector Boniface had been really good about keeping us informed as to what was going on, even to the extent of a midnight call the previous night.

He had also called Don Fisher to inform him that the Peer had flown to Rotterdam without the diamonds but nonetheless to assure him that we were getting close, and that the blackmailer would be punished. Apparently Don wasn't particularly impressed, and Boniface got the impression that he still wanted to kill the "old geezer". Odd that Fisher should refer to Hickstead as the old geezer when he was only six years older than the aging rocker himself.

A phone rang. We all went for our mobiles but it was DS Fellowes who received the call. He spoke for a while and the DS hung up, after issuing the instruction, "Stay with him, we'll get back-up."

He turned to the rest of us. "OK, that was DS Scott. It seems that Lord Hickstead has just entered number 2 Parliament Street, opposite the Palace of Westminster. According to the doorman, probably an MI5 operative, he's staying in the Chief Whip's private apartment on the fourth floor. DS Scott virtually had to get a warrant to extract that information."

"Thanks, Brad," Dee said in reply. I felt a small stab of disapproval. When had she started calling him by his first name? "That would explain why you couldn't find him registered at a hotel. If only we could get in there we might be able to close this case. He must be hiding the money, painting and diamonds somewhere."

We looked up the address on Google Streetview; it was a white rendered building which had probably been several separate buildings at one time. I had passed it many times and never looked at it twice, yet now it might be at the heart of the case against Hickstead. It was galling to hear that we were more likely to get a search warrant for Windsor Castle than for the Chief Whip's private apartment.

Chapter 42

No. 2 Parliament Street, London. Thursday, 9:30am.

DS Scott was standing on the other side of Parliament Street, from where he could see the entrance to the apartment building, and he was engaged in conversation with a motorcycle courier dressed in black with gold lettering on his jacket, which read City Slicker Couriers. The courier looked just like thousands of others in and around the City, but this one was very different. Constable Knott was a police motorcyclist from the traffic section, seconded to CID for covert surveillance. The reasoning behind the disguise was that no-one in London gives couriers a second look.

As they stood together talking, their attention was on the apartment entrance. The team felt sure that His Lordship would pass on the diamonds sometime soon and they wanted to be there when he did. Such had been the police focus on the Peer since he landed at City Airport that morning that they had not noticed he was also being followed by someone else.

***

Dirk stood at the corner of the street, watching the latest policeman to follow Lord Hickstead. It had been a busy morning. Dirk had been warned that the police would have a tail on the Peer, and so he knew he must be careful. Dirk had dutifully waited at the airport until Hickstead appeared. He hung back and watched as a plain clothes policeman followed at a distance, radioing in his location. The man then dropped back and allowed the target to head towards the DLR platform. Dirk felt a little uncomfortable. The boss had insisted he got himself a haircut and buy a dark suit. Dirk couldn't remember the last time he had worn a collar and tie.

Hickstead stepped onto the train and a casually dressed young man entered the same carriage, his eyes fixed on the target. The man had a phone fixed to his ear. Dirk was convinced he had spotted the new tail.

After an uneventful journey into the City, and a mad dash across Bank Station, the police tail nodded to a man standing on the platform and then walked away, almost brushing past Dirk as he exited.

The policeman who had picked up the tail at Bank Station was now standing opposite the building that Hickstead had entered an hour ago.

Dirk lifted his mobile phone to his ear. "Gordo, you still close by?"

"Yep, I can see you standing on the corner, but it's really difficult to keep parking up here. I've been moved on three times already."

"I need you in case he takes a taxi. If he leaves on foot I'll follow on my own, OK?"

"OK, Dirk."

***

Lord Hickstead had changed his clothes and was now standing at the kerb holding a briefcase. The doorman had walked to the corner to hail a cab for him. Luckily it was sunny and the cabs were looking for customers. In the rain you couldn't get a cab for love nor money.

"I think we're off," Sergeant Scott said to the motorcycle cop, who put on his full face helmet before testing the built in microphone. HQ answered immediately and made it clear that they wanted a running commentary.

The Peer stepped into the black cab, and after a moment it did an illegal U turn and headed towards the Palace of Westminster. As it passed Big Ben, or St Stephen's Tower as it is more accurately known, it had been joined by a motorcycle courier and a blue Vauxhall Astra.

"Bloody hell, Gordo, couldn't we run to something better than this?" Dirk asked as he slid the seat as far back as it would go, realising he was still bent nearly double in the compact space.

"Boss said it had to be something inconspicuous," Gordo muttered apologetically.

* * *

The unwitting convoy of cab, motorbike and Astra proceeded along Victoria Street and then north along Grosvenor Place, skirting Buckingham Palace Gardens.

Against the odds, they all made it around an exceptionally congested Hyde Park Corner to exit onto Knightsbridge and the A4. They hadn't travelled far along Knightsbridge when the black cab turned into Brompton Road and indicated a right turn. The motorbike followed, but the Astra, a few cars behind now, had to wait to turn.

Dirk and Gordo both swore, but they need not have worried because the convoy came to an abrupt stop just a hundred metres away on Cheval Place. By the time the Astra arrived on the scene, Lord Hickstead was climbing the steps into a building. The wall next to the front entrance bore a brass plaque on which was engraved the words CitySafe Depository.

This area of London was unfamiliar to the Astra driver, but he soon discovered that Cheval Place was actually a mews. It was very narrow and, whilst the motorbike could pull over to one side, the Corsa was not going to be able to squeeze past the cab, which was still standing outside the depository. Gordo turned right onto a one-way Street called Rutland Street, and then he turned right again onto Fairholt Street so that he was parallel to Cheval Place.

"OK, Gordo, His Lordship has obviously got a safety deposit box in there. We have to assume that he's retrieving something valuable.

Here's what we do." Dirk outlined a rough plan and Gordo agreed, even though he had extreme concerns.

***

Lord Hickstead pressed the buzzer on the security panel and announced himself. The door buzzed and a tough looking man in uniform opened the door with a smile, beckoning the customer inside. In a few minutes he was past the metal grillage which protected the strongroom security guard and at the entrance to the strongroom itself. The door stood open. It was about ten feet in diameter and it was at least two feet thick. A mixture of brass and titanium locking bolts were arranged in three rows. The safe was virtually impregnable and the depository was fully manned twenty four hours a day, every day of the year, so breaking in overnight or at a weekend wasn't possible.

The Peer looked into the vault. There were boxes of all sizes, from letter sized to kitchen cabinet sized. His personal box was one of the largest; it was called a 'half cupboard'. It was sixteen inches wide and half the height of the vault at around three feet six inches tall. He tapped in a six figure code and a small beep announced the opening of a discreet panel in the door. Behind the panel was a keyhole. Lord Hickstead took his key from his pocket. It was rather unusual in appearance, similar to a Yale lock blank key with no notches along the edge. Instead it had tiny depressions or craters drilled into the flat sides. He slid the key into the keyhole and heard tiny rods slip into the depressions. Once they were in place he was able to turn the key ninety degrees to the right, and the lock disengaged.

Inside the box sat the oversized briefcase containing the painting, a holdall courtesy of Don Fisher and a bag of diamonds donated by Josh Hammond. It was time to start converting the remaining goods to cash. He was meeting Van Aart's man in an hour, and he had a meeting tomorrow with a London based Sheik who used the Peer to gain access to the highest levels of the last government. The Sheik was also rather keen to own the Churchill painting.

The last item in the box was possibly the most controversial; it was a brown envelope containing a series of Polaroid photographs which had been taken last year. Hickstead was not a man for gadgets or technology, but who on earth uses Polaroids any more, he wondered. He already knew the answer. He had paid a German journalist ten thousand Euros for ten poorly composed and badly lit photos, taken by an impoverished but good looking German boy. The photos had no artistic merit, but the faces in them were recognisable and what they were doing was likely to disgust and shock many who saw them.

Lord Hickstead placed two items into the briefcase he had brought with him and locked his safety deposit box. He had a busy day ahead of him.

Chapter 43

Cheval Place, London. Thursday, 11 am.

Constable Knott was now about a hundred yards from the depository; he was sitting astride his motorcycle with a clipboard in his hand, trying hard to look inconspicuous.

He saw the target exit the depository and start walking up Cheval Place in the direction of Montpellier Street, where he would have a chance of hailing a taxi. The policeman put his full face helmet on and put his clipboard away. As soon as His Lordship reached the end of the road he would follow; until then he would be too obvious.

At first he wasn't sure whether or not he was seeing things. A short man appeared from nowhere and moved close up behind the Peer, before using his foot to kick at back of the target's knee. Naturally the older man's knees folded and he ended up on the ground, breaking his fall by instinctively stretching out his hands. In the process he let go of the briefcase, and his assailant picked it up, held it to his chest and ran.

The constable was already off his bike and was yelling into his headset that the target was down and a mugger was escaping down a side street. The policeman was normally very quick on his feet, but he discovered very quickly that motorcycle boots are not made for running. By the time he got to the Peer the uniformed security guard from the depository was already helping the man up, and so the policeman directed his attention toward the mugger.

The policeman ran around the corner onto Montpellier Walk and nearly ran into a smartly dressed man carrying a green Harrods bag who was coming in the opposite direction. The man looked alarmed, but he quickly regained his composure and said, "I think the fellow you're chasing turned left down Fairholt."

Knott called out his thanks as he ran around the corner in time to see the mugger starting a small car and driving away at speed. He read the registration plate out loud to Control, informing them that this was a one way system and the only way out was via Brompton Road. If they could block that quickly enough, they would catch the mugger.

The constable walked back to his bike and waited for back up.

***

The plan had worked well. As soon as Gordo was out of sight of the policeman he had passed the briefcase to Dirk, who placed it in the Harrods bag and walked nonchalantly in the direction of the crime scene.

The motorcycle cop raced around the corner and nearly knocked Dirk over. Dirk pointed in the direction the mugger had gone, and the policeman hurried on his way. The constable had seen a smartly dressed man in a suit carrying a distinctive green Harrods bag, and had no reason to suspect him of anything. He had been too preoccupied with chasing a mugger, after all.

Dirk crossed the road and pressed himself against a wall as a police BMW raced into Cheval Place.

***

Gordo slowed down as he put distance between himself and the crime scene, so as not to attract attention. He reached the end of the road and realised that he could only turn right. It was a one way system and cars were coming from the left. He manoeuvred into the roadway and realised that he was heading back to Cheval Place, but there was nowhere else to go.

At the next junction he could either go right and pass the crime scene, or left and up to Brompton Road. He took the left turn. He could see Dirk walking in the same direction carrying the Harrods bag, and was contemplating picking him up - although that wasn't the plan - when a police car headed straight towards him. The BMW screeched to a halt, and Gordo was trapped.

***

Dirk saw the police helping Gordo out of the car and hurried away from the area, eventually flagging down a taxi. He gave the Boss's address, and relaxed on the back seat of the cab before making the inevitable call.

"Boss, I have some good news and some bad news," he said, as if starting to tell some bad joke.

Chapter 44

New Scotland Yard, London. Thursday, 1pm.

By the time Dee and I arrived at Scotland Yard with Inspector Boniface, Lord Hickstead had been there for over an hour. So far he had been seen by a police doctor, who could find no injuries whatsoever, and he had been asked to identify the alleged mugger, which he could not do as the mugger had approached him from behind.

We were told by DCI Coombes that CCTV footage showed the incident in full, but quite honestly the mugger could have been anyone wearing dark clothing. Worse still was the fact that Constable Knott could not identify the mugger either, and he had to admit he had not actually seen the suspect getting into the car. He had assumed it was the mugger, mainly because of the timing of events and the fact that the streets were otherwise empty. A reasonable assumption, in my view, but not everyone shared that view.

"Nothing!" Detective Chief Inspector Coombes shouted in frustration. "We have nothing!" He stormed off, and Inspector Boniface rolled his eyes. We were all sitting in a meeting room, being briefed on the day's events, trying to piece together exactly how everything had gone so horribly wrong.

"So what was in the briefcase?" Dee asked generally. Gathered around the table were Detective Sergeants Scott and Fellowes, myself, Dee and Inspector Boniface.

DS Scott answered. "We don't know. We went through that car with a fine toothed comb, and no briefcase. We've even had uniform search the whole area, and they came up with nothing. The bloody thing seems to have just vanished."

"He could have thrown it away when the car was out of sight," Dee proffered.

"True, but why would he bother? As far as he was concerned he'd got clean away with only a courier on his trail." DS Scott was clearly irritated, and looked thoroughly miserable.

"What about Lord Hickstead? What does he say about the briefcase?" Boniface asked.

"He says that the briefcase contained some copies of private family papers, wills and that sort of thing, all of which he can have copied by his lawyers who hold the originals. He just wants to leave, and he isn't being particularly helpful."

"Sounds odd to me," I said. "Why travel halfway across London to get some copies of papers out of a safety deposit box when your lawyer has the originals? It doesn't make sense. I assume we're all thinking the same thing, that he's just had the diamonds stolen from him?" All heads nodded.

"He must be worried, because Europol informed us that early this morning Van Aart transferred a quarter of a million Euros to the bank account of Euro Union Financial Enterprises, the main signatory being one Arthur Hickstead. I guess that was the payment for the diamonds," DS Fellowes contributed.

***

"Is everything in place?" Inspector Boniface asked. It was. "Right. Thank Lord Hickstead for his assistance and offer to take him home. In any event, escort him out of the building, understood?" The person on the other end of the phone seemed to understand.

The video screen lit up, showing a blue screen bearing the name of the projector company. After a few seconds the picture changed to show a wide view of a comfortable room, where a middle aged man with a balding pate and overly long grey hair sat on a sofa.

It was my arch nemesis, Lord Hickstead. I didn't know how I felt. I should have been angry, but he looked so defeated, so unthreatening. He must have been really shaken up by the day's events, I thought. I had to remind myself that this was my blackmailer, and that I shouldn't be feeling sorry for him. He looked vulnerable. It was that very vulnerability which Inspector Boniface was hoping to exploit.

Assistant Commissioner Bryn Evans came into the picture. "Lord Hickstead, I am very sorry that you have been here so long, but the suspect is in our custody. Unfortunately he did not have your briefcase in his possession, and I'm afraid its whereabouts are presently unknown. I fear you may not see it again."

The camera caught a look of relief passing briefly across Hickstead's face, presumably because the diamonds would have tied him into the blackmail plots and the deaths of three people.

"Here is your watch, Lord Hickstead. You were quite right; it had no skin or blood or hair that we could have matched with the suspect's DNA profile. It's a very nice watch, I must say. Far too expensive for a policeman, though." He laughed at his own joke, and Hickstead smiled.

"Sergeant Baines will show you out." The two men shook hands and the pretty and petite policewoman led His Lordship towards the lifts. The camera view shifted to the lift lobby. After a minute of video of the reception area we saw the Sergeant and the Peer exit the lift and walk into a tastefully appointed area which serves as a waiting room.

At first the Peer was so busy chatting up Sergeant Baines that he did not look at the row of padded seats. These were occupied by two people wearing visitor badges and looking nervous. As they moved further into the lobby the screen split; one long shot, one close up of Hickstead.

The screen split at almost the precise moment that Lord Hickstead saw them sitting less than five metres away; Abasi Nour, the jeweller, and Kelvin de Montagu, the art gallery owner. His face registered shock, and he immediately turned his head away from the two men.

Under strict orders Sergeant Baines said, "Oh, Your Lordship, I'll need your badge so that I can sign you out." She left him standing in the middle of the lobby with every eye looking at him, each person wondering whether they ought to know him by sight.

The video screen reverted to a single wide shot of the reception area and I watched for a reaction from our two stooges. Whilst De Montagu registered nothing more than general curiosity, Mr Nour looked puzzled. After a moment he caught sight of the watch and stared intently at Lord Hickstead's face, before his jaw dropped and his face paled.

Confirmation, as if we needed it.

***

Lord Hickstead was being escorted home, hopefully feeling nervous, or at least unsettled, and Mr Nour was now showing on the screen. Inspector Boniface was sitting opposite him, smiling, trying to calm the old Egyptian.

"Mr Nour, I'd like to thank you for coming in today. Have you been treated well?"

"Yes, sir, I have. The young policeman who took me through my statement said that you were making progress. Does this mean I can have my money back? I have done nothing wrong."

"Mr Nour, we will release your money very soon, I can assure you. Now, one further question, if that's all right. The watch you were shown during your interview; was that the type of watch you saw on your Josh Hammond?"

"Yes, exactly the same. Where did you get it? They are very rare, I know."

"We have our sources. Why do you ask?" the Inspector asked, seemingly innocently.

"I don't know that I should say."

"Come along, Mr Nour, you can trust me. Anything else you can remember will speed up the release of your money."

The video screen showed a close up of Mr Nour. "I am not sure, I cannot say with firmness, but a few minutes ago I saw a man downstairs, Lord Hickwell or something."

"Lord Hickstead," Boniface provided helpfully. "Yes, go on."

"Well, he was wearing the same watch, and when I looked into his eyes, they were the eyes of Mr Hammond, the man who deceived me with his silly toupee."

Inspector Boniface registered shock on his face. "Mr Nour, are you saying that Lord Hickstead was the man posing as Josh Hammond in your diamond deal?"

"I believe so, yes, but I am sure no-one will believe me. He is a Lord, after all, and probably has an estate in the beautiful English countryside. But when I looked into his eyes I do believe he recognised me. I know it sounds foolish, but it is what I saw."

Boniface asked Mr Nour to keep his views to himself and, having added the latest revelation to the bottom of the witness statement as an addendum, he had Mr Nour sign it again.

***

Mr De Montagu could add nothing to his statement and had nothing to say about the set up in the reception area, and so he and Mr Nour were thanked and allowed to go.

The video screen was switched off and the bank of fluorescent lights came on. The same group sat around the table once again, with the addition of Assistant Commissioner Evans.

Clockwise around the table I saw AC Evans at the head, sitting under the video screen. To his left sat DS Scott and DS Fellowes, Dee was next, and I sat beside her. Boniface and Coombes completed the line-up.

Assistant Commissioner Evans summarised the day. "So far, today has had its ups and downs but, on the whole, I think we have our man on the hook. Now we just need to reel him in. I think we're unlikely to get a warrant to search the Parliament Street apartment, but I do believe we'll get a warrant for CitySafe Depository, or at least for one of its boxes."

I was surprised at that, and said so. "Assistant Commissioner, I thought that safe deposit boxes were sacrosanct, and that the banks protected their customers with their lives?"

"Mr Hammond, you're quite right, to a degree, but these depositories are not banks and nor do they share the same privileges. Perhaps DCI Coombes can explain."

We all turned to look at the grumpy policeman.

"In 2018 I headed an investigation into money laundering, and it led us to various safe deposit boxes at three locations; Park Lane, Hampstead and Edgware. We raided the premises simultaneously. There were at least fifty officers involved, and with angle grinders and other heavy tools we opened the suspect boxes.

Ninety percent of the boxes we opened contained evidence of criminality. As a result we arrested a significant number of criminals, as well as some of the depository owners, and recovered many millions of pounds in cash, jewellery and art."

Coombes fell silent and the Assistant Commissioner took over. "So, as you can see, Mr Hammond, in view of the circumstantial evidence we have, which is now rather substantial, and because of previous good results on other cases, we have a good chance of obtaining a warrant."

He had barely got the words out when there was a knock at the door. An out of breath young police officer was beckoned into the room and was eager to present something to the gathering.

"Sir, I have some news on the mugger. It's rather unexpected."

"All right, Constable, let's hear it."

The young man stood next to the Assistant Commissioner and read out his findings, which were indeed rather surprising. Or perhaps not.

"Ms Conrad; gentlemen. As you know, the man apprehended has denied any involvement in the mugging, pointing out that he was not in possession of any stolen goods when apprehended.

He's been calm and cooperative the whole time, and when asked whether he wanted representation he said he was happy to talk to us without a lawyer present, as he had done nothing wrong. However, he asked if he could seek advice from his employers.

He was allowed the phone call and he rang an Isleworth number. We later identified the company as the Distressed Media Group, who are the registered owners of the car.

The driver, Gordon James Coppull, who has no criminal record whatsoever, freely explained that he was a record producer for the said company and that he had a personal fortune of over two million pounds. We checked him out on the internet and before he went into business he was lead guitarist for The Regular Enemas, a popular grunge band from the 1990s.

As he had no history of criminality in his first thirty five years, and as he appeared to be as wealthy as he claimed, we more or less ruled him out of the mugging, until I received this back from Companies House."

The young man lifted a single page company search and read from it.

"Distressed Media Group is a PLC, formed in 1987. Directors are listed as Gordon J Coppull, Dirk Millman, Joseph Pettleman, Michael Dixon and the Managing Director is...." The young man paused for effect, holding the name back as if he was announcing the results on the X Factor.

"Donald Grainger Fisher, former lead singer of 'London's Burning' and founder of Rock Relief."

The young policeman received the reaction he must surely have expected. Every jaw in the room dropped.

Chapter 45

No. 2 Parliament St, London. Thursday, 2pm.

It was his third glass of the Chief Whip's Armagnac and the forty percent alcohol content was calming Lord Hickstead's nerves. He stared at the colourful liquid swilling around in the balloon glass, marvelling at the French talent for producing the world's best wine and then producing the world's best brandy from that wine. The oddly shaped bottle looked as though it should contain Olive Oil or salad dressing. It had a long neck, bulbous body and it was flat front and back. The label was old fashioned and appeared to be deliberately designed to appear aged. It read Clés des Ducs, with three stars under the name. As with other types of brandy, it had been given the appendage VSOP as it was a five year old Armagnac and, luckily, it was his favourite tipple.

Despite the mild alcoholic haze in his brain, his mind kept coming back to the disastrous day that was only half over. It had all seemed so simple in the depository. Go to Trafalgar Square, hand over the diamonds to Van Aart's man and drop the photos in the post to the anonymous 'Dr Crippin' who published the notorious Celebrity Leaks web site. He would have posted the Polaroids to one of the newspapers, but there was only one out of the batch of ten that could be considered suitable for publication by any newspaper, no matter how broad minded the readership. Still, by this time tomorrow the pictures would probably have appeared on a thousand web sites and blog pages around the world, especially considering the alleged celebrity of the subject.

He still couldn't believe that he had been mugged. The police seemed to think that the mugger had waited outside the depository, evidently reckoning that there was a good chance that anyone leaving the premises would be carrying some valuables. The police had a suspect, but no briefcase. That was just as well. How could he possibly have explained carrying a quarter of a million pounds' worth of diamonds? The only provenance or receipt he had which showed they had not been stolen would lead straight back to Abasi Nour.

That was another disaster. He had convinced the police that he had lost nothing of value, and they hadn't recovered the briefcase, so he thought he was in the clear. Then he saw Nour and De Montagu in the police station. Presumably they were sitting there waiting to talk to a detective about the blackmailer who used them to launder his money.

He thought that he had seen a glimmer of recognition in Nour's face when they had made eye contact, but he had convinced himself that he was over-reacting. In any event, who would believe that a Peer of the Realm would blackmail random individuals in the City? Nonetheless, the Egyptian had shown himself to be borderline criminal, and so Arthur would have to wait and see what happened next. His guess was that he would receive a call from Mr Nour and a request for his diamonds back. But the diamonds were gone, and Nour certainly wasn't the person he would have given them to, anyway. The Peer had already received polite but vaguely threatening calls from Van Aart demanding immediate delivery of the diamonds or his money back. The Dutch criminal also noted that if he did not receive the diamonds he would add an extra one hundred thousand Euros to the bill as compensation for lost profit.

Not a good day, on the whole. Almost a third of a million pounds down, an abysmal failure to humiliate that scumbag pop singer in Isleworth, and now a very real possibility that he might have to deal with Mr Nour.

Another glass of golden brown Clés des Ducs Armagnac slid down his throat.

Chapter 46

New Scotland Yard, London. Thursday, 4pm.

I was back in the conference room with Inspector Boniface, DS Fellowes and Dee. We had been summoned back by the Assistant Commissioner's secretary, having enjoyed a leisurely lunch in the canteen. The canteen food proved to be much better than I had been expecting. The roast lamb was moist, the roast potatoes crispy brown on the outside and white and fluffy on the inside, and the vegetables weren't overcooked, having the perfect degree of bite to them. The Metropolitan Police eat well, especially at those prices. I suspected that if Dyson Brecht had such a canteen we would all be much heavier than we are. Many of us are lazy thin; we simply can't be bothered to make the journey to buy food, either the healthy or junk varieties.

As soon as we were told that Don Fisher had been implicated in the mugging the Assistant Commissioner had blown his top and ordered DCI Coombes to "find him and drag him in, if necessary". No such action was necessary, however, as Fisher was already on his way to Scotland Yard to get his friend Gordon out of trouble.

DS Scott came in with Don Fisher and a churlish looking man whom I took to be Gordon James Coppull. They were followed a moment later by a man who was obviously a lawyer. He was carrying a green Harrods bag.

Introductions were affected, and then we sat down to await AC Evans. When he arrived he looked at Fisher and failed to completely mask his anger. Fisher had the decency to look embarrassed.

"Mr Fisher, you seem to have completely ruined a complex international surveillance operation, stolen a briefcase from a good friend of the Home Secretary, and put a suspect on notice that he is under investigation. Well done, and all in a single day."

James Loftus, the lawyer, began to speak, but Fisher caught his arm and shook his head. "I probably deserved that. However, I've got the briefcase here. None of my guys touched the handle or the locks, so you should be able to confirm it belongs to Hickstead."

The lawyer lifted the Harrods bag on to the table, the briefcase still inside. Inspector Boniface carefully slid the brown leather briefcase out onto the desk.

"Are you sure no-one has touched the handle or the locks?"

The former rock star nodded.

"We'll need your prints, of course, for elimination purposes," Boniface told him as he turned the briefcase to face him. Using a silver retractable ballpoint pen the Inspector pushed the right had side button toward the edge and the spring loaded fastener shot up. He repeated the operation for the left had side and, using the pen again, he opened the lid. It smelled of new leather. The inside was pristine. I suspected that Hickstead had bought it specifically for the diamond handover.

Inside the briefcase lay a large padded Jiffy bag and a plain manila envelope. Nothing else.

Inspector Boniface reached inside his pocket and took out a plastic ziplock bag containing a pair of pristine white cotton gloves. After slipping them on, he extracted the Jiffy bag. It was sealed. He looked at the Assistant Commissioner. He nodded and said, "The chain of evidence has already been broken, so you might as well open it."

I knew enough about these things to understand that any incriminating evidence we found would be unusable because the briefcase had not moved directly from Lord Hickstead's possession to the police, who would have sealed it to preserve any forensic evidence and recorded its processing from collection to trial.

Boniface carefully opened the Jiffy bag and removed a black velvet pouch. It had to be the diamonds. He opened the top of the drawstring pouch and looked inside. For a moment he said nothing, he simply stared at the contents. He then took the blue cardboard envelope file he had been carrying and placed in on the table where all of us could see it.

"Inventory please, Sergeant." DS Fellowes opened his notebook to a clean yellow page. The inspector carefully tipped the contents on to the blue folder. There were fifteen stones of different sizes, which meant they were worth an average of sixteen thousand pounds each. I could well believe it. I had never seen diamonds as large, as pure or so beautifully cut, and I see a lot of jewellery and gems as a loss adjuster. They sparkled from whichever angle one looked at them, even under the fluorescent lighting.

For the second time that day there was a collective sharp intake of breath around the table. DS Fellowes photographed the diamonds and the pouch from various angles, with his mobile phone. Taking great care, Boniface replaced the diamonds in their velvet pouch. He then placed the pouch in an evidence bag and sealed it, passing it to Fellowes, who wrote something on the label.

Inspector Boniface returned to the briefcase and lifted out the plain brown envelope, which was also sealed. Written on it were the words 'Dr. Crippin'. He carefully unsealed the gummed flap and then started to open the envelope.

"Stop!" Don Fisher shouted. "I need to explain something." The lawyer immediately advised him not to say anything that might incriminate himself. Don Fisher told him that they had gone too far for that, and that he needed to protect his family.

"Dr. Crippin is a filth monger," he explained. "He runs a website called CelebrityLeaks.org. It specialises in publishing private pictures, stolen movies and long lens shots of celebrities. Just yesterday he posted a video of that TV weathergirl showering topless on the beach in the French Riviera. Already that video has almost a million hits, and the ads on that page alone are raking in a small fortune.

I believe what you've got in that envelope are pictures of my daughter Lavender and some of her so-called friends, taken in Spain last year. I was approached by a German man who said he had ten Polaroids that he was sure I would rather have destroyed. He asked for a paltry sum of money, and I wish I'd paid him, but I get calls like that regularly and most of them are rubbish."

I thought to myself that he might be right, but Lavender was well known as something of a self-publicist, and if the Paparazzi don't snap her for a month she allegedly tells them where they can find her while she's out in some celebrity pool or on a beach, splashing around topless. Brand Lavender needed the oxygen of constant publicity.

Don Fisher was still talking. "Yesterday I got this text from the blackmailing shite, Lord Hickstead, signing himself off as Jim. It says, Thanks for the cash but keep your eye on CelebrityLeaks.org where your fragrant daughter will soon be making an appearance."

"So, that's why you had your men tail Hickstead and steal his briefcase after he had visited his safety deposit box?" Boniface asked.

"Yes. Believe me, that girl is in the deepest trouble of her short life. I told the TV company she's been working with to get her home today from Italy. They whined about their shooting schedule. I told them if she wasn't home tonight it would be a different and more fatal kind of shooting they would have to worry about. I was bloody angry."

"And you believe that these Polaroid photographs in this envelope are intimate shots of your daughter?"

The old rocker nodded unhappily.

"Then, why didn't you open the case and destroy them?" the Assistant Commissioner asked.

"Because, as much as I want to protect my family, I need the scum we keep calling Lord Hickstead to go down, to lose everything, to understand first-hand the disgrace that Lavender faces. I realise that the boys got a little bit overzealous and made an executive decision to snatch the photos before he could sell them on. But remember that Gordo here and Dirk have known Lavender since she was born; we have video footage of them both bottle feeding her at the studio. She's like a daughter to them. She might need a short sharp shock from you boys to bring her into line, but nobody deserves photos like those to be published on the internet."

"So she has admitted to you that the photos exist, and she has described their subject matter?" It was the Assistant Commissioner again.

"No. She can't remember. She was probably out of her head. It was the German boy who told me what was on them, but I wouldn't believe him."

"You realise, of course, that these photos are evidence that could be used to convict Hickstead. They will probably have his fingerprints on them, and that would be enough evidence to bring him in and sweat him, probably enough to get a warrant to search his safety deposit box."

The father nodded silently. There were tears in his eyes.

Inspector Boniface spoke gently to Don Fisher, father to father.

"Don, if we use these photos at all it will be to get him off the streets. I assure you that between the Met and the City Police we will be looking at charges that go way beyond threatening to post these shots on the internet. In which case, these photos will never see the light of day in court."

Somewhat mollified, Fisher thanked the Inspector.

"Mr Loftus, as Mr Fisher's legal representative you need to advise him that he and his two colleagues will be asked to accept a Simple Caution, and that whilst a Caution is a not criminal record, their fingerprints and DNA may be retained under the appropriate Acts of Parliament."

"Is this really necessary, Bryn?" the lawyer queried, revealing his familiarity with the Assistant Commissioner.

"Jim, you know full well that I am putting my neck on the block offering a Simple Caution at all. We should really be referring this to the Crown Prosecution Service."

Assistant Commissioner Bryn Evans responded reasonably.

The meeting broke up and Don Fisher approached Dee and I. "Sorry about all of this. If my interference stops you getting your money back, just let me know. OK?"

"OK," I agreed, and he left the room to receive his Caution.

"We could be rich after this," Dee said. "Two people have each offered us a quarter of a million pounds to put Lord Hickstead away." She smiled and linked my arm.

"We," I teased. "When did it become, we? Surely you mean me?"

"Oh no, you obviously haven't read the small print of our agreement. All recovered monies are split fifty-fifty. Why do you think I've been so nice to you?"

My face obviously fell as I searched hers to gauge whether or not she was serious, because finally she could hold it no longer and she laughed out loud.

"For a cynical City loss adjuster you are pretty gullible. By the way, did you know that the word gullible is not in the dictionary?"

I frowned, and she laughed out loud again.

Chapter 47

Ashburnham Mews, Greenwich, London. Thursday, 11pm.

I was lying flat on my back with my hands between my head and the pillow. I couldn't sleep. It seemed to me that if I was on a jury I would convict Lord Hickstead on the basis of the evidence that was already available. Although I understood that much of it was circumstantial, it was beginning to become overwhelming.

The police were testing the Polaroids for fingerprints and were quite hopeful of finding definite proof. When the fingerprint technician collected the photos, he said that the chemical process used by Polaroid to develop the picture in the camera leaves a soft residue on the surface which brings out the 'ridges and whorls' of a fingerprint very nicely.

The police had been busy, and had tracked down photos and other details of all those known to own an Old Navitimer Mecanique by accessing the DVLA database of driving license photos and the Passport Agency's database, which included details such as height and distinguishing marks. Lord Hickstead was the only man on the spreadsheet, provided by Breitling, who matched the description given by Nour and De Montagu in terms of height, build, ethnicity and eye colour. Nikon UK had helpfully taken the Breitling list and checked it against their registered owners of the P900. The only match had been Lord Hickstead.

Vastrick Security had also been working hard to build a full profile of Lord Hickstead, from his schooldays to the present. The file was thick with copies of his school reports and certificates, his university papers, his Trade Union activities, his numerous complaints about me and his insurers, press cuttings and a video from YouTube showing him being humiliated on screen by Don Fisher. There was whole section dedicated to his relationships with the victims of his blackmailing scheme. It consisted of lists of names derived from school, university, Trade Union

Membership records, director information from Companies House and AGP's list of individuals who travelled to the Partners' meeting with Andrew Cuthbertson.

Between them, the police and Vastrick could connect Hickstead with three dead bodies and two living blackmail victims. They could also place him in South Africa and Thailand, where 48hrs.co.za was based and registered.

Dee came out of the en suite bathroom and looked at me. She scowled.

"What's the matter?" I asked.

"Hmmm. Typical man," she murmured, climbing into bed and back towards me.

"Have I done something wrong, Dee?"

"You don't even know, do you?"

I scoured my memory banks for what I could have done to offend her, and came up blank. I tried again.

"I've had a lot on my mind. Have I missed something?"

Without turning around she said sharply, "Last night was our first week anniversary and you said nothing, did nothing and just let it pass. Hmmm."

I was taken aback. I hadn't realised that Dee needed that kind of reassurance. I turned on my side and placed my hand on her shoulder. "Sorry, Dee, it was thoughtless of me."

Her shoulders shook under my hand. Was she sobbing? She turned over and lay on her back and now I could see that she was laughing uproariously. I'd been had again. Was this the way it would always be; me as her comedy sidekick?

"You just like making fun of me, don't you?" I said, by way of statement rather than as a question.

There was amusement in her voice when she answered. "I do, for two reasons. One, you are an easy target and two, Josh Hammond, I think I might just be falling for you."

I was speechless, but happier than I could remember ever being before.

"Go to sleep Josh. We're bound to be busy tomorrow."

"I can't sleep," I answered. "I don't feel tired."

"I can help you there. If I place my hand on your shoulder and neck like this, and squeeze here, I'll cut off the blood supply to your brain, and you will be out in fifteen seconds."

"No, that's quite all right," I laughed nervously, switching off the bedside lamp. "I suddenly feel very tired."

Chapter 48

No. 2 Parliament St, London. Friday, 8:30am.

It had been a long night, and Arthur Hickstead had slept for a maximum of an hour or two of it. The two hours he had managed to sleep at all had been snatched in fifteen minute spells.

Yesterday afternoon and evening had been hectic. He had spent most of the time online, and on the phone to his bank, trying to send Van Aart his money back. Hickstead had explained about the mugging and Van Aart had seemed sympathetic. Nevertheless, he explained that the buyers he had lined up would be looking for compensation. Eventually the Peer decided that it was not in his best interests to upset one of Europe's most violent gang leaders. As a result, he had lost the diamonds and one hundred thousand Euros of his own. He had risked his liberty to blackmail that slippery loss adjuster and recover the insurance money he had been denied after his house had caught fire, only to end up worse off than he had been before. If he hadn't already had a hangover he would have had a drink to settle his nerves.

The console on the wall buzzed. It was Jeff, the doorman. The Peer picked up the handset.

"Lord Hickstead," he announced.

"Sir, we have two police detectives at the door who say they have recovered your briefcase."

Hickstead could feel the panic rising in his midriff. He had to stay calm; he could talk his way out of this. He took a deep breath.

"OK, Jeff, send them up, please."

***

DCI Coombes and DS Scott rode up to the fourth floor on what was the oldest and most elegant elevator they had ever seen. It had rich dark walnut panelling and a burnished brass console with worn enamelled buttons bearing the numbers of each floor. The door was a pair of iron lattice gates which had to be pulled across before the lift would move. A plate in the elevator proclaimed that the Otis Elevator Company had installed the lift in 1904. DCI Coombes was holding the briefcase in a clear plastic bag and so DS Scott operated the lift. As they arrived at the fourth floor, and opened the lattice gates, a door opened in front of them. They stepped out, then DS Scott closed the gates and the lift departed.

The detectives tapped on the apartment door and entered, closing it behind them.

"This way, gentlemen," a voice called from inside the apartment.

As they walked into what was probably called a sitting room, they marvelled at the ornate decor which was probably original. The painted walls were earthy colours but were not necessarily what one might choose for a modern house. Somehow, though, they seemed to work in these 19th Century surroundings.

Lord Hickstead was sitting in a high backed winged armchair with green leather upholstery; buttons secured the leather to the chair. He gestured to them to sit down on a matching Chesterfield sofa.

"It's a beautiful place, isn't it?" Lord Hickstead said as he looked around. "One could be in a country house anywhere in England. Sadly, it's not mine." He smiled and looked at the briefcase.

"I'm DCI Coombes and this is Detective Sergeant Scott. We believe that we have found your stolen briefcase."

"Oh, good," Hickstead responded, trying his best to sound pleased. "I'm delighted. Are my papers still inside? They are quite confidential."

"No, I'm afraid not, but shall we take a look inside, so that you can be sure that the case is yours?" DCI Coombes carefully set the briefcase down on a glass topped table in front of him. He suspected that if he broke the table it would cost his monthly salary to replace it. He looked at their host.

"This is your briefcase, isn't it, Lord Hickstead?"

"Yes, I believe it is, though they all look the same from the outside."

"We recovered the briefcase when the mugger eventually confessed that he had discarded it as he was being chased," Coombes explained. "It was found less than a hundred yards from where you were attacked. It has your fingerprints on the handle, and his on the sides. Once he heard about that, he knew the game was up."

Coombes opened the briefcase. Inside lay a sealed Jiffy bag and another sealed envelope addressed by hand to Dr Crippin. The police had carefully resealed the envelopes for the purposes of this morning's visit.

"Are these yours, sir?" DS Scott asked. "It's just that you didn't mention them in your statement, and we were reluctant to open them without you present."

Arthur Hickstead was on the horns of a dilemma. If he denied all knowledge of the envelopes, it meant that he lost the diamonds forever. If he confirmed they were his, he could be linked with the blackmail plots. He had to think quickly.

"No, they weren't in there when the case was taken," he said calmly.

"Are you quite certain of that, sir?" Coombes asked, looking Hickstead squarely in the eyes."

Hickstead felt a quickening of his heart rate. He didn't like the way this interview was going. Nevertheless, he answered calmly. "That is a puzzle, detective, but not one I can help you with, I'm afraid. Those packages do not belong to me. I've never seen them before."

DS Scott wrote copiously, being careful to record the Peer's words accurately.

"We didn't want to risk your safety, your Lordship, and so we scanned the packages for incendiary devices," Coombes said. "They were both cleared, which is why we have brought them here, but I think you might be rather sorry you didn't claim ownership of the Jiffy bag. That is, of course, if the scanner operator is right in his assumption as to what it contains."

Coombes opened the Jiffy bag and slid out the velvet pouch. He closed the briefcase, and very carefully he tipped the diamonds onto the brown leather lid.

"Bloody hell!" DS Scott exclaimed, acting his part well, and then added somewhat sheepishly, "Sorry, Lord Hickstead."

"No need to apologise to me, young man. 'Bloody hell' seems to cover it rather appropriately," the Peer replied, gazing at the stones with envy. "I suppose it's too late for me to claim the Jiffy bag now," he continued, smiling at his quip, even though he didn't feel like smiling at all.

"I'm afraid so, sir. DS Scott, could you take a record photograph, please?"

"Sorry, guv," Scott said, shrugging his shoulders. "I didn't bring the camera with me." Coombes seemed to be bristling with anger, and Scott added, "You didn't say anything to me about bringing a camera."

The situation seemed as though it might soon become embarrassing and so Lord Hickstead spoke up.

"Gentlemen, I have a digital camera you can use." He turned to open a Pilot case behind him. Coombes, unseen by the Peer, winked at Scott. The practised double act had worked again. His Lordship turned back to face them and handed a Nikon Coolpix P900 to the DS.

Scott took two photographs of the diamonds, and pressed the display button to check that the resulting images were satisfactory. He then pressed the back button surreptitiously, but there were no more photographs on the card. It didn't matter. They had what they wanted.

"I'll transfer the photos from the card onto my eBook," DS Scott said as he took a tiny Acer Notebook Computer from his bag and slotted the SD card into it.

***

When the stones had been safely restored to their pouch, DCI Coombes turned his attention to the other envelope and spoke solemnly to their host.

"Sir, I do not mean to offend you in any way, but the scans show that this envelope contains dense photo paper, the type usually associated with Polaroid cameras. Could there be any Polaroid photographs in here that may cause you embarrassment?"

Lord Hickstead laughed. "If that is your overly polite way of asking whether the photos are of me in indiscreet circumstances, then no. I'm a bit too old for that sort of thing."

"All right, sir, I am now opening the envelope," Coombes explained, "but I must warn you that the contents could either be innocent or explicit, we have no way of knowing."

"I think we are all men of the world here," Hickstead smiled. "I don't think I will be offended."

The photos dropped out of the envelope, and DCI Coombes slipped on a pair of cotton gloves and arranged them inside a transparent evidence bag so that they could all be seen. The reality, of course, was that they had all seen them before; indeed, the forensics lab had already extracted Lord Hickstead's prints from the Polaroids.

"Lord Hickstead, have you seen any of these photos before, or do they in fact belong to you?" Coombes asked. Scott waited to write down anything His Lordship might say, verbatim, when he denied all knowledge of the photos which carried his fingerprints, as he surely would.

The photos were in random order, but they all showed a girl, probably in her late teens, evidently inside a house. She appeared in various states of undress with two different men. Only one of the men appeared in the frame at any one time, suggesting that the other was taking the pictures. The girl seemed semi-conscious in most of the shots. Her tired, half closed eyes were unfocussed, her pupils massively dilated. Lines of what might have been cocaine could be seen on the table in front of the sofa the girl was kneeling on. Any one of these photos would end the burgeoning career of a young woman in the public eye and make any serious romantic relationship a thing of the past.

"No," Lord Hickstead responded after a moment's silence. "I have never seen these photographs before. Do you know who she is?"

DS Scott wrote assiduously in his notebook, as Coombes answered.

"I'm afraid not, Lord Hickstead. She might be a singer or a film star or something, or she just might be an ordinary girl. I'm afraid I'm not au-fait with current pop culture."

Both men looked at DS Scott, who was still in his twenties.

"Don't look at me," he said defensively. "I'm a married man. I have no idea who she is, either."

Coombes slipped the evidence back into the briefcase, speaking as he did so.

"Well, whoever she is, these pictures are unlikely to see the light of day, which is very fortunate for her. They will probably be destroyed, after they have been tested for fingerprints."

DS Scott had been watching the Peer closely, waiting for a reaction, and he got it. At the mention of the photos being dusted for fingerprints, the Peer blanched for a moment before regaining his composure.

"Is it really possible to lift decent fingerprints from photographs?" Hickstead asked, trying to sound nonchalant.

"Oh, yes," DS Scott replied. "As a matter of fact, the secretions from the human eccrine glands are particularly responsive to the chemicals used for film emulsions. In the seventies and eighties criminals would use Polaroids to photograph banks and shops when planning robberies and the like. More than one gang has been sent down by their careless handling of Polaroid photos."

DCI Coombes stood and offered his hand to Lord Hickstead.

"Sorry to have taken up your time, sir. We will return the briefcase to you in due course, but I'm afraid it could be a while."

"Not to worry, Chief Inspector, it wasn't expensive. As I explained, I was more interested in recovering my personal papers, which aren't inside any longer."

After the policemen had left, Lord Hickstead collapsed onto the Chesterfield sofa in a rage. He yelled out many obscenities but he didn't repeat any one of them twice.

Chapter 49

New Scotland Yard, London. Friday, 10:30am.

It had been almost a week, one hundred and sixty eight hours to be precise, since I had lost my money, and the net was closing in on my blackmailer. The police told me that the chances of me recovering my money had improved now that they had the diamonds and the frozen bank funds.

We were standing outside the new Scotland Yard with its iconic rotating triangular sign above our heads. Dee was on her mobile phone, with a finger in her other ear to try to hear the caller over the noise of the traffic on the Embankment.

I looked at her closely. She really was beautiful. Her hair was down today and the rich auburn locks were swept back over her shoulder and came to an end at her shoulder blades. Dee was slim but not thin. She was strong, but not muscular. I could easily see how someone might underestimate her. On the surface she was a beauty with a handsome cleavage, flat stomach and legs to die for. I was admiring her derriere when I felt a touch on my arm. Roused from my daydream, I discovered that a Japanese man was addressing me, more in sign language than in words.

"Please. You take photo. Me and wife?" A small Japanese woman next to him smiled hopefully at me.

"Of course," I smiled, nodding at him. He handed me a Sony camera and I framed the picture so that it included the couple and the world famous rotating sign. I showed them the resulting image when it appeared on the screen at the back. The couple seemed happy with the result, and bowed their thanks graciously. I wasn't sure whether I should bow in return, and ended up half bowing, half nodding.

A car pulled up and out stepped Inspector Boniface and his boss Chief superintendent Boddy. Both were wearing immaculate suits.

Dee finished her call and joined us.

"Ms Conrad, you look stunning today," Boddy commented, admiring her tailored suit and tight skirt.

"Chief Superintendent, you are such a flatterer," Dee responded as she flirtatiously slipped her arm through his. "Shall we go inside?" she asked as she led the blushing Chief into the building, though I noticed he made no effort to extricate himself. Boniface and I shared a smile.

**

The Assistant Commissioner and DCI Coombes were already in the room when we entered. We briefly reacquainted ourselves, and each took a seat in the same video conference room as before. For the first time I noticed that the room was called the Sir Robert Peel Conference room, after the founder of the police force.

I listened and made notes as we were updated on the latest developments. The first piece of news made me smile. Europol and the Dutch Police were closing in on Mr Van Aart and a Commissaris Bokhuis confirmed to the Met that Mr Van Aart's account had just been credited with three hundred and fifty thousand Euros, the money indisputably coming from Lord Hickstead's coffers. I was not alone in noticing that His Lordship had repaid the Dutch criminal about eighty five thousand pounds more than he had received.

Coombes explained in great detail what had happened that morning when they returned with the briefcase to Parliament Street. Having seen the Peer's reactions, the Met detectives were now more convinced than ever that Hickstead was guilty of murdering both Andrew Cuthbertson and Sir Max Rochester.

The video screen flickered into life, but instead of moving pictures a computer start screen was showing. A disembodied arrow floated across the screen and double clicked. A photo appeared of the diamonds, spread out on the lid of a brown leather briefcase. I was wondering why we were looking at a picture of the diamonds when the arrow clicked on 'more info' and the details of the photo came up beside the picture.

DSC100154

Nikon Coolpix P900

Autoflash on. Used.

1/60th sec

F5.6

Lord Hickstead's Nikon not only matched the previous shots but the numbering showed that the first shot of the diamonds was numbered as picture 100154, the next number in sequence after the shots of Richard Wolsey Keen, which finished at 100153.

"As you can imagine, bringing in a Peer of the Realm for questioning is a rarity, in fact until the 'Cash for Questions' investigation, during the last Labour Parliament, no Lord had been summoned for many years," the Chief Superintendent told us. "This means that both the Commissioner, who knows Lord Hickstead personally, and the Home Secretary, who has worked with Lord Hickstead in parliamentary committees, really need to be convinced that we have a case. I can happily report that they both agree the time is right to bring our man in for questioning under caution.

Additionally, we are bringing back Mr Nour and Mr De Montagu for an identity parade, for which Inspector Boniface will also invite an old friend of ours.

If we can reconvene here at three o'clock this afternoon, we should be able to proceed. A car is on its way to pick up His Lordship now. MI5 have confirmed that he is still in the apartment, as they have the responsibility for protecting those premises and their occupants."

Dee leaned across and squeezed my hand; she looked as happy as I felt.

Chapter 50

West London Magistrates & County Court, Talgarth Road, London. Friday, 12 noon.

Michael Lambaurgh paced restlessly around the small room, wondering what was going on. He had been in this courthouse a dozen times at least, and he had never been locked in a room before. Maybe this was a bad sign. Perhaps community service wasn't an option this time. He was nervous; this could mean a custodial sentence.

"Bloody stupid berk! Why did I have to kick the kebab shop door in?" he chastised himself aloud. He had been to the Chelsea match in between drinking sessions that ran from eleven in the morning until two o'clock the following morning. He had been out of his head by the time he decided he wanted a kebab. Unfortunately, by the time he arrived at Kebab Heaven the shop had been closed for an hour, and Michael was starving. In his drunken state he saw the light on in the flat above, and he reasoned that if he banged hard enough on the door they would come down and sell him a kebab. So he banged on the door.

Unfortunately for Michael, however, he always seemed to be unlucky with the police, and at that moment a patrol car had been passing by. The policemen, who recognised him, got out of their car to try to persuade him to go home. They were tired of arresting him, but one thing led to another and, in a fury, he kicked the door of the kebab shop, shattering the bottom pane of glass.

Now, three months later, here he was in the modern brick built courthouse with the grey architectural cladding. It was nicer than most of the magistrates' courts he had been in, but it smelled the same. If there had been a window he could have looked out and watched the traffic going over the Hammersmith Flyover, but the room was windowless.

***

The door opened and a smartly dressed man entered. Michael was puzzled, but he said nothing.

"Hello Michael, I am Detective Inspector Boniface."

"Detective Inspector, bloody Norah!" Michael exclaimed. "I kicked in a kebab shop door, I didn't rob a bank. Am I in real trouble this time?"

"On the contrary. I think we could persuade the CPS to drop the case and we could issue you with a conditional caution, if you were to be helpful to me."

Michael liked the idea of a caution; no jail time, he could keep his nose clean for a few months and he would be clear. He wouldn't even have to spend his weekends picking up needles and condoms in the park.

"What do I have to do?" he asked.

Chapter 51

New Scotland Yard, London. Friday, 3pm.

I was well aware that I would have to be back at work full time from next week, and so this would be my last day of sleuthing on the blackmail case. I was sure that Dee would help the police see it through to its conclusion, but I could take no more time off. I now had a mortgage to pay once again, until I got my money back - if indeed I ever did.

As predicted, Lord Hickstead had been awkward when the police asked him to accompany them to the Yard. He had demanded to speak to the Commissioner, the Home Secretary and his lawyer. By the time His Lordship arrived at Scotland Yard, the Commissioner had already taken calls from the former Labour Home Secretary, as well as one of the candidates in the race for the Post Corbyn Labour Party leadership.

It was all to no avail, however, and His Lordship was now in the interview room waiting to take his place in an identification parade. The screen in our room would remain blank until the Peer had been cautioned and told that the session was being videoed and recorded. Apparently, if he objected to the videoing, they would have to resort to audio recording only and we would have to wait for a summary from Boniface or Coombes.

There had evidently been no objection, because within a few moments the screen flickered into life and a wide angled shot of the stark interview room appeared. I was in the Robert Peel Room with Dee, DS Scott and DS Fellowes. The atmosphere was heavy with anticipation.

***

"Now that we are recording, I would just like to say that my client is a victim here and he is being treated like a common criminal. Furthermore, we strongly object to his being here at all," the pompous lawyer bleated, with obvious disdain for the two policemen facing him, both of whom he seemed to regard in much the same way as he might have looked at something stuck to the sole of his shoe.

"Mr Parsons, we aim to treat all suspects the same, whether common or uncommon. Now, shall we begin?" Inspector Boniface was smiling genially. DCI Coombes was not. He took over the interview.

"Lord Hickstead, would you give us permission to open your safety deposit box and examine the contents, please? Our enquiries in this regard relate to the investigation of a serious crime, and we have reason to believe that an examination of your safety deposit box will assist us."

"No, I most certainly will not give permission. Next question." Lord Hickstead spoke tersely, without consulting or even looking at his lawyer.

DCI Coombes opened the folder in front of him and extracted a piece of paper.

"This is a warrant which gives us permission to search that safety deposit box, with or without your cooperation." Coombes smiled unpleasantly.

"This is outrageous," the lawyer puffed, obviously caught unawares.

Hickstead leaned over to the lawyer and whispered to him for a few seconds.

"My client has papers in that safety deposit box that relate to European Commission business, and as such those documents are to be kept private, even from the police, under the Treaty of Rome. The box has a form of diplomatic immunity, if you like."

"Nonsense," Boniface retorted, and the lawyer looked affronted. Boniface continued. "My Masters degree is in European law, and under the Treaty of Rome there is no such restriction. The warrant is valid."

"This warrant, Inspector Boniface, is issued by an inferior court, and if you wish to terminate the day's proceedings while I race over to the High Court and obtain an injunction, we will do that. I'm sure that your Master's degree covered injunctions." The lawyer looked smug again, but the policemen had anticipated the refusal to allow them access to the box.

"Mr Parsons, we will not execute the warrant until noon on Monday, which gives you an opportunity to apply for an injunction, but I assure you we will be represented at any injunction hearing."

Lord Hickstead smiled, but the smile disappeared when DCI Coombes spoke.

"We had the box sealed this morning; the depository will not allow it to be opened until Monday at noon, assuming that no injunction is obtained. Furthermore, we have placed a uniformed officer outside the depository to ensure that your client's important papers are secure."

The lawyer and his client held a whispered mini conference before the lawyer spoke again.

"My client is most unhappy about the situation and will certainly make a complaint about your precipitate action but, as the papers are safe, he will wait until he has the injunction before opening the box privately and without hindrance."

"That will be fine," Boniface said as he lifted the brown leather briefcase onto the table. "For the purposes of the record, this is the briefcase which was shown to Lord Hickstead this morning by DCI Coombes and DS Scott. As agreed this morning, it is the same briefcase that was stolen from Lord Hickstead yesterday. We know this because it contains fingerprints from both the mugger and His Lordship."

Turning the briefcase to face the lawyer and his client, he asked, "Can you confirm for the record that this is the briefcase that you had with you when you left the depository?" The Peer nodded.

"For the tape, please, Your Lordship."

"Yes," the Peer said out loud, a little rattled.

"Turning to the contents, you reported that the briefcase contained only some family papers, is that correct?"

"Yes, that is correct."

"That does not conform to what the mugger claims. He says that the contents were quite different. In fact, he is certain that the contents were as you saw them this morning."

Boniface waited, even though he had not asked a question. The lawyer filled the silence.

"Inspector Boniface, I have to express some surprise that you are prepared to take the word of a criminal over the word of a Peer of the Realm who has served this country with distinction."

"Mr Parsons, in common with all policemen and lawyers it is my duty to believe the person who is telling the truth, irrespective of their social standing, and the reason for these questions is to see who has been honest with us and who has not."

"I can assure you that I have been honest and helpful, Inspector," Hickstead said through gritted teeth.

"Good. Then let us proceed. When we recovered the briefcase we found that the mugger had left it behind as he fled the scene. He left it just a hundred metres away from the site of the attack, whilst being pursued by police. When we recovered the briefcase it was kept closed, until I opened it in this building with other officers present.

When we opened it the briefcase contained two sealed envelopes, which are here in evidence bags." Boniface placed them on the table. "Do you recognise these envelopes, Your Lordship?"

The peer whispered to his lawyer and then answered.

"I recognise these envelopes as the envelopes I saw for the first time this morning, when Mr Coombes and his partner opened them. I'd like to make it clear I had not seen them prior to this morning." Satisfied with his answer, he leaned back in his chair.

"Before we move on, perhaps I should summarise for the tape," Coombes interjected, flipping open his notebook. "You signed out of the depository at twelve minutes past eleven yesterday morning, and then at around thirteen minutes past eleven, you were mugged. A witness chased the mugger, losing sight of him for no more than ten seconds. The mugger was then seen leaping into his car at around fourteen minutes past eleven, and was apprehended just two minutes later, at sixteen minutes past, without the briefcase. There are, therefore, three possibilities; Number one; the mugger, in the space of a few seconds and whilst running away, discarded your family papers, which have never been found, and replaced them with a quarter of a million pounds' worth of diamonds and some Polaroid photographs, before leaving the case behind." Coombes looked up and was pleased to see the lawyer's jaw drop. Clearly he hadn't been fully briefed.

"Number two; after the mugger left the case behind, and before we recovered it, an unnamed person stole your family papers and replaced them with a quarter of a million pounds' worth of diamonds and the Polaroids. Number three; you were mistaken about the contents of the briefcase at the time it was taken from you."

Coombes looked across the table. The Peer was poker faced. The lawyer was fidgeting with a pen. His nerves were beginning to show, but he rallied.

"My client does not have to explain how those items came to be in his briefcase after he lost possession of it. He has stated already that these items were not his, and surely no-one would disown diamonds of such value. It makes no sense."

Coombes looked down at DS Scott's detailed notes of the morning interview as Inspector Boniface lifted the photos on to the table, still inside the transparent evidence bag.

"My word!" the lawyer blurted out. "These photographs are shocking!" Nonetheless, he examined them closely.

"Lord Hickstead, this morning you said that the envelope containing these photos did not belong to you and that it was not in your briefcase when it was stolen. You have confirmed that again in the last few minutes. Could you also confirm your statement from this morning, to the effect that you had never seen these photographs before?"

"Yes, I can indeed confirm that they don't belong to me and I hadn't seen them before they were shown to me this morning. I would have remembered seeing material of this nature, believe me."

His lawyer interjected.

"Come on, now. Lord Hickstead has already stated explicitly that he did not have these items in his briefcase and that they were not his. Can we move on, please? It is Friday afternoon, after all."

"Of course," Boniface said politely. "If I could close this subject with one final question, please."

The Peer and his lawyer seemed relieved, and Boniface continued.

"Perhaps you could explain, Lord Hickstead, how your fingerprints come to be on each and every Polaroid photograph in this set, when you claim that you haven't seen them before, you don't own them, and they were never in your briefcase."

***

Lord Hickstead was preparing for his identity parade. The interview had terminated after his lawyer had advised him not to answer the detective's last question. Parsons, the lawyer, was standing in the corridor, speaking confidentially to Inspector Boniface.

"You know, Joseph, you were meant to be a Barrister, not a bloody policeman. Wasting all that expensive education. It's a shame. Your father was deeply disappointed."

"Alan, you are the only person, apart from Dad, who calls me Joseph. I've been using my middle name since college."

Alan Parsons shook his head. "In any case, what are you doing working with the Met? You don't normally play well together."

Boniface smiled. "I'm not going to tell you anything, Alan. I'll always be grateful for your help with my Masters degree, but you have to believe me when I tell you that the man you are representing has a wicked streak in him."

"Everyone has a right to a defence, Joseph, whether good or bad, innocent or guilty," Parsons stated.

Chapter 52

New Scotland Yard, London. Friday, 5pm.

Lord Hickstead looked decidedly uncomfortable, standing as he was at number four in a line-up of six. He had been advised that he could stand in any position in the line-up that he chose, and he chose number four. Inspector Boniface, DCI Coombes and Alan Parsons watched the proceedings.

The first person into the identification room was Mr De Montagu. He was informed that the man who had posed as the rich banker may or may not be in the line-up, and that he must only identify the man if he was absolutely sure.

One by one all six men in the line stepped forward, and spoke the agreed words, "Boris Johnson is our current Prime Minister". Then they stepped back and joined the line again. All six men were roughly the same height. They were all clean shaven, and they had varying degrees of hair loss.

Mr De Montagu asked for number four to step forward again and repeat the line. His Lordship did just that before stepping back into line.

"I believe that the man who took the painting is standing at number four," De Montagu said, "but I can't be sure without the disguise. Could you get him to affect a West Country accent?"

"No, I'm sorry, that would be prejudicial, but thank you for your help," Boniface said, shaking the art dealer's hand.

Mr Nour was ushered in and given the same instructions. As he looked along the line at each of the six men, his eyes immediately went to number four. The man looked different in a Metropolitan Police blue polo shirt, but he was certain this was the rogue who had tricked him. The polo shirts had been Alan Parsons' suggestion, whereas the instruction that no-one in the line-up wore a watch was at the police's request.

Each man stepped forward one by one, and Mr Nour remained silent until he was asked whether he recognised any of the men. The Egyptian spoke boldly and confidently.

"I am sure that number four is the man who posed as Mr Josh Hammond in my shop, and is the man to whom I handed the diamonds."

Alan Parsons blanched, and looked decidedly uncomfortable. He had been told by the police that documentary evidence proved that the diamonds he had been shown earlier were the same diamonds that Mr Nour passed to the man posing as Josh Hammond.

Mr Nour was thanked and then dismissed, and in came a rougher looking man dressed in an ill-fitting suit. The collar on his shirt was probably an inch too small for his neck. Nonetheless, it was fastened with a tasteful red tie.

Michael Lambaurgh, Medical Representative and sometime soccer vandal, took his place in front of the one way glass.

Boniface was ready to guide him through the process, to prevent him from saying anything inappropriate or ruining the identification process, but he need not have worried. Michael had switched on his medical representative persona; even his accent had been moderated. He came across as the well-educated catholic schoolboy that he was.

"The man who bought my credit card in South Africa was number four, though he had a South African twang then, not the plummy accent he used today."

After making sure that everyone was happy with the way the line-up had been arranged and executed, the participants were excused.

***

Boniface and Coombes were on their way out of the room when Alan Parsons called them back. The expressions on their faces told the lawyer that they were intrigued to hear what he had to say.

"I am sure that the three of us are patriots, and that this country means a great deal to all of us. Surely you can see that if a Peer of the Realm, a respected European Commissioner and friend of government ministers, past and present, was to stand trial, there would be public outrage. This would knock the expenses scandal into a cocked hat. This country would be a laughing stock."

"We can't let the guilty go free just because it would cause a stink," Coombes snarled.

"I don't remember anyone conceding guilt, gentlemen, but, guilty or not guilty, the country would suffer. If I can persuade him, could we work out a deal with the powers that be?"

"I don't think the Crown Prosecution Service will go for a deal, Alan," Boniface said, shaking his head.

"Look, I'm sure that you two have conducted a sound investigation, but whether this case is ever prosecuted will be decided several levels above the CPS. And, I suspect, the decision will not be made on the evidence alone, no matter how distasteful that may be to you and me."

***

Twenty minutes later Coombes was boiling mad, and was pacing up and down the Commissioner's office. Boniface appeared almost as angry, but was sitting at his allotted seat in front of the Commissioner's enormous desk.

The Commissioner tried to cool the atmosphere down.

"I quite understand that you are both disappointed, but there is no value in formally charging him today. We have agreed that he will stay within the confines of Westminster until Monday. Then, when we open the safety deposit box, as we surely will, we may find evidence that ties him into one or more of the deaths. At present he knows that he can't escape the Hammond blackmail charges, but he might just squirm out of the other two charges unless we can tie him to the painting and the cash. Take the weekend off. He'll still be here on Monday."

Coombes muttered loud enough for the other two to hear. "I bloody well hope so, for all our sakes."

Chapter 53

No. 2 Parliament Street, London. Friday, 7pm.

At the start of the day, Lord Hickstead could never have imagined how rapidly it would deteriorate, nor how quickly everything would begin to unravel. He had been so careful. Why had he allowed them to take his fingerprints after the mugging? Complacency, arrogance, everything he despised in others. He was evidently no longer the driven individual who had fought his way up from a rented house in Yorkshire to a seat in the House of Lords.

There were too many sycophants around him, telling him he was wonderful, powerful, influential and almost invincible. When he had embarked on the blackmail plot, he had convinced himself that it was a fight for justice. He wanted to right the wrongs which had destroyed him financially and robbed him of the opportunity of national recognition and, possibly, high office. His dear wife, Brenda, had sunk into a deep depression after the house fire, and his unnecessary tirade about her cancelling the insurance too soon hadn't helped. Despite all of the help she received, and despite being back in Yorkshire with her family, only strong antidepressants prevented her from attempting to take her life again.

What had begun as a righteous crusade had become an exciting, dark alternative life that set the heart racing and the adrenaline pumping. He had, quite simply, got carried away, and had gone too far.

Sir Max was a buffoon, but everyone knew it. He didn't carry the respect of his peers, just that of his blind followers. Arthur had killed him because he wouldn't pay a small fraction of his fortune to save his own life, and because he had insulted Arthur Hickstead one time too many.

Andrew Cuthbertson had asked for it. He was weak, and he would have exposed Arthur and sent him to jail. As for Richard – well, the man was a pervert.

The odd thing was that the person he had expected most trouble from was the foul mouthed Don Fisher, and yet the singer had paid up quickly and just let it go. The Peer certainly hadn't been expecting Josh Hammond to begin a witch hunt for his blackmailer. For heaven's sake! He'd only lost a quarter of a million. He would probably make that back in bonuses within a couple of years.

The more he thought about it, the more he realised that Andrew Cuthbertson had been right; Josh Hammond was the real danger in this scenario. None of the others had called in the police or threatened Andrew Cuthbertson. His alter ego, Bob, hadn't been worried about police involvement because he had covered his tracks expertly. No, it was Hammond's fault that his life had begun to fall apart.

Lord Hickstead felt the anger rising inside him but concluded that submitting to rage now would be counterproductive. He walked over to the drinks cabinet and poured himself three fingers of single malt whisky.

Catching sight of himself in the mirror, he saluted himself with the raised glass and swore an oath.

"I will not follow Jeffrey Archer out of the House of Lords and into prison."

***

An hour later the Peer had formulated a plan that he couldn't execute, and so he recovered the 'pay as you go' phone he had been using for the purpose and pressed the only number on speed dial. The phone rang out at the other end in long continuous tones, unlike UK phones. Eventually it was picked up, and Hickstead spoke urgently.

"You know who this is. I need your help and I'm willing to pay for it."

Chapter 54

Ashburnham Mews, Greenwich, London. Friday, 11:30pm.

I lay in bed looking at Dee's back; she was wearing a short strappy nightdress, similar in style to the dresses that many young girls would probably have worn going out to a nightclub. Her neck and shoulders looked so smooth and inviting that I wanted to kiss them, but she was asleep and I didn't want to wake her after another long and busy day.

Despite the hectic day, we had spent the night eating, drinking, and what passes for dancing. We had just one more night left together before she moved back into her flat. We were both due to be back at our desks on Monday, and Dee had lots to catch up on at home during Sunday.

Tomorrow night I would buy some take-away, chill some beers and we would snuggle up on the sofa before going to bed, where I intended to make love to her until the early hours of the morning.

After that, who could say? Tentatively we had arranged to stay over at each other's flats every weekend, but I had a feeling that it would not be enough for either of us. Was it too early to ask her to move in? I had known her for just a week or so, but it seemed like so much longer. And what a week it had been.

I wasn't sure how easily sleep would come for me tonight, but I guessed that it would come a lot more easily for me than for Lord Hickstead.

Chapter 55

Commercial Road, Tottenham, North London. Friday, 11:30pm.

"You know, this is insane, Dave. We never do a job with this amount of planning. The reason we aren't inside is because we strategise. We're better than those hot-headed gangsters in East London, that's why they keep doing time and we get to go on holiday with our families."

Dave merely grunted in reply. He seldom knew what to say in these circumstances. Johnny had always been the more articulate of the two, and he made some really good points. Dave didn't really know how to respond to them. But Dave knew that he was Johnny's equal in many other ways. After all, Johnny didn't know how to blow things up.

The industrial unit seemed dark and forbidding at this time of night. Dave's kids would have referred to it as spooky. The overhead lighting was adequate, but that was about all. Deep shadows fell across the floor. At one time this place had been a service centre for the electrical generators which ran the London Underground, but these days it was a printing press.

Dave and Johnny didn't work on the printing presses; they provided more specialist services. The industrial unit was far too big for the printing machinery. The presses looked rather lost on the floor of the building, which was about the size of a soccer pitch and rose a good thirty feet to the apex of the roof. The grey cladded walls and roof were supported by yellow painted steel portal frames, and in one corner stood a two storey block which housed an office, kitchen and toilets on the ground floor, with an open tread metal staircase leading to two big offices and a bathroom above.

The sign above the doors read Tottenham Press (2005) Ltd, mainly because the owners had allowed the old Tottenham Press to go bust to screw their creditors, only to set up in business again the following week with new directors.

During the working week the press turned out brochures, magazines, business cards and letterheads at almost cost price, but at the weekend it was a different story. On a Saturday and Sunday the special presses were running, the ones which produced forged tickets for pop concerts, sporting events and Premier League Football matches. It was no surprise that the forgeries looked just like the real thing; they were printed using the same technology.

Their most successful coup to date had been producing fifty thousand National Lottery tickets for Spain, all carrying the price of ten Euros and a nifty hologram in a transparent panel. The Tottenham Press had done themselves proud. The serial numbers, the metal strips, the watermarks and the foil pictograms had all been masterfully reproduced. It was even rumoured that it had been one of the forgeries which had scooped the main prize, but that was probably just an anecdote.

Johnny assembled the kit he had gathered from various lock ups in the area and placed them into the boot of the impressive car with cloned number plates.

"Dave, are you done with the Jelly?"

"Johnny, how many times have I told you we are in the twenty first century now? We use RDX high explosive. Gelignite probably hasn't been used in London since the 1970s."

"All right, smart arse, when will the RDX be ready?" Johnny asked, placing undue emphasis on the initials.

"Two minutes. I'll put it in the car boot with the other gear. Anyway, why aren't you going on this job, Johnny?"

"Because they're bringing their own team. We're just providing logistics, see?"

"Apparently I'm going."

"Dave, you're the best man in London for a box job. And on this occasion I think you count as logistics."

Ten minutes later the two men were closing the shutter doors and taping the laminated printed notice on to the outside. It read: "Closed for Holidays – Reopens after the Bank Holiday."

Chapter 56

Citysafe Depository, Cheval Place, London. Saturday, 3pm.

The sleek silver Lexus moved slowly down Cheval Place, the driver clearly looking for an address. After a minute of uncertainty, the luxury car with darkened windows pulled up level with the uniformed policeman guarding the entrance of Citysafe Depository.

The policeman watched as a man in a smart chauffeur uniform stepped out of the car, which was carrying diplomatic number plates and colourful sticker representing one of the states which had sprung from the breakup of the Soviet Union. Constable Davenport was familiar with most of the diplomatic flags - you had to be if you were a policeman in London - but he couldn't place this one. He scoured his memory banks for the country whose flag had a sky blue background and a bright yellow sun in the middle. He felt sure it would be one of the 'stans' but he wasn't sure which one.

"Excuse me, officer; we are looking for Citysafe Depository." The chauffeur was now standing by his side waiting for directions. The young policeman smiled as he looked at his own reflection in the man's large mirrored sunglasses.

"You're already here," he answered politely.

The chauffeur opened the car door and bowed slightly as a middle aged man stepped out of the car. He had one blue eye and one brown eye, disfiguring scarring on both cheeks and very prominent Slavic cheekbones.

"This is His Excellency Mr Muravi Dumatov, Ambassador to the United Kingdom representing Kazakhstan, and he would like to make a deposit."

"Good afternoon, your Excellency," the constable said respectfully. "I'm afraid that, owing to some additional security measures this weekend, I will have to accompany you to the vault. You will of course enjoy the same privacy as usual, but I will be guarding a particular box."

"Thank you, officer. Does your presence suggest my valuables may be at risk?" His Excellency made a determined effort to speak perfect English, but there was still the trace of an accent lingering.

"I can assure you that your assets are safer than ever," the constable said in a voice that he felt offered reassurance.

His Excellency Mr Muravi Dumatov reached into the car for his briefcase. It was an old battered leather case with two handles at the top which held it closed.

"Alexander, pass the treaty papers, please. You may wait for me in the car; I will be perfectly safe with the police officer." The man in the back of the car handed a banker's box to the chauffeur.

Constable Davenport, pleased with himself for recognising the flag and for reassuring the Ambassador, led the way up the steps to the Depository. At the top he pressed the buzzer and looked at the camera. The door clicked open. Weekends at the Depository were generally quiet, but security was paramount as usual, and so whilst one burly guard manned the desk, two more presented an intimidating presence in the lobby.

The fourth man on duty was downstairs in front of the vault.

The chauffeur placed the banker's box on the desk beside the Ambassador's battered briefcase.

"This is His Excellency, the Ambassador for Kazakhstan," the policeman announced, hoping that no-one would notice that he had already forgotten the man's name.

"Welcome, Your Excellency," said the guard, with little deference. "May I scan your Citysafe security card, please?"

"Of course," the Ambassador agreed, reaching into his briefcase. He did not extract a card, however, but rather he flourished a Czech Scorpion Machine Pistol. At the same time the chauffeur dipped his hand into the banker's box and took out a matching model. The Ambassador covered the policeman and the guard behind the desk, whilst the chauffeur covered the remaining two.

"Hands on your heads. No alarms, silent or otherwise, or we kill you all. No interference from any one of you or we kill you all. Are these rules simple enough for you?" They all nodded in shocked silence. No-one in that room was paid enough to willingly give up his life.

"OK, now all of you kneel against the far wall, facing away from me." The men did as they were told and the chauffer set about hooding all four and then tying their hands with plastic cable ties. The hoods had drawstrings which were pulled tight so that the men could not remove them easily. Now that they were secured, the two men from the car joined the fray.

The man posing as the Ambassador opened his mouth wide and removed two prosthetic fillers from his cheeks and his Slavic cheekbones disappeared as his face regained its natural gaunt look. Carefully he picked at his sideburns and peeled off a transparent sheet imprinted with pock marking and scarring. When he had removed both sides, his face was smooth and clear. Finally he popped out the brown contact lens, placing all elements of his disguise into the empty banker's box.

The three intruders in the lobby pulled on ski masks. By now the one dressed as a chauffeur was standing at the iron grillage that separated him from the last security guard and the vault. The man hadn't noticed him approach, as he was busy listening to live commentary of Chelsea versus Manchester City on the radio, which was strictly against company regulations.

The intruder coughed, and the security guard looked up.

"Sorry, sir," he said, hurrying to the gate. "Can you scan your security card on the panel, please?"

The intruder reached into his jacket and retrieved his weapon, which he pointed through the bars at the guard's face. The guard seemed so terrified that the intruder thought he would faint.

"If you don't open the gate in five seconds, I shoot you and we blow it open anyway. You choose."

The gate was open almost before his last syllable had died away. He hooded and tied the guard, securing him to his chair. The radio was still on, and the crowd cheered as Chelsea scored.

"I hope that you are not a City supporter," the chauffeur laughed grimly.

***

Dave, the safecracker or box man, was inside the vault placing his prepared charges. Plastic explosives worked to a strict chemical formula which Dave only partially understood; nonetheless, he was brilliant at shaping charges to blow inward or outward for point detonations as well as for the much less complex flat detonations. Dave was, quite simply, a natural.

Gregory had broken into the control room and found the server and the hard drive that stored the video from the CCTV cameras. He could have dismantled the hard drive and taken it, but this was a quick in and out job, so he placed one of Dave's charges on the server and closed the door.

Upstairs the fake Ambassador was talking to his captives whilst destroying the CCTV cameras with a crowbar. He lifted the ID card from the man who had been sitting at the desk; he would need it later. He placed it next to the phone.

Downstairs, Dave and Gregor were pushing the giant safe door towards the closed position. Whilst it was heavy it was so beautifully counterbalanced that it moved easily with just a gentle push. Leaving a small gap to allow positive air pressure to escape from the vault, Dave pressed the remote control.

A series of detonations filled the area with dust and debris, but the overhead fans soon cleared the air.

Gregor could see that the server was in ruins as the door was hanging open on one hinge. He, the chauffeur and James set about clearing the six largest boxes in the vault. As part of their haul they picked up a holdall and a large titanium case from one of the boxes.

They had been in the vault for two minutes when the reception phone rang. The Ambassador blew a whistle before he picked up the phone. The guys downstairs knew that they now had two minutes to get out.

***

The fake Ambassador picked up the phone.

"Citysafe, how may I help you?"

"Is that Chris?"

"No. It's Pete Maxwell. Chris is in the men's room." The intruder had assumed the identity of one of the lobby guards, Chris being the reception guard.

"You need to get Chris out of the bog right now and get him to the phone."

"OK, I've sent someone to get him. What's the panic?"

"You've gone offline. All your security lines are down. You are unprotected."

"No we're not. I'm looking at the screens now. The gate is locked, all personnel are on camera, and the vault cameras are showing green lights on all boxes."

"It must be the server, then. Is the server flashing red?"

"Hold on, I'll ask." the Ambassador said, leaning back in his chair and looking at his watch. "Yes, it is flashing red. Does this mean it's a false alarm?"

"Not necessarily. I can reboot the security system from here, but security protocol means I need Chris to give his secret data and the eight figure password before I can do anything."

The three men from downstairs were each laden down with bags when they passed through the lobby, nodding at their colleague at the desk.

"Hello, Chris here," the Ambassador said, moderating his voice and pitching it slightly higher.

"Chris, before I can reboot I need to ask the security questions," the technician said, on the verge of panic.

"Fire away," the intruder said, as he laid the handset on the reception desk and walked out of the building.

"Right, Chris. I have your details on the screen in front of me. The first question is, please provide the second and fourth characters of your mother's maiden name."

The technician was still awaiting a reply as the Lexus drove away towards Brompton Road.

"Hello? Chris, are you there? Hello?"

Chapter 57

Citysafe Depository, Cheval Place, London. Saturday 4:30pm.

Inspector Boniface drew his family car up to the police tape and parked, showing his warrant card to a uniformed officer. He was dressed in chinos and a colourful golf shirt which carried the logo of the PGA on the left sleeve. The crime scene was bustling. There were four police cars, an ambulance and a police van inside the cordon.

Boniface had been with his children in the park when the call came, a simple pleasure that the kids enjoyed all the more after the previous year of restrictions on movement and the closure of the City parks. The Superintendent told him he wasn't needed at the crime scene and that he had been called merely as a courtesy. Nonetheless, he had wanted to see the scene for himself, and so he dropped his two kids off at home, with his long suffering wife, and drove into central London on one of his precious days off.

He looked around to see whether DCI Coombes had made it to the crime scene and he spotted DS Scott, wearing denims, trainers and a brightly coloured Harlequins retro rugby shirt. In truth he was hard to miss, with the heady mix of blue, red and green adorning his torso.

DS Scott spotted him and waved. The young sergeant finished instructing the uniformed officer he was talking to and turned to walk towards Inspector Boniface.

"Inspector, I'm afraid we haven't tracked down DCI Coombes yet."

"Sensible fellow probably has his phone off. Well, Sergeant, this is a bit of a mess."

"Yes, sir, it is. We didn't see this coming, did we?"

"I'm not sure that we saw any of it coming. It seems to be spiralling out of control. What have we got so far?"

DS Scott flipped open his notebook and proceeded to explain that four or more armed men had gained entry by posing as Kazakh diplomats. They had blown open six boxes, removed the contents, and left the policeman and the guards tied up. The Citysafe central controller initiated the Metropolitan Police RVH Protocol, and the first squad car was on site four minutes later, with the first armed response vehicle arriving seven minutes later. The Robbery with Violence potential Hostage Protocol was initiated by a code word given to a police operator on a dedicated line, hence the quick response.

One of the six boxes hit turned out to be Lord Hickstead's sealed box, and the police constable in the depository said that the accents of the robbers sounded less Eastern European and more Dutch.

"So," Boniface responded as Scott fell silent, "Hickstead called in a favour from Van Aart, would you say?"

"Looks like it, sir. We have an enquiry out to Europol, who say they are close to finalising their operation and they don't want to jeopardise that. However, they confirm that Van Aart is still in Amsterdam."

"Maybe he sent a team over; he probably runs hundreds of men," Boniface thought out loud.

"I expect so, sir. Europol said that they trailed an SUV belonging to Van Aart to the Channel Tunnel and made sure that customs checked the passports and the vehicle thoroughly. The vehicle was clean. They are sending over the photo page of each man's passport."

"You know, Scott, on the surface this may look like bad news, but when criminals start rushing things like this they invariably make mistakes. They don't plan properly and they give us a chance to snare them." Scott wasn't sure he fully understood the Inspector, and so Boniface explained.

"Hickstead and Van Aart don't know that we have linked them. Van Aart doesn't know he is about to be closed down. His men in the UK don't know that we have linked them to this robbery, and they don't know that we know what they look like. I think it is also safe to assume that if their vehicle really was clean, then they are getting help from someone in London, and I'm sure it isn't Lord Hickstead. I think we will find that one of our local villains provided the hardware. How else could they have got hold of it so quickly? We know their car was clean, and they haven't been in the UK twenty four hours yet. No, Scott, they think that they're being clever, but I think that we are cleverer. What do you say?"

"I'm sure of it, too, sir," Scott agreed, feeling much happier than he had fifteen minutes earlier.

Boniface picked up his mobile and dialled Josh Hammond. He wasn't looking forward to making this call.

Chapter 58

Ashburnham Mews, Greenwich, London. 7:30pm.

Today was to be our last full day and night together before Dee returned to her flat and we both returned to work, and so I had intended it to be a wonderful, memorable day. Given my aspirations for the day, we probably should not have considered attending the West Ham versus Liverpool match. Even the most ardent West Ham supporter must have foreseen defeat at the hands of the de-facto Premiership champions, and the match did indeed run to form. It was a miserable day for West Ham fans. We were one goal down in the first few minutes to the Merseyside based champions. I had hoped rather optimistically for a draw at least, but when the second Liverpool goal went in a few minutes later, I decided to sit back and enjoy the company and forget that if we lost this match we would have played four games without winning a single point.

We did lose by three goals to one in the end, and had to bear the ignominy of being the only team in any league not have any points on the board. Less than a month into the season and we were already well behind the clubs that we had considered no hopers before the season began. We needed three points from our next home game against Tottenham. In the meantime, we shared the delightful experience of walking back to Stratford in the midst of a thousand loudly chanting Scousers.

While we were at the match, I had received a message on my smart phone from Inspector Boniface. He wanted to talk to me as soon as possible, and so as soon as we got back to the quiet of the flat I called the number he had left. The first twice I called I was diverted to voice mail, but the third time I called I spoke to the Inspector. For my own peace of mind I soon wished that I hadn't.

I laid my iPhone on the table and switched it onto loudspeaker so that Dee could listen too as the inspector explained that the Citysafe Depository had been robbed and a number of boxes had been cleaned out, one of which was the sealed box of Lord Hickstead. Boniface tried to play down the importance of the robbery by insisting that it changed nothing and that Hickstead would still be tried and convicted. But we all knew that with the money and the painting the case would have been a slam dunk, whereas now Hickstead would be well placed if he was looking for a deal.

I sympathised with Boniface for being called out to deal with the robbery in the middle of a family event, and asked him to pass my regards to DCI Coombes, who had eventually turned up at the scene and who was growing on me.

***

Dee had promised me that she had something planned that would cheer me up, and she did. It perked me up in every sense. I had seen a gaudy purple bag with gold coloured 1960s style writing on it on the bedroom floor earlier that day, and I had been curious. The logo on the carrier bag read Retro City, an odd shop run by a sixty something couple who could had been flower children in the 1960s and still dressed as if they were. I had been in the shop a few times, as it was close to where I lived on the High Street, and I had thought it strange. Stepping inside felt rather like going back in time. There were clothes made in the iconic styles of the period, Herman's Hermits singles, LP's and CD's and hippy paraphernalia all around. If anyone ever asked me if I knew where to buy fragrant joss sticks, I would direct them to Retro City without a moment's hesitation.

I had visions of Dee emerging from the bedroom in a flowing Kaftan with a beaded headband holding her auburn locks in place. I was wrong. Dead wrong. Wonderfully wrong.

Dee shouted for me to close my eyes, I did as I had been instructed. I could hear her walking across the room, and I sensed her standing in front of me. She said I could open my eyes, I did.

For a moment I couldn't catch my breath. I had often used the expression 'I was left speechless', but only now did I understand what it actually meant. I began to talk but just croaked. I tried again but nothing came out. I concentrated and eventually managed to kick start my vocal chords, but only to stutter like an idiot.

"That's, I mean it's, the way it fits. Wow."

"So you like it, then?"

If I could have connected my brain and voice box I would have told her that there was not a man in the known universe that wouldn't have liked it. I stared at her again. With her hair swept back and turned up at the ends and her face lightly made up, she glowed. At her neck was a buckled collar which topped out the figure hugging shiny black leather catsuit which had a zipper running down the front. I am quite certain it was the sexiest thing I had ever seen in my life.

I was immediately transported back to the 1980s when my dad used to sit next to me on the sofa and we would watch reruns of the 1960s cult TV show, The Avengers. My dad was in love with Emma Peel - he probably still is - and now he owns a complete boxed set, which contains all one hundred and eight episodes starring Diana Rigg. Mum doesn't seem to enjoy them quite as much, for some reason.

I guessed that the catsuit I was looking at was styled after the Diana Rigg costume, as it had definite 60's styling, although it could just as easily have been based on the Catwoman suit Julie Newmar wore in the Batman TV series of the same era.

Dee spun around on her patent leather boots.

"It's actually quite comfortable, and flexible." She ran through a few martial arts moves, including high kicking, but stopped when she noticed I was sweating.

"Get you shoes on and go and order the takeaway," she instructed. "I'll have a Chicken Korma with plain white rice and nan bread."

"But the Indian Restaurant is almost a mile away," I complained, knowing that I would pass two Chinese takeaways, a kebab shop and the Pizza & Pasta Palace before reaching the Spice Island Restaurant. Although, I had to concede that the food from there was wonderful.

"What? Don't you think I'm worth it, then?" Dee pouted as she started to unzip her catsuit.

"OK," I conceded. "I'm on my way. I'll be back soon."

It was beginning to get dark outside, and so I cut through the back garden and climbed over the small fence into Mrs Cattermole's garden before walking silently beside her house onto her driveway and onto the main road. Mrs Cattermole was a feisty white haired old lady who had scolded me more than once for using this shortcut. I vividly remembered one occasion when I thought I had got away with it. I was just exiting through her gate and she called me back.

"Joshua Hammond!" she called out, and like a naughty schoolchild I went to her and took the rebuke with head bowed. I might have been a man of thirty, but she was seventy and she made me feel like a kid again. She doesn't hold grudges, though, because when my downstairs neighbour told her I was in bed with the flu, she came around with a casserole, and by the time she left my flat was as clean as it had ever been.

On this occasion I made it without being caught and, having saved myself three hundred yards, I set off in the direction of Spice Island.

***

The Lexus circled the area for a second time and all was quiet. It came to a stop outside the townhouse. The light was on, as they had hoped. It suggested that their journey hadn't been wasted. The three men in the car were tired; it had been a long couple of days. They had left Amsterdam yesterday evening and driven to the Channel Tunnel to avoid as much customs interest as possible. They had expected a thorough search of their SUV, and so they hadn't carried anything illegal with them. That meant, of course, that they had to rely on Mr Van Aart's good friend Mr Holloway, the owner of the printing press, receiver of stolen goods and seller of humans trafficked from Eastern Europe, the Middle East, the Far East and Africa. Van Aart and Holloway had what they called a framework agreement. In Western Europe Van Aart would provide anything Holloway needed, and in the UK Holloway was the provider. If the balance swayed too far in one direction, a financial settlement was agreed. It was all very business-like, and very grubby.

The counterfeit Kazakh Ambassador, better known to his friends as Rik, sat beside Gregor in the back seat. Piet, now without his chauffeur uniform, was again in the driving seat.

"How long to open the front door?" Rik asked Gregor.

"A few seconds, that's all. It's on a movable latch that can be operated from the flats."

The three men exited the car and walked to the front door. Gregor took what looked like a wallpaper stripper bent halfway down the blade. The big man placed his weight on the centre of the glazed door until it flexed, then he forced the thin blade between the door and the frame exactly where the Yale lock was located. The door sprang open. They entered and closed the door behind them, allowing the lock to engage.

***

Dee decided that in ten minutes she would go to the kitchen and find some plates and cutlery, ready for the take away meal Josh was bringing home. She would just wait until this episode of Friends had finished. Dee had surprised herself this last week. She had always considered herself to be a strong, independent woman who could live happily without a man in her life. In her teenage years the closest she came to the boys was when she was throwing them around, kicking them or punching them in martial arts classes. Her sacrifice had seemed to be worthwhile when Dee had qualified to compete in the Commonwealth Games, held in Manchester, but she had been injured in training and lost her place. So, rather depressingly, she spent the duration of the Games in the arena seating, watching her 'Team GB' teammates.

Somehow, Josh had caught her unawares. He wasn't so handsome that he turned heads. He wasn't terribly intellectual, either, and whilst he was in reasonable physical shape, he was nowhere near as fit as she was. Then again, he didn't have to work in the kinds of dangerous and tawdry places Dee encountered on a regular basis. Whilst the largest part of her time was spent in close protection work, looking after people who considered themselves to be celebrities and at risk from fans, there were more testing duties from time to time. Vastrick Security had initially specialised in extracting people from cults and deprogramming them. About half of the rescued men and women went on to lead normal lives again, but the other half would go back, find another cult or even be sectioned under the mental health act. Some of the extractions were violently opposed, with weapons being used to try to keep Dee and her colleagues away from their targets. She still found it surprising how many cults with names like 'The Universal Congregation for Peace and Love" employed thugs to keep their members in line until the programming finally weakened their resistance.

Josh got under her skin. She was beginning to believe that she loved him, and it was difficult trying to persuade herself that this was not a sign of weakness. She was suddenly aware that Friends had finished, and she stood up just as the front door exploded against the wall.

***

Dee looked around to see three masked men rush into the flat, the third man closing the damaged door. It was this third man who spoke, as he looked her up and down, his eyes wide with obvious surprise.

"Good evening, Miss Whiplash. We are sorry we damaged the door but we forgot our key." Dee recognised the accent immediately. Van Aart's men, she thought to herself. She would play along for the time being, to see what developed. She put on a panicky girlish voice.

"What do you want? Who are you? I don't have anything valuable."

"Where is Josh Hammond?" the leader asked, his tenor suggesting he expected a helpful answer.

"Josh is out at a stag party for his friend. He won't be back until two or three in the morning. He might not be back at all, if they drink too much," she lied.

The leader swore under his breath, and told his colleagues to search the flat, to be sure that Josh was not around.

"And who, exactly, are you?" the man enquired.

"I'm just a friend," she answered, genuinely not knowing whether she was anything more than that.

The heavy set man returned to the room, carrying her nightdress.

"They're sleeping together, boss," he said, brandishing the lingerie.

The leader took his mobile phone and pressed a speed dial button. There was a brief conversation in Dutch before he hung up. All three were now back in the lounge. The leader said something in Dutch and the two others moved towards Dee.

"What are you going to do to me?" Dee shrieked, as if terrified. The men smiled at the seemingly frightened girl, and dropped their guard, as she had hoped.

"You're coming with us, to make sure Mr Hammond does as he's told."

Piet came up behind her and grabbed her upper arms, while Gregor approached from the front. Dee waited, and then made her move. She threw her head back and felt the satisfaction of her head crunching against the gristle of Piet's nose. Piet let go with one hand and clutched his face with a howl of pain. Dee lifted her right leg, and with her high heeled boots she scraped her foot down his shin. He yelped, let go of her other arm and doubled over, as she had anticipated. Dee threw back her right elbow until it connected with Piet's chin, and he went down. The big guy was almost on her, and so she deterred him by placing a well-aimed kick into his groin. The pointed toes of the boots did their job and she heard the wind go out of him. As he bent forward, her right knee came up to meet his chin and his head snapped back. He was teetering on his feet, and so Dee took hold of the ski mask, and a good chunk of hair, and pulled him towards her. She used his weight against him, and threw him on top of his groaning friend.

Dee was about to take out the third man when she felt a burning sensation in the middle of her back. Her muscles spasmed uncontrollably. She knew that she had trained for this eventuality, and so she forced herself to breathe so she would stay conscious, but her attacker did not stop sending the pulsing electricity down the wires in the same way the man leading her training session had done, and eventually she passed out.

Rik sniggered as his men began to lift themselves from the floor. He placed the stun gun back in his pocket. He had never had to use that much voltage to put someone down before. He just hoped she wasn't dead.

Chapter 59

Lambeth Road, London. 7:30pm.

Lavender Fisher couldn't remember the last time her father had been so angry, even thought he was a man who had built his career and reputation on being angry. When she had arrived back in the UK, her dad's head of security was waiting in the Arrivals hall to take her back to the family home in Isleworth. Declan was pleasant enough for a bodyguard. He warned her that she was in for a roasting when she got home, and he was right.

If she had been younger she would have been grounded. The worst thing about all of this was that she genuinely couldn't remember the photos being taken, although her father was apoplectic with rage about them. She remembered the nice German boy, Conrad; she remembered going back to his flat and meeting his flatmate. She even remembered the drink and the drugs, but everything else after that was a blur. What she remembered vividly was waking up shortly before noon the next day in a scruffy flat, in a double bed where the bed linens had not been washed for weeks. The place smelled awful. She couldn't believe that she hadn't noticed the night before. There was no-one else in the flat and so she picked up her clothes - a pair of panties and a short black dress - and put them on before heading back to her five star hotel.

The things her father described as being on the photos sounded sordid and dirty even to Lavender. No self-respecting girl could indulge in a threesome with people she had only just met and retain a scintilla of pride. But she had, and there was photographic evidence. What was worse, the police had the photos which showed her with the remnants of cocaine between her nose and top lip. She had an appointment to go and see the police with her father next week.

At this particular moment Lavender was in the back of the Chrysler 300C and Declan was driving. They were on Lambeth Road, heading towards Elephant and Castle and the Ministry of Sound.

Lavender wouldn't have been able to attend the reception, or the party afterwards, had she not been repatriated so urgently by the TV Company. This was a bonus for her. The fashion brand that was launching their autumn range also produced luxury goods and so the 'Goody Bags' would be stuffed with branded watches, bracelets, neck scarves and belts. It was not unknown for the value of such a gift bag to be worth over two thousand pounds. These freebies allowed Lavender to be extra generous to her friends on their birthdays and at Christmas.

Lavender was wearing a relatively modest mini dress with matching bondage shoes, and not a lot else. She noticed blue lights flashing behind her and turned to see a black SUV with flashing blue lights behind the radiator grille.

Declan saw the blue lights and instinctively looked at his speedometer. He had crept over the speed limit by ten miles per hour. He waited until there was a place to pull in off the busy road and then parked up in a recessed parking area. The SUV pulled in behind.

A man in jeans a tee shirt and a leather jacket approached the driver's door. He held a warrant card against the glass; the name read 'Detective Constable Gary Presswell'.

Declan wound down the window. "So when did detectives start pulling people over for traffic offences?" he asked.

"Don't worry, I'm not going to write you a ticket. We've been following you since you left the house because the young lady in the back is the target of a kidnapping threat we received this afternoon. Could you just show me your driving licence, please?"

Declan went into his pocket to retrieve his wallet. As he looked up, something was sprayed into his face. A second later the rear passenger side door flew open, and another man reached in and took Lavender by the arm.

"Come with me or you die where you sit," he snarled.

As the SUV drove away at speed, Declan rubbed his eyes. He was still blinded and in real pain. He tried to get out of the car by touch only, and when he was standing upright he leaned on the car horn until someone came to his aid.

Chapter 60

High Road, Tottenham, North London. 8pm.

Lavender had stopped crying. Dave the safecracker was sitting next to her. He felt rather sorry for the girl and rather wished he hadn't been so aggressive when he'd taken her. "Come with me or die where you sit" had sounded dramatic when he practiced it in head, but he knew that he would never harm anyone. She, however, didn't.

Johnny was driving the SUV.

"Those flashing blue lights worked a treat, bro; you're a bit of a genius on the side, aren't you?"

Dave enjoyed the praise, especially coming from Johnny who was a full timer in the organisation, whereas Dave had a real job and was only called on from time to time. If Dave's employers at the engine assembly plant knew he was so adept with explosives, they might be nervous. Dave had promised himself he would never use explosives to hurt anyone. That would make him no better than a terrorist, and he'd seen enough of those in Afghanistan.

Lavender was wearing a blindfold, the kind commonly handed out by airlines to those who want to sleep during a flight. It wasn't entirely lightproof, but her kidnappers just wanted her disoriented.

"Look at that. The floodlights are all blazing away, and they didn't even play at home today," Johnny commented as they passed Spurs new football stadium.

"They only managed a draw. They'll have to do better than that on Wednesday night or José will have their guts for garters."

They decided to change the subject before Lavender could work out where they were. Johnny's mobile phone rang. He answered at once.

"Yes, we have the package, and no, there were no problems. Why? What happened?" Johnny listened to the reply and a smile crossed his face. "OK, we'll be there in two minutes." He hung up.

"Dave, this'll make you laugh. Three of them went off to Greenwich and only managed to find the girlfriend."

"Are they bringing her, then?"

"Yes, but the funny part is that she beat two of them up. One had a broken nose and the other thinks he has concussion. England one, Netherlands nil, I think."

They both laughed as Johnny turned in to Commercial Road and manoeuvred to turn right again into the Tottenham Press car park.

Chapter 61

Ashburnham Mews, Greenwich, London. 8.00pm.

I struggled with my key as the hot take away food burned my arm. As soon as I had the front door open I ran up the stairs. I had some unzipping to do.

At first I thought that Dee had left the door open for me, but then I noticed the big black boot print on the door, and the broken lock. It didn't cross my mind in that moment that I might be in danger if I went inside, and to be honest, even if it had I would still have gone to Dee's aid. But Dee wasn't there, and the furniture in front of the TV was out of place.

I remembered that I was holding the take away food and so I went into the kitchen and set it down. I was in a daze. What I was seeing could not be real. I wasn't thinking clearly and so I shook my head. It made no difference. I splashed cold water on my face and walked around the flat.

The lounge was not as I had left it. On TV the detectives could always tell that there had been a struggle; there would be broken lamps, pictures askew, furniture on its side. But here there was nothing of note. The footstool was out of place and the rug had a corner turned over, but nothing seemed wrong otherwise. Yet there was clearly something wrong. Dee wasn't here, and there seemed to be an atmosphere of menace hanging in the air. The door had obviously been forced open, I had seen that much. My heart started to race as the likelihood of what had taken place began to distil on my senses like dew. I let the thought hang there a moment, still not entirely ready to believe it, and then I pulled myself together and called a number from my speed dial.

"Tom Vastrick." The voice was strong, bold and comforting. Mine was shaking.

"Tom, I think Dee has been kidnapped from my flat. What should I do?"

For a split second there was silence at the other end as he, too, digested the information, but then his voice reached me, sounding calm and decisive. "Do nothing Josh, I'll be there in twenty minutes with help."

***

Tom Vastrick hadn't been exaggerating. Twenty minutes later two Metropolitan Police squad cars were parked outside, blue lights flashing, and a Scene of Crime van was parked beside them. Curtains twitched as the neighbours looked out at them, obviously wondering what was going on.

A policewoman was sitting in the kitchen with me, having made me some tea. I sat sipping the tea, the aroma from the cooling take away making me hungry, although I no longer had the appetite to eat it.

A policeman came into the kitchen carrying my iPhone. "You might want to take this call; it's the City of London Police."

I took the phone and held it to my ear. "Hello," I said weakly.

"Josh, this is Inspector Boniface. I've just heard about what happened. Don't you worry, we've got two police forces and Vastrick on this. We'll get her back, even if I have to pull Hickstead's toenails out myself."

"Thanks," I heard myself saying. "It's been one hell of a shock, but I want to do whatever I can to help find her."

The real shock was how deeply I felt the loss. I couldn't live with the thought that Dee might be hurt, or perhaps worse. The shock did bring with it a sudden realisation; I loved Dee Conrad and would give my life to get her back.

"Josh, you may get a call from Don Fisher," Boniface added.

"Why?" I was puzzled.

"Lavender has been taken too!"

***

Tom Vastrick arrived fifteen minutes later than he had promised in a car that cost almost as much as my flat. Since receiving my call, he had been busy talking on the phone with two police forces and his own investigative staff. One of their own was missing.

When he came into the room I offered my hand but he ignored it, choosing instead to crush me in a bear hug.

"Josh, Dee is family as far as we're concerned, and that makes you family, too. Every resource we have will be made available. I should tell you that Dee is also trained for this kind of eventuality, and she will most probably come up with plans of her own to remedy her situation, so try not to worry too much. She's a very capable girl, as I'm sure you're aware. Now, we need to get ready for the inevitable contact from the kidnappers. I have people with Don Fisher, too. As soon as these people make contact, we're going to use every means available to us to track them down, legal or illegal."

I didn't know it then, and Tom certainly would not have vocalised it, but Dee was like a daughter to him, he had plans for her to take the reins at Vastrick when he retired. This was business for Vastrick the company, but personal for Vastrick the man.

Chapter 62

Commercial Road, Tottenham, North London. Friday, 9pm.

The journey from Josh's flat had been uncomfortable, or at least the part of it she could remember. Dee had woken with a shocking headache to find herself tied up, hooded and lying in the footwell in the rear of the car. Not the best of circumstances to find herself in, she thought, but not irretrievable, either.

The leader of the kidnapping team was sitting on the seat with his feet on her back. He felt her move.

"So Miss Whiplash has woken up. You need to lie still until we get where we're going. It won't be long now. Then I suggest you don't give either of my friends here any excuse to punish you, because they've both requested that privilege. However, under the Geneva Convention we will treat you humanely," Rik laughed.

A few minutes later the car stopped and waited as a roller shutter door rattled open nearby. Dee knew that it was important to gather as many clues to her whereabouts as possible, and she concentrated on doing just that. The car moved forward and stopped. She heard the roller shutter door close behind them.

Dee was taken from the car by Rik, who handed her to Johnny and said, "Take her upstairs and put her with the other one. We need to get cleaned up before we move to stage two."

Johnny smiled because he knew that getting cleaned up was code for attending to the injuries inflicted on them by a mere girl.

Dee concentrated and identified a strong smell. She recognised it, but where from? She was being taken somewhere but the hood was hampering her efforts to climb up the narrow steel mesh staircase.

"I'm going to loosen the hood so you can see your feet, OK? Don't do anything silly," Johnny warned her as he created a gap at the bottom of the hood that enabled Dee to see her feet and the area immediately around them. At least she wouldn't fall over.

Taking advantage of the narrow strip of vision available to her, Dee looked to her left and saw that she was in some kind of factory or warehouse with a grey painted concrete floor. She pushed her luck and moved her head a little more, but this earned her a sharp poke in her ribs. By the time she reached the top of the stairs she had been able to work out that they were in an industrial unit, with dust proof floor coatings and some boxy looking machinery. It was at that point she remembered where she had come across that smell before.

***

Dee had her hands untied before being guided to a chair. A hand pressed down on her shoulder, so she sat. She could hear sniffling from close by. Her captor took each hand separately and applied handcuffs. Once she was secure he lifted the hood from her head. Squinting in the harsh fluorescent light, she glanced around quickly and saw that she was in a small windowless room with a distraught young woman.

"I'll leave you two to get acquainted," Johnny laughed as he left the room, closing the door behind him. They both heard the key turning in the lock.

"Lavender Fisher, I presume," Dee said as she took in her surroundings. She was sitting on the long side of a rectangular metal framed table with a wood effect laminated chipboard top, and Lavender was directly opposite. The table was screwed to the floor and the chains attached to their handcuffs passed through a hole in the middle of the desk, probably intended for computer cables, to be padlocked onto the legs. The chain allowed only a few inches of movement in any direction. Dee was already trying to come up with a way out of this.

Lavender's face was smeared with mascara, and she looked miserable and scared, which was hardly surprising. Dee wanted to take advantage of their time alone. Firstly she introduced herself to Lavender, trying to keep her voice calm and steady.

"Lavender, as you can see we're both in the same boat here. My name's Dee. I know your Dad and I intend to get you back to him safe and sound, but I'll need your help. Do you understand?"

"Yes. Yes, I understand. I'll help you if I can. Just tell me what to do."

Lavender had almost broken down at the mention of her father, but she had managed to hold herself together. She didn't feel quite so terrified now, knowing that she was not in this alone. Whoever Dee was, she seemed to know what to do. At least, Lavender hoped so.

"All right, Lavender, I believe that this building is a commercial printing press. I think we're in an industrial unit, possibly on an estate of similar units. There's a motorised roller shutter door at the front of the building, but there are bound to be emergency exits as well."

"How do you know all that?" Lavender asked. "They had you blindfolded."

"I'm a trained investigator. I was taught by the best, over in the USA. Also I recognised the smell of printing ink from when I picked up our company brochures a couple of weeks ago. What I don't know is where we are geographically, and you can help with that."

"I don't think I can. I was blindfolded like you all the time," Lavender wailed, afraid that she was being negative.

"Lavender, please just stay calm. Listen carefully to my questions and answer them as best you can, OK?"

The young woman nodded, and actually managed a brief smile.

"Where exactly were you kidnapped?"

"About a mile and a half from Elephant and Castle, on Lambeth Road."

Dee absorbed the information and asked another question. "From being kidnapped, how long did it take to get here?"

"About thirty five minutes," Lavender said with some certainty.

"Are you sure?"

"Yes. They didn't take my watch. I was taken just after half past seven, and I was in this room being chained up at ten past eight."

Dee smiled back at her encouragingly. "Excellent. Now, concentrate. Was the car moving quickly most of the time, or did it stop and start in traffic?"

"I guess we spent about five minutes at traffic lights and such, but most of the time the car was in fourth gear. It's amazing what you hear when your eyes are covered up and all you have is your ears."

"It certainly is," Dee agreed. "Lavender, I suspect that if we were in West London they would have grabbed you closer to home. So, assuming we are North, South or East of London, thirty minutes at an average speed of about thirty miles an hour means you could have travelled around fifteen miles at the most. That would put us in Croydon to the South, Blackheath in the East or in North London or Essex. Did you cross a bridge?"

Lavender concentrated. "I don't know. I couldn't see."

"Think back. If you crossed the Thames from Lambeth Road you would have crossed Blackfriars Bridge. Most of the bridges across the Thames have expansion joints. They allow the bridge structure to move a few millimetres without cracking the road surface. When cars cross these joints, there's always a small shudder and a sound like this." Dee banged her fists on the table a fraction of a second apart. "There would probably be four or more of these across the bridge. Do you remember anything like that?"

Lavender thought hard. "Maybe. I think I can remember that, but I don't know whether I'm making myself believe it because you just told me about it."

"That's all right. Don't worry. You're doing very well," Dee smiled. "Your dad will be proud of you. Take your time and try to remember. At the moment we can't rule out any options. Did they say anything during the journey? Anything at all?"

Lavender's brow creased in concentration. "Yes, they did, they were talking to each other, but nothing that's any use, really. It was just a few minutes before we arrived."

"Lavender, try to remember exactly what they said. It might be vital."

"I think they said something about it being odd for the floodlights to be on when they weren't even at home today. They also said José wouldn't be pleased with the draw today and they would have to do better on Wednesday night. Does that even make sense to you?"

Dee took a deep breath. "Yes, Lavender, it does. You've done very well to remember all of that. I think I do know where we are, more or less. But we mustn't let anyone know about this conversation, OK?" Lavender nodded, smiling properly for the first time.

***

Floodlights suggested a sports ground, presumably a large one. Not being at home today suggested football or rugby. A draw suggested football or cricket, but only football would be played again on Wednesday night.

Of course, Dee realised, it was probably Champions League. She remembered Josh talking about it to one of his friends at the match this afternoon. If only she could remember which team had drawn today and was also playing again on Wednesday.

Dee quite liked football, but didn't know a great deal about it. She would certainly not have considered herself a fan, but some football news was hard to miss. She knew that Arsenal, Spurs, West Ham and Chelsea were the London teams in the Champions League, so it had to be one of those four. She had seen Liverpool beat West Ham today, and Chelsea had played at home, so it couldn't be them. The ground Lavender had passed was not Chelsea's or West Ham's.

So that left the two North London clubs, Arsenal and Tottenham. She couldn't recall what their scores had been today, or whether either one had been at home, but she did know that Spurs' next home match was against West Ham. Tickets had been advertised for sale on the hoardings dozens of times during the match.

She had narrowed their position down to North London, which was something. The trouble was that the Emirates Stadium, the home of Arsenal, was close to the A1, and the new stadium, where Spurs played, was close to the A10, both quite fast roads and both easily accessible from the river.

Something else popped into her mind. She looked at her new friend.

"Lavender, did you mention someone called José?"

Lavender nodded. "Yes, they said Harry would have their guts for garters if they didn't play better."

"José could be a manager. I think Mikel something is the manager at Arsenal, good looking guy used to be at Manchester City, I took his wife around London shopping once. ButI don't know if Tottenham's manager is called" José, Dee mused out loud.

"Of course he is," Lavender almost shouted. "José Mourinho. He's the manager of Tottenham, he used to be at Chelsea. I saw him at London Fashion Week. He's really quite nice."

"Lavender, I could kiss you!" Dee said as she realised that they were within a few hundred yards of the Tottenham Hotspur Stadium, in Tottenham, North London. So, she knew approximately where they were, and what kind of building they were in. Now all she had to do was work out how they were going to get out of there.

Chapter 63

Commercial Road, Tottenham, North London. Saturday, 10pm.

Lavender had been talking for a while and Dee had explained why she was dressed in a jumpsuit. Lavender didn't need to explain why she was dressed the way she was.

The last hour had been something of a confessional, where Dee had listened to a little girl lost who thought she was an adult and so behaved like one. When Lavender listened to Dee and heard about her experiences, she suddenly realised that here was a substantive woman who was beautiful and tough and who felt no desire for celebrity or recognition.

Was her shrink right, she wondered for the first time? Was Lavender Fisher a lost soul seeking fame through notoriety, just as her mother and father had done? They had settled down eventually, and no doubt Lavender would, too, one day, but they had both enjoyed successful careers in the full glare of celebrity. Lavender had hosted a few TV shows because she was Don Fisher's daughter, but she hadn't actually achieved anything in her own right.

Lavender confided in Dee that when they eventually got out of this mess, she would go into rehab and come off alcohol and drugs.

Dee spoke to her like a kindly older sister. "Lavender, that's the wrong move. All you would be doing is making someone else responsible for getting you sober and clean. Even if it works, because you didn't do it yourself, you'll slip back. You need to do something constructive, something to give your life direction. Why don't you come and work with me for two months as an intern? Live at home. Get yourself sorted out and I'll show you what a real job looks like."

"You would do that for me?" Lavender asked, surprised.

"Yes, I would. Believe me when I say that I've helped girls in a much worse state than you. Girls who have been trafficked for sex and exploited by evil people in the name of profit or cult religion. It worked for them, and it can work for you, too, if you really want it to. Now, remember the plan. We have to stick with it, OK?"

***

From the first minute she had been taken, Dee had expected that this moment would come, and so she had prepared herself and coached Lavender.

Two of the masked men stood at the end of the table with a video camera. They were the two whom Dee had injured. They were clearly still suffering, judging by their fidgeting and complaining.

Piet gave the girls their orders. "This video will last a minute and not a second longer, so choose your words wisely. I will introduce you both and you will each tell your people that they must stop the police pursuing the blackmail case, first of all. The police must then come to an agreement with Lord Hickstead by Monday evening at six, or your families don't see you again."

Piet stood behind the camera and counted Gregor in.

"Three, two, one." Gregor pressed record; both girls were in shot, sitting either side of the table, still chained as before. Their captor introduced them to the camera.

"As you can see, we have Lavender Fisher and Diane Fraser. We guarantee that they will both be returned safely, just as long as you have the police reach an agreement with Lord Hickstead by Monday at six in the evening."

Piet fell silent and pointed to Lavender, who fell straight into her prepared speech, although her voice quavered with nerves.

"Dad, I'm so, so sorry. I caused all of this. I promise that if you make the police do as these men say, I'll give up the celebrity lifestyle and take that office job on the first floor."

Piet pointed at Dee, or Diane as he had called her. Her voice was much stronger.

"Josh, please don't go into print with your statement. Press the police to agree to the terms these guys want. If you don't, you'll find your next opposition right here."

Piet spoke from behind the camera again. "Remember, Monday, six o'clock, or you never see either of them again."

The camera was switched off, and Piet announced sardonically, "That's a wrap, folks."

Chapter 64

Vastrick Security, No. 1 Poultry, London. Saturday, Midnight.

We all sat around the conference table waiting for the inevitable call, well aware that it might not come until tomorrow. I was still having trouble grasping the reality of the situation. The police were busy examining both crime scenes and each force had a representative in the room with us.

Around the table were Tom Vastrick, Inspector Boniface, DCI Coombes and an agitated Don Fisher. At the head of the table with a mass of electronics was a young man called Levi, whose Jewish heritage was not in question once one had seen him in his yamulke.

Both my iPhone and Fisher's mobile phone were plugged in to a speaker and we had been given headsets that we could don as soon as a call came in. The idea was that any calls be traced, recorded, decoded and analysed by voice stress analysts sitting at Scotland Yard.

In the end it was a waste of time, as two text messages came in simultaneously from a Dutch mobile phone number. The message was simple.

"Follow the link www.flickr.com/48hrs/Videos."

Levi wasn't fazed by the unexpected turn of events, and within a few seconds the photo storage and networking site was on our screen. There was one video in the collection and Levi clicked on it. A play arrow was displayed.

"Before we run this, I want full transcript, enhanced video stills and full analysis of any key words or signals. I suggest we conference call in 30 minutes to swap war stories," Tom Vastrick said to the people in his office and to Scotland Yard via the open communication link.

Levi pressed play.

A man appeared on the video, which was exceptional quality, and spoke. His voice was slightly muffled because of the ski mask, and he was trying to conceal his accent by exaggerating a British twang. He had chosen his background well, as on first look there were no clues as to where he was.

"Mr Fisher, Mr Hammond and associated representatives of the Police Force. There follows a message and I urge you take it seriously. I would not say this in front of the hostages but they will die if our demands are not met. I cannot help but notice they are both attractive women, the kind that men dream of having on their arm and in their bed."

The video picture faded and a new scene faded in. On the screen we could see Lavender and Dee either side of a long table with chains on their wrists. A disembodied voice spoke, again muffled and this time affecting a Mid Atlantic accent.

"As you can see, we have Lavender Fisher and Diane Fraser. We guarantee that they will both be returned safely, just as long as you have the police reach an agreement with Lord Hickstead by Monday at six in the evening."

I was taken aback. Who was Diane Fraser? The others looked puzzled, too. We couldn't dwell on the anomaly at that moment, however, as a nervous Lavender began to speak to the camera.

"Dad, I'm so, so sorry. I caused all of this. I promise that if you make the police do as these men say, I'll give up the celebrity lifestyle and take that office job on the first floor."

"What job?" Don Fisher blurted.

But any conversation was curtailed as Dee spoke.

"Josh, please don't go into print with your statement. Press the police to agree to the terms these guys want. If you don't, you'll find your next opposition right here."

It was my turn to say "What?"

The second kidnapper spoke from behind the camera again.

"Remember, Monday, six o'clock, or you never see either of them again."

***

As soon as the video ended there was a flurry of activity, and analysts were poring over every work spoken for clues.

"Mr Fisher, Josh, let me start by saying that at Vastrick we train all of our operatives in surviving hostage situations. Just like the military, we use certain key words and phrases that signal useful pieces of information. After that, it's up to the ingenuity of the hostage, and Dee is ingenious, believe me. I know because I've watched her in action. Now, can I have your initial thoughts on what we just saw and heard?"

I spoke out first.

"The very first thing that puzzled me was the way the man called Dee, Diane Fraser. I can't explain that. Why give a false name?"

"I think I know," Levi said, staring at his screen where a picture of a young woman was prominent. "The Vastrick database has thrown up a reference to a former case where we recovered a cult member after her parents made a donation to 'The New World Order for Tranquillity'."

"I remember that case," Tom Vastrick interrupted, frowning. Obviously it hadn't ended well. "The cult leaders said if the parents paid half a million pounds in donations, they would excommunicate their daughter and expel her. The parents paid up, and our operatives were directed to an industrial unit where we found Diane Fraser fit and healthy and angry, having been chained up. Sad thing was, after a month she went straight back to the cult. It was probably a ploy. OK people, analysis please."

A voice came over the speakers.

"Tom, this is Luke. As there is no cult involvement here, could it be that Dee is sending us a message that she is being held in an industrial unit?"

Tom looked around the table, and Boniface and Coombes both nodded their agreement with the analysis. We moved on to Lavender's statement, and Don Fisher spoke up.

"I don't know what the girl is on about. I've never offered her an office job and our offices don't have a first floor, anyway."

"I think she's a clever girl," Coombes commented. "Surely she means that they are being held in a first floor office. So far we have them in an industrial unit, with two storey offices, and they're on the first floor."

Boniface leaned over and squeezed the DCI's shoulder. DCI Coombes beamed as the table accepted his analysis. The door opened and a full printed transcript was given to everyone. We were then told that the video stills were being printed. Boniface took the lead for a moment.

"Josh's statement was taken days ago, and he signed it in Dee's presence. It would seem to me that the first part, about going into print, must also be a coded message."

We all pondered what it could mean, and the analysts set algorithms away that would analyse all possible meanings of the words.

"Luke again," the speaker chirped. The computer is showing that the word 'print' can be associated with the word 'press' in the next sentence, as in 'printing press'. This could be code for Dee telling us that the industrial unit houses a printing press." DCI Coombes and Inspector Boniface whispered to one another before Coombes said in a loud voice, "DS Scott, are you still sitting with the voice analysts at Scotland Yard?"

"Yes, Guv. We can hear and see everything that's going on."

"Good. The Inspector and I would like you to run a check on all print companies inside the M25. Don't bother with print shops, just the ones operating out of industrial premises. Oh, and see if we've had any suspicions or reports on any of them."

"OK, Guv, I'm on it now."

We all looked at the next section of the transcript, and Tom continued.

"So, we know that Dee thinks that there are at least four men holding them, did everyone see that?" Everyone nodded but me and Don Fisher.

"Run that part again, Levi," he said, seeing our puzzlement. "Watch her hands."

Dee had been sitting with her hands in closed fists, and as soon as she said the words "these guys", she opened her right hand and tucking her thumb underneath tapped the table gently with four fingers.

I didn't know who was cleverer, Dee for coming up with it, or the detectives in the room who noticed that imperceptible movement. Along with a strong feeling of pride in Dee I also felt a quick stab of pain at the loss, no matter how temporary, of the woman I loved.

***

Things had been going well and everyone was exuding a confidence and bravado that lifted Don Fisher's spirits and my own, but then they faltered. The clumsy phrasing of Dee's last sentence obviously meant something, but neither the analysts nor the computer had a reasonable interpretation of what it meant.

They all turned to me. Inspector Boniface voiced the opinion of them all.

"Josh, we think this message is specifically meant for you. She deliberately says:

"If you don't, you'll find your next opposition right here."

I guessed that they were right, but other than the obvious meaning that the kidnappers would be my opponents if I didn't persuade the police, I couldn't see what else it could be.

"Luke again. The computer has these suggestions for 'your next opposition'. First a political opposition, which given the fact that he is a Labour Peer seems most likely. Second a sporting opposition, an individual or team attempting to overcome you."

How could I have been so dense? I put it down to tiredness and stress. A light went on in my brain, and suddenly I knew what it meant.

"Thanks, Luke. Sporting opposition is exactly what it means. Today at West Ham, Dee and I watched as they lost to Liverpool. West Ham have now gone four games without a point, so everyone was saying we must win our next home match, where the opposition is Tottenham Hotspur."

***

It was now nearly two in the morning, and computers were working overtime, looking for printing companies in the vicinity of Tottenham. There were six possibilities and so Levi typed in the first address provided by DS Scott from Scotland Yard.

Up on the video came a satellite view from Google. Levi dragged a little man figure onto the road in front of the printing press. Immediately a picture looking down the road appeared. Levi clicked on an arrow and the view was to our right.

There in the middle of the picture was a 1930's single storey brick building bearing the sign, Norman Betteridge, Printer and Binder. This was clearly not our building.

Levi carried out the same routine for all six addresses. We were left with two possibilities. Offset Litho (Tottenham) Ltd on Brantwood Road, and Tottenham Press (2005) Ltd, on Commercial Road.

Offset Litho was a two story flat roofed building with offices at the front and the factory space behind. Tottenham Press was a big shed with a pitched roof.

Something had been niggling at me for an hour and I couldn't bring it to the front of my mind. I flicked through the video stills again, in case I had missed something important. I was about to put to one side the first picture of the masked man facing the camera when I saw something that took me back a couple of years. In the background, just behind the man, I could make out a column of what seemed to me to be yellow steel. They were quite clearly inside a yellow steel framed building.

In 2018 I had been called to a fire where a mini industrial unit had burned down. The site was a tangle of cladding insulation and twisted yellow steel. The insurer paid for the rebuild, which I certified at each month end as the work proceeded. The original steel contractor had been employed to rebuild the frame. The company were called Conder

Structures, if I was remembering correctly, and their director told me that three of the major construction steel suppliers used their own patented colours; blue, green and yellow respectively. Most other contractors' steel was usually primed with red or grey. The interesting point as far as I was concerned was that Conder specialised in portal frames because they provided greater strength with less steel and gave a completely free floor area with no columns. A portal frame building would typically also have pitched roof.

I quickly explained to the weary team my theory and preference for Tottenham Press being the kidnappers' hideout. No-one disputed my analysis, but just to be sure the Metropolitan Police asked a local car to drive by both premises and look for signs of life. Tottenham Police Station obliged, and promised to call back in fifteen minutes.

DCI Coombes' mobile phone rang and he answered it. He grabbed a pen, making notes on a pad in front of him.

"Thanks for that, Sergeant. That might just be the information that tips the balance."

He set down his phone and spoke to Inspector Boniface, speaking loudly enough for us all to hear.

"Have you heard of the Holloway family?"

"Yes. We caught one of their teams unloading a dozen Chinese illegals at one of the big office blocks in the City, but the Chinese wouldn't talk to us and so they were deported and a couple of Holloway's boys went to prison for acting as gang masters to illegal immigrants. Neither of them would say a word about Pops or Sonny, though."

DCI Coombes turned to the rest of us.

"Alfred Clement Holloway is in his sixties now but he's been a villain all of his life. We've linked him with stolen goods, drug trafficking, human trafficking and prostitution but so far he's always managed to get away with short sentences, having pleaded guilty to the minor offences and knowing witnesses wouldn't come forward. For the last twenty years he has been known as Pops Holloway, as a sign of respect and because his son Adam Alfred Holloway, joined the family business."

This was all very interesting, but I couldn't see where this was taking us. Coombes was still talking.

"Pops Holloway was a Director of Tottenham Press when it went bust in 2005. He was disqualified as a director for ten years because Companies House thinks he deliberately siphoned off creditors' money before he went into administration. He still owns the lease, and his son is one of the directors.

DS Scott says that the Fraud Squad think that it was Holloways that printed all of the fake tickets for that Diva's concert at the O2 Arena last year. Almost half the tickets were fakes, but the gate staff couldn't tell them apart. We had fifty officers there breaking up fights between fans who had booked the same seats as others."

Vastrick was in conference with the two police officers, who were trying to decide if we had enough certainty to mount a raid on Tottenham Press. The phone rang and Vastrick put it on speaker.

"DCI Coombes, this is Sergeant Hall at Tottenham. We did a drive by, and Offset Litho is dark and quiet. Tottenham Press is showing a narrow strip of light under the roller shutter door, which is odd."

"Why is it odd, Sergeant?" Coombes asked.

"Well, there's a sign on the door saying it's closed for holidays and reopens after the Bank Holiday."

Chapter 65

Commercial Road, Tottenham, North London. Sunday 6am.

Dee and Lavender were lying under the table on a sleeping bag which had been opened up for use as a thin mattress. Both were still chained to the table, which meant it would be virtually impossible to make themselves comfortable. Nonetheless, Lavender had fallen asleep quickly and showed no signs of rousing soon. The night had been warm enough to sleep through, and Dee had managed a few hours of fitful sleep herself. Now, though, she felt cold and thirsty. She could look forward to another thirty six hours of this if things didn't go well.

Dee lay on her back, thinking. She trusted Tom Vastrick and she believed that Josh would move heaven and earth to save her. That was the type of person he was. Between the two of them, and Boniface and Coombes, Dee was sure her message would have been received and understood. At least, she hoped it had been received and understood.

Lavender stirred and turned to face Dee. Then, much to Dee's surprise, she smiled. The girl had been kidnapped and had spent the night on an uncomfortable floor, chained to a table, yet she was still smiling. Dee involuntarily smiled back. Without layers of make-up, the young woman facing her looked like the vulnerable young girl she was.

"Good morning, ladies. I trust you slept well." The voice made them jump. It was the leader, who had just entered the room. "If you promise not to do anything silly, I will allow you both fifteen minutes in the bathroom. If you don't promise, I'll have to keep the door open and watch you, won't I? So, do you promise?"

Both women promised. Quite what this man thought either of them could possibly get up to in a bathroom was anyone's guess. There was no external wall to the bathroom, and no window; it was a Portakabin, inside a factory unit.

***

When Dee returned to the room, having allowed Lavender to go first, she held her hands out dutifully to allow herself to be handcuffed. A two litre bottle of still water had been placed on the side table, and Rik moved it to within their reach.

"I hope you don't mind sharing. Breakfast will be along shortly. Oh, it will probably be more continental style than 'full English'." He laughed and left.

Lavender reached for the water at once, but Dee stopped her. She picked it up and turned the bottle upside down before squeezing it hard. She seemed satisfied with her efforts and turned to examining the plastic bottle closely, concentrating on the section above the water line.

"What are you doing?" Lavender asked, clearly puzzled.

"If they want to keep us subdued for the day they may try to drug us. The easiest way is to inject a sedative into our drinking water."

"Oh." Lavender was beginning to realise how dangerous this situation really was.

Dee broke the seal on the water and handed it to Lavender.

"I think this is safe, but just in case we'll have only a mouthful now, just to take the edge off our thirst, and if we're both still OK in an hour we'll be able to drink as much of it as we want. All right?"

Lavender took a mouthful thankfully. She passed the bottle to Dee and asked, "Do you think we'll get out of here today?"

Dee didn't want to crush her hopes. "Only if we escape, but that may not be as unlikely as it seems. I've got an idea."

Chapter 66

Vastrick Security, No. 1 Poultry, London. Sunday, 8am.

I had managed to snatch five hours' sleep on a bed set up in a small room at the back of the offices. Obviously the Vastrick staff stayed overnight regularly because there were two such rooms ready for use with fresh linens and a towel. Don Fisher had retired to the other room.

DCI Coombes and Inspector Boniface had gone home after a raging argument with their superiors. They had both wanted to go into the printing press 'hard and heavy', in the early hours of the morning, but they were ordered to hold off for twelve hours, until after the planned timing of an intervention from Europol. Tom, Don and I were livid.

We were told that Europol would be taking down Van Aart and his organisation in a coordinated series of raids spanning the Netherlands, Belgium and Northern France. Van Aart's home, offices, brothels and drug dens would all be hit by a variety of well-armed national police and security forces.

The Koninklijke Marechaussee, the Dutch Military Police, would also hit two industrial units where East European girls were held until they could be transported to a place where they could earn money by selling their bodies. Europol were tracking a container lorry from Bucharest, which they believed was heading for one of the units in Pernis on the outskirts of Rotterdam. It would arrive within the next hour and disgorge its cargo of teenage girls.

At twelve noon, European time, or one o'clock in the UK, the raids would begin. Unbeknown to either DCI Coombes or Inspector Boniface, the Metropolitan Police had been secretly planning to coordinate raids on the Holloways' premises at the same time. The secret plans had been codenamed Operation Tango, and we couldn't act until the raids were over. The Assistant Commissioner had explained that almost four hundred officers would be involved in the raids in four countries, and that they couldn't take the chance of Holloway or Van Aart's men reporting back to Amsterdam that the police were onto them.

Despite the Assistant Commissioner's pleas, Don Fisher still had to be threatened with a night in the cells before he accepted the decision. I had serious qualms about the idea, too, but we reached a compromise that I was able to live with.

The police now had three men watching the Tottenham Press building; they had taken up their positions at four o'clock in the morning, and were in constant radio contact. One was in a highly specialised vehicle parked in the car park of the factory across the street, and the remaining two were concealed where they could see the two personnel doors that also served as fire exits. Nobody would go in or out of the printing press without being observed.

In less than an hour we would be meeting with DS Scott, DCI Coombes, DS Fellowes, Inspector Boniface, Tom Vastrick and a new face, Geordie Lowden, who would lead Vastrick's assault team.

Geordie, as his name suggested, was travelling down to London from Tyneside on a chartered helicopter, which should have landed by now at London Heliport in Battersea. Given that the roads would be quiet, as they usually are early on a Sunday morning, I reckoned that the car journey from the heliport would take twenty minutes or so. Geordie, it appeared, was Dee's right-hand man at Vastrick. I managed to pull myself away from my bed and head towards the shower.

Chapter 67

Commercial Road, Tottenham, North London. Sunday 11am.

Piet entered the room where Dee and Lavender were secured and removed the coffee cups.

"I'll be back in an hour with your famous British roast beef dinner, or another packet of sandwiches." He sniggered and left, closing the door behind him.

So far they had been provided with water, coffee from a vending machine and sandwiches. In each case the food had been delivered on the hour. Dee was working on the theory that they had an hour until the next visit.

"Lavender, our hands have only about nine inches of movement, and so I need your help. I'm going to lean forward, and I want you to unfasten my necklace."

Dee leaned over the table so that her nose was almost touching the table top. Lavender reached over and unclipped the necklace. The necklace was sterling silver and consisted of a thin chain and a loop which attached just below the throat, from which hung three sterling silver rods. The outer two rods were the same length, which was around an inch, but the middle rod was slightly longer, perhaps by half an inch. Their diameter was about three sixteenths of an inch.

Lavender watched as Dee pulled the rods in opposite directions, opening the silver loop which held them. The three rods came free.

"Lavender, please listen very carefully, we don't have a lot of time. Handcuffs are not that difficult to unlock. The fact is that the main reason you can't unlock them is that they are often fastened behind your back. These police style speed cuffs are rigid, which means that your hands are held three inches apart and so you can't reach the lock with either hand. Do you see?" Lavender nodded.

"Our friends downstairs have overlooked the fact that I can reach your handcuff locks, and you will then be able to reach mine, as your hands will be free. Now, hold out your hands and watch me work."

Dee took Lavender's right hand and turned it so that the lock was facing upwards. Taking one of the shorter rods from her necklace, she pushed it into the keyhole until it met resistance.

"Handcuff keys have to be simple and universal, because while one policeman might lock you into them, an entirely different one will probably have to release you. So they usually only have two tumblers. The key will have a space, a ridge, another space, another ridge. Like a tiny house key. The way a key works is that the ridges line up with the levers, and the spaces line up with fixed stays, so that when you turn the key the ridges open the tumblers whilst the spaces pass over the blocking stays. If you put in the wrong key the ridges will hit the fixed stays and the key won't turn. Now, we don't have a key but we have these three rods, and we should only need two of them."

Lavender held her breath, watching carefully as Dee pushed the longer rod into the lock.

"I'm going to use the first rod to slide over the first lever like this." Dee wiggled the rod until she could move the lever. "Now, this exposes the second lever and we do the same again. If we now push both levers at the same time, they should get to the point of equilibrium."

"What does that mean?" Lavender asked.

"When you use a key to a deadlock, like the one over there on the door, you place the key in the guide, which we call a keyhole. As you turn the key you feel resistance don't you?"

"Yes, I'm with you so far."

"Well, that resistance is the key ridges hitting the levers. They are called levers for a reason. When the levers get to the mid-point, the point of equilibrium, gravity takes over and the only reason you keep turning the key is to remove it from the keyhole. Take notice next time you unlock a deadlock. When you get halfway through the rotation, the lock clicks open."

Dee used the two rods to push the levers, and seconds later there was a click and Lavender's right hand was free. Lavender unwound the chain from around the handcuffs and she was free to move around, albeit her left hand was still handcuffed.

It took Dee twenty minutes of patient coaching to teach Lavender how to prise the right-hand side of her handcuffs open, but when she did she almost whooped with joy. She was so proud of herself that Dee couldn't suppress a laugh.

Three minutes later both sets of handcuffs were off. Dee decided there wasn't time for any more on the job lock pick training, and so released the left hands herself.

***

It was a quarter to twelve and Dee was standing at the open door on the upper level, looking out over the factory floor. There was no-one to be seen. Carefully she stepped onto the steel mesh landing at the top of the stairs.

So far, so good, she thought to herself. Since breakfast and the toilet visits, their captors had not bothered locking the door to their room, assuming the chains and cuffs would be more than enough to hold them.

Dee wanted to protect Lavender, and so she gave her explicit instructions that would ensure her safety. Now she had to act before their captors made the rounds again.

There were two cars in the unit; a Black SUV with EU plates, and a Lexus with UK plates. At the bottom of the steel staircase she could see an open half glazed door leading to a small office, and voices were coming from inside. She counted four separate voices. That was good. They were all together.

Rather than use the metal stairs, which would certainly make a noise, she removed her boots and climbed between the landing and the handrail. She hung on to the steel railings, lowering herself down until she was dangling six feet above the ground. A second later she dropped silently to the floor, landing like a cat on all fours.

The fire exits were at the far end of the factory unit, and so Dee circumnavigated the floor, keeping the bulky printing presses between her and the open office door. A few moments later she reached the fire door and her heart sank.

"This door is alarmed," the notice read, as did the notice over the fire door opposite. They could not go through either of those doors without alerting their captors.

It didn't really make any difference, Dee reasoned to herself. The difficulties would be the same. As soon as she exited the building the men would be alerted, and she would have to run over unknown terrain barefoot. She had no way of knowing how far she would have to run before finding somewhere to raise the alarm, but she had come too far to back out of this now.

***

The alarm on the fire door was really more of a buzzer, but it was enough to alert the four men in the office. They ran out on to the factory floor, looking around to try to discover what had set the alarm off.

"You two make sure our guests are secure, and we'll find out what's going on."

Rik and Gregor had their guns at the ready as they ran out of the open fire door.

***

Dee had micro seconds to take stock of her location and try to work out which direction she needed to take. The building was an anonymous looking industrial box, with a car park on two sides and a concrete paved path leading to the front entrance. A fence, perhaps seven or eight feet tall, enclosed the site. The fence posts were concrete, with a galvanised steel chain link mesh strung between them. The top section angled inwards and was threaded with barbed wire, so there was no chance of climbing it.

She ran along the paved pathway towards the front of the building, a distance of some seventy five yards. As she got to the front of the building she heard the sound of the fire door crashing open, and she looked back to see two men in pursuit.

She raced across the car park and through the open gateway onto the deserted road, where she almost knocked over a man with a carrier bag who was walking by. Dee wasted no time.

"Please, sir, will you help me? There are armed men chasing me. We both need to run. Find somewhere safe."

The man looked rather alarmed, but instead of running for his life he did something she wasn't expecting. He punched her in the face.

"Shit, there were five of them," she thought to herself as she tried to get up. Her plan was in tatters, but she had to try to keep Lavender safe somehow.

"Lavender, run!" she yelled at the top of her voice, until the taser disabled her for the second time in a few hours.

Chapter 68

398 High Rd, Tottenham, North London. Sunday 11:30am.

Number 398 High Road in Tottenham is a huge Georgian red brick building with stone features around the Georgian paned windows and a carved stone portico around the door, into which is carved the word POLICE.

The ornate police station stands on a busy dual carriage way and so we had to wait for a change in the traffic lights before we could turn into the car park. The reason we were being hosted at this location was its proximity to the Tottenham Press, which was less than a mile away.

In the past week I had been in four different police stations and I didn't really like it. I wanted my own life back. I needed to get back to dealing with clients who didn't seek to destroy the lives of others because they couldn't accept that they had made a mistake themselves.

Don Fisher and I were led into a bare and unfriendly waiting room whilst the four policemen went to the operations room. Tom Vastrick and three of his people were on their way.

The plan was simple, although not everyone had agreed on strategy. The four policemen who had been living and breathing this case for days wanted to storm the building from every angle with overwhelming force, a strategy the Americans refer to as "Shock and Awe". The commanders who were charged with designating personnel to the task felt that the Risk Assessment demanded a softer approach, a standoff where a negotiator would talk the men out of the building, leaving their hostages safely behind. In the end the final decision was to be left to the men on the ground.

Unless things changed, the plan was simple enough. Don Fisher and I would be sitting in an unmarked van parked a hundred yards away from the Tottenham Press car park, ready to comfort the hostages on their release.

The telephone landline would be disconnected at the exchange, and the white van already parked over the road would switch on its electronic jammer. Then, for the next few minutes, every mobile phone in that cell, about half a mile square, would be silenced with the notorious message "No Network Coverage" being displayed on their screens.

Armed police with protective vests would then form an outer ring around the building, and two armed police with full body armour and helmets would enter via each fire door. Another six similarly clad officers would go in through the roller shutter door.

The roller shutter door had presented a problem to the police during the planning stage, as they knew it was designed to be raised by inserting a key into a weather protected housing and holding the key whilst the shutter crept up an inch at a time. The police didn't have the key, and nor did they have the time to wait for the door to open so slowly.

Vastrick, who provided security to many such buildings, referred the police to an electrical contractor whom they knew, who could bypass the key, but he would need at least five minutes to do so. The electrician was being briefed by the police upstairs. The roller shutter door was also secured at the bottom with a padlock that fixed the door to the concrete base, but that could be removed in seconds with bolt cutters.

Don Fisher wasn't a man who could sit still for long and he was anxious to get on with the raid, even though nothing could be done until we heard from the Assistant Commissioner that Operation Tango was well under way. That would probably be closer to two o'clock than one o'clock.

"You know, Josh, yesterday I wanted to hang that Hickstead creep from the nearest lamppost. Now I don't give a damn what happens to him. I just want my daughter back safe. Her mother will blame me if anything happens to her and I'll probably not disagree."

"Don't worry, Don," I said, feeling none of the confidence I was expressing. "We'll get the girls back safely. Dee will care for Lavender like a mother hen. I certainly wouldn't want to be the man that tried to hurt Lavender while Dee was around. The woman fights like a demon. She's also a trained protection officer. She knows what to do in this kind of situation."

The door burst open. DS Scott came in with a hand held radio.

"You need to hear this! Okay, Charlie two, say again."

The radio produced a second of static and then a strong male voice came through.

"A female in a leather catsuit came flying out of the fire exit a minute or two ago, and ran barefoot to the road. She stopped a male on the street and he decked her. Two other males ran off searching the area, while the suspect on the street and one of the kidnappers dragged the female back inside."

"Who were they looking for?" Don Fisher yelled, ignoring radio protocol. The man didn't hear the question and so Scott repeated it.

"That's the odd thing. We've been watching the place for hours and the female we saw was the first and only person to leave the building. But if the male with the carrier bag full of supplies is one of them, there are now six hostiles counted. Two searching, two dragging the female and two who came to the door to see what was going on."

"Your woman is definitely a fighter, I'll give her that. And in these circumstances that has to be an advantage," Don Fisher said, sounding a little less afraid now.

I hoped that he was right, but I was worried. Dee was obviously trying her best to find a way out of her current predicament, but her plan had failed. The captors now had two hours, during which they might well make her pay for the escape attempt.

Chapter 69

Commercial Road, Tottenham, North London. Sunday Noon.

"Johnny, what the hell is going on here? I thought you had these women chained up?"

"Sorry, Sonny, but the 'cloggies' have been looking after the women. They wouldn't let us near them once they were upstairs."

Sonny Holloway and Johnny closed the fire door and joined the others, who were all gathered around the chair to which a hooded Dee was tied. Sonny took Rik to one side and kept his voice low.

"I come around to bring you some food and what do I find? A hostage running to me for help, that's what. I could have been anybody. How did they even get out of the room, let alone the building? Those chains are supposed to be solid."

"I don't understand it. They got the handcuffs open, but I'm the only one with a key. But even if they got out of the room, they still had to get down the stairs and past the door, and we didn't see or hear them."

Rik knew that he was to blame. It showed on his face. The older woman had beaten up two of his best men as if they were rank amateurs, and she had also escaped from a seemingly secure environment. Rik's career prospects were looking slim.

"OK, we are where we are. Where's the other girl?"

"We don't know," Rik admitted.

"Go and bloody well find out, then!" Sonny growled through gritted teeth.

Rik turned to Dee and addressed her in a moderated tone. "Diane, we need to know where Lavender has gone. Please tell us, because we don't want to cause you any more pain."

"I don't know," Dee replied. "I told her to run as fast as she could to get help. I wasn't going to get far in bare feet, was I?"

"I'm going to give you one more chance. Where is she? We've searched the factory, and she's not here, and we've searched the area outside and she's not there either. Last chance." Rik waited.

"Look," said Dee, "I realise that you aren't English, and so I'll speak slowly. I.... don't ....know!"

Gregor had heard more than enough from this woman, who clearly derived pleasure from humiliating them. He stepped forward and shot her.

***

Blood spattered everywhere and Sonny tried to jump out of the way, but he was too late. The woman's blood was on his coat.

"What the hell do you think you're doing, you lunatic?" Sonny screamed. "This is my place. If the police forensic people get around to looking in here I'll go down for years. Put the guns away."

"We haven't got our answer yet," Rick said, nodding to Gregor.

Dee had been shot in the thigh. She had no way of knowing whether her femoral artery had been damaged, but she knew that if it had she would have only minutes to live. What she did know was that she had never felt pain like it. She was in shock; she was fighting unconsciousness. She couldn't give Lavender up. She had to convince them.

Gregor leaned over and pushed the hot barrel of his gun into the wound. Dee screamed and felt herself sliding away. Just before she drifted into the blackness, she heard Lavender's anguished voice.

"Stop it! Please, no more! Leave her alone!" She started sobbing, but Dee heard nothing more.

"Go and get her down, Johnny. You too, Dave," Sonny ordered. "And you three can stop this one bleeding all over my floor."

***

When they had escaped from the chains, Dee had checked the factory floor below and, finding that they were not being observed, she helped Lavender climb onto the flat roof of the two storey office building. Dee handed up the remaining water and said, "No matter what happens, lie flat and still in the middle of the roof and don't make any noise at all. Someone will come and get you."

"Can't I come with you?" Lavender had pleaded, afraid to be left on her own.

"No, darling," Dee replied, her voice soft and calming. "We won't make it far and they have guns. We have to make it look as if you got away. OK?"

Lavender remembered that conversation, and the promise she'd made, but she couldn't let Dee die just so that she could stay hidden. Dee was the closest thing she'd had to a real friend since school.

Dee now lay on the table on the sleeping bag. She seemed to be drifting in and out of consciousness. Sonny had ordered Johnny and Dave to look after the hostages. He didn't want to leave them with the Dutch thugs. Johnny had cut off the leg of the cat suit to expose the wound. It wasn't the neat round hole that might have been expected. The wound was ragged. It was black on the edges, and he could see the white fat layer under the skin. It was surprisingly white. He stepped back when he suddenly realised he could see the muscles beneath.

Dave took over. He lifted the leg and placed his hand underneath; he could feel the bullet under the skin.

"It's not a through and through, mate," he said to Johnny. "I'm not an expert, but I reckon if it doesn't come out, by tomorrow night she'll be in real trouble."

"What a mess. Can we get it out, do you think?"

"No choice, Johnny. Go and get my toolbox, it's in the next room."

Lavender listed to the conversation with increasing horror.

"You can't cut her open! You're not a doctor. You don't know what you're doing!" she sobbed.

"Look, Miss, that isn't strictly true," Dave answered. "I was in the army, in Afghanistan, and we often had to do emergency medical on our mates or they would never have made it to the field hospital. I promise I'll do my best, if you help."

Lavender shook her head, shrinking back. "I can't watch you cut her, I just can't."

"I know, it's tough. I'm going to roll her into the recovery position which will protect her if she vomits. It'll also give me access to the bullet. I want you to roll up some of that leather until it's about an inch thick and put it between her teeth on top of her tongue. That'll stop her biting her tongue while I'm working."

Johnny opened Dave's bomb making tool kit and wasn't surprised to see the neatest and most organised tool box in London.

Dave took a Stanley knife, or box cutter, out of the box and took a brand new blade out of its waxed paper. He then picked up a small bottle containing clear liquid.

"This is pure alcohol. I use it to clear residue from the ends of wires before I terminate them. It gives a better connection."

Dave cleaned the new blade with the alcohol and slipped it into the knife. He swabbed the area around the bullet, which was clearly visible below the surface.

"Right, you both need to hold her down. The squaddies in Afghanistan were doped up with Morphine and they still kicked."

Lavender took Dee's head and shoulders, and Johnny took her legs. When he was happy she was restrained, Dave made the one inch cut. The new blade parted the skin with alarming ease. Dee moaned but didn't struggle.

Dave laid down the knife and picked a pair of alloy pliers with a pointed nose. He had to use non-magnetic pliers when making or disarming bombs, as lots of wires and bomb components would become magnetised during assembly and the last thing you wanted to do was to attract the wrong wire to your pliers.

After dousing the pliers with alcohol and cleaning them thoroughly, he told his helpers to brace themselves. Dave put the closed pliers into the middle of the cut and opened the jaws. The bloody bullet stared out at him. Dee started yelling and trying to move her leg but Johnny held on tight. Realising he didn't have much time, Dave prayed that his first effort would succeed and fixed the jaws of the pliers around the bullet, then retracted them slowly.

He dropped the bullet on the table and examined it closely. It appeared to be complete. The bleeding was minimal and so, wrapping the jaws of the pliers in a hygienic wipe, he cleaned the wound inside and out. Dee was back to moaning.

Dave would have stitched both wounds if he'd had some means of doing so, but he didn't have anything close to a needle and thread. Improvising, he securely taped a cotton bud to each side of the wound and had Johnny pinch the sides of the wound together. This caused Dee yet more agony, whilst he taped two more cotton buds across the first two. Satisfied that the framework of plastic cotton bud shafts was holding the wound closed, he reinforced the structure with more medical tape before applying sterile dressings front and back. The task was completed by wrapping a bandage around the leg and tying it off.

Dee was in shock, but there was little they could do about that.

"Will she die?" Lavender asked, her voice trembling.

"No, but she'll be in bad shape for a few hours. You'll have to nurse her through it. And make her sip some water. Don't let her gulp it down, though." Dave closed the door.

"Johnny, what have we got ourselves into here? We took that girl. We're responsible her safety."

"I know, Dave. I felt bad about this from the off, do you remember me saying?" Dave nodded. "Dave, at least one of us stays with the girls at all times, right? When we hand them over tomorrow I want them in good order. I don't want some mad boyfriend chasing me because we killed his girl."

"All right, Johnny. Kidnapping's is one thing, murder is something else entirely. We need to agree to protect these girls, whatever it takes!"

"Whatever it takes," Johnny repeated, as they closed their fists and touched knuckles.

Chapter 70

398 High Rd, Tottenham, North London. Sunday 1:30pm.

Don Fisher and I had been ushered into a marginally more pleasant meeting room, its walls adorned with posters about the collection and disposal of used needles, child abuse and a particularly gruesome one picturing a victim of domestic abuse. Her face was so distorted with bruises, stitches and swelling that she did not look human. It struck me as a little tactless to sit us under that particular poster when Dee and Lavender were in the hands of brutal criminals.

DS Scott joined us in the room.

"Right, gents, we should be moving into position in five minutes or so, but let me update you on where we are."

DS Scott looked down at a clipboard that had around half a dozen sheets clipped to it. The clip on the top was blue, the corporate blue of the Metropolitan police. The sheets it held were a mix of printed and handwritten, but all carried the police logo.

"At noon Europol launched simultaneous armed raids in The Hague, Amsterdam, Brussels and Strasbourg. Local police forces were also scheduled to hit targets in Estonia, Latvia and Lithuania but they won't report back any time soon.

In The Netherlands there was some armed resistance and five suspects are being treated for injuries. Van Aart instructed his people to stand down, preferring to fight with lawyers rather than guns. In all over one hundred and fifty arrests were made and sixty two young East European girls were freed from a holding camp in The Hague.

France and Belgium reported little resistance, and were equally successful but in smaller numbers.

Here the Metropolitan Police Armed response units hit Pop Holloway's known haunts and his house. They have arrested eight people on suspicion of drugs, firearms and human trafficking offences. Pops Holloway is under police guard at the hospital, where he is reported as suffering from the symptoms of a stroke, or else he's faking it. They're doing tests to find out. We couldn't find Sonny Holloway, but guess what? His Range Rover is parked half on the pavement outside a sandwich shop on Commercial Road, less than a hundred yards from Tottenham Press. Any questions?"

Don Fisher beat me to the punch.

"Can we go in, then?"

"Yes, as soon as we're ready. Listen, this is off the record, you didn't hear it from me. I just think you have a right to know what's going on, that's all." DS Scott leaned over the table towards us and lowered his voice.

"An hour or so ago one of our observers at the scene heard something that could have been a gunshot, he wasn't too sure. But there has been no activity as far as they could see, and so we're assuming that everyone in there is still OK."

I looked at Don Fisher and wondered whether my face had turned as pale as his. We would have been angry if all emotion hadn't already been drained out of us.

***

Thanks to the Police psychologist, who said that the girls would need to see their loved ones as soon as possible after being freed, to reduce the post-traumatic stress, we were allowed to watch events unfold from close by. We sat in an unmarked white van in a parking space reserved for deliveries to the sandwich shop, which had closed for the day. We could see the Tottenham Press building through the front windscreen. One of the two plain clothes policemen sitting in the cab of the van was wearing headphones with a microphone curling around in front of his face. He was listening, and occasionally contributing to the radio chatter. The headphones were operated by Bluetooth and were wireless, but they were connected to a secure closed network radio with encryption. Just in case anyone in the area had a police scanner.

Commercial Road was sealed off by a sign that read "Road Closed: Gas Leak" and which was manned by a uniformed officer. There were very few people around the industrial area on a Sunday afternoon, but those that were around were inside the building, which was being observed closely.

The officer with the headphones repeated to us what he had heard.

"Armed response has arrived. Their adrenaline is up after a good result with the Holloway raid. They're moving into position. The plan is a go. The electrician is kicking us off any time now."

I had to admit, I felt somewhat useless as a spectator. The police were trained to handle such situations, and in that respect I was happy to leave it to them, but I couldn't help feeling that I had let Dee down. I hadn't been able to do anything to help her, and I felt frustrated and perhaps a little bit weak. I was also afraid to think of what might happen if all of this went wrong. I had known Dee for a matter of days, yet suddenly the prospect of life without her seemed inconceivable. I had no idea what I would do if anything happened to her, but I knew that if – when – she did get out of there, I would make damned sure I took better care of her in future.

Fisher and I leaned forward and observed as two men wearing overalls with a logo on the back appeared from the gap between Tottenham Press and the building next door. Their overalls looked bulky and I guessed they were wearing protective vests.

When I looked closely I could see the older man working quickly whilst the younger man was constantly looking around. He was holding a handgun.

The next few minutes were going to seem like an eternity.

***

Ben Tyler should have been at home snoozing on the sofa with a stomach full of Sunday lunch while his grandkids ran wild in the garden, but instead he was in Tottenham working. Ben couldn't remember when he had been more scared. The presence of an armed policeman, intended to make him feel secure, achieved exactly the opposite result.

Nonetheless, he had to concentrate. This was a tricky job. For a start, the system was live and electrocution was a distinct possibility. Fortunately, the wiring to this unit passed through the steel column that took the weight of the door and the roller mechanism, and would remain concealed until the front plate was completely removed. Whereas house wiring was simple three core cable with a plastic coating, this cable was copper sheathed and mineral insulated. The copper that wrapped the cores, or wires, was packed with magnesium oxide, an inert chalky substance which insulated the wires from one another. In order to keep the chalky substance in place when the cores were exposed, the wires had to be terminated with small aluminium pots. Had this not been the case, Ben would not have been able to carry out this operation on a live system.

Now they were in the third minute and he was just now exposing the cores. He loosened the terminal screws and the switch with its key control came off in his hands. Ben had to ensure that he did not touch either wire on any metal parts of the switches. He also needed to make sure that the two wires did not touch, or the roller door would try to open. The electrician tucked the key operated switch inside his overalls and extracted a much simpler switch. This unit was plastic and had a simple red switch on and off. Very carefully Ben attached a tiny crocodile clip to each exposed core, inserting a plastic spacer between them to ensure they did not touch, and allowed the plastic switch to hang suspended from the copper MICC cable.

Ben nodded to his guard who signalled a 'thumbs up', and whilst he was leading Ben away to safety another man ran towards the door.

***

We had been watching nervously as the electrician did his job, but the man deserved a medal in my opinion. Under extreme pressure he took less than four minutes.

As he was led away, Geordie from Vastrick, armed with bolt cutters, appeared from behind a green telephone junction box and ran towards the door. In ten seconds he had removed the padlock and was heading back to his hiding place.

The telephone landline had been cut off over an hour ago, and the mobile phone jammer had been in action since before the Europol raids. We had noticed during the short journey from the police station to our current position that the people in the van, and the few we saw on the streets, had all lost their phone signals.

I found it amusing that almost everyone with a mobile phone did the same thing. They saw the message, ignored it, pressed a few buttons and held it to their ear. Seconds later, realising that they were not connected, they looked at the message again and frowned. Finally, the majority of them shook the phone and looked again to see whether the signal had been restored, because of course everyone knows that sometimes the electronic signal gets trapped at the top of the phone and a good shake will loosen it allowing the phone to work. At least it took my mind off the seriousness of what was about to happen.

A few seconds passed, and six battle clad men ran to the roller doors carrying deadly looking rifles. The policeman in the headset held up three fingers, counting down by bending one finger at a time. No sooner had all of his fingers closed than there was a muffled explosion.

Chapter 71

Tottenham Press, Commercial Road, London. Sunday 1:30pm.

Dee had been awake for a while now, albeit in some pain. The man who tended her wounds had given her a foil of painkillers which he had found in the secretary's desk drawer downstairs. Dee had taken two, but as yet they hadn't made a lot of difference. She concluded that she would need something a bit stronger than over-the-counter aspirins to tackle this amount of pain. Nonetheless, she thanked him for his help, and she thought that he might be blushing under his ski mask.

Before he left the room, he closed the door behind him and spoke to the two girls in hushed tones.

"I realise that you think of me as the enemy, but I've never hurt a woman in my life, and what happened downstairs was out of order. We certainly didn't agree to any of that. My mate and me will be watching you from now on from the office at the other end of the corridor. If you need the toilet just go, but please don't give them a reason to hurt you again, all right?"

He began to leave, but as an afterthought he added, "If we're not up here, or if we're asleep and anyone worries you, yell for help and we'll come running. We just want you to get home safe. We're in enough damn trouble as it is."

Dee was standing up and trying to walk using the fixed table to lean on. If she was being honest it was no more painful than it had been lying down. At least the bullet had missed the artery and the bone. The muscle would repair itself, in time.

***

Rik stood at the office door on the lower floor of the little building, and looked around. Piet was sitting halfway up the stairs to his right, and the soldier was upstairs making sure there were no more escape attempts.

Gregor was asleep in the passenger seat of the Lexus, which was parked next to the Subaru 4x4 with Dutch plates. He would be glad when this was over and they were back on the other side of the Channel. Rik always felt uncomfortable on islands. They were surrounded by sea and too easy to close down if you wanted to escape. No, Rik preferred the mainland where, if you needed to run, you could drive thousands of miles whilst avoiding manned border crossings.

Holloway and his friend Johnny were in close conversation at the back of the factory unit, almost halfway between the emergency exit doors on either side of the building.

The factory unit had too much wasted space, in Rik's opinion. The printing presses and machines were in the middle third of the floor, like an island. On the far side of the unit, opposite the offices, were huge steel racks filled with giant paper rolls and box after box of paper in smaller sheets. Next to the racks stood a heavy duty steel walk in cupboard with a built-in fume extraction box above. Presumably that was where they store or mix ink, he thought.

At the rear of the unit, where the two Englishmen stood talking, there was more open space which housed a few lockers, a coat rack and a few mismatched tables and chairs.

Had it not been for the cars parked just inside the roller shutter doors, that space too would have been empty. They could be paying half the rent and still have plenty of room, he thought to himself.

His musings were disturbed when he heard a click. It appeared to have come from the shutter doors. He looked quickly at the two Englishmen. They had heard it, too. Sonny Holloway shouted over to Rik.

"Don't worry Rik, it's probably kids. Johnny'll go out and scatter them in a minute, before they start spray painting their gang tags on my doors."

Rik leaned against the door frame and polished his Sig Sauer P226 handgun, specially adapted for left handed users, by rubbing it on his trousers. The two-tone Sig Sauer was a compact yet powerful pistol, known to be used by US Navy Seals, and more importantly it was easy to conceal.

Rik returned to the table, laid his gun down and took his seat. He was about to drink his lukewarm coffee when all hell broke loose.

Chapter 72

No. 2 Parliament St, Westminster, London. Sunday, 1:30pm.

Whilst Arthur Hickstead wasn't under house arrest, his confinement wasn't far short of it. The police had his passport, his accounts were being monitored and if he wanted to leave the building, Donald on the front door would accompany him whilst one of the back office staff manned the door.

It didn't really matter. There was nowhere he wanted to be, and by tomorrow night the inevitable deal would have been reached with the authorities. The Establishment didn't want a newly ennobled peer of the realm all over the tabloid newspaper front pages; the country would become a laughing stock. Whilst he had been very careful, he considered himself fortunate that there was as yet no evidence linking him to the murders of Sir Max or Andrew Cuthbertson. As it had turned out, the deaths were being reported as natural causes and suicide respectively.

He relaxed into the leather upholstery of the wingback chair as he reasoned that since the money and the painting were now in the possession of Van Aart's men, the police would have trouble persuading the CPS to do any more than prosecute him for the Hammond blackmail. The peer had been told that the CPS would probably recommend a deal on that basis. Still, a deal would be assured if Hammond and Fisher refused to give evidence, hence the temporary absence of Lavender Fisher and Hammond's girlfriend.

The bright spot of the weekend had been the visit of that awful policeman, Coombes, who had to 'sadly inform you that your safety deposit box was broken into and your papers have gone'. The message had been delivered with bad grace and more than a hint of malice, because both men knew what had really been in the box and who had initiated the break in.

The Sunday papers hadn't picked up on the scandal yet, albeit one of the more sensationalist tabloids carried the headline "Unnamed Peer in Criminal Conspiracy" under an 'Exclusive' banner on page 2. He read the article twice. It was a mixture of rumour and speculation, but there was no suggestion that he was the peer involved.

He jumped when the phone rang. He hadn't been expecting any calls. It was Faik, his Iraqi friend.

"The documents you requested are ready. Do you want me to deliver them to the hotel?"

"Yes, Faik, thank you. Are they as discussed?"

"You pay for the best, you get the best. Yussi wants his money."

"I have it at the hotel. Meet me there at seven o'clock tomorrow evening."

"OK, I will bring the documents."

Hickstead terminated the call and justified the expense to himself. It always paid to have a contingency plan. Anyway, once Van Aart had taken the million-pound Churchill painting in payment for his services, he would have a million pounds in cash. A man could still travel a long way on a million pounds, and travel in style.

Chapter 73

Tottenham Press, Commercial Road, London. Sunday, 1:50pm.

Dee was still trying some tentative walking when she was rocked by two explosions, which occurred almost simultaneously. Seconds later there was pandemonium downstairs. She heard lots of shouting, and a moment later a machine pistol rattled off a dozen rounds.

Lavender was terrified. Dee told her to get under the table because she would be safer there but, without knowing what was happening, she had no real way of knowing. It might turn out that nowhere in this place was safe.

***

Rik grabbed his gun and was at the office door in time to see two armed men in combat gear run into the building, rifles raised, screaming orders. As he turned he saw two more identical figures coming in from the other fire door. Light poured in through the spaces where the fire doors had been, silhouetting the policemen.

The first two people the police approached were Sonny and Johnny, who were so surprised that when they were told to drop their weapons and put their hands on their heads they forgot they weren't even armed. As a policeman came towards them signalling that he wanted their arms up, three shots rang out from an automatic gun. The policeman was hit and fell to the floor. Sonny and Johnny's eyes widened in horror, expecting a violent reaction from the police.

Gregor, awakened by the explosions, had slipped out of the car and concealed himself behind a print machine. Confused and still dazed, he was uncertain as to who he was facing. He stood up and fired a controlled burst at the first person he saw. He swore under his breath when he noticed the word 'police' painted on the helmet of the man he had just shot.

Gregor ducked down again. He saw Piet running up the stairs and so he stood up to give him some covering fire. Before he could aim, his head exploded as he was shot from behind. Gregor's body shuddered, and then he fell as he was impacted with more bullets, his machine pistol firing wildly before falling silent.

The roller shutter door had been rising so slowly that the policemen outside decided to lie flat on their stomachs to get an angle of fire into the building. When they saw a masked man raising a machine pistol, intending to fire at their colleagues, three of them shot at once. Usual protocol; one to the head two to the chest, except that this time it was three to the head and six to the body.

Johnny had dropped to the floor when the firing began, and was now lying spread-eagled as speed cuffs were fastened onto his wrists. He wondered why Sonny was not being subjected to the same treatment, but then he saw why. He looked across the floor into the flat, dead eyes of his boss. Gregor had unknowingly sprayed Sonny with bullets as he fell to the floor in his death throes. Two bloody holes were left where 9mm slugs had pierced Sonny's coat, and the third slug had taken off part of Sonny's right ear as it passed into and out of his skull at an angle of forty five degrees.

***

Dee pulled Lavender to her feet and stood protectively in front of her as she heard someone running up the stairs. A second later the door crashed open and Piet burst in. He wasn't wearing his mask, which was a pity because his face was contorted with rage, and Lavender whimpered.

"This is your fault! Die, bitch!" Piet snarled as he raised his gun.

Dee braced herself, spreading herself wide to offer Lavender maximum protection. She closed her eyes just before the shot.

***

Rik heard the shot upstairs and took advantage of a lull in the firing to race up the metal staircase. As he ran he was accompanied by a symphony of clanging metal as bullets hit the staircase. One bullet grazed his leg and another gouged out a wickedly painful groove in his left side just below his ribs. He dived through the door.

***

Dave had been dozing when the explosions woke him into instant awareness. He took off his mask as he saw the police burst in, mob handed. He put his gun down on the table and decided to leave the girls where they were. They were probably relatively safe in there, he thought. Then the lunatic Gregor shot a policeman, and within seconds it had turned into carnage. From his window he could see Johnny being cuffed, Sonny lying dead, and the twisted ruin that had once been Gregor's body.

Piet rushed in to the accompaniment of gunfire and went straight to the girls' room. Dave reacted instantly, reaching for his gun. As he closed his hand around the grip he heard Piet screeching "Die, bitch!" and watched as Piet raised the gun, ready to fire. Dave's finger found the trigger but he wasn't sure he would find his target in time. His gun was still swinging in an arc when he bit his lip and fired.

***

Dee opened her eyes to see Piet's hands drop to his sides. There had been time for Piet's brain to register shock before half of it hit the wall beside him. He collapsed onto the floor. Lavender was hysterical, and a moment later Dave came running in.

He wasn't wearing a mask, and his face registered concern, not for his colleague but for the girls. He could see that both were fine. He spoke in a reassuring tone. "It's OK now. It's almost over."

"Is it really, soldier boy?" Dave turned to see Rik standing in the corridor with his gun aimed at Dave's chest. Dave lifted his arms and held his gun away from his body, to show that he wasn't a threat.

"Come on, Rik. It's all over. There's been enough killing. We need to give ourselves up." Dave kept his voice calm, but Rik shook his head.

"Well, I don't think it's over. Not yet. We still have two hostages."

"Rik, I can't let you do this. It's insane." Dave was watching for any sign that Rik might shoot, and he saw it in his eyes. Dave brought his gun down into shooting position and began to move into a crouch to offer a smaller target, but he was too late. Rik's bullet took him in the chest and threw him against the wall.

A smear of blood streaked the wall as Dave slid down into a sitting position, his head lolling to one side.

Rik came into the room, holding his gun ready in his left hand. When he was satisfied that Dave was no longer a threat to him, he turned the gun on Dee.

"Move out of the way! I'm taking the girl."

"No, you're not! " Dee spat out defiantly.

"Come on, lady, you've already been shot once today. I don't want to kill you." Dee held her ground whilst Rik found a position to shoot her where the bullet wouldn't pass through her and hit Lavender. Then he fired.

Dee spun around when the bullet hit. Her leg gave up and she fell to the floor. The room was spinning. She was on the verge of passing out again. How much blood had she lost today? She clamped her right hand around her upper left arm. At least this time the bullet had gone right through.

The blood was oozing through her fingers, but she had to get to Lavender before that madman got them both killed by a stray marksman's bullet. Dee tried to stand up, but couldn't, so she dragged herself along using her good right arm.

She got to Dave when she heard Rik say to Lavender, "We're going down the stairs now. Behave yourself and you'll be fine."

He took Lavender by the arm and led her through the door. "Get back!" he shouted to the figures below. "I have a hostage."

Dave opened his eyes. He was alive, just. He lifted his gun.

"Take this, get Lavender," he grimaced, and coughed. There was blood on his lips but he still tried to smile.

Dee took the gun from him and shuffled towards the stairs, inch by agonising inch.

***

Once Rik pushed Lavender ahead of him onto the staircase, the policeman on the stairs backed away and the others pointed their weapons towards him. He was probably the only hostile left standing.

Keeping Lavender in front of him with his right arm across her throat, he pressed his gun into her neck with his left hand. Step by step he moved down the stairs, not allowing anyone to get a shooting angle. The Armed Response team were frustrated, but they kept him in their sights all the way. Sooner or later one of them would get a clear shot.

***

Dee had managed to drag herself to the door and look out. Rik had Lavender by the throat, and they were almost half way down the stairs. Dee lay down on her stomach and, ignoring the pain in her left arm, she levelled the gun and took aim.

Dee knew that a poor shot could injure Lavender, and so she took a deep breath, then aimed and fired.

***

Rik was concentrating so much on the policemen below him that he had no idea he was in Dee's sights. Suddenly he felt a great pain in his chest. It felt like his heart was exploding. He was almost right. Dee's bullet had passed through his right armpit and careered through his ribcage before destroying his heart.

Rik let go of Lavender with a gasp. He collapsed and slid on his back down the stairs, landing in a heap on the concrete floor. He lay still, mouth and eyes wide open as blood pooled under his body, the effects of gravity draining the blood from his body in the absence of a working heart.

Lavender rushed up the stairs to cradle Dee in her arms.

"I thought you were dead!" the younger girl sobbed. "Oh, Dee, please don't die! I can't lose you!"

Two voices shouted "Clear!" and a paramedic raced up the stairs to attend to Dee.

"There's a man in there who needs you more than I do." Dee pointed to Dave.

The paramedic was back inside a minute. "I'm afraid he has passed, Miss. Nothing can be done for him now. Well, you've certainly been in the wars, haven't you?" he remarked, somewhat undiplomatically.

Lavender stood up and looked around at the carnage below her. She had seen two men killed in front of her and another two lay dead on the concrete floor. The armed policemen were gathering around a colleague who was just getting to his feet looking disoriented. His black chest protection had two holes in it and white material showed through.

She watched as his colleagues removed his jacket and chest pad to show a pristine white tee shirt beneath. There were grins all around. The relief was palpable and the policeman's colleagues were slapping his back and saying, 'You'll have a lovely bruise there tomorrow.'

Suddenly there was a disturbance of some kind downstairs as policemen shouted, "You can't come in here! It's a crime scene."

Chapter 74

Tottenham Press, Commercial Road, London. Sunday, 2pm.

When we heard the words "all clear, hostages have been secured," Don and I forgot about the promise we'd made to Inspector Boniface and leapt out of the van. We ran towards the building, ignoring the howled protests behind us.

For a man of his age, Don Fisher could cover a hundred yards surprisingly quickly. He was close behind me all the way. We ran into the unit, and two armed policemen blocked the way. I wasn't about to let them stop me, and I body swerved between a Lexus and a black 4x4 before coming to a halt at the bottom of a set of steel stairs.

Lavender Fisher, barefoot and wearing a stereotypical little black dress, came down the stairs. She looked drawn and dusty but she still looked beautiful to me, and probably more so to her father.

Don Fisher swept her up in his arms. "You, young lady, will not leave my sight until you are at least thirty." He hugged her as tightly as a man could without physically damaging her.

I looked to the top of the stairs, searching anxiously for any sign of Dee. When I eventually caught sight of her I was shocked. Dee was still wearing the leather catsuit she'd been wearing the last time I'd seen her, but the left sleeve and right leg were missing. Around both limbs were copious amounts of bandages. A Paramedic was half carrying her down the stairs, whilst another walked carefully down backwards in front of her, in case she stumbled. They reached the bottom safely, and headed towards the door.

At that moment another two intruders broke through police lines. This time it was Geordie and Tom Vastrick. Geordie handed the paramedic a card and said, "Take her to the Highbury Clinic, please. They're expecting her."

Tom turned to Dee, and placed his palm on her cheek.

"I'm very pleased to see you, Dee. Don't expect any time off, by the way. You got kidnapped in your free time, after all," he said.

I took her in my arms, taking her weight and hugging her tightly.

"Will you marry me?" I asked.

"If I don't die," she quipped, managing a weak smile. There was a round of applause from the same policemen who had objected to my presence in their crime scene.

"I have been shot, you know. Twice!" she giggled.

The paramedic winked at me, and explained in a single word.

"Morphine".

Chapter 75

Highbury Clinic, Blackstock Rd, North London. Sunday, 2:40pm.

The journey to the hospital had taken only a few minutes, and I sat with Dee in the ambulance, holding her hand whilst the paramedic attached her to a drip and a variety of machines.

The hospital was a modern brick building of two storeys, sporting a colourful blue sign depicting the name of a well-known provider of private medicine. The sign below read 'No A&E facilities'. I wondered why we had come here, until Dee was wheeled in and was in the operating theatre within two minutes.

I waited in the lobby with Don Fisher and Lavender, who had followed the ambulance in the paramedics' sitting ambulance, basically a Volvo Estate car. A Doctor approached us and explained that Dee would be treated and back in her room within the hour.

"Now, if you will come with me, young lady, I need to examine you," the doctor said. Lavender stood up to accompany the doctor, as did Don Fisher. Lavender frowned and said "Dad!" and Don Fisher sat back down.

As they disappeared into a room, a police car drew up outside. A young policewoman came into the lobby and addressed us both.

"Mr Hammond, Mr Fisher, my name is Andrea Farrell and I am the police constable assigned to guard your two rooms for the night. The hospital has kindly assigned Ms Conrad and Ms Fisher companion rooms next to each other on the first floor. We can go on up and wait for them there, if you'd like."

It didn't sound like a question, and so we both followed her to the lift. Once we emerged from the lift we entered a corridor that was more like a hotel than a hospital. It didn't have that hospital smell which is prevalent in all NHS premises, but smelled like a newly built hotel. WPC Farrell checked the piece of paper in her hand and led us to rooms 35 and 33. The doors were close together.

Andrea opened number 35 and said, "This room has been assigned to Miss Conrad." We followed the WPC inside, and looked around. The room was spacious and beautifully decorated, and could easily have passed as an upmarket hotel. The cream painted walls were adorned with tasteful, bright watercolours. The bed looked as though it contained enough technology for space travel, and against the wall stood a sofa and a matching armchair with a high back. On the wall opposite the bed hung a flat screen TV which was operated from the bed via a remote control.

"The sofa folds out into a bed, should you wish to stay the night," WPC Farrell informed us.

I saw the brightly lit en suite bathroom, with its sandy coloured marble effect tiles and full sized bath, and I suddenly felt grubby. I realised that we had all been wearing the same clothes since Friday.

"I'll be next door, Josh," Don Fisher said, his hand resting on my shoulder.

"OK," I answered, noticing that his face was pale and drawn. All the worries of fatherhood seemed to be resting on his shoulders. Seeing him vulnerable and exposed as he was made me realise that, no matter how rich you may be, you can't keep your kids entirely safe.

I decided I should have a bath, and rang downstairs for extra towels. A nurse arrived in the room a few minutes later. She laid the towels and some other linen on the bed.

"I thought you might need these," she said, holding up a pair of plain white boxer shorts. "They look the right size." She grinned at my obvious embarrassment as she held them in front of my groin.

"Also, if you're staying overnight, you might need these."

She laid out what looked like a lounging suit consisting of dark blue track suit trousers and a matching zip up top. The colourful hospital logo was embroidered on the left had side of the chest. To my dismay it looked a lot like the Arsenal football club badge.

"If you need anything else, just let me know. Oh, by the way, you can see the Emirates Stadium in the distance from this window." She left, closing the door behind her. I went to the window and closed the curtains.

Chapter 76

Tottenham Press, Commercial Road, London. Sunday, 5pm.

Inspector Boniface and DCI Coombes left the Tottenham Operations Room as soon as the operation was over, arriving just after the paramedics had left. They had been here for almost three hours and the scene was still buzzing with people.

The last of the bodies had just been taken away in the coroner's black van, and some of the crime scene investigators had also gone, but the doctor was still in the building.

The armed response team had been quizzed by the Internal Investigations Branch, standard procedure in a fatal shooting, and their recollections matched the findings of the crime scene investigators. Now they were all piling into cars and minibuses to return to base.

The doctor, still wearing his white protective overalls and plastic overshoes, strode over to the two senior detectives.

"What a bloodbath. Six suspects, five of whom are dead, and a hostage shot twice. There is some good news, if you can call it that. We only took one of them down. Preliminary analysis suggests that Sonny Holloway was killed by a machine pistol, almost certainly by the suspect who was killed by the firearms squad. Then, it gets confusing. We know that one of the hostages shot the last man but there were two more bodies upstairs. My best guess is that the one on top killed the one underneath before our last man killed him.

If you're keeping score, we killed one, three were killed by other suspects and the hostage shot one. With one still alive, that's all six accounted for, gentlemen." The doctor removed his latex gloves and unzipped his overalls.

"You'll have the full report tomorrow," he volunteered as he walked away.

***

DS Scott and DS Fellowes had joined the two senior detectives and were reporting their findings. DS Scott offered to lead, and Fellowes nodded.

"All firearms used in the shootings today have been recovered and bagged. Additionally we discovered a small armoury in a steel lockbox concealed in the paint store. The contents have been logged and removed. There were two blocks of RDX explosives in there, as well. DS Fellowes also had a memorable find."

DS Scott looked at Fellowes, who took up the story. "Hidden with the spare wheel was a carefully wrapped painting. It has Churchill's signature on it and is probably the one De Montagu sold to Hickstead. As we suspected, it had been kept in Hickstead's safety deposit box.

Also concealed in the body panels were necklaces, bracelets, rings, cash in numerous currencies, and a collection of gold Krugerrands in a coin collector's album. There were at least a hundred in there, and they usually sell for about five hundred pounds each.

Best of all, there's a holdall in the office packed with fifty pound notes. The bag weighed just over twenty three kilos. A million pounds in fifties weighs twenty two kilos. What's the betting that the numbers match those given to us by Fisher's bank?"

Suddenly the weariness lifted from all four men and they smiled. Tomorrow Lord Hickstead would come looking for a deal, fondly imagining he still had the bargaining chip of hostages. That interview would now be much more enjoyable. The four men all shook hands, and Boniface spoke.

"You three go home and get some rest. I'll call in at the hospital and see if our victims want to see his Lordship squirm tomorrow. I think they deserve that."

Chapter 77

Highbury Clinic, Blackstock Rd, North London. Sunday, 5:30pm.

I sat on the edge of the bed talking to Dee when she was awake. If we stopped talking, even for a few seconds, her eyelids would flutter and she would be drifting away again. The doctor explained that she would be 'dopey' until she had enjoyed a good night's sleep.

There was a tap on the door.

"Come in," I shouted, and Dee opened her eyes.

Don Fisher and Lavender came into the room. He was wearing a blue lounge suit like mine, and Lavender was wearing the equivalent in burgundy. Rather inappropriately I thought, if I took a picture of them dressed like that I could blackmail them for a million pounds and get it, no questions asked.

Lavender went to Dee and hugged her, kissing her on the cheek, before running her fingers down the other cheek.

"Oh Dee, your face is all bruised. Is it OK?" Sonny's fist had indeed left an ever developing bruise that ran from her jaw line to her cheekbone. All hues of yellow, blue and purple were now represented in the swelling.

"It'll heal quicker than the bullet wounds," Dee joked weakly.

Lavender came over to me and gave me a hug, too. She hung on for quite a while before Dee reminded her that I was 'her man'. Lavender kissed me on the lips for devilment.

"Oooh, he's a good kisser," she said to Dee, laughing at my blushing face. "I'm Lavender, by the way."

"I know," I replied. "I've seen your pictures." The room fell silent. "In the papers," I added hastily, but too late. "Not the Polaroids. I didn't look," I spluttered, digging myself deeper in. "Sorry."

Lavender, Dee and Fisher laughed out loud.

***

Don Fisher asked if he could speak to Dee privately, and so Lavender and I retired to her room, which was identical to Dee's but in mirror image. We sat and spoke for a while, and she told me about Dee's sacrifices on her behalf, which included her pushing Lavender onto the roof of the offices and pretending that she had escaped, even though she knew she would be punished.

The plan had been to make them believe that Lavender had escaped, so they would have been forced to abandon their hideout, leaving Lavender to raise the alarm by calling the police from the phone in the office.

She was in tears as she recounted how Dee had been shot and tortured whilst stubbornly refusing to give Lavender up. After tearfully explaining how Dee had stood in front of her, ready to take a bullet, Lavender said something that touched me. Taking my hands in hers, she began.

"No-one has ever done anything like that for me before. All the time I was thinking to myself, why is she wasting her life for me? She's so much more valuable than me. I'm just a spoiled child, like people say, and I couldn't see it until today. I thought we were going to die. Josh, why was she prepared to die for someone she had just met, someone so shallow and selfish like me?"

I had to think for a while, but then I found the words. "I've only known Dee for a week and a half, but she entranced me from the beginning. Isn't there a song called 'You had me from hello'? Well, that's how I feel. A person like Dee is rare. If you want my opinion, I don't think she was protecting the spoiled child in you, I think she was protecting the vulnerable person underneath. She was protecting the person you have become, not the person you were on Friday."

The tears were flowing freely now, and Lavender squeezed my hand. I hoped that she would find her way in life and be happy. She seemed like a good kid on the whole. She didn't deserve a shallow celebrity life; she deserved so much more.

Don Fisher came into the room and, for the sake of something to say, he joked.

"I've tried to get Dee to see sense, but the drugs are messing with her head and she's still insistent on marrying you."

"Can I be a bridesmaid?" Lavender trilled, her eyes widening in expectation.

"You can be the chief bridesmaid," I replied.

The phone rang and Fisher answered it. He listened for a moment and then explained that we needed to go next door. Inspector Boniface was on his way up.

***

Once he had explained what they had discovered in The Tottenham Press building, Inspector Boniface asked the girls to confirm the sequence of events leading to their eventual rescue. Other than the fact that "Dave the soldier" had given his life to save them, things had unfolded pretty much as the police had surmised.

Having expressed admiration for their courage and resourcefulness, the Inspector explained that Dee and Lavender would each be required to give a formal statement later.

"Now," he said brightly. "I need to explain what happens next."

He paused to ensure that we were all paying attention. I could see that he was relishing this next part.

"Lord Hickstead has been kept in sterile conditions all weekend. That is to say, he's heard nothing of the day's events, and nor will he. There is a press embargo on the Europol action until a press conference is held tomorrow afternoon, aimed at the evening news programmes.

At ten o'clock in the morning he will be back at Scotland Yard. As far as he's concerned, the only evidence we have consists of the fingerprints on the photographs and a lot of circumstantial evidence. He will also believe that Josh and Don are pressuring the police to allow him to plead to a lesser charge and walk away with a non-custodial sentence. I think we can expect him to be unbearably smug, at least for a while.

My question is this. Do the two of you want to watch that interview from the conference room?"

"I suppose it's too much to ask for me to be left in the same room alone with him for five minutes?" Don Fisher asked, without any hope of a positive answer.

"The offer is restricted to watching on a video screen, I'm afraid, but if you do want to see him face to face, I have an idea."

I was torn between staying with Dee and watching Lord Hickstead's world collapse around him. In the end, both Don and I agreed we would be there.

"Will you be wearing those attractive matching tracksuits?" Boniface asked, barely holding back a guffaw.

We both scowled at him, and bid him farewell.

Chapter 78

No.2 Parliament St. Westminster, London. Sunday, 8pm.

Alan Parsons, Lord Hickstead's solicitor, sat on the Chesterfield sofa facing the peer, who looked comfortable as he sat in the wing chair sipping brandy.

"Arthur, we have a difficult meeting tomorrow morning, and based on what I have heard, the police are close to arresting you. I appreciate that the safety deposit box is now empty and that your papers have gone. I also understand that whatever the police hoped to find in there is not there, either. But - and this is a big but, Arthur - they still have witnesses who can connect you to the blackmail plot, and blackmail in this country carries a sentence of up to fourteen years."

"Relax, Alan. They'll do a deal. They won't want the publicity, and by the time the politicians put the pressure on..."

"Yes, Arthur. Actually I was coming to that."

Hickstead thought that this sounded rather ominous, and he was right.

"I did a ring around Friday and yesterday. No success, I'm afraid. The Commissioner wouldn't speak to me, but had his assistant tell me that he couldn't interfere in an ongoing investigation. The Home Secretary and Shadow Home Secretary wished you well in establishing your innocence, but they will not take your calls. The two Labour Leadership contenders you asked me to call said that the charges were so serious that they were unwilling to intervene, although one of them did say that if there was any hint of a political element in the prosecution he would try to help."

"So, basically, they're all running for the hills, are they?" Hickstead spat bitterly. "I'm on my own after all that I've done for them individually and for the Party."

The lawyer looked down, in order to avoid the look of self-pity in his client's eyes. For goodness' sake, he was at least a blackmailer and probably a murderer, and he was behaving like some kind of martyr. 'Everyone deserves a good defence', he reminded himself, before imparting the last bit of bad news.

***

The lawyer had gone and Hickstead was pacing around the room. He was livid. Tomorrow he would strike some sort of deal with the police, the hostages would be released, and then he would get his payback.

They would be made to pay for betraying him. The former Prime Minister would be first on his list.

Alan Parsons had been contacted by the leader of the Labour Party in the Lords, who had said that they expected Arthur to resign if he was charged. He then reminded Alan of the changes to the legislation relating to their Lordships, legislation that the Labour Party had commenced in 2009.

Arthur read the text once more.

The Baroness has today commented that she will implement the new rules that include the ability to expel Members of the House of Lords from their duties if they are guilty of an offence, and she has said that in the cases that we know about, she is prepared to bring forward emergency sanctions to deal with those issues.

The underlining had been provided by the Party apparatchiks.

Arthur would get his deal and defy his party. If the whole house wanted to vote to suspend him, so be it, but it wouldn't be so easy when they heard that he had walked away from Scotland Yard with a Conditional Caution.

Chapter 79

Highbury Clinic, Blackstock Rd, North London. Sunday, 8pm.

A bright young woman from Vastrick Security had delivered some clean clothes and a suit from my flat. She also brought Dee a couple of outfits. That was a little optimistic, as I didn't think Dee would need them for a while yet. I was also informed that a new door had been fitted to my flat, courtesy of Vastrick, and that it had a seven lever security lock. I took the key for my new front door. The young woman kissed the sleeping Dee's forehead and took a second to arrange her hair before departing.

Don Fisher had gone home with his tail between his legs after a tongue lashing from the redoubtable Mrs. Fisher. I could tell that she was a rock journalist by her extensive vocabulary of swear words. There was a time in the verbal tirade when she had used up her entire vocabulary of expletives, and she'd had to resort to foreign swear words.

Having heard this through the wall, I was more than a little scared when she came into Dee's room. I stood up nervously. Maddie Fisher was still a good looking woman, and when she smiled she looked quite stunning.

"You must be Josh," she said in a matter-of-fact way, taking hold of my chin between her thumb and forefinger, turning my head from side to side as if examining a racehorse. "Mmm. Lavender was right, you are a handsome boy."

I hadn't been a boy for close to twenty years, but who was I to argue with such an icon of good taste?

Maddie spoke to a smiling, and awake, Dee for a few minutes, and then said to me in conspiratorial tones, "Josh, if the arrangement Don made with Dee isn't generous enough, let me know. Don can be a tight bugger if he isn't watched."

Dee said she would see Maddie in the morning, and wished her goodnight. Maddie responded in kind and added, "Oh, I almost forgot. Lavender said she wanted my opinion as to whether Josh was a good kisser."

She walked towards me, put her manicured hand on my cheek, and said, "Just kidding." I relaxed visibly, and she kissed me anyway.

"Mmm. Not bad," she said, winking at Dee, who would laugh her stitches out if she wasn't careful.

I yawned so widely that my jaw almost locked. I kissed Dee, and lay down on the sofa bed that the nurse had made up for me. I lay on my side and looked at Dee as she looked at me. I closed my eyes for a few seconds, and suddenly it was morning.

Chapter 80

New Scotland Yard, London. Monday, 10:30am.

The team that had parted on Friday afternoon had now reconvened. Alan Parsons was sitting next to Lord Hickstead, and opposite was Inspector Boniface and DCI Coombes.

We were watching from a room down the corridor via CCTV. When I say we, I mean myself, Don Fisher, Tom Vastrick, the two Detective Sergeants and an interloper, Lavender Fisher.

When I had been waiting for the car to take us to Scotland Yard, Don Fisher joined me on the kerb. A second or two later someone linked my arm, and I looked around to see Lavender linking arms with us both and grinning from ear to ear.

"The doctor said I could go, and Mum thought it was a good idea."

I was about to ask a question when Don Fisher said, "Don't ask, Josh. It isn't worth it."

So now here we were, the six of us, in a semi darkened room, looking at our tormentor.

***

After the necessary procedural niceties, DCI Coombes got straight down to business.

"Lord Hickstead, I trust you had a relaxing weekend. Ours was rather hectic."

"Yes, you mentioned to me on Saturday that my Citysafe box wasn't as Citsyafe as I'd thought it was. I understand its contents were stolen," the peer smiled.

"Quite a coincidence, I think you will agree."

Alan Parsons interjected before Lord Hickstead could respond.

"Come now, Chief Inspector, you can't be suggesting that my client robbed his own box, surely?"

"Luckily for your client, Mr Parsons, we can only prosecute on evidence," Coombes stated. "What I believe or do not believe is neither here nor there."

"If we could set the animosity aside for a few moments, perhaps we could discuss how this case is to proceed," Parsons continued irritably. "I have spoken with my client and, faced with the evidence, whilst he admits nothing, he understands that there is a possibility he would be convicted of the Hammond blackmail, but I think we would all have to concede that there was at least reasonable doubt about the other charges."

"What are you suggesting?" Coombes asked.

"Well, we could reach some kind of agreement, to save ourselves and the courts a lot of inconvenience. Perhaps his Lordship might plead guilty to a lesser charge, and the CPS could be persuaded that my client was emotionally disturbed when he acted as he did, trying to recover money he believed he had been entitled to. We could then look at a suspended sentence, perhaps some probation, and keep the whole thing off the front pages of the tabloids."

Coombes and Boniface whispered to one another as if considering the offer, and Hickstead smiled. Boniface looked at them and spoke.

"We would have to consult with the two alleged victims, to ask them if they could accept these terms because, although it isn't necessary, we don't want any action taken against the police."

"Unusual but entirely understandable," Parsons replied reasonably.

"As a matter of fact, they are in the building at this very moment. Perhaps we could bring them in?"

"Absolutely not!" Parsons spluttered. "That is a disgraceful suggestion. You are suggesting exposing my client to his accusers, who will naturally assume his guilt!"

"Oh, quiet down, Alan," Lord Hickstead said. "I think I'm man enough to face my accusers. I've been facing up to my opponents since I was twelve. I say let them in, and we can see what they have to say." His smile was wider now.

Alan Parsons strongly advised his client against it, but he was silenced by His Lordship.

***

I had never before seen Lord Hickstead in person, and when I did it was not a pleasant experience. Despite his despicable actions, and the pain he had inflicted on everyone, he sat smirking beside his lawyer. Don Fisher was standing next to me, the very model of restraint. I knew that Don would happily have squeezed the life out of the peer, given the chance.

As rehearsed, the two policemen explained to us what a deal meant and how it would be final. They concluded by saying that they would proceed on all charges unless we said otherwise.

I was the first to speak, and although I was addressing the policemen I was looking straight into Hickstead's eyes. The man was brimming with confidence.

"Inspector, I have listened carefully to what you have suggested, and it is my view that we should...." I hesitated. "We should proceed on all charges, and seek the maximum penalty the court could impose."

Alan Parsons leaned over to Hickstead, whose face was now blank, and whispered none too quietly.

"Bloody hell, Arthur, I could see this coming a mile off. Why couldn't you? Why on earth would they agree?"

Don Fisher stepped forward. Looking at Hickstead, he said, "Inspector, I agree with Mr Hammond. Criminals should have to face the full consequences of their actions, especially when they are scum eating bottom feeders."

"Inspector, really!" Parsons protested. "Get these men out of the room at once." We started to leave, and Hickstead stood up from his chair, veins bulging on his neck and forehead.

"You realise what this means," he yelled angrily in our direction. We continued walking and closed the door behind us.

***

"What does it mean, Lord Hickstead?" Boniface asked. Parsons looked bemused, as if everyone in the room was in on a joke except him.

"Figure of speech, that's all," Hickstead replied in a surly tone.

"One of the reasons we had such a busy weekend is that Lavender Fisher and Delia Conrad, Mr Hammond's girlfriend, were kidnapped on Saturday." Boniface looked at Hickstead, who maintained his poker face.

"You can't seriously be suggesting that my client is in any way involved in that kidnapping? It's simply absurd!" He said the words, but Boniface could see fear in the lawyer's eyes.

"We don't make any accusations, Alan, but if you watch this perhaps you could tell me what we are meant to think." He clicked the remote control and they all turned to watch the monitor.

A masked man appeared on the screen, threatening that the hostages would die unless an agreement was reached with Lord Hickstead by this evening. The camera then showed Lavender and Dee chained to the table. Boniface switched it off.

"My God!" Alan Parsons blurted out, but Hickstead remained resolute.

"I need some time with my client," the lawyer said. "I want all cameras and sound off. Understood?"

"Of course," Coombes agreed reasonably.

***

"Arthur, what have you got yourself involved in?" Parsons demanded, clearly flustered.

"One of my less straitlaced friends may have become a little, shall we say, overenthusiastic in an effort to protect me. But you heard the threat the same as I did; unless there is an agreement, the women die. I suggest we concentrate on reaching an agreement so that these young women can be returned safely to their families." Lord Hickstead did not look at his lawyer once during the exchange.

"Arthur, I don't see how we can expect an agreement when the people involved are insistent that you be prosecuted to the fullness of the law."

This time Hickstead looked into the eyes of his lawyer as he spoke. There was menace in his voice, and his face was unreadable.

"Alan, that is a negotiating position. We hold fast and call their bluff. They will come around. We've only just started, and you want to throw the towel in already."

"That video clip is extraordinarily prejudicial," Parsons pointed out. "That could send you to prison for life if it was played to a jury."

"It never will be, Alan, trust me. It will be part of the bargaining that will result in an agreement, and which will free the two women."

"And if we don't get an agreement, Arthur, what then?"

"Then I expect the women will die. That is what the video said. After all, I have no control over those men."

Parsons stared at him wide eyed. "That is a blatant lie! How would they find out we'd got a deal, unless you tell them? You must be able to contact them." The lawyer sat back, waiting for the peer to concede the point.

"At last, Alan, you're earning your fee. You asked a question I hadn't considered. I think I must say that I have been told to send an email to an anonymous email address. That sounds plausible. At least plausible enough to get across to those two morons that their loved ones might die just so they can have the satisfaction of seeing me being sent to an open prison for a couple of years. We've wasted enough time. Get them back in."

Alan Parsons sighed. He was beginning to wonder whether absolutely everyone deserved the best defence they could get.

***

The video in our room clicked back on. The client conference had obviously concluded. The two policemen followed the protocols again, naming the room occupants and stating the time.

Alan Parsons then spoke up. "Lord Hickstead denies any involvement in the kidnapping. He was unaware of the abduction until he saw that clip of video. He does acknowledge, however, that there is a possibility that a misguided friend may have acted in what they thought was his best interests. Now, having expressed his outrage at what has been done in his name, he is even more eager to reach a deal so that the women can be returned safely."

"Thank you, Mr Parsons," Boniface replied. "If that turned out to be true, then it would be very public spirited of his Lordship to accept punishment just to save the life of two women he does not know. Albeit he has been in possession of some extremely explicit and unpleasant pictures of one of them." He paused before turning his gaze to Hickstead. "But, of course, everyone sitting around this table knows that this is all crap. Your client is up to his neck in blackmail, kidnapping and armed robbery. He may even be responsible for one or more deaths. How am I going to persuade the CPS to go for any sort of deal in those circumstances?"

Hickstead smiled nastily. "Because we have a common goal. I want a deal, and you want the hostages back. This is a win-win scenario. If the deal doesn't happen, it becomes a lose-lose scenario, where two women die unnecessarily, and I take my chances with a jury."

Coombes stepped in, for the first time playing the good cop. "Lord Hickstead, you may have crossed some lines but I cannot believe that you would let two women die just because you had to face a trial for a blackmail plot that you yourself hatched."

"Just watch me!" Hickstead snapped.

"Arthur, be quiet! Let me do the talking," Parsons advised him quickly. "This isn't helping your cause one iota." Hickstead fell silent, and the lawyer sighed.

"Might we have some drinks brought in? It might cool things down a little."

"Of course. I'll see to it." Boniface excused himself, and the tape was stopped. A minute later he was in our room, with an audacious plan that he had cooked up with DCI Coombes during the break. He told us what he had in mind.

"Is that legal? Are you allowed to do that? It seems rather underhand," I said.

"It's borderline, but hey, when DCI Coombes joined the force they were still slapping suspects with wet towels." Boniface smiled. "Timing is everything, remember." The plan was already underway.

***

Coombes was chatting amiably to Alan Parsons, recalling previous cases where they had faced one another. Boniface entered, and set down a tray of soft drinks and chilled water, both still and sparkling. There were also the ubiquitous biscuits that were so common in meetings. The chocolate ones and the cream filled ones would be consumed, but the Rich Tea would be passed over for the next meeting to ignore, as usual.

I looked at my watch. Any second now, I thought, and a moment later there was a tap on the interview room door.

"Enter," Boniface shouted, without looking up.

A young girl entered the room. She was smartly attired in a modest burgundy dress, trimmed with lace. She was wearing black tights and was wearing smart black shoes with a low heel. Her hair was tied back to show that her face was lightly made up.

I watched as Hickstead dropped his glass, spilling water over himself and his lawyer.

"Oops," said the girl. "I'll see if I can get a cloth for that. Dad said you might need these papers, Inspector."

Boniface took the papers from her with a smile. "Thank you, Lavender. Don't worry about the cloth, though. I have a fresh handkerchief here. Close the door on the way out, please."

***

Alan Parsons railed at the two detectives for a full five minutes as Hickstead sat looking blankly at the table. He looked rather like a marionette whose strings had been cut.

"Right, Alan. Your complaints have been registered on the tape. Now, would you like to hear what kept us busy the rest of the weekend?"

"Go on," the lawyer said wearily, knowing that nothing good was to come from this summation.

Boniface explained the Europol operation and the part that the Holloway family had played in the events. He explained that Van Aart had been persuaded to become a prosecution witness to reduce his own jail time, and that Van Aart had met with his Lordship in Amsterdam.

He explained how an innocent woman lay in a hospital bed with two bullet wounds, and five men lay dead in a morgue because Hickstead wouldn't face up to his crimes and tried to cover them up by conspiring to commit even more serious crimes.

Hickstead and his lawyer were then shown a statement from a man called Johnny, who said that the Holloways had been assisting Van Aart's men to recover a holdall and a painting from Lord Hickstead's safety deposit box at Citysafe. Johnny confessed to kidnapping Lavender in order to give Lord Hickstead leverage over Don Fisher, and he related the story of Dee Conrad's trials at the hands of the Dutch criminals.

By the time Boniface concluded with the facts that Lord Hickstead's fingerprints were found on the holdall and the painting, Parsons had already given up hope of keeping his client out of prison for the rest of his days.

***

"You are joking, surely, Commissioner!" DCI Coombes was back at his livid best. "This man has been charged with blackmail, conspiracy to commit armed robbery and conspiracy to kidnap two women. A banker, a philanthropist, an accountant and five other men lie dead because of his direct and indirect actions."

"Coombes, please remember where you are," the Commissioner said by way of warning.

"Well, obviously I've strayed into some banana republic where politicians can do what the hell they like and just walk away!" Coombes spluttered. Boniface grabbed his arm and looked into the DCI's face.

"Terry, will you please calm down? This won't get us anywhere. Let's see what we can do to make the best of the decision."

"Listen to the Inspector, Coombes, and I will try to forget your intemperate outburst," the Commissioner said. "I don't like this any more than you do. Whilst Hickstead's friends are deserting him with the rapidity of rats leaving a sinking ship, they do not want another scandal. We already have four MPs on trial for electoral fraud. When the public find out that a peer has been involved in serious crimes like these, there will likely be an outcry the likes of which we have never seen before.

The establishment wants time to prepare. This week there will be an emergency debate in the House of Lords, and if necessary special legislation will be rushed through both houses to expel Hickstead. By the end of the month you will have all of the evidence together, and we will be in a better position to arraign him. We will oppose bail, of course, and he will sit on remand for months while we prepare for trial.

Gentlemen. For the next few days he will be under virtual house arrest with MI5 'protecting him from a terrorist threat'. I can assure you that he will never see the light of day again after that, except through prison bars."

"Thank you, Commissioner. Can we assume that our colleagues elsewhere in the Yard and in Europol will freeze all of Lord Hickstead's assets in the meantime?" Boniface asked.

"Yes, with two exceptions. First, we cannot touch his pension funds without agreement from the Union that holds those funds. But in any event he cannot access his pension for another year, by which time he will not need it. Second, we are obliged to allow him to operate a simple credit account so that he can honour his commitments to his creditors. The bank and credit card companies cannot lend him money, or accept any new money. He can only expend funds that he has in his account as of today."

"Thank you, Commissioner," Boniface said. "We will ensure that he is securely delivered to Parliament Street."

Chapter 81

Highbury Clinic, Blackstock Rd, North London. Monday, 6pm.

I realised, as I travelled to the hospital, that I had been quite selfish in my pursuit of Dee Conrad. It was true that I loved her, and it was true that I had sensed that love was reciprocated, but for the last twelve days her life had been on hold whilst she stayed with me. We had talked about her flat mates and her social life, but I actually knew very little about her, and had never seen her flat. I had glibly assumed that if we loved one another we could just cohabit at my flat and perhaps get married. I was not considering her wants or needs; not because I thought mine were more important, but because they had just not entered my mind in the busyness of our lives for the last twelve days.

I was somewhat pleased, therefore, when I heard laughter and girlish giggling coming from Dee's room. I walked into a girly fest; there were balloons, cards and all things pink, adorning the room. Two women, almost the polar opposite of Dee, stood either side of the bed. These women were dressed fashionably but in clothes that would have suited them more if they had been perhaps ten years younger. Their make-up was exquisite, though. I wondered whether their flat would maybe have three bathrooms, because if it didn't then surely they must work in shifts in front of the mirror.

One was blonde and the other brunette, but both had long hair, expertly cut by a stylist who was worth every penny of whatever fee they charged. Either one of them could have fronted an advertising for L'Oreal; they both seemed 'worth it' to me.

I was introduced to Dana and Gemma by a much improved Dee, who was looking the picture of health, despite her bandages and bruises.

"Ooh, he's older than I thought he would be," Gemma said, curling her lip.

"Yes, I imagined he would be more handsome, too," Dana agreed, contributing to what was obviously a well-practised double act.

"I wonder if his talents lie elsewhere, perhaps?" Dana continued, whilst looking me up and down but holding her gaze over my groin area.

In spite of myself, I blushed. I knew that was what they were expecting but I just couldn't help it. Dee was laughing too.

We all had a sensible conversation for ten minutes or so, and then Dana and Gemma had to leave so that they could attend their 'Boxercise' class at the gym. After spending another ten minutes hugging and kissing their way through their goodbyes, I was left alone with Dee. I wasn't sure where to start, so in the end I took a deep breath and simply came out with it.

"Dee, I've been doing some serious thinking. I realise you probably feel that I may have taken you for granted. I know how I feel about you, but I haven't really stopped to consider your needs, or your life, or what you might want."

She smiled at me.

"There will be plenty of time for all of that, Josh, but for now the girls are looking for a new flatmate. Of course, it's also quite likely they will convert my bedroom into a giant dressing room with all of their clothes on racks and their shoes stored in transparent stacking boxes."

"Where are you going?" I asked nervously, knowing that there was only one answer I could live with. She looked me in the eyes.

"I rather thought that I might move in with you. You'll need help to pay the mortgage now that you have so recklessly frittered away a quarter of a million pounds."

***

We decided not to make any immediate plans, and to wait until Dee was out of hospital and back with me.

The next hour was spent explaining the events of the day and Lord Hickstead's spectacular fall from grace. Dee seemed to understand the peer's motivations, and whilst she couldn't condone anything he had done, she expressed her opinion that the case would never reach a jury.

"What are you suggesting?" I asked.

"Josh, I love your innocence, but just think this through and then judge the likelihood of a trial being held. It seems to me that there are a number of options here, the least likely being incarceration and trial. First option, release his Lordship on his own recognisance, let him consider his future and give him the opportunity to take the easy way out."

"Suicide, you mean?" I asked, surprised.

Dee nodded before continuing. "It's a real possibility, Josh. He will be expelled from the Lords, he will lose the proceeds of his crime, he will be in prison for the rest of his life, and it certainly won't be a cosy open prison, given the nature of his crimes. The second option is that he doesn't have the nerve to end his own life and so he is, shall we say, helped along a little."

I was aghast at the suggestion.

"That would be the equivalent of a state execution!" I stated. "Surely you're not suggesting that sort of thing actually goes on these days?"

"Think back, Josh, and not too many years ago you will recall individuals who had, or would have, embarrassed the establishment. Scientists, spies and specialists in Weapons of Mass Destruction have died rather conveniently, or have apparently taken their own lives. Some of these people are placed under such enormous pressure that suicide seems to be the only way out, and if they still don't act then there a thousand ways they can be assisted. Hickstead proved that, with Sir Max and Andrew. Josh, if Lord Hickstead goes to trial it will be broadcast around the world. The Press would have a field day. The ex-Prime Minister will be made to look incompetent for nominating him as a Peer. The new PM will be embarrassed that he allowed the nomination to stand. They will both blame the security services who carry out the checks before anyone gets a peerage, and the House of Lords itself will be damaged. The hereditary and the life Peers will all be pilloried and discredited in the same way that the expenses scandal tarred all MPs, guilty or not. There will be outrage from the public when they hear of the deaths and the distress he caused; I wouldn't be surprised if there were calls for the House of Lords to be disbanded. That part of the establishment is already deeply unpopular, and Hickstead has handed its opponents a potentially lethal weapon.

The unions will disown him, his party already have, and he will have made dangerous enemies that he could not have foreseen when he started all of this. Our Secret Intelligence Services will be deeply humiliated and angry that they're being blamed for a political blunder, and will already be preparing their defence.

What I'm saying is this, Josh. If he goes to trial there will be parliamentary commissions, committee hearings and so on, and none of them will show the system in a good light."

I still couldn't believe that a country like ours would stoop to those depths to save face. It seemed to me that such mistrust was at the heart of all conspiracy theories.

Dee could see the doubt in my face. She squeezed my hand and asked a question that sent a chill through my body. "Josh, earlier today, against all the odds and against all common sense, the Commissioner of the Metropolitan Police was instructed to release Hickstead on police bail. Into whose hands was he released?"

She had a point. Number two Parliament Street was guarded by MI5.

Chapter 82

No.2 Parliament St. Westminster, London. Monday, 6pm.

Lord Hickstead had concluded that the life he had carefully built for himself had gone forever. With his credit cards cancelled and his bank account frozen he had to rethink his strategy.

He had around four thousand pounds in his current account that he was free to use. His other accounts had almost seventy thousand pounds deposited in them, but he would never see that money again. They would claim it as the proceeds of crime, even though it wasn't true. He did have a very good pension with the union, but it would not pay out until next year. He did, however, have two aces up his sleeve.

Lord Hickstead made a call to his Swiss Bank and checked the balance for the numbered account in the name of Euro Union Financial Enterprises. The balance had been reduced as a result of paying Van Aart a hundred thousand Euros in compensation when the diamonds went missing. Still, the figure quoted to him was the euro equivalent of almost half a million pounds.

Several years of milking the EU coffers had served him well. When he had worked for the Trades Union they had wanted to see receipts for all his expenses. They didn't particularly care how much was spent, but they wanted receipts. He could hardly believe his luck when he took up his new post and found he was allowed the cost of flying home on a Friday, first class, and back again after the weekend, whether he travelled or not. He could also travel widely in his role as European Commissioner for Labour Relations and rack up all kinds of alleged expenses along the way. But not until the last year or so of his posting did anyone ask for receipts. There was simply a presumption that he had travelled home each weekend at a cost of over five hundred pounds a week, and that he had indeed expended what he had claimed. He wasn't alone in recognising that loophole.

The only other source of cash he could access was waiting for him across London, and to collect that he would need to find a way to bypass his MI5 minder at the front desk. Lord Hickstead's problem was that, whilst there were many exits leading to external fire escapes, they were all alarmed. He couldn't use any of those exits as he hadn't the first idea how to disable an alarm. That left him only the front door.

***

Quite why this building was so secure Hickstead didn't know, but then he had never researched its history. Since 1895, number 2 Parliament Street had been used solely as civil service office accommodation until apartments had been created from the offices on the top two floors during the 1970s. At that time the doorman would traditionally have been an ex-serviceman. However, following the assassination of Airey Neave on 30th March 1979, within the confines of the Houses of Parliament, there had been a sea change in security arrangements. The recently converted apartments were seen as potential targets for terrorists, as they housed senior government officials. To offer better protection, Special Branch's SO12, 'S' squad, took an office suite at the back of the building and equipped it with firearms, and staffed the lobby with armed officers.

After the 11th September 2001 attacks on New York, SO12 had their hands full with other commitments and so they had been more than happy to let MI5 use the offices as long as they also handled the doorman duties. It was also a coup for MI5. Because all of the bills for this satellite office were covered by the building owners, Crown Estates, very few people at MI5's HQ at Thames House even knew it existed. This made 'the cubby hole', as it was known to operatives, an ideal place to carry out operations without the continuous oversight of the bean counters at Thames House.

***

Arthur Hickstead had left the apartment carrying nothing but his cash card. He knew that he could not risk taking anything with him. He had no way of knowing what bugs or transmitters they might have hidden in his personal belongings. Having come to the ground floor via the service stairs, he was now in the photocopier room close to reception. With one quick look through the small window in the door leading to the lobby, he satisfied himself that Malcolm was at his desk.

The peer lifted the internal telephone and dialled zero.

Malcolm picked up the old fashioned looking telephone that was in keeping with the decor. "Front Desk," he said, sounding bored.

Feigning breathlessness and inflecting his voice with pain, the peer stuttered.

"This is Lord Hickstead……..chest pain……..can't breathe……..help me!"

With that, he hung up the phone.

As anticipated, Malcolm raced up the stairs to the apartments with his mobile to his ear, yelling "Paramedics to Number two Parliament Street immediately! We have a suspected heart attack."

Lord Hickstead smiled to himself as he let himself out of the glazed internal security doors and out of the original wooden doors onto Parliament Street. No doubt they would review the CCTV footage and realise they had been tricked, but by then he would be long gone.

Chapter 83

Thames House, Millbank, London. Monday, 6:30pm.

Until the 1980s Thames House had been occupied by ICI, for whom it had been constructed in the 1930s. MI5 had moved into the building in the early 1990s, and it was then officially opened by the Prime Minister John Major in 1994. Used as a backdrop before being blown up in Skyfall, a recent James Bond film, the impressive building overlooks the Thames and Lambeth Bridge. Tourists often visit the office block looking for the entrance familiar to them from the BBC TV series 'Spooks'. Sadly they are disappointed, because the BBC uses Freemasons' Hall for their external shots of MI5's offices.

Timothy Madeley stood in his second floor office looking out over the Thames. His office was neither as ornate as M's office in the Bond films, nor as high tech as the offices depicted in Spooks. The carpet was beyond office quality, and the furnishings were custom built, not assembled. On the wall was a fabric wall hanging from Afghanistan and an impressive oil painting, on loan from the National Gallery.

The phone rang and he walked over to his desk to pick it up. He stated his surname.

"Sir, this is Malcolm, at the cubby hole. Lord Hickstead has gone."

There was no hint of fear in his voice, nor was there any expression of surprise from his superior.

"Excellent. Did he escape on his own, or did you have to intervene?"

Malcolm then explained how the peer had hoped to draw Malcolm away from his post, and how Malcolm had played along, pretending to call an ambulance.

"Excellent. So, if another agency manages to pick him up, he will be convinced he escaped using his own prowess. In your view, he is entirely unaware that we allowed him to go?"

"Yes sir, that is correct. Sir, are we running a sweep on this one?"

"We are, Malcolm. We're guessing which country he runs to. Do you want in? It's a tenner entry fee and we draw lots on Friday. If he doesn't make it out of the country, all stakes are refunded. If he settles in a country we hadn't considered, it goes to the nearest geographically. Agreed?"

"That's fine, sir. I think he'll make it across the Channel, that's child's play, and after that Europe and Scandinavia are open to him without him even needing a passport."

"Malcolm, did I ever tell you that I spent a couple of years in the "cubby hole" when I was Liaison with SO12?"

"You did, sir," Malcolm confirmed, but it made no difference. Timothy Madeley told his funny story about the premises anyway, pausing at the appropriate points for Malcolm's forced laughter.

Chapter 84

City Club Lounge, City Wall Hotel, London: Monday 7pm

The journey across London had been uneventful and now Lord Hickstead was sitting in the club lounge at the City Wall Hotel, giving instructions to the concierge. The concierge disappeared briefly, to return a few minutes later with a briefcase and a holdall.

While he was waiting for his guests he slipped into the leisure club changing room and switched from his suit and tie into a more casual travelling outfit. He placed the discarded clothes carefully in the holdall.

Back at his seat and sipping complimentary champagne which had never seen France judging by the taste of it, the concierge appeared.

"Your guests, Your Lordship," he announced, distaste written on his features as he ushered the Iraqis into the hallowed surroundings.

The two Iraqis sat down opposite the peer and gawped at their surroundings before their client could attract their attention.

"You have the papers?"

"Yes, here they are." Faik, the young Iraqi whom Hickstead had been championing for residency, handed over an envelope.

Hickstead looked at the papers. All were genuine; the passport had his photo and carried the name Martin Wells. Even the next of kin section had been completed with the epithet 'Janine Wells, Daughter'. In addition to the passport he also had a birth certificate, marriage certificate, library card for Hounslow Public Library, a National Insurance Card and a soon to be redundant E111 EU Medical Card.

The Iraqis had done well. Hickstead had given them a good start but they had done most of the work. Martin Wells had served in Northern Ireland under Hickstead and had taken a sniper round to the head. He was now in a half-way house for psychiatric patients in Camden. Martin had turned up at a public meeting where the peer was speaking, and to his credit he hadn't asked for anything, he had simply wanted to greet a familiar face.

Hickstead had bought him a meal and listened to his terrible story. This was four months ago, and Hickstead spotted an opportunity to provide himself with a completely new identity without the chance of being caught with fake documents.

He said that he needed Wells' documents so that he could raise his case in the House and hopefully save other soldiers from suffering the same indignities. Wells cooperated fully, handing over dirty, tattered and torn certificates and an old driving licence.

Fail and Ali had set to work obtaining new copies of all the certificates and applying for a passport and a new style driving licence. With the photos of the new Martin Wells, authenticated by a Lord, the applications were successful and Lord Hickstead was now looking at his photo in Martin's passport.

Hickstead asked if they had everything in place. They said that they had, but there was a small problem. Their contacts wanted ten thousand pounds, not five thousand as previously agreed.

Lord Hickstead was livid, but his two guests were insistent that there was nothing they could do. Reluctantly he opened his briefcase and paid them half the money he had in there.

"If your friend isn't there when I land, the two of you will be back in Basra by the weekend. Understood?"

They nodded and left.

Time was tight, and he needed to move quickly if he was to make the ferry.

Chapter 85

Highbury Clinic, Blackstock Rd, North London. Monday, 8pm.

I could have stayed the night, and I wanted to stay, but tomorrow I had to show my face at the office and clear my desk, ready to start work again. With that in mind, we reluctantly agreed that I would go home and that we would talk more tomorrow. We had plans to make and now that Hickstead was out of our lives for good, we could move on. I was on the verge of leaving for the night when the bedside phone rang.

Dee answered it, and listened intently before saying, "Send her up, by all means. We would be pleased to see her."

Jayne Craythorne walked into the room with an elegance and assurance that spoke volumes about her status. She was dressed elegantly but casually. She was every inch the multi millionaire's wife, the beautiful aristocrat with whom Jason Craythorne had fallen in love. I looked into her face as she approached Dee, and fancied that I could see some resemblance to her late father, Sir Max Rochester.

"Dee, I'm so sorry. I feel responsible for this. If I hadn't asked you to pursue Arthur Hickstead you wouldn't be here. I never imagined so much violence would intrude into my world so quickly."

She held Dee's hands firmly in her own, and tears filled her eyes as she looked at the bandages and visualised what was underneath.

"Jayne, Josh and I are pretty stubborn. We would have pursued Hickstead anyway." I wasn't sure that we would have, but I let it ride.

"I heard from the Commissioner that the police have enough evidence to put him away for life, even if they can't link him with my father's death." Jayne turned her head and looked at me.

"I owe you a great deal, Josh. You did everything you could and more. I think I would have shot Hickstead myself if he had escaped prosecution."

Jayne Craythorne sat down and listened as we explained everything that had happened since our last meeting in my flat. We all agreed that the whole episode seemed rather surreal, and only the deaths and injuries turned it into a terrible reality for those who lived through it.

Jayne had heard about my proposal and asked, if it wasn't too indiscreet, whether we had any plans.

"He might not have any plans, but I do," Dee stated. "What else is there to do when you're sitting in a bed most of the day with only daytime TV?"

This was news to me. Perhaps this was one of the things we were going to talk about tomorrow.

"That is such wonderful news," Jayne said warmly. "You will make a lovely couple, and don't worry about how long you've known each other; I fell for Jonas inside an hour. If you're having a traditional white wedding I can help. I have lots of friends."

I almost said that most millionaires probably have lots of friends, but didn't.

"I might just take you up on that. I intend to have the whitest of white weddings," Dee said excitedly.

***

When Jayne left I accompanied her to the lift. She held my hand tightly and thanked me again, and kissed me on the cheek.

"When Dee is fit again you must both come over for dinner. We don't get a lot of 'real' people over these days, and Jonas is very down to earth. He soon tires of the trendy set and their affectations. Oh, by the way I have brought a thank you card."

"There was no need. I'm glad we could help." She handed me an envelope. I slipped it into my pocket and bid Jayne goodnight.

When I arrived back at the room I tossed Dee the thank you card and told her I would have to be going soon.

"Josh." Dee was holding the card and grinning from ear to ear. "This isn't just a card. There's a note, too." Dee read the note and passed it to me with a smile.

'Thanks for everything. It will take months to get your money back. Until then Jonas has wired a quarter of a million pounds to your account. Think of it as a loan. We can discuss repayment over dinner some time. Jonas and Jayne.'

Dee then explained that Don Fisher was paying all of the bills for Vastrick, including a six figure sum in compensation for Dee's injuries. He also wanted to give me my quarter of a million pounds back because his cash would be returned very quickly, whereas my money was tied up until after the trial.

As excited as I was, I didn't think I could accept the money. Nevertheless, this was the happiest we had been for days, and so I didn't want to dampen the mood.

Unfortunately the mood wasn't destined to last. My phone rang. I answered it, and swore. As soon as I had finished the call Dee asked me what was wrong.

"Bloody MI5! They've let Hickstead escape! He's on the run!"

Dee didn't seem at all surprised.

Chapter 86

Bogaz, Northern Cyprus. November 20th 2010, 2pm.

The journey to Turkish controlled Cyprus had been much easier than he had anticipated. Despite security checks at the Port of Dover, the Border Agency staff had not been looking for a Michael Wells and luckily Arthur Hickstead was average height, average build and Caucasian. The crossing was quick, and he was able to secure a taxi to the Aero Porte Calais-Dunkerque at Marck, just a few miles from Calais.

When he arrived at the white painted aerodrome it was deserted but well lit. The restaurant displayed a sign announcing its permanent closure, and another building announced that customs had to be contacted twenty four hours in advance of any arrivals to arrange attendance. The aerodrome was in the middle of grass pastureland but it had a well maintained tarmac apron, taxiway and runway.

Having paid the taxi driver, he had walked towards the only aircraft showing any lights. It was a Cessna 172 with four seats. The pilot was French speaking but was originally from Iraq, judging by his accent and colouring. Hickstead held onto the strut supporting the wing and lifted himself into the small aircraft. He had paid ten thousand pounds for this journey, and to protect his anonymity. Dozing from time to time, he dimly recollected touching down at some deserted airfield to unload something - he didn't want to know what – and to refuel.

It was light by the time the plane touched down in Cyprus at Ercan Airport, which was a charter airport and so had some basic immigration checks, which were quickly dispensed with when his pilot, Assif, handed an envelope to a Turkish official.

A forty minute drive took him to The Mercure Hotel in Kyrenia, where he slept the day through in a luxury suite.

Now, almost two months later, he regretted his initial extravagance. After a month he had been obliged to move from the hotel into a small rented cottage to eke out his initial funds. He was safe from extradition here. The weather was warm and dry; even in November the daytime temperature reached the mid-20s Celsius. He also had beautiful view over the sea where he could watch the sunset, which made up, in part, for the modest accommodations.

Living as Martin Wells, he had become known as Mr Martin to those locals who had a smattering of English. In the evenings he would sit in the bars at the local hotels and strike up conversations with English tourists. Working class to a man, they would generously include him in their group and buy his drinks.

When his initial cash began to run out he sent off a letter to the Bank in Switzerland that held the Euro Union Financial Enterprises numbered account, requesting transfer of all funds to Mr Martin Wells' account at the Cyprus Turkish Bank of Commerce. That was two weeks ago, and he had heard nothing yet, but the post from Cyprus was notoriously unreliable and he no longer had constant internet access.

In desperation he tried to make a withdrawal from his UK Barclays current account, but the account had insufficient funds. Presumably Brenda had cleaned out the four thousand that had been in there. He wasn't surprised; he had left her high and dry, after all. If he valued his freedom he could not contact her. Brenda had become very fragile of late, and her depression had developed into bouts of paranoia and memory loss. She couldn't be expected to keep a secret.

He had just worked out that he had enough cash to pay the rent for the next month if he ate frugally, when there was a knock at the door. It would be Bajram, the soup man. It amazed Hickstead that in the heat of the Cyprus day a vendor could come around the streets and sell hot soup to locals, who brought out their own tureens or bowls. He had to admit, though, the soup was good and it cost almost nothing.

He walked to the door and opened it, but it wasn't Bajram. It was an English face he hadn't seen in a while. For a moment he was speechless, but finally he found his voice.

"Josh Hammond. This is a pleasant surprise. Have you come to kill me?"

***

The figure facing me now was a lot less prepossessing than the Lord Hickstead I had seen previously.

"No, Arthur, or Martin, or whatever you call yourself. That would be more your line of work than mine."

"Touché," he said. "You had better come in."

I walked along a roughly plastered corridor with whitewashed walls. On one side was a kitchen and on the other a bathroom. The corridor opened into a bright lounge area that was modestly furnished in typical holiday cottage style. There was a radio and a TV but no air conditioning or heating. The view from the large picture window, however, was to die for. It was spectacular. I sat on a cane sofa with flowery upholstery and he sat in a matching chair. From my seat I could see a tiny lobby area leading to two bedrooms.

"Sorry about the accommodation. I'm taking a villa on a new development just along the coast. It's amazing what you can get in Northern Cyprus for around fifty thousand pounds."

As I had been told by Inspector Boniface, Hickstead still believed that he had over half a million pounds safely secreted away in the Euro Union Financial Enterprises account. That account had been closed some time ago, but the security services had asked the bank to keep that information to themselves until he gave the bank his permanent address.

"So, Josh, what brings you all the way to Cyprus?" the peer asked conversationally. "Surely you haven't flown all the way here just to gloat?"

"Not at all, Arthur. I was in the area on my honeymoon and thought I'd call in and keep you up to date with the news from the UK."

"Well, well, I would have thought you would have taken the lucky lady somewhere a little more exclusive. After all, I imagine you now have your money back."

"To be honest, Arthur, Cyprus is just one port of call. An old friend of yours has generously allowed us the use of his family yacht and crew to cruise the Mediterranean for two weeks."

The former peer frowned in puzzlement, and so I expanded on my brief explanation.

"Jayne Craythorne and her husband Jonas have become good friends of mine, thanks to a common interest in what happens to Lord Hickstead. In fact, you've done me more than one favour."

"Really?" His confusion was as enjoyable for me as his despair would be later.

"Oh, yes. When you threatened to kill me I was given a bodyguard, Dee Conrad, who as of last weekend is now my wife. You probably remember her as the woman you had kidnapped and shot twice."

The peer blanched and it looked as though he was going to distance himself from the actions of the Dutch thugs in Tottenham, but he obviously decided against it.

"I notice that your Navitimer has gone. It was once a fixture."

"Well, there really is little need for a watch these days, especially here. I rise with the sun and sleep when I'm tired. Anyway, what a poor host I am. Would you like a glass of wine?"

Pain showed in his eyes, a regret at having to sell his watch simply to survive. A regret, I fear, he had not experienced when he killed Sir Max Rochester or Andrew Cuthbertson.

"Actually I have something better than the local wine," I told him. "It's a small gift."

I lifted a bottle of Clés des Ducs Armagnac from my bag and handed it to him.

"How perceptive of you!" he beamed, surprised. "It's my favourite. Would you like a glass? It is an excellent brandy."

"Actually, the brandy is a gift from DCI Coombes and the newly promoted DCI Boniface. They noted your preference when they cleared your belongings from the Chief Whip's apartment."

The forlorn figure facing me took the bottle. He opened it, and poured a generous portion into a tumbler. As he took his first taste he closed his eyes. The pleasure he took in savouring the taste was obvious. This was just one more thing he missed from his old life.

"Well, Josh," he said after a few moments. "I imagine you would like to get back to screwing your wife in the master suite of the Craythornes' yacht, so what's the news you are bringing to me?"

I ignored his jibe and his vulgarity.

"Well, first of all you've been listed as missing, not dead, and so all of your assets are taking some sorting out. Brenda's sister has sold the house and the furnishings, as Brenda is unable to do so herself. If you're interested, Brenda is in a really pleasant care home on the edge of the Yorkshire Moors, and she is now well enough for her sister to take her shopping and on outings. I went to visit her a little while ago and she thought I was someone called Danny."

I paused when I saw him flinch. His sister in law had explained that he and Brenda had one child, Daniel, who had died in his cot, and with no apparent cause of death his passing was ascribed to Sudden Infant Death Syndrome. They had never been able to have more children, but Brenda was adamant that he had survived and had grown to adulthood.

"The care home is expensive, but the funds from the sale of the property will keep the payments going for around three years."

"How did she manage to sell the house? It was in joint names. I should be entitled to half of that money." His lack of concern for his wife was sickening.

"Well, I was able to help there. I found an underwriter who would issue a single premium insurance policy that would pay out your share should you ever return and make a claim. I think you have five years.

By the way, they sold most of your belongings, too, but there was one thing they thought you might want to keep."

I lifted the second package out of the bag. It was a varnished oak box with a hinged lid and brass clasp.

"How did you get that through customs?" he asked, taking hold of the box and opening it.

"What customs? When you land at the Marina there is a notice above a telephone which states that if you have anything to declare, pick up this phone."

I looked at Hickstead as he carefully lifted his old service pistol out of the velvet lined box. I could see memories flooding back as he felt the weight of the gun in his hand. The Browning Hi Power 9mm semi-automatic handgun had replaced the old Webley Service Revolvers in

1963 and the army were still using them in many units. I had taken the precaution of ensuring that there was no ammunition in the box.

"Arthur, you will be pleased to hear that when your pension is due next year the Union are paying it to Brenda to pay for her care. They said it was the least they could do, as you had gone missing. Unless, of course, you pass away before then, in which case the whole pension pot is paid to her as a lump sum."

Hickstead clamped his teeth together; he had obviously made other plans for that pension.

I continued. "On the employment front, things have moved along quite quickly and quietly. The new government, at the request of the Lords, passed a bill allowing you to be expelled from the House of Lords and for you to have all your attendant privileges withdrawn. But I guess you were expecting that. There is some good news, though. Alan Parsons, your solicitor, won't be charging you for his services now that he knows you are impoverished."

The former peer bristled at this.

"Tell him to submit his bill, for all the use he was. I am expecting a large sum of money soon, and he will get his money."

I went into the nearly empty bag one more time.

"As I was coming to see you anyway, I was asked to bring you this letter."

The franking on the accurately addressed envelope denoted that it came from his Swiss Bank. He opened it and looked at the statement. I already knew that there were only five transactions shown on it. The last was the most important. It was dated the day he fled London. It read:

'Transfer to UK Security Holdings Ltd. €645,000.00, balance remaining €1,326.00.'

Hickstead stared at the letter. I watched his eyes dart to and fro across the words as he read and reread the contents. When he finally spoke, he was almost shouting.

"This isn't right! This is a disgrace! It's a clear infringement of my human rights. In fact, it's downright criminal. I'll sue the bank and whoever took the money!"

Hickstead was seething, but he knew that his prospects of recovering any of his money were now zero. He was almost penniless, and unless he returned to the UK he would never see any of the money that had been taken from him. He was clearly tired of me now, and suggested rather impolitely that I leave.

"Yes, I need to get back, but you might want a copy of this." I withdrew a sheet of paper from my inside pocket and handed it to him.

"It's a European Arrest Warrant for Arthur Hickstead, also known as Martin Wells. It seems that whilst the Turkish authorities will not deport you, they will notify Interpol if you leave Cyprus, and if you fly through European airspace or land anywhere in Europe you will be arrested on landing and returned to the UK. By the way, I'm sure you know already, but the arrest warrant also applies to the southern half of Cyprus, which is administered by Greece."

I stood and walked to the door. He followed.

"You want me to go back to the UK and be tried for my crimes, don't you? That's what this whole exercise was all about."

I smiled, because he still had not worked it out.

"Arthur, nobody wants you back. You are already in a prison of your own making. You're stuck in the northern half of a small island.

Even worse than that, you have no money and no earnings and you're living in a down market holiday apartment where you wouldn't have dreamed of staying overnight two months ago."

The truth hurt, and he remained silent.

"I think it's safe for me to give you these now."

I handed over half a dozen 9mm parabellum bullets.

"Enjoy your freedom, Arthur."

He slammed the door behind me as I left, and I walked down the street. I hadn't gone far when a young MI5 operative stepped out of the shadows.

"All done?" he asked, and I nodded.

Chapter 87

Thames House, Millbank, London November 20th 2010, 3pm.

Timothy Madeley stood in his second floor office looking out over the Thames with his mobile phone to his ear. He listened as one of his operatives checked in from Turkish Cyprus, one of the favourite destinations in the sweep, won by Audrey in administration.

"Mr Hammond has done his part, sir. Hickstead is now in possession of the means and he has sufficient motive."

"But does he have the courage, Boyle, or will he need helping along?"

"Hard to say, sir. I guess if he doesn't do it this evening he might rally tomorrow and start considering his options."

"We can't allow that to happen, Boyle. Either he goes himself or someone will have to help him along. But it must look like he took his own life, or Hammond will smell a rat. Giving the old man the means to take his own life was one thing, but knowing he had participated in his execution might just be more than Hammond's morality can take."

"Understood, sir. I'll be in touch again before you retire for the night."

Madeley clicked off his phone and sat down at his desk. In his view, Hickstead had two options. First, accept that he was penniless and defeated and end it all before he lost what was left of his self-esteem. Second, get drunk tonight and wake up tomorrow realising that the tabloids would pay a small fortune for his story.

The second option was unacceptable. Lord Hickstead would be reported as having taken his own life in Madeley's report to the Prime Minister tomorrow, one way or another.

Chapter 88

The Janus, Northern Cyprus. November 20th 2010, 5pm.

Dee climbed off the jet ski onto the jetty and removed her life jacket. She was still laughing. I suspected that she had used jet skis before when she continued to circle my jet ski and spray me with surf as she banked. I tried banking my jet ski just the once, and fell off. I wondered if the whole of our married life would be as competitive as this, or whether two weeks after the whitest of weddings her affection for me was waning.

I had to admit, however, that for a wedding arranged at just four weeks' notice, Dee, Jayne and Lavender had done an amazing job. We tied the knot in a historic chapel which had probably looked much the same nine hundred years ago when it was built in the grounds of Falsworth Hall near Reading. My heart skipped a beat when I saw Dee in the dress for the first time. She looked spectacular. When I heard that Jayne's friend, and Avant-garde fashion designer, Li Li Sung, was making the dress, I had imagined something offbeat and probably weird. I was wrong. It was a traditional white bridal gown, decorated with white Swiss embroidered love symbols from every continent.

Now to be honeymooning on a private yacht – well, my parents would be boasting about it to their friends in the Midlands for years to come.

Dee lay on the recliner, covered with a towel to dry off. I sat on the recliner beside hers. I stared at her but couldn't tell if she had her eyes open or closed through her densely tinted sunglasses. My eyes were drawn to her recent wounds; the scarring would diminish over time, but she had refused reconstructive surgery. Her arm had circular scars front and back, but her thigh had only one noticeable scar, at the front. The emergency surgery in the Tottenham Press office had been done so well that there was now just a small line of scarring where the stitches had been.

Dee wasn't worried about the world seeing her scars, and had been moving around the deck in her swimsuit the whole voyage. She had seen me looking and beckoned me closer, pulling me onto the recliner and pressing her lips to mine.

"Josh, it seems to me that you've done your job for Queen and Country, and now is the time for some recreation."

"We've just been jet skiing," I pointed out.

"Bedroom based recreation," she said coyly, before sitting up and nodding towards the stairs to the lower deck.

***

Arthur Hickstead fully understood the message that the Establishment wanted him to take from Hammond's visit. Essentially, it was expected that he would take the quick way out, drink the Clés des Ducs Armagnac, watch his last sunset over his panoramic window view, and blow his brains out with his service weapon.

He had to admit they had given him little option. With just a couple of thousand Euros left to his name, he would be penniless in a month.

It had crossed his mind to go to town and use his gun to rob a bank, but he knew he would be no good at it, and on this small part of the island they would probably track him down inside an hour. There was nowhere to run to.

But Arthur Hickstead had come up with a different plan. The Establishment hadn't won yet.

***

Stuart Boyle rang Thames House. He needed instructions. Madeley answered the phone.

"Sir, Hickstead in on the move, and he is carrying."

"Hell's teeth! Can't he take a hint?" Madeley said impatiently. "OK, you'd better follow him. He might have decided to make his exit sitting on the sand watching the sun drop over the horizon. If he doesn't take care of it himself, you'll have to make the message a little clearer. Use his own gun, if you can."

Boyle strode off in the direction Hickstead had taken.

Chapter 89

The Janus, Mediterranean Sea. November 20th 2010, 6pm.

We were still making love when the engines started up. We were both surprised because we had expected to cast off after dark.

"Shall I see what's going on up there?" I teased.

"Don't you dare. Your duties down here aren't even close to being completed yet." She was becoming excitable, and I was inclined to stay the course.

***

"Lord Hickstead, this is insane. Put the gun down and we'll talk this out," Boyle shouted from the jetty.

Hickstead held the gun steady against the first mate's head as he shouted back. "Radio me when we have a deal that lets me live my life out in luxury. I will kill everyone on this boat if I have to, but this is just to show that I'm serious."

Boyle took his gun from his holster, but by the time he raised it he had taken a bullet from Hickstead's gun. At this distance the Browning Hi Power had sent a 9mm bullet through Boyle's stomach and out of his back, just missing his kidney. Boyle fell to the floor cursing, as uniformed men poured onto the jetty. As one of the men pressed a pad onto his wound, Boyle used his mobile to stutter out a brief report to Thames House.

***

I was lying on the bed with Dee beside me; we were both covered with a sheen of perspiration and feeling dozy when we heard shouting. Dee sat up, immediately alert, and signalled for me to remain silent. A shot rang out. It was unmistakable, and it was very close. A powerful handgun had been discharged from the deck.

Dee quickly pulled on a pair of shorts without taking the time for underwear and then grabbed my sweatshirt and pulled it over her head. By now I had pulled my shorts on and was about to leave the saloon and make my way to the deck to see why we were accelerating away from the dock. Dee pulled me back.

"Josh, it must be Hickstead. Don't ask any questions, just keep him busy for a few minutes while I get organised. Don't forget, he's armed, but we're not."

***

I reached the deck to find the Captain operating the yacht from the auxiliary console. Normally the Captain would be in the deckhouse running the yacht from where he had full radar and radio coverage. But there was an auxiliary console and wheel on the top deck for those occasions when the owner wanted to be in the sun and feel the salt in his face. From his position below, Hickstead could ensure Captain Poulter did as he was told whilst still holding the first mate hostage.

When I came up onto the deck I found the first mate sitting down on a bulkhead with his hands fastened behind his back by his own belt. I looked into the distance and saw a group of uniformed men running around with radios. Good, I thought; help would soon be on the way.

"Sorry, Boss." The first mate's voice was slurred, and I noticed that blood was pouring down his cheek from a wound on his temple. "He asked permission to come aboard to give you a message from home, and as soon as I turned around he belted me with the gun."

"It's OK, Sean, it's not your fault. It's mine. I should have shot him myself earlier, when I had the chance. No-one would have cared."

Hickstead overheard our conversation, and laughed.

"Josh, you don't have it in you. You're not man enough. When Sir Max had to go, I dealt with it. Then Andrew was about to cave in and I had to kill him, too. As you said earlier, I am a killer, you are not, and that's a weakness."

"Or a strength, for most people," I retorted.

"Why don't we give your lady wife a call? I'd like to congratulate her on your recent nuptials."

"Leave her out of it. You are quite mad. You do know that, don't you? You've strayed way over the line that separates sanity from insanity." I hoped I was giving Dee enough time to do whatever she needed to do.

"You have a lot to say for a man with a gun pointed at him," Hickstead spat. "Now, call your wife or I'll shoot you in the gut, just like your spook friend on the jetty."

Sean confirmed that Hickstead had fired a potentially killing shot before I had reached the deck. I had heard it for myself, after all. I made a play of shouting for Dee to join us on the deck. I was surprised when she replied.

"Coming, Darling."

The boat shuddered to a halt, and the Captain looked surprised. Hickstead pointed the gun at him.

"What's going on? Don't try me. I have plenty of bullets for you all."

"I have no idea," the Captain answered nervously. "I'm not doing this. It should be working fine. All of the gauges are showing normal readings. I don't understand it."

"Oh, that might have been me," Dee said in mock apology, holding up a length of cable with exposed copper cores at each end.

"Sorry, Captain. Is this piece of wire important?" She sounded calm and actually smiled. The Captain was incredulous. He spoke angrily.

"What are you doing, Ma'am? This man has a gun on us and you go and pull the main ignition cable out. It'll take me an hour to put that back in, and that's if you haven't damaged the terminals."

Dee ignored him and walked straight towards Hickstead, extending her hand.

"Lord Hickstead, we haven't met. I'm Mrs Josh Hammond. My, you are a handsome man." She flirted outrageously.

Hickstead, in no mood for this, pointed the gun at her head.

"Not another step, Mrs Hammond. The last time you got close to two of my confederates they needed hospital treatment. I want you to keep your distance."

Hickstead actually seemed more afraid of her than she seemed of him, even though he was the one holding the gun. He had recognised that Dee was the main danger to his plan, and he was going to neutralise her. I hoped she had a plan, because I had no idea what I should do, and was more than a little worried.

"OK, Sean, stand up and seat yourself against the deckhouse wall." Hickstead was positioning us where he could cover us all easily. He kept the gun on Dee as he gave further orders.

"Now you, Captain. Sit on your hands until I get a chance to tie you up. Josh, you do the same." We obeyed, because it seemed sensible to do so. "That's it, sit on your hands. This is just like serving in the Middle East, except I wasn't allowed to kill them, even though they were killers themselves."

He removed his leather belt.

"Now, dear lady, turn around, please. I am going to tie your hands."

Dee giggled.

"Oh, Hicky, I'm not that sort of girl, and I'm married now."

She held out her left hand to show off her engagement and wedding rings. Old habits die hard, and out of politeness Hickstead looked, as Dee knew he would.

"Shit!" Hickstead shouted, berating himself for falling for the oldest trick in the book.

Before he could look back at Dee's face and loose off a shot, Dee swung around and whipped him across the face with the cable. Cuts opened up across his cheek. Hickstead fought the pain and brought the gun around, but Dee blocked his swing with her forearm and a shot fired into the superstructure. My new wife grabbed his wrist, and squeezed the pressure points until he dropped the Browning and it skittered across the deck towards the stern.

Hickstead knew that he couldn't beat Dee like this, and so he decided to use his height advantage. He grabbed her in a bear hug, lifted her up and squeezed. Two of us were on our feet.

"Sit down or I'll break her back!" He carried on squeezing, and reluctantly we sat down again.

Dee yelled. "Josh! In the lounge…" and then she went limp.

"That's better," Hickstead said, relaxing his grip.

But he had been deceived again. Realising that she would not win a battle of brute strength, Dee allowed her body to relax. As soon as her feet touched the deck she launched a vicious head butt into the former Peer's face. His nose disintegrated and blood sprayed everywhere, but he was fighting for his life and would not let go. She butted him a second time, smashing his cheekbone as he turned, trying to avoid her head. His left eye socket was broken and only skin was holding his eye in place. Still he held on, until Dee took hold of his left arm and forced it backwards to the point where she heard ligaments tear. Hickstead's left arm fell uselessly to his side, and he moaned.

Unfortunately the double head butt had also disoriented Dee, and they both collapsed on the deck in a heap. Dee was the first to recover and she got to her feet. Apart from Hickstead, we were all on our feet now. It looked as though it was all over. And, still teetering on unsteady feet, Dee looked for the gun.

Her luck wasn't holding. Hickstead had landed on his Browning. Summoning all the strength he had left, he gripped the gun, pointed it upwards, and without aiming at anything in particular, loosed off a shot.

Dee yelled, stumbled and fell over the rail into the Mediterranean Sea.

***

I looked on in stunned disbelief, standing motionless as I heard the splash of my wife's body hitting the water. The Captain pushed me towards the lounge and I half fell inside. The Captain dived over the side to save Dee.

I didn't know what I was looking for until I saw it. I picked it up, set it and stepped onto the deck, aiming at the slowly rising form of an unrecognisable Hickstead.

He had the gun in his right hand and was trying to raise it to a firing position. His face was destroyed and looked like something from a horror movie. The left side of his face had collapsed and the whole of his eyeball was visible.

"Don't raise that gun or I'll shoot," I stated firmly. It was my voice, but it didn't sound like me.

Hickstead gurgled a laugh from the bloody mouth that hung open to gasp at the air.

"I'm the killer, Josh, not you," he reminded me as he began to level the gun.

I pulled the trigger on my spear gun and the stainless steel shaft flew straight and true. In a fraction of a second the barbs had penetrated Hickstead's chest and showed through the back of his jacket.

I thought he would be dead instantly, but he fell to his knees, holding onto the bulkhead for support. I took the gun from his hand.

"Finish it!" he yelled, spraying bright red arterial blood all over the deck.

I left him leaning on the bulkhead and went to find my wife. Expecting the worst, I looked over the side to see the Captain assisting Dee to the ladder. With relief flooding through my body I lifted her into the boat. She was soaking wet, but I couldn't see any blood. She lifted her left arm and there was a new bullet hole just inches from the other one.

I led her to a recliner and laid her down. The Captain bound the wound tightly, but it was difficult because the bullet had entered underneath her armpit and exited behind the shoulder.

The Captain said he would get the yacht started and we would be back onshore in five minutes.

"I thought Dee had damaged the main ignition cable," I said, a little naively.

"No, she didn't. She pressed the emergency fuel cut off in the engine room and came onto the deck brandishing the cooker cable. So I had to get inventive."

I smiled and held Dee tight. I looked across at Hickstead. There was still life in him, although it was ebbing fast. He certainly wouldn't make it to shore. As he kneeled, breathing his last, he looked up and saw Dee sitting up, holding her arm. He must have realised at that point that he had robbed me of nothing, nothing at all.

Epilogue

I kissed Dee goodbye at the tube station entrance. She made her way to No. 1 Poultry and I headed off to Ropemaker Street. Dee still had her left arm in a sling, but I knew for a fact that she would discard it as soon as I wasn't looking.

I arrived at the office to find the Times on my desk, open at the obituary page. I read the most prominent of the articles.

'Arthur Hickstead, formerly Lord Hickstead, has passed away peacefully whilst on a retreat in Cyprus. Former Trade Union President and European Commissioner, he was a committed public servant. Friends say that the reason the Lords withdrew his peerage was so that he could try his hand at helping Labour back into power as an MP.

At his request the burial was a small family affair. A spokesman for the family said that Arthur never liked pomp and ceremony and so didn't expect it at his funeral.'

I folded the paper and looked at my messages. DCI Boniface wanted a statement from me to confirm that Lord Hickstead had freely confessed to the murders of Sir Max Rochester and Andrew Cuthbertson. I would probably walk over to Wood Street at lunchtime and do what I could to ensure that Charlotte Cuthbertson benefitted from Andrew's life assurance policy.

We loss adjusters have hearts as well.

Read the Next Book in your Box Set:

CHAMELEON

A City of London Thriller

J JACKSON BENTLEY

Ouroboros Publishing

Printed in Great Britain
by Amazon